By Ada Piper

More than an Act

Published by Dreamspinner Press
www.dreamspinnerpress.com

Ada Piper

MORE THAN AN ACT

Published by
DREAMSPINNER PRESS

8219 Woodville Hwy #1245
Woodville, FL 32362 USA
www.dreamspinnerpress.com

More than an Act
© 2025 Ada Piper

Cover Art
© 2025 JP Designs
Cover content is for illustrative purposes only and any person depicted on the cover is a model.

Trade Paperback ISBN: 978-1-64108-854-1
Digital ISBN: 978-1-64108-853-4
Trade Paperback published August 2025
v. 1.0

To anyone with a dream that seems impossible

Acknowledgements

It may seem strange to thank the coronavirus for anything, but it is unlikely that I would have written this book without all the chaos and heartache that it caused. In Hong Kong, we were never in complete lockdown as in mainland China or the West, but we endured many frustrating restrictions and mask mandates until March 2023.

During those uncertain times, I discovered a love of romance novels, particularly MM ones, in my search for joy, as well as Kpop and Cantopop boy bands like BTS and Mirror. And then I was inspired to try writing myself.

Although I've worked in an editorial capacity for most of my professional life, I knew little about writing a novel. But I found many excellent resources online from writers and coaches such as Savannah Gilbo, Daniel David Wallace, Jane Friedman, Kate McKean, and Golden May Editing. I'm also grateful to the Hong Kong International Literary Festival for organizing workshops about romance novels and publishing with local authors Brian Lancaster, Jordan Rivet, Larry Feign, and Chris Maden.

Through Bianca Marais, I connected with beta readers Alexandra, Leticia, and Margot, who provided insightful comments that helped me refine my descriptions and characterizations. My dear friend and reading buddy Rebi went above and beyond throughout the writing process by offering feedback on countless ideas, Hong Kong elements, and at least two finished drafts.

Other friends who knew about the book were a great source of encouragement as well, including Amy, Wing Sum, and Erin. I would also like to thank all my friends in Hong Kong then and now. They truly became more like family in those years when we were so far from home for so long.

When I started this book, it was more as an exploratory project than with a desire to become an author. Needless to say, I am thrilled to be published by Dreamspinner Press and am ever grateful to them for this opportunity.

Much to my mother's chagrin, she encouraged my curiosity in the world beyond Missouri from a young age. I must thank her, and the rest of my family, for tolerating my life in Hong Kong for fifteen years, and for all their love and support.

Finally, although he isn't much of a reader, my husband is a wonderful source of information about movies and music. Our relationship has infinitely broadened my entertainment horizons, which in turn helped me grasp key storytelling concepts. He has also been incredibly patient with me throughout this entire process. Thank you, David.

STUDIOHK CASTING CALL

Dreaming of a career in Hong Kong's entertainment industry? StudioHK wants to hear from you! Male Cantonese speakers aged 18-25 are invited to apply for this once-in-a-lifetime open call for a number of full-time positions in music and television at the city's premiere production studio.

Submit your application online at studiohk.com.hk by January 5.

Chapter 1

A DROP of sweat trickled down Aden Wong's forehead, its salty contents precariously close to his eye, but he made no move to wipe it away. Instead, he jutted his chin a bit more vigorously than usual as he danced in time to the retro Cantopop beat. His legs scissored open into a flawless grand jeté, and once his feet were back on the ground, he spun out into a series of traveling turns that sent his wavy black hair into a perfect circle round his head.

But this wasn't his usual daily workout nor one of the many jazz or aerobics classes he taught each week. He'd spent the morning filming the dance portion of his audition for StudioHK's citywide casting call—his chance to break into Hong Kong's entertainment industry. It was an opportunity far beyond any of the few minor gigs he'd booked so far, one that might give him everything he'd ever dreamed of, certainly a whole lot more than his current position as a dance teacher slash fitness coach slash *tai tai* eye candy.

And this take, along with several that preceded it, had been practically perfect. Aden wasn't about to spoil the choreography with any unnecessary movements. He needed at least a few decent recordings to prepare his final video submission, due tomorrow, which also included clips of him singing and performing lines from a sample script.

For the big finish, Aden dropped to the studio's polished wooden floor and slid forward on his knees, with a little help from his shiny black leggings. He sailed downstage toward his best friend, Winnie Chan, who was currently filming him via smartphone, and stopped just shy of her feet. But his triumphant smile wavered ever so slightly after a glimpse at Winnie's surprised face, her mouth open in a perfect O.

When the music ended, Aden rose to his feet as his heart sank. Had this run-through not gone as well as he thought?

"Was it that bad?" he asked Winnie half-jokingly.

She stood unmoving, dark eyes glued to his phone screen. "Wh-what?" She visibly jumped at Aden's voice next to her.

"I said," Aden began, dragging out each word in annoyance, "was the take really that bad?" Then another thought occurred to him. Grinning, he added mischievously, "Or perhaps it was just that good?"

"Oh. Well...." Winnie swallowed nervously, avoiding Aden's gaze. She struggled to remove his phone from the tripod, then held it to her chest protectively. Something was definitely up.

"Please don't tell me you forgot to press Play," Aden moaned, wiping a palm down his sweaty face. Singing and dancing were two of the things he loved most in the world, but though he was fitter than most people thanks to teaching as well as his own rigorous exercise regime, he wasn't a machine. He needed a break. And something to drink.

"N-no, I didn't. I… I think it was fine," Winnie replied, though her tone was less than reassuring.

"Really?" Aden wasn't convinced. He lunged for his phone to see for himself, but Winnie was too quick. She retreated toward the mirrored wall, twisting her hand behind her, still clasping the phone tightly against her oversized chunky sweater.

"*Diu,*" Aden swore under his breath. He scowled at Winnie, who looked like she was waiting for a hole to open up in the floor and swallow her completely.

Seeing her distress, Aden softened, though he wasn't giving up yet. "Come on, Win," he urged. "What's this all about?"

He glared at her until she peeked up, then nodded in encouragement.

"You got a message from Simon," Winnie finally said in a soft voice as she reluctantly handed over Aden's phone.

Aden winced at the name of his most recent fling, though he wasn't exactly sure why. They hadn't officially dated, and Aden had been the one to end things a month earlier. Just like he always did. He'd never met anyone he couldn't live without, and he always made sure to cut all ties before he did anything careless like fall in love. He had other priorities right now, like becoming a professional actor, dancer, singer, or any combination of the three. He didn't need any distractions.

Still, Simon had been sweet and surprisingly supportive of Aden's dream, unlike a lot of guys, who would never consider anything outside the standard expectations of many Asian parents: doctor, lawyer, accountant, banker, boring office jobs that paid well. If he'd met Simon later, after his career had taken off, Aden could almost imagine them staying together for the long haul. They'd been instantly compatible, from their shared interests in old films and fitness to their irrational fear of butterflies.

But who was he kidding? Aden didn't know the first thing about being in a real relationship, except what he'd learned from watching his parents over the years. They seemed happy enough, though not in the rapturous way that Winnie talked about being in love. Maybe someday he'd understand what that felt like, but not today.

Momentarily lost in thought, Aden stared unseeing at his phone. Then Winnie, who so far had remained silent, stifled a yawn. Glancing up at her face, which somehow managed to look both concerned and sleepy, he smirked.

"Simon who?" Aden asked innocently, giving Winnie his best sweet smile. He may have felt more wistful than usual about his most recent non-breakup, but what was done was done—there was no point in dwelling on it, even if Winnie had other starry-eyed notions.

"Aden Wong, you are ridiculous!" she exclaimed in frustration.

Pushing past him, she walked over to the stereo cabinet, grabbed her takeaway coffee cup, and took a long drink. Aden's mouth suddenly felt even more parched. He hurried over to join Winnie and gulped down the rest of his soymilk latte before replying.

"Okay, so what if I got a message from Simon?" He tried to keep his tone light. "It's not a big deal. I'm over it already."

"So over it that you were stunned into silence when you hadn't even read it yet?" Winnie eyed him closely.

"I… I'm exhausted. You know, from rehearsing my audition nonstop and recording my submission multiple times?" Though what Aden said wasn't untrue, there was a nervous pitch to his voice. He took a deep breath to steady himself before continuing, "I was just surprised, that's all."

"Is that so?" Winnie raised an eyebrow. Dropping her gaze to the floor, she added quietly, "You know, you can have goals and still be human too. It's okay to admit that you liked Simon or that you might miss him even a little bit. We can talk about it, if it helps."

When they were young, Aden and Winnie had told each other everything, all their hopes and dreams to travel the world, become famous dancers, and find their great loves. There was even a brief, awkward period when Winnie had thought Aden might be hers, and though she may have wavered when he'd explained that would never happen because he was gay, their friendship had remained solid ever since.

But if Aden's star was soon to be on the rise, Winnie's experience showed just how quickly things could fizzle out. After skipping university to join the local professional ballet training program, she'd made it into the corps only to have her promising career cut short after a back injury. Now she spent her days teaching kids at Miss Sally Wu's World of Dance under the tyrannical watch of the proprietress of the same name.

Winnie had never had much luck with dating either, and she'd put in significantly more effort than Aden. If he hadn't already decided to prioritize his career over love, helping her recover from multiple heartbreaks over the years could've easily pushed him in that direction.

And her most recent breakup had been by far the worst. She'd been dumped for a younger woman that her ex met while they were on a couple's holiday in Thailand. For their anniversary. Aden's self-inflicted melancholy paled in comparison.

"Thanks, Win. I guess moving on isn't necessarily easy, and maybe this time seems a little harder than usual." He smiled ruefully, knowing he alone was to blame. Though if he made it through the casting call to the next round of auditions, it would certainly be worth a little temporary heartache. "But I've made my choice and I'm stuck with it."

Winnie's forehead wrinkled with concern. "Maybe so, but…."

Aden held up his hand before she could launch into one of her speeches about true love and other romantic ideals. He'd heard it all before, and while it was sweet in theory, he wasn't looking to find his soulmate or happily ever after anytime soon. It would be hard enough to become a successful performer to begin with—long, erratic hours; intrepid paparazzi and muckraking tabloids—even more so as an openly gay man in still-conservative Hong Kong.

"I promise to let you know if I need a shoulder to cry on." Aden paused, noting the slight nod of satisfaction that made Winnie's single long braid bounce. "Today I just want to focus on my audition, and I think it's good to go."

"Yep, the last run-through was almost perfect I think," Winnie replied warmly, then glanced nervously at her watch. "It's a good thing too, since I've got a class to teach in about thirty minutes."

"*Aiya*, sorry. I didn't mean to keep you so long." Aden was quick to apologize and also grateful for the change of subject. He reached for his lightweight silver down jacket. "I'll head off, then. Back to our usual time next week?"

Like many Hongkongers, Aden and Winnie weren't usually early risers. Today's 8:00 a.m. start had been a rare exception so that Aden had enough time to film multiple run-throughs. Normally they met later in the morning for a quick workout before their respective classes began. Aden always supplied the coffee and, on special occasions, the pineapple buns.

"Yes, please. I love our friend dates, but today was a bit too intense." Winnie sighed, causing her thick black bangs to flutter.

"Well, with any luck, it'll be the last time I need to audition for anything." Winnie rolled her eyes, and Aden laughed lightly. He pressed a kiss onto her cheek on his way out.

That evening, once Aden was alone in his tiny childhood bedroom, he finally allowed himself to check the message from Simon. He'd been putting it off all day, which honestly hadn't been too hard since he'd taught several high-intensity dance classes in a row. Still, he'd thought about it more than he wanted to admit.

But when he looked for said message, he had no new notifications on his phone whatsoever. Had Winnie imagined what she'd seen? Or had she just pretended because she wanted to check in on him?

Puzzled, Aden sighed, then shook his head in an attempt to clear his thoughts. His glance fell on the few framed photos he kept on his otherwise sparse oak desk: him and Winnie the last time they'd danced a pas de deux in early secondary school, his winning performance at the Hong Kong Dance Gala set to Leslie Cheung's version of "I Am What I Am," him as Danny in his university's production of *Grease*.

Right. He had more pressing things to focus on than a message he may or may not have received from a person he was trying to forget.

He set down his phone and opened his laptop. He spent the next hour reviewing his application form on StudioHK's website, to be submitted together with his audition videos. There were no typos or missing fields, and the video files were in the correct format. All that remained was to press "apply now" and send everything out into cyberspace.

Aden took a deep breath and clicked the button. It was done. He tried not to think about whether he'd make the cut, especially since he wasn't at all sure what he'd do if he didn't. It had been a year and a half since he'd finished uni and started teaching dance while auditioning for bit roles on the side, but he'd had his fill of working with out-of-shape office ladies and eager grannies.

He yearned for something bigger, something more to give him that wonderful feeling he'd only ever gotten on stage. Besides, this summer he'd be twenty-four, and while that wasn't old, per se, age worked a little differently for dancers and people who made their living in front of a camera.

Aden's phone buzzed with an email notification confirming that his application had been received. But he wasn't quite finished yet. To really make it in Hong Kong's entertainment industry, Aden needed more than just his talent and good looks. He needed fans. So he made a highlight reel with the best bits of his audition videos and shared it across his social media accounts. Hopefully his followers, or at least his friends, would be impressed, even if StudioHK wasn't.

Only then did he notice a tiny red alert in the top right corner of his phone screen. After tapping it, he saw that he did have a notification from Simon after all. Except it wasn't really from him. It was simply the app informing Aden, along with all of Simon's followers, that he'd been live earlier that day.

Against his better judgment, Aden clicked the notification and Simon's tanned face and glossy dark hair appeared on his screen. Apparently he was traveling—on a tropical beach somewhere—and showing off the sparkling white sand and crystal-blue water. Compared to the cloudy chill of the Hong Kong winter, it looked amazing, but then there was a shadow, and the video blurred.

Oh.

When the image was clear again, another Chinese young man had joined Simon on camera. Aden barely had time to register just how handsome the man was before he kissed Simon's cheek. It didn't seem like a friendly kiss either, especially not when the man moved his mouth to Simon's neck and started nibbling on it. And then the man and Simon were fully kissing, really going at it for everyone to see for a few seconds before the video cut off.

Well. Winnie would certainly be interested to know what Aden had just watched, but not nearly as excited as she'd been that morning. While she'd been dreaming up romantic notions about Aden reuniting with Simon, he'd been making out with another guy on camera under perfect sunny skies. Obviously he wasn't thinking about Aden, as Aden shouldn't be thinking about him.

Aden slammed his phone down, struggling to ignore how much he might've been glad to get a message from Simon, after all. He was tempted to blame Winnie and her wild speculations for putting ridiculous ideas into his head, but the truth wasn't so simple. Still, what Aden wanted most was the chance to pursue his dream. He had to take it, no matter what else he might end up sacrificing along the way.

TWO WEEKS later, Aden was trying his best to get warmed up in the only free space he could find at StudioHK—a small open section of the corridor between a vending machine and the toilets. Down the hall and around the corner from the registration table and the audition room, it was somewhat removed from the hubbub of the main waiting area.

Not only did that room not even have enough seats for all the auditioners, it was drafty and cool on a winter's day. So Aden had retreated to someplace marginally warmer and more private, yet still close enough to be ready when his number was called.

Thanks to Winnie's help with his audition video, he'd made it to the casting call's final round. When he'd told her the good news a few days earlier, her response had been an endless stream of emojis: clapping and praying hands, shocked and excited smiley faces. Since then, she'd messaged him more than usual with friendly reminders about his health and his technique, which Aden had replied to but then mostly ignored. This morning, however, she'd absolutely made his day with one simple sentence: *Sell it, baby!*

Those three words had been the pre-show mantra of their childhood recitals. Aden smiled every time he remembered how their old queen of a dance teacher had shouted the words backstage before each performance. For most kids, it mainly shocked them out of feeling nervous, helping them to focus on the show. But for Aden, who felt more alive than afraid on stage, the phrase seemed to speak directly to his innermost soul as a performer.

Unfortunately, right now he was finding it difficult to get into the pre-performance mindset. He'd dressed the part, in his best black jazz pants and a black tank top that showed off his toned arms, but he was constantly being interrupted by the beep of buttons on the vending machine and the dull thud of items dropping into the collection tray.

Aden had (wrongly) assumed that most people at the auditions would take advantage of the free catering, leaving the vending machine unused. He himself had no plans to go near either—he rarely ate snacks or junk food, though he usually kept an apple and some almonds in his bag just in case. Nor did he want to run the risk of bumping into someone he knew and having to make small talk. So far he hadn't seen any familiar faces, but it was always a possibility, given people were still arriving.

"Attention, number twenty-five. Please make your way backstage." Aden's ears pricked up as a female voice came over the intercom. He double-checked the slip of paper he'd received at registration, though he knew it by heart: number forty-five. With twenty people to go, he still had plenty of time to prepare for his audition.

Aden had already done some basic stretches for his arms, legs, and back to make sure he wouldn't injure anything. So he moved on to vocal exercises, keeping his voice low to avoid attracting any more attention than he already was.

"Mi me ma mo mu," he hummed up and down a scale, followed by a few rounds of "E-e-e-e-a-a-a-a-e."

Now he was ready to mentally run through his routine—another technique he and Winnie had learned from recitals in their youth. Aden cued up the music on his phone and put his earbuds in, turning off the hear-through function before pressing Play.

As he psyched himself up to audition, Aden tried to let his excitement about performing overtake his annoyance with the warm-up conditions. But mostly, he felt a little more anxious than he wanted to be. He'd rehearsed so many times he could probably perform in his sleep, but that didn't mean he couldn't feel the incredible weight of the moment.

If things went well today, his entire life could change. He might just get everything he'd been working toward all these years. He'd be able to leave teaching behind for something he truly loved and maybe even move into an apartment of his own too.

But what if they didn't?

When the music started, Aden closed his eyes and pictured himself on stage. He tried to ignore any negative thoughts as well as his current surroundings—the glare of the fluorescent lights, the hum of the vending machine and water cooler and most of all, the numerous human distractions. He made small movements with his hands and feet, marking out the larger dance steps while lip-synching the vocals.

A couple of times, Aden thought he could sense another person nearby, but he didn't open his eyes to check. It would only be someone using the vending machine or going to the toilet. Another distraction.

In time with the beat, he hopped lightly to one side, barely lifting off the ground since it was just a warm-up. Yet when he landed, there wasn't only the cold gray linoleum floor underneath his right foot. Suddenly he was rolling and slipping around everywhere.

"*Aiya*," Aden wailed, flailing far out of time with the music.

So much for a flawless warm-up, he thought with a grimace. Then as he continued to struggle to find his balance, panic set in. His mind flew to all the different worst-case scenarios where he might pull a muscle, break an ankle, or worst of all, jinx his audition. His blood ran cold in his veins.

Aden's spiraling worries were interrupted when a pair of warm, strong hands clasped him firmly under the arms. They pulled him backward slightly, and then somehow he was standing upright on solid ground again.

He whirled around, ready to pounce. Though grateful for the help, he was still reeling from his pseudo-disaster, not to mention angry at being disrupted in the first place. "What the—"

But the rest of his accusation died on his lips as he came nose to nose, or more like nose to throat, with an angel. At least he looked like everything an angel should be to Aden's scrambled brain. The tall man standing before him was dressed all in white, and even his unruly curls were dyed an iridescent silver. He wore a simple metallic chain around his long, slender neck, and he smelled deliciously of vanilla.

Aden opened his mouth, then closed it again, unable to speak. He just stared at the gorgeous mystery angel, err man, in silent wonder. As quickly as it had surfaced, his irritation faded, replaced by a mixture of desire and jealousy. Whoever this was, if he was also auditioning today, he'd be a shoo-in with even the tiniest drop of talent. There was no doubt that fans, girls and boys alike, would fall all over themselves for him. Aden could only hope he would be so lucky.

But right now the man was looking down at Aden anxiously with big dark eyes framed by long thick lashes. Apparently he was talking too, though Aden couldn't hear any words.

He frowned, wondering if there was more to his near fall than just losing his footing. Surely he was too young to be having a stroke. Reaching up to scratch his head, Aden's hand brushed against something hard and plastic. An earbud, still playing his audition music on repeat.

Aden held up one finger, signaling the man to wait. Removing the earbud, he asked, "Err, what?"

"Ahh." A flush spread over the man's cheeks and down his throat, and Aden found himself wondering what it would be like to kiss the delicate skin below the man's Adam's apple. Yikes. He needed to take a step backward, but he was frozen in place. "I was trying to ask if you're okay?"

Aden swallowed. Although he'd heard the question this time, he still couldn't answer. Physically, he was unharmed, but mentally, he felt like he was spinning, not quite touching the ground. Instead of the music he'd been listening to just before, now it was his heart pounding loudly in his ears. Slowly, he forced himself to nod.

"That's great." The man flashed a sunny grin that made Aden feel even fainter. But after a moment, his face resumed its worried expression. "I'm so, so sorry. I—I got too many things from the vending machine and my hands were full."

He gestured sheepishly toward a pile of snacks on the floor, balanced atop a stack of notebooks. From the bits of paper sticking out of the sides, they appeared to be full of handwritten sheet music. Aden's eyebrows shot up at the substantial spread: spicy potato chips, chocolate-coated biscuit sticks, cup noodles, gummy bears, lemon tea, and a bottle of water. Was all that really just for one person?

"I couldn't catch the mints when they fell and rolled away," the man continued. "And I don't think you heard me calling out to warn you, but I wanted to make sure you didn't fall. Are you sure you're not hurt or anything?"

Aden glanced back toward the ground, where he saw the fateful, flattened roll of chewy mints slightly apart from the other food. He closed his eyes, but that didn't quiet his galloping pulse. It wasn't every day he got literally swept off his feet by a guardian angel, albeit one with rather questionable dietary choices and the absolute worst timing.

But then Aden's thoughts took a darker turn. What if this seemingly kind stranger had an ulterior motive? Perhaps he'd tripped Aden on purpose to sabotage the competition. A young, handsome man with sheet music at StudioHK would most likely be here for the casting call as well.

Then again, Aden was unhurt, so the sinister plan he was imagining hadn't exactly worked. Still, he didn't feel ready to face the biggest audition of his life. He couldn't even form basic sentences, let alone sing and dance for an audience. His momentary enchantment at being rescued was forgotten as his initial annoyance came roaring back.

"I'm fine." Aden gritted his teeth, eyes narrowing. It was hard to believe there could be anything remotely unsavory about the beautiful human standing in front of him, but the entertainment industry was nothing if not a cutthroat business. He needed to find out for sure. With a regretful sigh, he bit out, "Besides, wouldn't it be better for you if I was injured anyway?"

Either the man was an incredible actor, another reason he'd definitely pass the audition, or he was innocent of any terrible thing that Aden could imagine. Horror and mortification flooded his face.

"Oh my god," he moaned weakly. Shaking his shining head vigorously, he backed away from Aden. "I would never…. I—I don't even know you."

"Not yet," Aden retorted. He'd meant to sound confident in his chances of becoming a star, a household name that everyone would know, but somehow it came out sounding rather suggestive instead. Now it was his turn to blush, doubly self-conscious that he'd both insulted and possibly flirted with someone who'd only been trying to help. God, he was such a jerk.

And yet the man was now watching him with what appeared to be mainly confusion, or even amusement, rather than disgust. He opened his mouth, and Aden's heart hammered away in his chest, desperate to know what else this captivating stranger might say.

But the next thing he heard was another announcement over the intercom.

"Attention, number thirty-eight. Please make your way backstage," the same woman's voice said.

"Oh, that's me." The man cocked his head to one side, though incredibly, he seemed perfectly calm. Not that Aden was typically a bundle of nerves, but he certainly wasn't ready to audition right this minute. Had this guy even warmed up yet? Or had he been too busy buying food?

"Right. I'm sorry, I...." Aden trailed off. He didn't know how to apologize for what he'd said, especially not now when every second counted. But the man hadn't rushed off yet. Perhaps Aden could recover somehow. Gesturing to the pile of snacks still on the floor, he tried to offer some help of his own. "Be careful, and maybe don't eat all that at once. Sorry again, and um, *gaa jau*, break a leg...."

Though he felt like an idiot for delaying the man even longer in this career-making moment, Aden hoped his words might partially make up for his earlier rudeness.

"Thanks. You too." With a small smile, the man bent down to collect his vending machine haul, and Aden definitely didn't sneak a peek at his ass as he hurried away. Though it wasn't for lack of trying. Unfortunately, the man's loose trousers made it impossible to see anything clearly.

Aden sighed. There were fewer than ten people to go before his number was called, but now he was even less prepared. Whatever had just happened—whether he'd been helped or hindered by a far-too-handsome stranger—he didn't have time to think about it. He scrubbed a hand down his face before starting to warm up all over again and tried not to picture how radiant the angel of a man might look on stage. Or in his bed.

Re: Casting call follow-up
From: leon.ho@studiohk.com.hk
To: peter.siu@studiohk.com.hk
February 1 11:24am

Dear Mr. Siu,

Attached please find the shortlist of male candidates with the highest overall scores in the callback auditions. My suggestions for our top picks are highlighted in blue.

For your reference, I've listed out another group of candidates who also showed potential in a separate tab. We may consider inviting some of them to join the studio's training program to monitor their progress.

I'll share similar summaries from the female auditions by EOD at the latest.

Best,
Leon

Chapter 2

Aden waved to the last of the students leaving the dance studio, mostly middle-aged or older women in this afternoon time slot. Then he rushed to pick up his phone as he'd done after every class the past few days. It had been almost a week since his callback audition at StudioHK, and so far, he hadn't heard a thing. No missed calls or new notifications, no public announcements of any new bands or TV shows featuring his gorgeous guardian angel.

He kept telling himself that it wasn't time to panic yet. The studio was probably just getting caught up after the recent Chinese New Year holidays. Still, Aden was starting to think that he wasn't going to have much luck in the new year after all.

Wait. There was an unread email in his inbox. With his heart in his throat, he opened it and quickly scanned the text.

> *Re: StudioHK casting call audition results*
> *From: casting@studiohk.com.hk*
> *To: aden.wong@hkmail.com*
> *February 2 5:32pm*
>
> *We're sorry to inform you….*
> *Thank you for your participation….*
> *Best of luck in future….*

No, no, no. It couldn't be. Aden let his head drop back against the mirrored wall as his knees gave way, sending him sliding down onto the wooden floor.

Even though his warm-ups had definitely not gone to plan due to the memorable disruption by a handsome stranger, Aden's actual audition for StudioHK had been good, great even. He'd seen the impressed looks on the producers' faces and heard the enthusiasm in their voices.

But apparently it hadn't been enough. Maybe Aden's guardian angel hadn't been so helpful after all, or perhaps he, along with the other hopefuls in the hallway that day, had just performed even better. Aden's chest was tight as he blinked back tears, setting his phone aside. He didn't want to read any more—right now he couldn't see much anyway.

Two classes later, the studio was finally closing for the night. Aden was grateful that the younger, but still almost exclusively female, students in his last class, dance aerobics, didn't tend to stay behind and chat.

In the staff changing room, Aden pulled on a purple hoodie over his fitted gray V-neck and slammed his locker closed with a bang. Next to him, Ernesto Mendoza, the studio's lead salsa teacher, who was one of several Filipino employees, jumped, nearly dropping the towel he was using to dry his full head of black hair.

"Man, what's that door ever done to you?" he asked, chuckling to himself and revealing a set of perfect white teeth. Seeing Aden's stormy face, he placed a firm but caring hand on his shoulder. For some reason, Aden's brain took this moment to remind him of the last time he'd been touched by another man, and now he was thinking of the sweet-smelling stranger. Again. "C'mon, it's not the end of the world. We've both won and lost loads of auditions, and you know there will always be more."

Aden sighed. He appreciated his colleague trying to cheer him up, though it was an impossible task. It wouldn't be so bad to miss out on a small role in a music video or film, but this was a contract position with a huge industry player. There was nothing left to do but go home and wallow in this disappointment to end disappointments for the rest of the evening. He might even eat some ice cream, vanilla-flavored like the man from the audition, in spite of the calories and the cold weather. That couldn't be any worse than letting someone he didn't know take up so much space inside his head.

"Thanks, Ernesto." Aden smiled weakly. "Though I'm not sure things like this come around too often."

"Oh really? What makes you say that?"

"Well, this wasn't just a one-off or a short-term gig," Aden explained sadly. "It was an open call for full-time talent at StudioHK, and you know they do everything—reality shows, dramas, online concerts, records...."

Ernesto's encouraging smile dimmed as he grasped the scope of Aden's lost opportunity. He squeezed Aden's shoulder tighter and let out a low whistle.

"Shit."

"Yeah, exactly." Aden clapped his hand onto Ernesto's shoulder in return, then grabbed his bag to leave. "See you tomorrow, after I've eaten my weight in dessert."

Ernesto's eyes widened in surprise. He, like most everyone at the studio, was aware of Aden's well-deserved reputation as a health nut. Long ago, they'd learned to stop offering him cake when it was anyone's birthday or even mooncakes at Mid-Autumn Festival. He simply never allowed himself to eat that stuff. Except tonight.

"Yeah sure. Actually, I'm gonna stop by Tonic for a drink or two, if you wanna drown your sorrows instead." Ernesto was nothing if not consistent. For the past year, he'd asked Aden to join him at a nearby gay bar around once a week after work. And just as regularly, Aden had refused almost all his invitations. Not because he didn't like Ernesto (as a friend) or like to have fun (on occasion). An evening at Tonic, with its rainbow lights, disco ball, and frequent drag appearances, was always a great time. But he was so focused on his career—and relatedly, his health—that he rarely made time to socialize.

Ernesto waggled his eyebrows suggestively. "Might help you turn that frown upside down."

Tonight, Aden felt more tempted to join Ernesto than he had in some time. Though hookups weren't usually his thing, it would be nice to lose himself in another person's body for a short while. Forget his flagging career and his deflated dreams. Get the man from the audition out of his head once and for all. But he was tired and grumpy and way more heartbroken than when he'd called things off with Simon or any other guy. No one in their right mind would want to be around him.

"No *la*, not this time," Aden replied glumly. "I appreciate the offer, but I wouldn't be good company for you or anyone else tonight."

Later, once he was sitting on the express bus home, Aden felt a brief pang of regret. If ever there was a time to let loose, surely tonight was the night. He'd missed out on the opportunity of a lifetime to do something he'd always wanted. Now he'd be stuck teaching dance to elderly aunties and chubby office girls, fighting off their unwanted flirtations forever.

Right now he could be drowning his sorrows in cheap vodka and grinding against a hot guy on the dance floor. Instead he was going back to his apartment, where once again his mum would ask if there was any news about the audition. Tonight he finally had an answer, though not the one they'd hoped for. And once he told his mum, she'd have even more questions—her standard coping mechanism for anything she didn't understand.

With a sigh, Aden opened his email for the first time since the afternoon. He had no desire to read the studio's message again, but he needed to make sure he was armed with all the details. Then he'd be prepared for at least some of what his mum might ask, though it was unlikely he'd ever know the real reason for his rejection.

[Recall] Re: StudioHK casting call audition results

Aden blinked. Besides several promotional emails for coffee and athleisure wear, he had two new emails from StudioHK. Not only had they recalled the first email—the one Aden had been dwelling on all day—they'd sent him another one minutes afterward, which of course he hadn't seen since he'd been avoiding his inbox.

He opened it with trembling fingers.

> *[Resend] Re: StudioHK casting call audition results*
> *From: casting@studiohk.com.hk*
> *To: aden.wong@hkmail.com*
> *February 2 5:35pm*
>
> *Congratulations! You've been accepted….*
> *Please ignore the previous email with apologies….*
> *We look forward to seeing you on….*

Aden gasped so loudly that several passengers seated nearby heard. They turned toward him with expressions ranging from slight worry to obvious annoyance.

"Sorry," he muttered, holding his hands up, palms out contritely.

His eyes returned to his phone, and he willed himself to breathe normally, though he was still in shock. Apparently the first email had been a simple clerical mistake, albeit one with temporarily devastating results. Aden had been right all along—he had done well in the audition, so well, in fact, that he'd been chosen to join StudioHK's ranks. The latest email didn't specify what he'd actually be doing, but right now Aden didn't care. All that mattered was that he was in, and so close to getting what he'd always wanted that he could almost taste it.

Most evenings, Aden's commute from the dance studio to his childhood home in Tsing Yi took about an hour, as he traveled from one side of Hong Kong to another on highways that ran past soaring skyscrapers and vast container ports. Tonight, however, the rest of the journey could've taken minutes or days and he would've neither known nor cared. Once the bus reached his stop, the end of the route, he rushed home as fast as he could, beyond relieved that there was no longer any reason to pick up unhealthy comfort food along the way.

Breathless, he unlocked the front door and kicked off his shoes.

"Mum," he called out huskily. "Mum!"

In the living room, Evelyn Wong paused the K-drama she was watching and stood up from the maroon leather couch. She hurried past the glass dining table to meet him in the entryway wearing a fluffy pink housecoat and a look of concern.

"Shhh, Aden dear," she said in a low voice. "You know your dad's already in bed at this time of night."

Like most young adults in Hong Kong, Aden still lived at home with his parents. Rent in the city was crazy expensive, and buying a flat had been out of the question until he'd found a job that paid more. If everything went well at StudioHK, he'd probably be able to afford a place of his own, but it was still too soon to be thinking about that.

"Right. Sorry, Mum." Aden tried to seem apologetic, but a silly grin had been plastered on his face since the second he'd checked his email on the bus.

"Is everything all right?" Evelyn peered up at him, searching, though the entryway lighting was too dim to see clearly. "I'll heat up your dinner, and you can tell me all about it."

As she moved toward the apartment's tiny galley kitchen, Aden held out an arm to block her way. When she reached him, he curled both arms around her waist, scooping her up into a hug. He lifted her off the ground and spun the two of them around, just like his parents had done with him as a child.

"I'm in, Mum! I passed the audition." Though he wanted to roar the words triumphantly, he settled for excited shout-whispering into her ear. "You're looking at one of Hong Kong's newest soon-to-be stars."

Evelyn's arms tightened round him, and the pride in her voice echoed around the flat. "Oh, my beautiful boy, congratulations!"

When Aden set her down and they were facing each other again, Evelyn wasn't the only one with tears in her eyes. Aden's heart was full, though he felt a momentary pang remembering the last time he'd celebrated a success at work—Simon's promotion to manager in an insurance company—which had involved a lot more than just hugging. Maybe it was going to be harder than Aden had thought to keep his mind out of the bedroom and on his career alone.

"Thanks, Mum." Aden beamed once the lump in his throat had eased. "But I think we better be careful not to wake Dad."

Evelyn clicked her tongue in response, shooing him out of the way as she once again headed for the kitchen.

A SHORT week later, Aden found himself back at StudioHK's compound on the outer edges of the city. He'd woken up hours earlier, too full of anticipation to sleep any longer. After much debate about what to wear— he'd spent the past year or more mainly in workout clothes—he'd chosen acid-washed skinny jeans and a white long-sleeved tee with a burgundy blouson jacket. Still, he left home with plenty of time to spare, but after navigating through the gated entrance to the main building and then the administrative wing, he wasn't as early as he'd hoped.

But it turned out that someone else was running even later than Aden. For the past fifteen minutes, he'd been sitting in a conference room with three other local guys—young hopefuls like himself who'd presumably passed the callback auditions—waiting for one more person to arrive before their introductory orientation could begin.

At first, Aden had chatted with the other three, briefly yet awkwardly. So far he'd learned their names, Phantom Kwok, Mingo Lee, and Shine Cheung, and their key interests, singing, vlogging, and rapping, respectively. Unsurprisingly, they were all handsome, but each had his own unique appearance. Phantom was well on his way to looking like an idol, whereas Mingo brimmed with innocence, and Shine had an edge about him.

Now the legendary producer Mr. Peter Siu and one of his younger colleagues named Leon had taken their places at the head of the conference table. With his navy double-breasted jacket and gray combover, Mr. Siu looked more like a banker than a producer, while Leon sported typical

Hong Kong office casual: black trousers and a fitted T-shirt with white canvas sneakers.

For a while, the room was quiet except for the occasional whisper and the ticking of the clock on the wall. Next to it, built-in glass shelves neatly displayed StudioHK's most recent awards in film, television, music, even marketing.

Then, for at least the third time, Mr. Siu turned to Leon and said, "Still no word from Calvin. Should we go ahead and get started?"

Across the long mahogany table from Aden, Phantom sat up straighter, his fleece-lined leather jacket squeaking against the back of the chair. He casually flicked his swooping side part out of his face, revealing a diamond stud in one ear. "I bet he's in one of the practice rooms downstairs. I can go get him if you like."

Huh. He seemed very confident, as if he knew the mysterious Calvin Leung, as well as the layout of the studio's office space. But how? The casting call hadn't been open to current or former StudioHK performers. Aden was intrigued, almost suspicious.

"Thanks, Phantom," Leon said, seemingly unfazed. "Let's give him a few more minutes before we send out a search party."

So the room fell silent again, and everyone returned to scrolling through their phones. Aden inwardly cursed the missing Calvin, who was making him wait to find out just exactly how his dreams were going to come true. He still didn't know if he would get to be on TV, on the radio or what, and the suspense was making him antsy.

When the door behind him finally flew open with a thud, Aden nearly jumped out of his seat.

"Sorry, so sorry," a male voice said, and Aden wondered if he'd heard it somewhere before.

He looked on with interest and no small degree of trepidation as a tall man in loose gray trousers and an oversized flannel shirt came around the table carrying an armful of messy binders with a cup of instant noodles balanced precariously on top. These items and a black baseball cap pulled down low obscured his face as he sank into the chair next to Phantom, but Aden didn't miss the nod of recognition that passed between them. He, on the other hand, couldn't place the man, even if his voice seemed familiar.

"Thank you all for coming here today, and nice of you to finally join us, Calvin. Now let's jump right in." Looking over the top of his thick gold-framed bifocals, Mr. Siu addressed the young men as if they were his naughty grandchildren. "First, let me say that you were all chosen based on your strengths, which will complement and contribute to the group as a whole."

"And by 'group,' he means the newest boy band in Cantopop," Leon added with complete nonchalance, as Aden's eyes widened in surprise. He wanted to jump for joy, but the younger producer only shrugged and ran a hand over his naturally spiky hair. "We're still working on the name."

It was a good thing that Aden didn't need to talk because he was too shocked to speak. He'd known the casting call was a big deal, but being part of a pop group was far beyond his expectations. For probably the thousandth time, he thanked the universe that he hadn't blown his callback audition and he'd received that revised acceptance email.

He scanned the room, curious to know more about the rest of the guys and how he measured up. Phantom had said he was a singer, and perhaps Calvin was too if, in fact, he'd been in a practice room just before. Were they friends as well? Presumably Shine and Mingo also had some singing ability, or they wouldn't have been chosen for the band. At least Aden was fairly confident that he'd be the best dancer in the group—he'd never seen any of these guys before, and he'd come across most of the dance pros in Hong Kong.

There was a loud slurping sound, and Aden's gaze flew to Calvin opposite him, or at least what he could see of him behind the stack of binders. His cap was still covering the top half of his face, but his flushed cheeks were just visible. At the moment, his full lips were pursed as he inhaled a mouthful of noodles, and Aden couldn't quite look away. He was fascinated, and at the same time, a little bit horrified that Calvin had decided to eat in the meeting.

"That's right, you'll all be in a band together, but there will be other sorts of opportunities too," Mr. Siu was explaining. "We're excited to introduce you to the city as the next generation of all-round world-class entertainers."

He seemed to have a knack for speaking without really saying anything. Aden could tell he was accustomed to giving speeches, as any industry leader and award winner would, but he wished he would include some actual details. He was finding it very difficult to concentrate on this vague business-speak.

Across from him, Calvin was now drinking the broth from his cup noodle container, tilting his head back to reveal a long, delicate neck. Aden spotted a silver chain peeking out from underneath the collar of his white undershirt. Hmm.

Soon Calvin's head returned upright, and he placed the container onto the table much more quietly than he'd eaten its contents. He looked up, directly at Aden, and Aden was about to be mortified that he'd been caught staring when he realized that he and Calvin had met before. Very recently.

Now Calvin's cap had shifted backward on his head, the brim sticking up at an odd angle, to reveal a head of silvery hair and dark eyes with long lashes. There was no mistaking it: he was none other than the handsome guardian angel from the callback auditions. Aden's mouth dropped open, and he watched as Calvin's rosy cheeks blushed even harder. He didn't need to wonder what had happened to the vanilla-scented stranger anymore—he'd be seeing him regularly from now on.

A shuffling at the head of the table brought Aden back to the meeting. He tore his gaze away from Calvin just in time to see the producers stand up and leave the room as a stern-looking middle-aged woman took their place. Shit. Aden hoped he hadn't missed anything important. He gulped. Just how long had he been distracted by Calvin?

"Okay, everyone, I know you must be excited about everything you've heard from Mr. Siu and Mr. Ho," the woman began. "But before you can get started at StudioHK, we've got to go through the terms of your employment. I'm Ms. Yeung from HR, and please feel free to ask me any questions you might have."

Ms. Yeung proceeded to pass out several items of paperwork—the company's spiral-bound handbook, separate informational packets about their health insurance and mandatory provident fund, and most importantly, their contracts.

With a no-nonsense suit and severe bangs, the not-so-young Ms. Yeung was quite an imposing figure. Except that when she spoke, she had the squeakiest voice Aden had ever heard. It didn't lend much credence to what she was trying to share—the sound of nails on a chalkboard would've been soothing in comparison. Still, he renewed his efforts to listen closely, as her presentation, though boring, was pretty important.

First Ms. Yeung covered the contracts, insurance, and investment information before moving on to the company policies in the handbook.

There were guidelines for new talent from the studio's legal advisors (don't do anything illegal, or if you do, don't get caught), PR department (promote yourself on social media, but don't share too much about the real you), advertising team (as a spokesperson, you're also a product) and more. And now she was going through the code of conduct.

"We want you all to know that StudioHK is an open, welcoming employer that prioritizes diversity and inclusion." Ms. Yeung paused as she turned to the next page of the handbook. "Discrimination of any kind based on race, gender, nationality, sexual orientation, et cetera, will not be tolerated. We expect all employees to be respectful of everyone's identity and what they do outside work in their private lives."

Though Aden wasn't planning to come out to a room full of people he'd just met—he needed to find the right time and place—he was pleased to hear that the studio had joined the twenty-first century like most other corporations, at least in theory, even if the local government had not. How closely they'd stand by their principles if challenged would be another question, one he hoped to avoid for as long as possible.

"However, we also expect our talent, as representatives of StudioHK, to conduct themselves in an appropriate manner at all times." Ms. Yeung stopped reading to check if each band member was listening. Except for Aden and possibly Calvin, they weren't. Phantom and Shine were blatantly on their phones, and Mingo might've even been asleep. She snapped her notebook shut and waited until all eyes were on her.

"Look, I know there's a lot of information to process, so let me just say this. Whatever you do, be discreet, for your own good as much as the studio's. If you don't already know, you'll soon find that fame is a tricky business. Oh, and one more thing. No dating is allowed between members of the band or any StudioHK employees unless—"

"Oh my god, seriously?" An incredulous Phantom cut her off, and a tightness began to form in Aden's chest. Then Phantom placed a protective hand on Calvin's shoulder, and Aden's eyebrows rose. He'd been expecting Phantom to be angry that he couldn't date beautiful actresses at the studio, or at the assumption that he was interested in men, but now he had a feeling there was an altogether different reason for his interruption.

Ms. Yeung, seemingly taken aback by the degree of Phantom's outrage, was frozen in place, with only her pupils flicking nervously back and forth between the band members.

Calvin gave Phantom a resigned look and shrugged his hand away. "It's fine," he muttered, before addressing the room hesitantly. "It had to be said at some point. So, obviously I'm not planning on dating any of you guys, but just FYI that I'm gay."

Aden's heart kicked into overdrive, beating faster each second that no one said anything in response. At least no insults had been shouted out, but there were no words of acceptance either. Not even from Ms. Yeung with her diversity and inclusion policy. Still, if Calvin was willing to stick his neck out so soon, he should know that he wasn't alone. Aden had to tell the band members about himself sooner or later, and this way he might be able to make up for being rude to Calvin at the auditions as well.

He gritted his teeth and took a deep breath in and out through his nose.

"Me too, actually, but I don't really date. At all," he said, his eyes locked on Calvin, whose full lips parted in surprise, then formed a small, relieved smile.

"But you guys would make such a cute couple!" Mingo squealed. With his round face scrunched in excitement beneath a blue Doraemon beanie, he almost seemed like a child.

Flustered, Aden looked away immediately. He'd found Calvin attractive the instant they met, but he certainly didn't need to think about that now that they were colleagues. Although it was nice to know that Mingo wasn't worried about sharing a stage, or a dressing room, with two gay men. With any luck, Phantom and Shine would feel the same way.

"Whatever, dudes, you do you," Shine drawled, saving Aden from what would've been an awkward attempt to reply. Turning to Ms. Yeung, he continued, "But I won't be held responsible for what happens when the ladies of StudioHK meet me. I can't help it that most women, even mature specimens like yourself, find me irresistible."

Aden kept his focus on the papers in front of him, biting his lip to stifle a grin, or even a giggle. With a bleach-blond tipped fade, a goatee, and gold chains, Shine had perfected his own retro gansta rap style. But given that he was even shorter than Aden's five nine and only average in terms of looks, it seemed unlikely he was quite the stud he claimed to be.

"Really?" A skeptical Ms. Yeung had finally found her voice, though long overdue. "Even so, please remember that no dating of studio employees is allowed unless an official declaration is made to the company and all paperwork has been signed. For all other relationships, you are strongly recommended to inform us as well. Trust me when I say it's for your own protection."

Ms. Yeung surveyed them ominously, and when she was convinced there were no further objections, moved on to the rest of the StudioHK handbook. This time, Aden didn't even try to pay attention. He was too shell-shocked. So far today, he'd learned he would be in a Cantopop band (amazing!), he'd been reunited with the handsome stranger from his callback audition who just so happened to be gay (double amazing!), and he'd come out to a room full of new colleagues (yikes!). When would this meeting be over?

Fairly soon, it turned out, and it seemed that Aden wasn't the only one who was relieved.

"Later, guys," Shine said as he headed toward the door. "If I hurry, I can catch the end of the live news broadcast in the next building. And I just might get a chance to meet Serafina Chan, that beautiful witch."

Shine waggled his eyebrows, and Aden chuckled, though he didn't quite agree that the studio's longtime news anchor was as much of a cougar as his new bandmate seemed to think.

"Were you even listening to what Ms. Yeung said? You can't date another StudioHK employee!" Mingo shook his head in exasperation before following Shine out of the room.

Across the conference table from Aden, Calvin had stood up yet seemed reluctant to leave. Beside him, Phantom was still seated, eyes glued to his phone.

"So…," Calvin began, looking like he wanted to hide underneath his cap.

"So…," Aden replied, unsure how to move beyond the awkwardness—of their first real meeting since he'd been in Calvin's arms, however briefly; of whatever you were supposed to say after finding out that someone attractive was queer, yet also very much off-limits.

Before either of them could speak again, Phantom jumped up and threw an arm around Calvin's shoulders. Given their height difference, it couldn't have been an easy reach, but that didn't seem to bother Phantom at all.

"You guys must be glad to see each other," he crowed, and Aden could almost hear the missing "again" in that sentence. He had a terrible feeling that he might be blushing, so instead of answering, he asked a question of his own.

"And you all too, I guess?"

"Sure, Calvin and I go way back. Platonically speaking, of course." Phantom squeezed Calvin toward him in a friendly gesture, yet Aden thought the latter seemed more uncomfortable than pleased. Perhaps there was a complicated history there. "But don't worry, you can be yourself around me. I'm an ally or whatever they call it."

"Oh, err, that's great." Aden should've been genuinely pleased to hear that, but he was more focused on Calvin's eye roll than Phantom's words until another thought occurred to him. He added dryly, "Good to know that the studio is all about diversity too."

"Yeah, my dad said it's really—" Phantom broke off at Calvin's snort.

"I wouldn't get your hopes up," Calvin said, looking even grimmer than before. His jaw was set, but his voice grew impassioned as he continued. "But don't let that stop you from living your life either. I certainly haven't, and I won't start now."

His eyes were flashing, and Aden really wished he hadn't noticed how dark and sparkly they were. Despite everything he'd learned today about his new career and his new colleagues, it was mainly Calvin's eyes that he thought about on the way home.

Re: MK5 schedule
From: leon.ho@studiohk.com.hk
To: selina_mak@agentart.com.hk
Cc: peter.siu@studiohk.com.hk;
*   janus.so@studiohk.com.hk*
February 10 2:56pm

Dear Selina,

Great to have you on board managing our new Cantopop group, MK5. Attached please find a list of the band's upcoming commitments and appearances as we prepare for the launch of their brand and their first single. This document was compiled by my colleague Janus (cc'd here), and she will keep you updated about all band-related admin going forward.

Just let me know if you have any questions.

Best,
Leon

MK5 schedule

February 12:	Hair, makeup, fashion appointments
February 13:	**AM** Medical, nutrition, fitness consultations
	PM Photo shoot (individual and group shots)
February 14-22:	Music rehearsals (rest day: February 18)
February 23:	First public appearance: Interview on *StudioHK Live Tonight* [TBC if the band is ready to perform, but this would be ideal]
February 24:	Appearance debrief @StudioHK, additional rehearsal time if needed **10PM** StudioHK Radio 1 with DJ Uncle Tam
February 25:	**2-2:30PM** Harbour City mini-stage concert **7-7:30PM** Central Harbourfront outdoor concert [Detailed rundowns to be provided ASAP]
February 26-28:	Recording studio @StudioHK
March 2-6:	MV rehearsals and filming @ StudioHK

CHAPTER 3

OVER THE next few weeks, the band members spent most of their waking hours together. After signing their contracts, they had to clear their schedules of anything not related to StudioHK. Aden wasn't sorry to say goodbye to his teaching job, though he was surprised at how much he missed seeing Ernesto, and of course Winnie, regularly.

As a group, the band was whisked from point to point to acquire the necessary trappings of their new lives: studio-approved hairstyles, coordinated outfits for public appearances, headshots for press releases. They even got full medical check-ups, together with diet and exercise recommendations. The studio's nutritionist had been so impressed with Aden's current lifestyle choices that her only suggestion was to remind him that relaxing and having fun were also important to overall well-being. He'd smiled and nodded, but he had no intention of taking it easy just yet.

Not when it was time to start making actual music together. At the studio, the band spent countless hours rehearsing a selection of different songs before Leon and their studio-appointed manager, Selina Mak, chose a few to be recorded as potential singles.

Despite the hectic schedule, Leon managed to remain mostly unruffled. In fact, Aden couldn't quite figure out how he'd made it in the music industry—he seemed too nice, even when giving feedback on some of the band's worst takes.

Selina, on the other hand, was organized chaos in human form. Her petite frame was rarely still, always multitasking with a phone or tablet in hand, and she spoke in clipped sentences even when not giving orders. At first Aden had wondered if she was a fellow member of the LGBTQ community, given her pixie haircut. But as he got to know her, he realized she wasn't a tomboy lesbian, just a badass.

Along with all the busy-ness, Aden found himself doing a significant amount of waiting: for the recording equipment to be properly set up and tested, for Leon to listen to playbacks again and again, for Selina to arrive from gigs with her other clients. Forming a new Cantopop group involved a lot of effort and input from different people working together.

It was in all those in-between moments that he and the other members of the band (now called MK5) really got to know one another. Phantom, the studio's choice as the lead singer, had a tendency to brag about his four-octave range and his famous father (a record producer at another studio), but underneath he was a good guy. Someone who was overly protective of his friends, like when he'd tried to defend Calvin against Ms. Yeung, would be a loyal asset to the new act. It didn't hurt that he had almost model-level good looks that would appeal to the fans—high cheekbones, thin nose, and even the double eyelids that many Asians craved.

Shine talked a big game too, as if just by saying things out loud he'd manifest his credibility as a rapper. He certainly dressed the part in streetwear like wide-legged jeans, colorful graphic tees, or sports jerseys that hid his muscular arms, but perhaps he'd switch to cut-off shirts when the weather got warmer. And though he'd grown up none too well-off in a single-parent home, his success was more likely due to open-mic nights and poetry slams than illicit triad connections.

At twenty-one, Mingo was the youngest of the group, and he seemed even younger with his rice bowl haircut and round rosy cheeks. Still, he'd been vlogging and singing about the comical adventures of his overgrown house cat for years. He was sweet and funny and rarely got upset about anything, even when everyone else around him was hangry and exhausted.

And then there was Calvin—the band member Aden felt closest to, though they'd only known each other a few weeks. Turns out it was even nicer than Aden expected not to be the token gay in MK5. It wasn't just that he had someone to talk to when the other guys veered into discussions about hot girls that didn't appeal to him. He and Calvin had a fair amount in common.

They'd both come out in their early teens and had never even dated girls. They'd been blessed with parents who fully accepted their sexuality yet still had those annoying relatives who were convinced they just needed to find the right woman. Since childhood, they'd dedicated untold hours to perfecting their crafts—in Calvin's case, music; in Aden's, dance— more than they'd spent doing regular things like gaming or watching cartoons or, later on, hanging out and partying. Though Calvin could be better described as an intuitive artist, Aden's success was mainly due to a combination of hard work and sheer determination.

At the moment, both of them were also single, but Aden tried not to dwell on that thought too much. And in some ways, it wasn't that hard. Sure, Calvin was gorgeous, even in the loose-fitting artsy clothes he nearly always wore, but he was also genuinely nice. They were colleagues who were becoming friends, and even without the studio's no-dating rule, it would be simpler for everyone if they stayed that way.

So today, when Calvin seemed unusually quiet, Aden definitely didn't consider hugging him tighter than normal or think about all the creative ways to try to smooth the worry lines on his handsome forehead.

"Are you okay?" Aden nudged Calvin's white leather sneaker with his own. They were sitting on stools in one of the smaller recording studios at StudioHK, waiting for Leon to return from lunch. On the black leather sofa nearby, Phantom and Shine were deep in conversation about the best placement for a song's rap break, and Mingo was happily doodling cartoon cats in the margins of his sheet music.

"Sure, I'm fine," Calvin replied without looking at Aden. He continued to stare, or more accurately, glare at the music stand in front of him. His hands were clenched on either side of it, knuckles white, and the tension in his hunched shoulders was obvious.

"You don't seem fine," Aden observed. "But even you can't be hungry since we literally just had lunch. So what's up?"

If Aden had learned anything about Calvin over the past few weeks, it was the fact that he could eat. A lot. And much to the dismay of the studio's nutritionist and her spreadsheets, Calvin was overly fond of junk food in pretty much all forms. He brought snacks with him everywhere yet somehow managed to remain perfectly thin.

"The lyrics have been changed," Calvin mumbled, more to himself than anyone else. Reaching around the mics between them, Aden pulled the top of the music stand down so that he could see exactly what Calvin had been staring at: the sheet music for one of the songs they hadn't rehearsed yet.

"Oh really? You know this one already?"

"Of course I do," Calvin snapped. "I wrote it."

"What?" Aden asked breathlessly. Though he knew Calvin could sing and play the piano, Calvin being a songwriter was news to him. Apparently they hadn't grown as close as he'd thought. "Are you serious?"

"Yes. Here, look." Calvin returned the stand to its upright position, then spun it around to face Aden. He pointed a finger just below the title, "No Other Love," at the byline in a significantly smaller font which read "Music and lyrics by C. K.-W. Leung." Oh. Aden had barely glanced at the text, so he certainly hadn't twigged that Leung was Calvin's surname. Obviously the C. was for Calvin, and no doubt K.-W. stood for his Chinese name. Below that, he saw the first two lines of the opening verse:

My girl's always there for me
There's no other love I need....

"*Waaa*, that's amazing! Why didn't you say so before?"

"I'm not like Phantom." Calvin shrugged. "I don't make a habit of telling people how good I am."

"Literally no one talks about themselves as much as Phantom does." Aden rolled his eyes. "But in this case, maybe you should. You're a published songwriter—that's way more impressive than being the son of a hot-shot executive who also happens to have a good voice."

"A published songwriter with more than five top ten hits in the past two years, actually. First with Phantom's dad at MusiCity and now at StudioHK." The corners of Calvin's mouth rose briefly, but then his frown returned. "Though if you ask my mother, that's nothing to be proud of."

"What? Of course it is!" Talented, modest, kind, not to mention good-looking. A successful songwriter and member of a boy band. As far as Aden was concerned, Calvin's mother should be nothing but proud.

"Not when you raise your son to become a classical pianist and he chooses pop music instead."

"Oh. Right." Aden didn't know what to say. Though his parents had never understood much of what he did in ballet or musical theater as a child or even now at the studio, they'd never pressured him to do anything else. They were willing to let him take a chance on his career, at least while he was young.

Something hit the top of Aden's head, interrupting his thoughts, and he jumped. He looked up just as Phantom threw another wadded-up piece of paper at Calvin but missed.

"Come on, dudes. We're tired of waiting. Let's do something," Phantom moaned.

"Such as?" Aden asked.

"Want to hear the latest song I wrote about the Grand Meowster?" Mingo offered, as behind him, Shine vigorously shook his head no.

"Play us a tune, maestro." Ignoring them, Phantom spoke to Calvin, waving a hand toward the keyboard off to one side of the room. He was telling, rather than asking him to play, but apparently Calvin didn't mind. He made his way to the full-size electronic keyboard as requested, black trousers swishing as he moved. At first his fingers fluttered over the keys aimlessly, picking out a few chords here and there. Aden wondered if they were from "No Other Love," but figured that might be a rather sensitive topic.

"Sorry, Mingo. No cat songs today. Let's try something more people will know." Calvin smiled wanly, then without any music, began to play the opening bars of Leslie Cheung's 1995 ballad "Chase." With its melancholy melody and slower tempo, it wasn't the most upbeat way to pass the time as they waited in the dark soundproof room, but it was a fitting choice given Calvin's current mood.

Logically, Aden already knew that Calvin was a pianist. He'd played a few chords here and there at previous rehearsals and had even mentioned it in their conversation moments before. But seeing and hearing him play an entire song, either by ear or from memory, was entirely different. Aden was transfixed by the virtuoso in front of him: the intense concentration in his eyes, the quiet power in his hands, the way his silver hair fell across his face.

By now Calvin had reached the first verse, but no one was singing along, not even Phantom, the ultimate show-off. Although the song had debuted before any of the band members were born, it was a classic. Aden couldn't believe that the others didn't know at least some of the words about chasing love and dreams, sung by one of Hong Kong's gone-too-soon LGBTQ icons. Perhaps they were just as captivated by Calvin's piano playing as he was.

So Calvin himself began to sing, quietly yet beautifully, and though Aden's brain was still stunned and his heart was pounding, his mouth somehow managed to form the words to join in. Soon after, Phantom was harmonizing with them in his falsetto range, and by the next chorus Shine and Mingo were singing too.

When he got to the end of the song, Calvin kept right on playing, moving seamlessly through a mixture of Cantopop and Western hits, new and old. He was like their own personal karaoke machine, except without the lyrics. But his song choices weren't too obscure, so there was always at least one other person who knew the words and could help the others along.

One by one, the band members moved to stand around Calvin at the keyboard in a cluster, and though they'd been singing together for a while now, this time was different. No producer, no click tracks, no one watching over their shoulders. Just five young men who loved music and shared a dream of making it big.

Once or twice, Calvin looked up at him midsong, and Aden's chest tightened. Calvin was smiling now, beaming even, and though it was a perfectly normal reaction to the situation, to Aden, it felt like it was just for him. He had to close his eyes, otherwise he might cry. Still, he hoped Leon wouldn't return anytime soon—he never wanted this moment to end.

Over three whirlwind days, MK5 made their first appearances in front of the Hong Kong public, and suddenly they were everywhere all at once. First, they were interviewed on the set of *StudioHK Live Tonight*, where the questions were all softballs and the audience had been instructed to be supportive of the new band no matter what.

Then they joined StudioHK's Uncle Tam, one of the city's longest-running DJs, for a radio broadcast that Aden could almost forget was actually supposed to be work. Chatting to a local legend about the golden age of Cantopop and listening to classic hits made him nostalgic as well as eager for MK5's upcoming debut.

But the real test came in the form of two live performances at different venues on the same day. Aden knew they were far from perfect—flubbed lines, dropped notes, minor issues with the sound equipment. No matter how talented each member of MK5 was, they needed more time to fully gel together as a group. Still, the warm feeling at the end when they'd bowed and the small crowd cheered had filled a part of him that had been empty for too long.

Selina and Leon had seemed pleased too, though they'd mainly been focused on the next items in the band's schedule—more sessions at the recording studio. And not only rehearsals this time.

A week later, it was somehow March and MK5 had recorded not just one, but four tracks in total—their first single and the dance remix, plus two additional songs that were reserved for future use as singles or album tracks. They were given one whole day off, which Aden unsurprisingly spent at the gym, before heading back to the studio to rehearse and shoot their first music video.

"YSim" (which stood for "You Smile, I Melt") was an upbeat pop number, a throwback to Cantopop of the 1980s and '90s. So the video was appropriately going to be retro themed—all the visuals (to be added in post-production) would be in dreamy pastel shades straight out of an ice cream parlor or a roller-skating rink.

For now, Aden and the rest of MK5 stood in front of a green screen in regular workout clothes. They, along with their female backup dancers, were watching Louis the choreographer (pronounced *Louie*, not *Lewis*) reteach a few tricky moves from the dance break. Though, if he was being honest, Aden wasn't looking for any tips on the sequence—he'd mastered it already. He was purely interested in the teacher himself, with his long legs and muscular shoulders. Just because Aden had sworn off dating didn't mean he couldn't enjoy an attractive man when he saw one.

Still, Aden followed along with everyone else, enjoying the sensation of being the best in the room for a change. Most of the time he could hold his own with Phantom and Calvin, the standout musicians in MK5, but he wasn't sorry to have an opportunity to really shine.

To start, they did a series of alternating kicks to the left and right, four steps forward, four steps back. So far, so good. Then spin around, stick the landing, arms out wide. Now came the part where Calvin and Mingo had struggled all afternoon—each band member had to twirl a backup dancer into their chest and then dip them down to one side.

Calvin danced just like you'd expect a classical pianist to, too stiff and refined, whereas Mingo's movements were scattered, as if he were in one of his cat's viral memes. But the main problem was that they were both trying too hard to guide their partners toward them, when what they needed was the freedom to turn on their own. By offering too much help with their hands, the men were just getting in the way, which made them late to dip the girls backward. Mingo was beginning to look like a sad puppy, and Calvin's shoulders were tense underneath his baggy white tank.

"Yeah, okay. We're getting there." Louis sounded far from convincing. He made no attempt to hide his disdain at working with the young band members who weren't up to his standards.

Next to him, Aden's partner clicked her tongue disapprovingly. She knew, as Aden did, that the previous run-through hadn't been one bit better than any of the several before it. Yet it seemed Louis wasn't going to simplify the choreography or even offer any help except to take everything from the top again. Louis may have been good-looking, but a good teacher he was not.

"Um, actually, Louis. Would you mind if I tried something first?" Aden ventured. As a former dance instructor himself, he knew he needed to tread carefully to avoid stepping on any creative toes. But something had to be done, and he had an idea. After all, he'd been twirling Winnie around practically since the day they met.

"Be my guest," Louis replied with a sneer.

Aden walked over to Calvin, motioning for Mingo to follow, and took the place of Calvin's dance partner. Of the two, Aden had chosen Calvin without thinking, but it was fair to say that he'd probably be more comfortable dancing with a man than Mingo. It had nothing to do with the fact that their height difference was exactly right so that Aden could twirl just under Calvin's nose and look up into his beautiful dark eyes.

"Okay, Calvin, put your arms out and then don't move. Just watch. You too, Mingo."

Both band members did as they were told, and while Mingo seemed grateful at the chance for some extra support, Calvin's face was harder to read. He was more uncomfortable than Aden had expected, or perhaps he was just nervous about having his flaws pointed out in a very public dance lesson.

Aden raised his left arm in the air, as if Calvin were holding his hand, and proceeded to do two turns to his left, which brought him directly in front of Calvin's chest. It was awkward, both because there was no one holding his hand and because he normally danced the man's part, but he managed to complete the move unassisted. And that was his whole point—in partner dancing, you weren't necessarily supposed to be helping the other person. It was about finding ways to work together equally.

"So, what did you see?" Aden asked, stepping backward to look at Mingo as well as Calvin.

"You danced the girl's part," Mingo said in the same tone he would've used for words like "duh."

"Yes. But why did I do that?"

"To show us how not to get in the way?" Calvin asked. His tone was dry, but there was a glint in his eyes as he reached into the pocket of his low-slung athletic shorts and casually took out a mint. The same kind of mint that had ended up under Aden's foot at the callback auditions when Calvin had most definitely been in Aden's way.

"*Hai yaa.*" Exactly. Aden chuckled at the thought of their memorable first meeting. "Okay, let's try it again. This time, put your hand up as if you're going to twirl me, but don't. We'll just barely touch."

Aden repeated his movements just like before, though now his left fingertips were brushing against Calvin's smooth palm as he turned round and round. This close he could smell the mint Calvin had eaten, along with traces of his familiar vanilla scent tinged with sweat. That wasn't surprising, given they'd been rehearsing for a few hours now, but Aden wasn't prepared for how much he enjoyed it. He quickly took a step backward.

"Good. Ready to do it for real?" Aden prayed that his voice sounded confident despite the strange fluttering in his stomach.

"Yes, *si fu.*" Calvin bowed in mock seriousness, as if Aden were his kung fu master, and Aden rolled his eyes.

He took his place on Calvin's right once more. This time he clasped Calvin's hand as he turned and let him guide the twirls ever so slightly. Before Aden could be surprised at how well Calvin was doing, he was wrapped tightly in Calvin's arms. He closed his eyes for a moment, almost dizzy from the rush. Apparently the girl's part in pair work was a lot more fun than he'd ever considered.

Aden hadn't managed to catch his breath when he found himself moving backward, and at first, he thought he was falling. His eyes flew open wide, and he came face-to-face with Calvin's tentative smile, full of hope but somehow still uncertain.

"Don't worry, I've got you," Calvin murmured so low that Aden could feel the vibration in his chest, tingling all the way to his toes.

Then Aden felt Calvin's hand splayed across his back, and he knew he was being dipped. Calvin had seamlessly moved on to the next step in the sequence, thanks in part to Aden's guidance. He beamed as an inkling of pride took hold in his chest, along with something else that he couldn't quite name.

Seconds later, Aden was standing upright again, now at a more reasonable distance from Calvin, to a chorus of cheers and whistles. He blushed, only just remembering they'd had an audience the entire time.

As the clapping died down, Aden realized he and Calvin were gazing at each other in a way that was starting to seem more than friendly.

Quickly, he looked away and turned to find Mingo. "Your turn?"

"Yes, *si fu*," he replied with a grin, parroting Calvin minutes before.

So Aden began a similar process with Mingo, working up to the twirl step by step. His body went through all the same motions, but his mind was far away. He was thinking about how good, natural even, it had felt to dance the traditionally female role with Calvin, though he'd never done so before. He'd twirled more turns and danced more parts than he could count, but nothing had ever been quite like that. It was the most he'd ever enjoyed teaching too.

After a few tries, Mingo seemed to be making progress as well, so Aden gladly handed the rehearsal back over to Louis. All the band members and backup dancers resumed their positions to begin the sequence as a group once the music started. As Aden twirled and dipped his partner, his thoughts drifted away from "YSim" and back to Calvin. Suddenly he remembered the words to Calvin's song "No Other Love," the one he'd been so upset about days before.

My girl's always there for me
There's no other love I need....

Of course. Aden hadn't understood it then, but now it was obvious what word had been changed. Unless he was talking about his dog or his mother (and presumably he'd never pen a song about a parent who disapproved of his career choices), Calvin wouldn't choose to write or sing a love song about a girl. That wasn't his truth. Just like Aden partnering with a female dancer would never come close to those few moments he'd shared with Calvin earlier.

The music ended and everyone scattered. A long day of rehearsals was over, and tomorrow they would film the music video for "YSim," MK5's debut.

As Aden bent over to pick up his gym bag, he could feel someone standing behind him.

"Err, thanks for your help today," Calvin said carefully. He seemed awkward somehow, and Aden sensed that perhaps he needed something like closure or reassurance. A return to how things were between them before they'd danced together so closely.

"No problem. That's what friends are for. I'm sure you'd help me write a song if I asked."

Aden tried to act casual for both their sakes, not to mention the group dynamics of the band. Still, something funny happened to Calvin's face, so maybe he'd miscalculated.

"Of course," Calvin said, though it didn't quite sound like he meant it.

"Speaking of which, I get it now," Aden continued. At least he could tell Calvin about what he'd come to understand earlier. Surely that would be a consolation.

"What do you mean?"

"Why you were so upset that your lyrics had been changed. It was the word 'girl,' wasn't it?"

"Oh yeah. Right." Calvin sighed.

"You want to write love songs about boys just like I want to dance with boys." It was only after the words were out of his mouth and Calvin was looking at him with the widest eyes that Aden realized what he'd said. It was perfectly true, but now he could see how it not only sounded cheesy, but also kind of bordered on a bad pickup line. He'd been hoping to make things better, not worse.

"I mean…." Aden cleared his throat as the silence stretched between them, though he didn't know what to say.

"Well, maybe we can someday," Calvin said wistfully. With a wry smile, he added, "If we're popular enough, we might just be able to do whatever we want."

"Here's hoping." Aden raised his hot-pink flask in a pretend toast before slipping it into his gym bag, but he was far from convinced that fame would open quite so many doors.

Realistically, he knew that revising Calvin's lyrics and using female backup dancers made sense—there were three straight members of MK5, and as a boy band, most of their fans so far were girls. Even if things were slowly changing in Hong Kong, he couldn't imagine that he and Calvin would soon have many opportunities to make art that truly represented everything they were, not just as a dancer and a pianist but as proud members of the queer community.

That was something to think about in the future. Maybe. Aden had worked too hard to get where he was right now, on the verge of living out his dream. And now that MK5 was about to release their first single, they'd soon find out if all their efforts had paid off.

Is this the start of Cantopop's return? New boy band MK5 making waves
HK Entertainment 101
March 7

IN RECENT years, Hong Kong music lovers have turned to K-pop and Mandopop, as the local music industry waned following the deaths of superstars Leslie Cheung and Anita Mui, among other setbacks. But after backing a string of hitmakers last year, and with the launch of their newest boy band, StudioHK might just manage to usher in a new era of Cantopop.

Formed with the cream of the crop from a citywide casting call, MK5 features five multitalented young men: Phantom Kwok (lead vocalist), Calvin Leung (vocalist, songwriter, pianist), Aden Wong (dancer), Shine Cheung (rapper) and Mingo Lee (vocalist).

Though their first single is yet to drop (we're waiting!), MK5 attracted large groups of fans to recent performances at a Tsim Sha Tsui shopping mall and Central's waterfront promenade, after appearing on various StudioHK TV and radio programs. At last count, the band's social media accounts had amassed tens of thousands of followers, which is only expected to grow.

StudioHK has announced a press conference later this week, promising more details of the band's next moves. Could MK5 become Cantopop's new heavenly kings?

CHAPTER 4

THE DAY after filming wrapped on their first music video, the members of MK5 sat around the table in one of StudioHK's meeting rooms. It wasn't the same one where they'd first met, but it was somewhat similar, if even less notable.

Aden was bent over, resting his forehead on his hands, eyes more than half closed. He was tired; they all were. They'd been working pretty much nonstop for days, weeks even. And this was just another example of how their precious free time was wasted by waiting, though it wasn't Calvin who was late today. It was Mr. Siu.

At the head of the table, Leon checked his watch for at least the tenth time in the same number of minutes, and Selina continued to type violently onto a tablet keyboard, oblivious to everything else. Finally, the door opened and Peter Siu strode in. He walked over to the chair reserved for him but didn't sit down, choosing to stand behind it instead.

"Phantom, Calvin, Shine, Aden, and Mingo," Mr. Siu called out each band member's name individually, but spoke over their heads rather than toward them. "It's so good to see you again. I've heard about the great work you've done on your first single, and I know we're all looking forward to it going live. It's also time to think about what's next in the pipeline."

Aden sat up, intrigued, though he didn't expect to learn too much from Mr. Siu. He spoke in sweeping generalizations and rarely cut to the chase. It seemed pretty straightforward what the band's next moves should be anyway. They'd already recorded a few other songs. The most logical thing would be to choose one as their second single, make a music video, and release it. There was no need to have a big formal meeting about it.

"Right. So, we'll do some Q and A prep for the press conference after this," Leon explained, fiddling with his pencil. He seemed on edge, which was unusual, but surely he wasn't worried about a simple media event to launch MK5's first song. Maybe he just didn't like Mr. Siu hovering over his shoulder. "But we have a few other things to talk about first."

"Obviously we're in the process of choosing another song as your next single, but it won't launch for another couple of months. In the meantime, we've got several exciting projects lined up for you all, and Leon is going to tell you more details."

With a cunning smile, Mr. Siu clapped Leon on the back vigorously, then proceeded to walk out of the room. Aden sighed. He certainly wasn't sad to see him go but also wondered why he'd bothered to come at all. The meeting might've been over by now if they'd actually started on time. Then he'd already know what was next for the band and his career.

Leon stared at the papers on the table in front of him until the door had closed behind Mr. Siu. He cleared his throat loudly.

"As I'm sure you remember…" Leon's voice seemed to have gone up an octave, and his gaze flicked rapidly from one band member to another. He was definitely nervous, which didn't inspire confidence, but at least Aden had signed a three-year contract. He knew he wasn't about to be fired. So, whatever else he had to do, how bad could it be? "… the studio's plan is for everyone in MK5 to release their own singles at some point, and now we're ready to kick things off. Phantom will start recording his solo debut next week."

As soon as his name was mentioned, Phantom grew taller in his chair and somehow managed to look even smugger. Interestingly, he didn't seem too surprised or even that excited. Neither did Calvin, who gave a loud pretend cough that sounded a lot like "shock." Though Phantom truly was a great singer, Aden got the feeling this decision wasn't based on his talent alone and had something to do with Phantom's famous father.

To his right, Aden heard Shine heave a heavy sigh, and Aden silently agreed. He shuddered to think how insufferable Phantom might be if, or presumably when, his single got good reviews and countless plays. He didn't even want to consider how Phantom might react if a song by one of the other band members outperformed his own.

"Don't worry, guys," Selina spoke for the first time, eyeing them all closely. As if she was concerned the rest of MK5 would be unhappy with Phantom taking the spotlight first, she reiterated what Leon had said. "You'll all have a chance to record music as solo artists later. For now, we're going to feature other aspects of your talent."

Now Aden was fully paying attention. He'd only just gotten used to being in a band after focusing mainly on dance the past few years. What could possibly come next?

"Exactly!" Leon continued. "Now, for example, Shine and Mingo will be starring in a new TV show...."

"Like *The Bachelor*?" Shine asked, waggling his eyebrows suggestively.

"No—"

"Like *X Factor*?" Shine interrupted again.

"No, just hang on," Leon snapped. Finally he didn't seem uncertain, just annoyed. "As I was trying to say, it's going to be a combination of many things, actually. A lifestyle infotainment magazine show, if you will. Getting to know Hong Kong and letting the city learn more about you through food, art, culture, and so on."

"Let me explain a bit more," Selina chimed in, and for once her words were almost gentle. "It's not a competition show, Shine. That said, we can certainly include music in some of the episodes. For instance, maybe you all can spend a few hours with a radio DJ or have a rap battle as part of an open mic night."

"Wow, that sounds pretty fun!" Mingo exclaimed brightly.

Aden's lips lifted at Mingo's enthusiasm, but his chest was tight. He was anxious to know what StudioHK had planned for him and prayed that it wasn't a similarly vapid show. That seemed like a waste of his time and talent, though his opinion made little difference. His general contract with the studio meant that he mostly had to do whatever they told him to.

"What about me, then?" he asked quietly. Across the table, Calvin smiled encouragingly, as if he was telling Aden not to worry. And yet Calvin also didn't know what was next for him, though perhaps he'd just go back to songwriting for a while. Almost before he realized what he was saying, Aden added, "And Calvin?"

"Well, the two of you get to work on something quite interesting indeed." Leon's voice started to pitch higher again, and he paused. This guy really needed to work on delivering uncomfortable news in a less stressful way.

"In fact, I would call it groundbreaking." Selina, too, spoke carefully, as if it were a delicate situation. "The studio is producing Hong Kong's first-ever BL drama, which will be called *Hooked on Love*. It's a love story set in an old fishing village, and you both will have two of the starring roles."

Aden's mouth fell open, and a quick glance at Calvin revealed that he was equally stunned. His sweet smile had faded entirely. Maybe a harmless lifestyle show wouldn't be that bad after all.

"I'm sorry, what?" Aden asked in case he'd misheard. His mind reeled, and his emotions ranged from delighted to terrified to just about anything in between. What could possibly go wrong pretending to love his very attractive friend/colleague on TV while also opening himself up to criticism from conservative groups and online trolls?

"You know, BL, as in 'boys love,'" Phantom sniffed. "I believe you're both pretty familiar with this topic."

"Yeah, I know what it means," Aden replied sarcastically. He didn't need Selina to explain the term. He just wanted to understand how it could possibly be true. Airing a BL show would be a huge risk, albeit a historic one, for the studio, not to mention Aden and Calvin's budding careers.

"So my lyrics were changed to be more heteronormative, but now we're going all out on TV?" Calvin snapped. He threw a piece of gum into his mouth and chewed it violently.

"That was a tricky situation, and I understand that you were quite upset." Now Leon looked even more discomfited. Aden hadn't been there, but apparently Calvin and Selina had had a meeting about changes to Calvin's work some time the week before. He'd discovered revisions in multiple songs and wanted to convince the studio to let him do rewrites in the future. No doubt Leon had been involved, so he knew that Calvin's complaint had been logged, but the revised lyrics had stayed, and the studio had made it clear that they had the last word on all content approval.

As StudioHK's representative, Leon couldn't officially apologize without causing the company to lose face. But it was in his, and their, interest to smooth things over. The songs Calvin had written for other groups had done well on the charts, and now they wanted him for a TV role. Tentatively, Leon suggested, "Why don't we consider this an olive branch and a step in the right direction?"

"Hmm. Does this mean we'll be out for real too? Or are we only supposed to pretend to be gay?" Calvin countered. Apparently he wasn't ready to play nice just yet. His eyes flashed and his cheeks flushed, and Aden found himself unable to look away.

Aden could fully understand Calvin's anger, but all he felt was shock. First a member of a boy band, now a star of a BL TV show. He wondered if he should pinch himself in case this was actually a dream and he was still in secondary school imagining fame and all its possibilities with Winnie. Then again, a gay love story was nothing if not controversial, not to mention Aden hadn't done any acting since university. There was no guarantee the show would be a success.

"I think the current advice still stands," Selina replied evenly. "Keep your personal life private for everyone's benefit, and no dating StudioHK employees without approval. Once you're in a serious relationship, we can talk about how much information needs to be shared with the general public."

Though he didn't want to hide who he was, Aden was more than happy with Selina's response. His sexual preferences were his own business. Besides, he had no plans to date until his career was well-established, so it was really a moot point.

"I understand this is quite a change for all of you," Selina continued, addressing the whole band before returning her attention to Aden and Calvin. Now she almost sounded like her usual brisk self. "Especially you two. You can have a minute to think it over, but I'm afraid the decisions have mostly been made."

"You really think this is a good idea?" Aden asked, though he was pretty sure he was on board. "I don't want people to hate me before they even know who I am."

Although Aden was nervous about the role, something about it felt right too, like the dance rehearsal a few days before. He couldn't believe that Calvin's wishful thinking that day might just become their new reality. And even if the show was a flop, at least he and Calvin would be in it together. Yet another special bond they would share.

"Remember, Aden, StudioHK is first and foremost a business. I can promise you that we've done our research about the market and the latest trends." Leon spoke earnestly. "We're confident in this decision, and we support you and Calvin 100 percent. Get ready to make history as well as great TV."

Aden glanced over at Calvin, expecting him to still be sulking, or at the very least, skeptical. Instead, he seemed quietly hopeful and was looking at Aden tentatively, almost tenderly.

"Well?" Aden asked, his stomach fluttering in a way he hadn't felt for the longest time. "I suppose I'm game if you are."

"Let's do this." Calvin beamed, and Aden wished he could agree all over again so he could memorize every curve of his soon-to-be costar's mouth.

"Best of luck, you two," Shine whistled, tipping the flat brim of his MLB cap in their direction.

"Just make sure you don't actually fall in love, and then everything will be fine." Mingo grinned. He was teasing, but somehow his warning made Aden feel uneasy.

ONCE THE meeting was over, the band members lingered near the studio entrance, reluctant to part despite the chill in the air. Though they'd soon be going their separate ways, they'd still see each other now and then. They even had a press conference the next day, but Aden supposed they could all sense the finality of the moment. This was one of the last times they'd be together as just themselves, not famous singers or TV personalities or celebrity crushes.

"It's early and everything's set for tomorrow, so I know nobody has any more work to do. Let's celebrate!" Phantom sounded more like he was making a demand than a suggestion.

"Dinner?" Mingo offered. Though Aden had eaten with the band many times during their long workdays, usually takeaway ordered to the studio, he'd never had a meal at a restaurant with them. He knew that Phantom and Calvin hung out outside of work—they'd been friends before MK5 was formed—and sometimes the others had gone for late-night drinks or snacks after rehearsals.

Although Aden had been invited, he hadn't joined for a combination of reasons. At first he'd been juggling the band's schedule along with his last classes as a dance instructor during his one-month notice period. Then even after he'd finished teaching, he'd found he still had other things to do, like fitting in his own workout or seeing Winnie or his parents. But today his schedule was open, and he was very much inclined to participate.

"Nah, man." Shine wasn't impressed. "Dinner is how you celebrate your mum's birthday. We're young and free. Let's make a night of it!"

"Actually, I was probably going to go to a bar tonight anyway," Calvin said, a mischievous gleam in his eyes.

"Perfect!" Shine exclaimed.

"Yeah, some friends of mine are going, and there are great deals on drinks. But—" Calvin paused to flash a grin. "It's a gay bar."

"Oh." Shine's face fell, and for a second Aden was worried. Though Aden hadn't even thought about where to go, now that a bar he'd genuinely like had been mentioned, he didn't want to consider anywhere else. His mind flashed to an image of Calvin's silver hair shining under a rainbow disco ball, and his pulse picked up speed.

"Not my first choice, I'll admit. But since you guys are about to make gay history, I guess I'll allow it." Shine shrugged, playing it cool.

"Which bar did you have in mind?" Aden asked, slightly breathless.

"Tonic," Calvin replied, and Aden felt like he'd been slapped. Tonic was Ernesto's usual hangout, the bar that Aden had been to a handful of times, though he'd been invited countless others. If he'd've gone more often, would he have met Calvin one night? Possibly, but they were friends and colleagues now anyway. Why did it seem to matter so much?

"Cool." Aden tried to keep his tone neutral. "I have a friend who goes there a lot. Let me see if he's going tonight."

"Great! Why don't we all invite our friends, if they're free?" Mingo suggested, to which Shine and Calvin nodded in agreement.

Phantom, on the other hand, had picked up on the fact that Aden had finally decided to hang out with the rest of the band. "It's about time you joined us," he snarked.

In the taxi on his way home, Aden messaged Ernesto, asking him to invite all his former colleagues from the studio. Then he figured he might as well invite Winnie too. She'd met his old coworkers before, and now she could meet his new ones while they had a chance to catch up. Their weekly dance workout sessions had tapered off as of late, due to Aden's unpredictable rehearsal and filming schedule.

He shouldn't have been surprised when they both replied with similar versions of the same message, seemingly more excited to meet his cute bandmates than see Aden. And while Aden didn't think Winnie would find her next romance with one of his new colleagues—Mingo was too innocent, Phantom too stuck on himself, and Shine too ridiculous—

he didn't even want to consider the possibility that Ernesto might get lucky with the only other gay member of MK5. Calvin and Aden were friends, so that would be too weird.

At home, Aden took a nap before eating dinner with both his parents for the first time in ages. Then he changed into his tightest ripped black jeans and an off-the-shoulder long-sleeved purple tee and told them not to wait up.

Tonic was heaving when Aden arrived, even though it was a weeknight. The few booths and tables at the side were already full, and the line at the bar was three deep with people waiting for their late-night happy hour drinks (50 percent off). Most were young, fit Chinese men, but there were a few who were older, along with some expats and women thrown into the mix.

Hong Kong was a city that never slowed down, much less slept—some bars stayed open till the sun came up. Aden had no plans to stay out that late, though he let himself remain open to whatever possibilities the night presented. It was the first time in a long time that he'd been out with friends, and he intended to make the most of it.

So he found himself spinning and laughing and drinking on the dance floor with Phantom, Mingo, and Shine. Tonic may not have been their first choice, but after their initial awkwardness faded, they'd fallen all over one another to show off their moves to anyone in sight. Thankfully it seemed most of the notice they'd received was friendly appreciation and nothing more—no overeager *haam sap lo* on the prowl, and more importantly, no one who recognized them. Aden felt a warm glow in his chest that wasn't only from the press of too many bodies and copious amounts of vodka.

"And to think, you just wanted to go for food," Aden shouted into Mingo's ear in between songs. "Dancing Queen" had just finished, and Mingo's had been one of the loudest voices in the bar.

"I can admit it when I'm wrong. This place is great." Mingo clinked his glass to Aden's and then Calvin's before downing the rest of his drink.

At the moment, Calvin was rather preoccupied with his two female friends: Christelle, a blonde, curly-haired Cantonese-speaking *gwai mui*, and Naomi, a pale, waifish local who was as quiet as a mouse. Both women, to an extent, but especially Christelle, were using Calvin like their own personal prop for a raunchy pole dance, as he bopped in place to "SexyBack," looking bemused. They weren't the dirtiest dancers by far—

see the couple who were downright dry humping over Aden's shoulder or the guy in short shorts twerking so hard that everything underneath them was fully on display—but something about their movements left a bad taste in Aden's mouth that wouldn't quite go away.

Ernesto and Winnie both arrived a bit later, after their evening classes had finished, and then proceeded to tease Aden mercilessly about how he'd finally learned to stop working and have fun. When Aden had grown tired of their sass, he grabbed Winnie's hand and spun her close just as Lady Gaga came over the speakers.

"May I have this dance?"

"I thought you'd never ask. Time to sell it, baby."

And it was like they were teenagers all over again, each following the other's lead to create a quirky combination of moves based on whatever popped into their mind. Moonwalking followed by the hand jive, swing dancing, and then quick salsa footwork before switching it up once more. Other people on the dance floor stopped what they were doing to watch, but Aden wasn't fazed. Unlike Phantom, it wasn't his goal in life to draw attention to himself, but he wasn't shy either. Even in a bar, he loved performing for an audience, something he hoped to be doing a lot more of in the near future.

As Winnie twirled toward him, Aden caught a glimpse of Calvin behind her. Dressed all in white clothes that actually hugged his tall frame for once, he was hard to miss. Though his body was still swaying in time to the beat, the line of his mouth was firmly set. He appeared to be looking in Aden's direction, brow furrowed, while Christelle whispered in his ear. Even when the song changed and Aden and Winnie were no longer in the spotlight, Calvin remained stern, not at all the expression you'd expect in a club.

The night wore on, and people drifted off and on the dance floor. At one point, Aden could've sworn he saw Winnie go outside with some guy, but later he thought he must've imagined it. He was considering following Phantom and Mingo to the bar to buy another drink when Christelle appeared at his side and pushed him toward Calvin with a twinkle in her eye.

"Hey," Aden shouted, realizing they hadn't talked all night. Oh. Maybe that was why Calvin had seemed so pissed off before.

"Hey. Having fun?" Calvin shouted back, leaning his head down toward Aden's but still keeping a friendly distance between them as they danced.

"Yep. Best. Idea. Ever." Aden grinned. Then a new song came on, and somehow the dance floor was even more crowded than before. Aden found himself pressed up against Calvin, so close that he could smell his sweet vanilla scent and feel the roll of mints in the front pocket of his tight jeans. At least Aden assumed that's what it was. His mind didn't need to think about what else it could be, not at this distance with Calvin looking down at him so intently. They were just friends having a casual dance on a group night out.

Glancing to his left to avoid Calvin's gaze, Aden realized that Christelle was no longer beside them. She and Naomi had drifted farther away in the crush. They too were standing chest to chest, eyes locked, seemingly more interested in each other than they had been in Calvin earlier.

"Not very subtle, is she?" Calvin's lips brushed against Aden's ear, and he shivered. Though he assumed Calvin was talking about Christelle, he wasn't exactly sure if he was referring to her wild dancing earlier, her golden hair in a sea of black, or something else. Still, he nodded because it seemed like the easiest thing to do.

For some reason, Aden was almost nervous, so he kept watching Christelle and Naomi, even though it felt more and more like he was intruding on a private moment. At the same time, he could identify every single place that his body was touching Calvin's—chest, hips, thighs— and it occurred to him that neither of them had danced so closely with any of the other members of MK5. He had no idea what to do with that information.

As he turned back toward Calvin, Aden debated if he should try to put some space between them, though he felt strangely reluctant to do so. And at the sight of Calvin's rosy cheeks, Aden felt momentarily breathless as his heartbeat rose, not necessarily due to his movements on the dance floor.

Then Calvin's hands slid round Aden's waist and he let out a little gasp without meaning to. Before he could think about what he was doing, Aden's own arms were around Calvin's neck. And then Aden was most certainly floating, though he wasn't on drugs and had been carefully moderating his alcohol intake all night, alternating between vodka soda and soda alone.

Not long after, someone on Aden's right bumped into him, squealing even louder than the music as he embraced his friends in a drunken group hug, and a light bulb went off in Aden's brain. Though he'd been mindful of his drinks that evening, the rest of his friends probably hadn't. So there was a perfectly reasonable explanation for Calvin's flushed face, shining eyes, and warm touch—he was drunk and feeling overly affectionate, as were many other people in the bar.

Before Aden could register anything like disappointment, Calvin managed to find space to dip him sideways in the crowd. Though it caught him by surprise, this time he wasn't worried about falling, like at rehearsal a few days earlier. Instead, a joyful laugh burst from his chest, releasing some of the tension from all the emotions raging inside.

Songs changed again and again, and still Aden and Calvin were dancing together. It felt like they were completely alone, yet they were entirely surrounded by strangers. At some point, Aden was aware that all their friends had returned. Soon after, he noticed the space between him and Calvin had adjusted to a more appropriate level, but he couldn't say who had pulled away first. Given how much he felt the absence of Calvin's touch, it was hard to imagine it had been him.

With nothing to hold on to, Aden's hands suddenly felt empty. So he made his way to the bar to order another drink, definitely with alcohol this time. As he waited, he scanned the crowd, observing the different ways people were living it up, but his focus kept returning to just one person.

"You were so right. He's even more gorgeous in real life." Winnie's voice in his ear made Aden jump.

"Who?" he asked innocently, not looking at her.

"The tall man dressed all in white that you're currently ogling."

Aden didn't even consider trying to deny that he'd been doing just that. He knew Winnie would see right through him. Instead, he simply said, "So what?"

"You like him," Winnie pressed.

"Of course I like him. We're friends and colleagues."

"That's not what I meant, and you know it." Winnie swatted his arm lightly. "When you first told me what happened at your audition, I could tell you were really intrigued by that guy, even if you didn't want to admit it. And then once it turned out to be Calvin, you got really good about finding ways to mention him in your texts. Your whole body literally lights up when you're together, for goodness' sake."

"I have no idea what you're talking about." Aden reached for the glass the bartender had recently placed next to him and took a long pull through the straw. In fact, he knew exactly what Winnie meant—she'd perfectly described how he'd felt dancing with Calvin earlier that evening and in rehearsal days before. Something had shifted between them, but Aden didn't know how to put it into words. For now, Calvin was his friend and bandmate, and soon they'd be breaking new ground on Hong Kong television together.

In the darkened bar, Aden could feel Winnie peering at him. She clearly knew he wasn't telling the whole truth, so Aden was surprised when she didn't interrogate him further. It wasn't like her to let things go so easily, but then again, a crowded, noisy bar wasn't an ideal place for conversation. Maybe she was planning to question him again later.

"Riiiight. Well, tonight's been fun anyway," Winnie said. "See you back out there."

With that, she headed toward the dance floor, threading her way through the sea of bodies until she reached the other members of MK5. Aden watched as Shine cupped his hand to Winnie's ear, saying something that made her laugh. Then he must've asked about Aden because Winnie waved one hand in the general direction of the bar, all the while looking happier than she'd seemed in a long time.

Sometime later, Aden let Ernesto drag him away from the bar toward a group of his old colleagues. It was time to stop letting his mind, and his eyes, wander into dangerous territory. He needed to get back to drinking, dancing, and listening to the music, and definitely not thinking about Calvin.

Morning Entertainment News Roundup
HK Star Watch
March 8

Breaking news: Super Fan Arrested After Uninvited Sleepover in Celeb's Bedroom
>>Read more

Music update: StudioHK's Newest Cantopop Sensation MK5 to Debut their First Single
>>Watch live today at 3pm

Photos: MK5 Members Spotted Around Town: See Phantom's Basketball Game and Shine on a Date(?)
>>Check it out

CHAPTER 5

THE NEXT morning, Aden woke up to a string of texts from Winnie. First, she thanked him for inviting her to the bar, then apologized for disappearing without saying goodbye, which Aden didn't exactly remember. Of course she couldn't pass up the chance to tease Aden about Calvin and their new project.

Can't wait for u to spend more time with your new "fake" bf!

Rolling his eyes, Aden moved on to her next messages. She'd also wished him luck at his first-ever press conference and attached a link to a crazy bit of celebrity news.

See what u have to look fwd to [upside down smile emoji]

The headline was "Super Fan Arrested After Uninvited Sleepover in Celeb's Bedroom." Though Aden lived on the thirtieth floor and his apartment door was always locked, he shuddered to think that that could happen to him or any member of MK5. He refused to read the full article—just because the tabloid was capitalizing on the invasion of someone's privacy didn't mean Aden had to as well. Yuck. Aden had always wanted to become a successful entertainer, though preferably without any midnight stalkers.

Returning to his messages, Aden saw he had one from Calvin too. He held his breath as he opened it. Although it wasn't the first time he and Calvin had messaged each other privately, they usually used the MK5 group chat instead.

Hope you made it home ok

Calvin had actually sent the message the night before (technically in the early hours of the morning), but Aden had missed it. Sometime after Winnie had gone, Christelle and Naomi had dragged Calvin off to Tsui Wah, a Hong Kong staple for late-night dining. But the rest of MK5 had decided not to go, so Aden had stayed with them at Tonic, as much as he'd been tempted to get food instead.

Thanks, you too, he belatedly replied.

As he thought back to the events of the night before, Aden's pleasant memories faded and his stomach clenched at the idea that any paparazzi could've been there. Not that he, or anyone in MK5, had done anything wrong, though Christelle and Naomi had been pretty salacious in some of their dance moves. Remembering how flush his body had been against Calvin's in the crowd, he couldn't help but imagine the possible headlines: "From Boy Band to Boys Love" or "Members of MK5 Spotted at Gay Club in Compromising Position." That wasn't how he wanted to tell the general public he was gay, assuming that he ever did.

Aden was beginning to get used to seeing his name in the news, but so far only for studio-approved reasons. StudioHK's marketing and PR teams had left no stone unturned in promoting the launch of "YSim." Besides the interviews and performances that MK5 had done, there were countless clips and photos posted on social media along with ads and announcements on the studio's TV and radio stations. They'd even created fan clubs, one for MK5 itself and one for each band member, all of which had ever-growing numbers of followers. All that was left was to introduce the band's new song.

When Aden arrived at the launch venue that afternoon, he found himself face-to-face with the real-live results of the studio's promotional efforts. A decent crowd of fans had already gathered outside a few hours in advance despite the damp spring air. People of all ages, mainly women, stood in a long, orderly queue that wrapped around the ground floor of a five-star hotel in the city center, the uppermost levels of its glass tower shrouded in mist.

It was surreal to think that all these people, far more than at any of the band's previous appearances, were here to see MK5. And just for a press conference and music video, not even a live performance. The size of the audience at Aden's childhood dance recitals, or even his university's musical theater events, could in no way compare.

But as happy as Aden was to see such a crowd, it was unnerving too. Especially when the only thing separating it from him was a simple velvet rope strung between a series of brass posts.

Too late, Aden realized that he needed to walk nearly the entire length of the line in order to enter the hotel himself; there was no sidewalk on the other side of the road and no safe place for him to cross anyway. He gulped, then quickly found a surgical mask in his bag and put it on beneath his black bucket hat and dark sunglasses. But it seemed that by covering up his face, he only managed to attract more attention.

Behind him, a female voice cried out, "Look, it's Aden!"

Several other shrieks followed, together with an increase in the murmurs and movements of the crowd, though thankfully they remained behind the barrier for now. Aden quickened his pace and kept his eyes straight ahead, occasionally giving a slight nod to a particularly eager fan.

When he finally reached the hotel entrance, Aden passed in front of the line and flashed his event badge to the doorman with trembling fingers. Relief washed over him when he was waved into the brightly lit, lily-scented lobby. It was only in the quiet elegance of the pale gray interior, with its enormous floral displays and shiny marble floors, that he noticed his pulse was racing and his breath was coming in quick, shallow gulps. Maybe success and fame were going to take more getting used to than he'd thought.

Once inside, Aden sped toward his destination, a large meeting room a few floors up, taking no chances in case any overzealous fans had snuck in. Seeing them in a fancy hotel wasn't nearly as bad as having one in your bedroom, but it was still better to avoid both if possible. He'd almost reached the room when another unfamiliar voice called his name in the otherwise empty hallway.

"Aden," purred the beautiful, well-dressed middle-aged woman in front of him, who seemed to have appeared out of nowhere. Her long manicured nails were black and white with rhinestones, which matched her designer handbag and the sequined headband in her short bobbed hair.

Aden had no idea who this person was, nor did he intend to find out. He looked over her head to avoid her steely gaze as he tried to walk by, but she wouldn't let him. Like an octopus with many tentacles, she alternatively reached out a tiny arm or a leg to block Aden's way, allowing him to move forward only slightly.

"What's the hurry, Aden?" she drawled. "Slow down and let's have a chat. Don't worry, I'm not a crazy fan. I just want to help you."

The woman's voice was silky smooth, and Aden was momentarily intrigued. If she wasn't a fan, as she claimed, then perhaps she was an agent or someone else in the industry. The last thing he wanted was to offend anyone important. But he already had a manager, and the studio handled everything else. Right now, what he needed most was to get to the launch event.

Unfortunately, the only way to the meeting room was straight ahead, through the mystery woman. Aden held his bag in front of his chest protectively, his jaw set. As he searched for another possible escape route, he continued to inch down the hall slowly, the woman still mirroring his every move.

Then a door opened on his left, and Aden almost cried. There was Calvin, smiling and laughing and seemingly coming to his rescue once again. He looked great in a pair of skinny black trousers and a chunky sweater in sky blue—his studio-selected outfit for the day. Aden would soon be wearing the same trousers, with an icy pink top instead. But Aden wouldn't have cared if he'd been wearing the worst clothes imaginable or nothing at all.

"Aden!" Calvin exclaimed, his dazzling smile fading at Aden's pained expression. And once the mysterious woman turned toward him, Calvin downright scowled.

"Helga Sze, so glad you could make it today," Calvin remarked, his tone implying the opposite. Aden vaguely recognized the name, but he couldn't recall where he'd heard it or why.

"Calvin dear," Helga crooned, unfazed. "It's been too long. How are you and your dear mother?"

"Just fine, no thanks to you," Calvin snapped down at her, eyes flashing. "I don't think you're supposed to be back here asking questions yet."

"Well, I was just getting to know Aden a bit better," she said sweetly. Whoever she was, Helga Sze was a smooth operator, oily as a snake. Aden didn't even try to speak.

"Hmm, I wonder what our manager would have to say about that?"

Still leaning on the door, Calvin glanced back inside and waved a hand toward someone that neither Aden nor Helga could see. Realizing that this must be another entrance to the event space, Aden took a step closer, and Calvin's familiar vanilla scent surrounded him like a warm blanket.

"You're no fun at all," Helga chided, feigning innocence, though her worried expression revealed that Calvin's threat of finding Selina had hit its mark.

"See you later, Helga," Calvin said, and his lips crooked into a wicked grin. He placed an arm on Aden's shoulders, and with a gentle tug, pulled him into the meeting room. The door clanged shut behind them in Helga's face, and Aden hoped it could only be opened from the inside.

"Thanks, man," Aden sighed, sagging into Calvin's embrace. It wasn't quite a hug, but at this point he'd take what he could get. He was more rattled than he cared to admit, and the press conference hadn't even started. "Who was that?"

"Helga's one of the finest arts and entertainment reporters in the city," Calvin explained grimly, without looking at Aden. His voice suddenly seemed much less steady than before. "Which means she's the best at digging up dirt."

"I see." Now Aden remembered where he'd seen the name—in the bylines of countless celebrity news stories, including the article Winnie had shared that morning. It was obvious there was no love lost between Helga and Calvin, but Aden had no idea why. He didn't keep up with entertainment gossip, and he'd never searched for details about the members of MK5. "So she's, err, published something about you?"

"No-o, not me exactly." Calvin shook his head, letting his arm slip off Aden's shoulder. Only then did Aden notice that Calvin was trembling. "My mum and dad."

"Oh!" All Aden knew about Calvin's mother was that she didn't approve of his career. He'd never heard him mention his father. Yet something in Calvin's manner made him reluctant to ask for more details—he seemed sad, unnerved even, and that wasn't often the case.

"I'm sorry," Aden said quietly. "I didn't realize…."

"That they were famous? They're not, or at least not to most people." Calvin's tone was bitter as he picked up where Aden had trailed off. "My mum's a well-known pianist in the classical world, but my dad's just a regular guy. Except for when they got divorced, and Helga described all the gory details in her columns while I was in secondary school. I believe she called it 'In the Mood for an Affair.'"

Aden pressed his lips together. For most of his life, his parents had seemed happy enough, though they tended to socialize independently of each other these days. It was difficult for him to imagine them not being together, much less having to deal with their separation in such a public way. Like most teenagers, he'd had plenty to worry about—exams, friends, puberty, as well as figuring out his sexuality—but Calvin's situation had been even more complicated. No wonder he'd been less than pleased to see Helga.

"*Aiya.* And now you've got to face a room full of fans and reporters, including Helga I assume. Are you gonna be okay?" Aden peered up at Calvin in concern, his earlier worries forgotten.

Calvin let out a short, harsh laugh and muttered something that sounded like "We'll see."

Then he smiled weakly, and Aden's chest ached. "I think I could ask you the same thing. You looked pretty shaken up out there."

"Definitely better now, thanks to you." Aden forced himself to sound cheerful, at the same time resisting the urge for another side hug.

Soon afterward, the launch event kicked off with a literal bang—MK5 and their producers pushed a giant red Start button on stage that popped confetti into the air before the "YSim" music video rolled on a massive LED screen. Then they all took their seats at a long table overlooking the rows of chairs filled with journalists as well as the fans who'd been waiting outside.

Aden had felt nervous at the start—a press conference wasn't the same as a performance—but in the end, the band members didn't need to answer many questions themselves. Leon and Selina did most of the talking.

Still, Aden gripped a pen tightly in his hand, and his leg bounced up and down involuntarily more than once. When it was time for the announcement about *Hooked on Love*, Aden wasn't the only uncomfortable one. Calvin had started to fidget next to him. Not fully aware of what he was doing, he shifted under the table until his thigh was just touching Calvin's, and he was rewarded with the slightest amount of pressure in return, which was surprisingly soothing.

For the rest of the event, Aden struggled to stay focused on what was being said instead of the warmth coming from the man beside him. He told himself that, just like Calvin had done earlier that day, they were simply two costars looking out for each other. But he couldn't shake the feeling that some imaginary lines were being crossed, and that was before they'd even started to pretend to fall in love.

WHEN ADEN got home, his mum was in the kitchen wrangling a fresh fish from the wet market. Although the fishmonger had already killed, cleaned, and prepared it, she was inspecting it carefully, suspiciously, for any traces of scales or gills.

"Steamed fish for dinner? What's the occasion?" he asked, though he had a pretty good idea. Holding his breath as he neared the odorous main course, Aden lightly brushed a kiss onto Evelyn's cheek, careful not to smudge her foundation with his stage makeup.

"Can't I make fish any time I like?" Evelyn countered, still examining the food in question. "Your sister is joining us tonight, and for once, you're not coming back at all hours. Besides, I think you both have something to celebrate."

"We do?" For a moment, Aden wondered if his older sister was pregnant. But given how much his mum had longed for a grandchild, he would've expected a seven-course meal at a Michelin-starred restaurant if that was Mimi's news, not just steamed fish at home.

"I got a new job. And it was a big day for you, little brother!" Mimi squealed as she came in from the living room. Though she was slim, it was still a tight squeeze for the three of them to fit into the small kitchen at once. Aden noticed that her long, straight hair was now dyed a rich brown, not maroon-tinged like before, and was reminded that they hadn't seen each other in a while. "I caught most of the live stream during my break, but Mum hasn't seen it yet. I promised to show it to her and Dad after dinner."

"Oh thanks! What did you think?" Aden eyed his sister closely, but her expression was unreadable. He hadn't told any of his family yet about *Hooked on Love*. With his busy schedule, he'd only seen his parents early in the morning or late at night, and he was usually in a rush. But if Mimi had watched the entire event, then she'd heard about it already, along with the media and thousands of other viewers.

When she didn't reply right away, Aden quickly added, "And err, congrats on the new job too."

He felt guilty at being so caught up in his own life recently, though he and his sister hadn't been great at keeping in touch since she'd moved out. He vaguely remembered that she hadn't loved her job at an urgent care clinic and was curious what she'd decided to do instead. But unless Mimi was going to become a private nurse to the stars, it seemed that Aden's news was probably a little more exciting.

"Thank you," she said and continued to toy with the glass bottles on the counter next to the gas stove: soy sauce, rice wine vinegar, chili oil. Finally she looked up at Aden, frowning, though the corners of her mouth threatened to turn upward.

"Well, 'YSim' is no 'Thriller,'" she began, referring to Aden's performance at the school talent show in primary three. He'd spent months perfecting Michael Jackson's dance moves, only to break his arm in PE a week beforehand. His otherwise flawless routine had ended up more like a comedy sketch as he attempted to fling his cast around to the beat on stage.

"Though even without any hilarious dancing, I have to admit that it's pretty catchy." Mimi chuckled. "But at times, I wasn't totally sure if you were singing or not."

"My own sister can't recognize my voice!" Aden feigned shock, but he knew Mimi was right. There were too many unison parts in MK5's new single by design. It was much easier for the new stars to sing cleanly, especially live, than multipart harmony.

"I'd know the sound of my wonderful son's singing anywhere." Evelyn tutted at Mimi over her shoulder. She set aside the fish and started washing the spring onions and coriander that would garnish it. "Besides, when Aden releases his own single, then everyone will be able to hear him clearly."

Mimi opened her mouth to reply, closing it again when Aden shot her a warning look behind Evelyn's back. He didn't know what she'd planned to say, but it was his career, after all. He should be the one to set the record straight.

"Actually, there's been a bit of a change of plans," Aden began tentatively. By now, he'd gotten over the initial shock of playing one of the first openly gay characters on television in Hong Kong. With the studio and Calvin on board, he felt confident it was a good career move. His mum, however, had no idea, and he certainly didn't want to upset her—just because his parents supported him privately didn't mean they'd be thrilled if their only son was out on TV. A glimpse of his sister's eager face told him that she knew what was coming, though she held her tongue.

"As it turns out, Phantom is doing the first solo song. Mine will be later, though I'm not sure when," Aden explained. "The studio wants me to do a TV show next instead."

"Well, there's nothing wrong with that. Andy Lau and Tony Leung were on TVB well before you were born, and look at them now," Evelyn replied knowingly. Aden smiled in appreciation, though his situation wasn't exactly comparable to the early work of two of Hong Kong's aging stars. Still, his mum had always been his biggest cheerleader, even if everything she knew about show business was from a viewer's perspective only.

"That's true, but maybe things are a bit different now, Mum." Aden paused as his courage momentarily wavered.

"I don't think it's the idea of a TV show that's the issue," Mimi interjected.

"So what's the problem, then?" Evelyn, still washing the herbs, glanced over at Aden with slight concern on her face.

"Well, it's not a police show or an old Chinese story…." Aden may not have been alive when they first aired, but he knew a thing or two about the programs his mum had mentioned. "It's a BL drama, which is kind of incredible but, you know, controversial. It's never been done here before." Aden spoke rapidly in an effort to force the words out. "So it will be historic, and hopefully not a total disaster."

For a minute, everything was silent in the kitchen except the water flowing from the tap. Aden held his breath and waited for Evelyn to react.

"BL means boys love, Mum," Mimi said gently. "It's a show about a gay romance."

Evelyn gave the last bunch of coriander a final rinse and shook it, perhaps extra vigorously, before setting it on a plate next to the sink with the rest of the greens.

"I know, *gaa je*." Evelyn nodded at her daughter, using the familial term for "older sister" like she'd done since they were kids. Then she turned off the water and faced Aden.

"I'm sure the studio wouldn't take such a risk unless they knew it would be worth it. They want you to become more popular, not less. But either way, your father and I are behind you no matter what. You're our son, and we're your family. Period."

Her tone was firm but infinitely warm. Aden's eyes felt wet, and he was about to pull Evelyn into a hug when she took a step back. Once she could see both her children more easily, she spoke to Mimi instead.

"The same goes for you, of course," she added, a hint of frustration creeping in. "Even if you're too busy working to start a family and rarely bring your handsome husband home to visit."

"*Aiya*," Mimi huffed dramatically. "I've just turned twenty-nine and only got married a year ago. Be patient, Mum!"

With a heavy sigh, she grabbed a rag and a bottle from the cabinet of cleaning supplies and trudged into the combined living/dining area, dragging Aden behind her. Mimi sprayed the dining table and wiped it down silently but aggressively.

"I'm sorry. Tonight doesn't need to be all about me. It's great that you've got good news too," Aden said quietly. "And I know she puts a lot more pressure on you about these things, which isn't fair."

"It's not your fault," Mimi murmured. She gave the glass table a final squeaky pass, then straightened up, brushing her hair away from her forehead with the back of her hand. "It's just different for you."

"Because I'm a guy?"

"Maybe, but also because you're younger and her favorite."

She paused, raising an eyebrow at Aden, to which he simply shrugged in return. When they were kids, he'd been closer to their mum, while Mimi had been a daddy's girl. Even now that they were adults, not much had changed.

"Plus, it's not that easy for you to have kids anyway...." Mimi toyed with the cleaning cloth in her hands. Momentarily lost in thought, she seemed sad, though Aden wasn't sure if it was for herself or him. Then, eyes dancing, she continued, "Even if you were still with Simon, or somebody else. What's your new costar's name again?"

Aden shook his head. Like Winnie, Mimi had a tendency to tease him about his sex life, or lack thereof. Though since her marriage, she'd been less focused on Aden finding true love and more interested in him playing the field with any number of attractive young men.

"Nope, not a chance." Aden was defiant, though inwardly he felt less certain than he'd like. "No Simon, no Calvin, and no one else. I'm not letting myself get distracted now that my career is finally taking off. Besides, with rehearsals, recording, and filming, I don't have the time."

"Hmm. Suit yourself," Mimi mused. "But I guess you can have a little fun with Calvin, even if it's just acting. Then again, you never know. I'm pretty sure the great Tony Leung met his wife on set."

Aden's lips parted as he prepared to tell his sister off for meddling in his love life once again. But he found himself unable to say anything. His thoughts returned to how right it had felt dancing with Calvin the night before and their interactions earlier that day. It wasn't exactly going to be difficult to act like he was in love with him, and hopefully that wasn't going to be a problem.

Re: MK5 single follow-up
From: janus.so@studiohk.com.hk
To: peter.siu@studiohk.com.hk;
*   leon.ho@studiohk.com.hk;*
*   selina_mak@agentart.com.hk*
March 8 8:43pm

Dear all,

I've received the first report from the media relations team after today's press con as attached. It looks like there's been online coverage of MK5's new single from all major local outlets, and we should have more details on print media tomorrow.

Responses on social media so far have mainly been positive, with some of the expected negativity regarding pop music and boy bands in general, as well as the LGBTQ issues around *Hooked on Love*. The team will let us know if any major concerns arise.

Regards,
Janus

CHAPTER 6

AFTER DINNER, during which Aden had to explain the process of filming a music video and then recap all the events of the day's press conference, he retreated to his room. It was quiet and clean, mainly because he'd barely been there except to sleep recently. After opening his laptop, he scanned through more junk emails than he wanted to count, including too many notifications from his social media accounts.

In the past few weeks, he and the rest of MK5 had steadily been gaining followers, and just today it seemed Aden had at least a few hundred more. Already he'd received far too many unsolicited nudes, declarations of love, as well as a variety of abuse from angry trolls. Thankfully, there were no unwanted visitors in his bedroom.

As far as Aden could tell, the band's launch event seemed to have gone well. Selina had shared multiple articles in their group chat, all with a positive spin, and he'd gotten quite a few messages from old friends and colleagues. There were bound to be negative comments thrown in the mix, about their song or their outfits and presumably *Hooked on Love*, but the studio's PR team could handle it.

Finally, Aden found what he was looking for—an email from Selina with the script for *Hooked on Love* attached. So far he'd only had time to skim it, but he was eager to dive in and find out what he'd gotten himself into. Filming wouldn't start just yet, but in a few days he'd be back at the studio for table reads, costume fittings, and more preparatory work.

Though the show was set in a seafood restaurant in one of Hong Kong's traditional fishing villages, most of *Hooked on Love* would be filmed on set at StudioHK, with a few on-location shoots scheduled later in production. Aden was going to play a character named Mok, a new server at the restaurant, who pursues his coworker Ting (played by Calvin).

Since every love story needs a rival, Calvin's character, Ting, was also being pursued by one of the restaurant's regular patrons. Aden still couldn't believe that Reynold Tam had been cast to fill that role as Mr. Yue, a middle-aged man on a coming-out journey after his wife leaves him. He wasn't quite on the same level as Andy Lau and Tony Leung, but Aden's mum, and most Hongkongers, would still be impressed. And presumably surprised, given that Reynold Tam usually starred in action-heavy roles that were rarely romantic, much less queer.

The supporting cast for *Hooked on Love* included Ting's female best friend and a couple other restaurant staff. There also seemed to be a few guest-starring roles, and Aden was curious which local celebrities might be brought on board. Although cameo appearances were relatively common in the industry, this wasn't exactly an ordinary project.

Skimming through the first episode of the script, he found the scene where Mr. Yue professed his love to Ting.

```
    EXT.   SEAFOOD   RESTAURANT,   NEAR
SEASIDE—EVENING


    Ting strolls along the waterfront
promenade after his shift. Mr. Yue
steps out from where he has been waiting
behind a tree, surprising him.


            MR YUE
    Ting Ting! What's a handsome young
      man like you doing all alone on a
        beautiful night like tonight?


            TING
    Mr. Yue?! I didn't expect to see you
      here. Actually, I was supposed to meet
        some friends, but they canceled at
      the last minute. Thought I'd get some
        fresh air before heading home.


            MR YUE
    That's a shame, though it seems their
            loss is my gain.
```

<pre>
          He comes to a stop in front of Ting,
           then suddenly kneels down and wraps
           his arms tightly around Ting's waist.

         Ting Ting, you are the most wonderful
         creature I've ever met. Will you go on
                    a date with me?

                      TING
                     Whaaat?
</pre>

Aden chuckled as he imagined Reynold Tam hugging Calvin dramatically while the latter made a wacky face that would no doubt be adorable. With the right mix of humor and sincerity, this scene would hopefully appeal to a wide range of fans. And yet, for some reason, Aden also felt rather wistful.

He scrolled farther down until another scene caught his eye. Now the love story was getting more complicated, as Ting explained to his friend over drinks.

<pre>
                      SHER
           Wait a sec. One of your customers
           told you he loved you, and then your
           coworker kissed you? But I can't even
                     get a date!

                      TING
           I knowwwwww. What is happening to me?
               And what am I going to do?
</pre>

Aden inhaled sharply, then re-read Sher's line until he'd memorized it without meaning to. He hadn't even read the actual kiss scene between his and Calvin's characters—he must've skipped over it accidentally— but his pulse quickened just thinking about it.

He'd known all along that he and Calvin would have to kiss at some point, given they were playing lovers on the show. But seeing it in black and white made it much more real. For a moment, Aden allowed himself to consider what it would be like to brush his mouth over Calvin's full lips and run his hands through his silvery hair as Calvin's fingers skittered over his hips. He could almost taste one of Calvin's mints on his tongue, and his mouth watered.

Startled at the direction his thoughts had taken, Aden jumped up from his desk, his wooden chair squeaking on the smooth tile floor. It was no secret that Calvin was attractive and talented and also seemed to be a genuinely good person. But they were just colleagues and friends who cared about each other, and somehow Aden's overimaginative brain had carried those feelings a little too far.

Aden smiled to himself at the irony. He'd sworn off men and relationships for the foreseeable future in order to focus on his career. He'd also been worried that his sexuality might not be well-received by the fans, yet now he was going to publicly "date" another man, Calvin, as part of his job.

Returning to his chair and the script, Aden couldn't resist the urge to skip all the way to the end. As long as he didn't tell anyone, it wouldn't really be a spoiler—TV shows weren't necessarily filmed in chronological order anyway. He let out a long breath as he read through the last scene.

```
          INT. COFFEE SHOP—MORNING, OPENING
DAY


     Ting is putting the final decorative
     touches on the trendy coffee shop that
     he and Mok now own in a revitalized area
     of the city, far away from the fishing
     village and the restaurant. From the
     kitchen, Mok enters and stands behind
     Ting, wrapping his arms around him.


               MOK
          Happy?


             TING
     Well, these flower arrangements aren't
       exactly cooperating, but otherwise,

               yes.
```

```
                    MOK
               Good. Me too.


                   TING
                 Really?


                    MOK
      Of course. Just as long as I have you,
                  my love.


          Mok  reaches  into  his  pocket  and
      pulls  out  his  phone  to  snap  a  selfie
      of  the  two  of  them.  In  the  final  shot,
      he  turns  his  head  to  kiss  Ting  on  the
      cheek.
```

Aden's heart was full. He felt more pleased than he cared to admit that *Hooked on Love* had a happy ending, but he didn't pause to consider why. After his more-than-friendly thoughts about Calvin earlier, he wasn't interested in digging too deep into his current mood. Besides, everyone loved happily-ever-afters, right?

On his desk, Aden's phone buzzed. For some reason, his heart fluttered when he saw the sender's name: Calvin. Another private message, not in the group chat.

Just reading the script and want to give you a heads-up. Don't worry, it's good news :)

Aden frowned at his phone, waiting for Calvin to finish typing.

Christelle's been cast in the role of Sher. Guess we're going to be childhood friends on TV and real life ha ha

Oh wow, really? Aden replied. *Thx for letting me know*

Aden had only met Christelle the night before at Tonic, and though it had been a challenge to talk over the music, she'd chatted with all the band members and even Winnie. He hadn't realized that she was an actress, but that wasn't what was making him uneasy. If Calvin's oldest friend was around on set, Aden wondered if he'd end up feeling like a third wheel throughout the filming of his television debut.

No problem. Just another case of life imitating art, or vice versa. Looking forward to working with you both ;)

Huh. Aden stared at Calvin's last message for far too long, his eyes stuck on the word "both" and the wink emoji. He was being stupid—of course Calvin was happy to work with two of his friends on a groundbreaking TV show. But if that was all, why hadn't he used a regular smiley face instead? Maybe he was just getting ready to flirt with Aden on camera, or it could've even been a typo. Aden decided it was better not to ask.

So he typed a one-word reply, *Same :)* before returning his attention to the script.

A FEW days later, when Aden made his way to the studio for the first table read, the "YSim" music video had already reached half a million views. Thousands of people had streamed the replay of the launch event, and enrollment in the MK5 fan clubs had to be paused because they'd run out of T-shirts and souvenirs for new members. Even Aden's dad had started his own fandom of sorts in their apartment, carefully clipping out every article or advertisement about the band from his daily newspaper.

Aden was still getting used to the idea that his childhood dreams were coming true. Of course it was amazing, but it was rather surreal too. Thankfully he hadn't encountered any more large crowds or overeager reporters since the press conference. Though when he'd picked up coffee for himself and Winnie the morning before, he'd heard the hushed whispers of other (female) customers and seen their (unsuccessful) attempts to sneakily snap a photo. The barista, however, had acted the same as usual—with the quiet aloofness and extreme snobbishness characteristic to his profession.

At StudioHK's headquarters, Aden's stomach was taut with anticipation. Today was the beginning of the next phase of his career. He and Calvin were going to become TV stars as well as pop idols, provided that the general public kept an open mind about the theme of *Hooked on Love*. And as long as Aden didn't let his wandering imagination get the better of him.

Sitting comfortably next to Calvin in yet another of the studio's conference rooms, Aden knew that they were just friends and colleagues.

But whenever he read the script alone and encountered the multiple kiss scenes between them, Aden's mind got a little too fixated on the details. As if they weren't just actors on a set, as if they could do much more than kiss. Either he'd suddenly become a believer in all of Winnie's ideas about love, or perhaps it was just the fact that he hadn't so much as touched anyone for… too long.

Oblivious to Aden's racing thoughts, Christelle and Calvin were quietly discussing a song he'd somehow found time to write for StudioHK's new Cantopop girl group, BB852, as Calvin munched a luncheon meat and egg breakfast sandwich. They fell silent when the door opened and Kenny Tsui, the director of *Hooked on Love*, walked in with Reynold Tam.

"Welcome, everyone," Kenny began, moving to stand behind his chair. "Before we get started, I'd like to thank you all for being here. This project is so important, and I'm forever grateful to StudioHK for taking a chance on me and my vision. It isn't every day you get to work with a legend like Tam Sir, as well as fresh young faces from the next generation."

Kenny folded his hands in front of his chest and bowed slightly to the cast, causing his round red glasses to slip down his nose. Once he stood up, Reynold clasped his shoulder warmly.

"From what I hear, I may be the lucky one." A few wrinkles appeared around Reynold's eyes when laughed, but otherwise he looked just like the star he was: thick, wavy hair; glowing skin; silk cravat around his long neck. With a nod in Aden and Calvin's direction as he sat down, he added, "You guys in MK5 are really something else."

Whatever Aden had been expecting from his first day, being praised before they'd even gotten started wasn't it. Had Reynold Tam, an actor he'd watched on TV growing up, really given him a compliment? Aden's pulse thrummed in his ears, and he felt himself blush. Out of the corner of his eye, he caught a glimpse of Calvin positively beaming that took his breath away.

"Besides, I may be an experienced actor, but this is definitely new territory for me," Reynold continued with a chuckle. "Feel free to share if either of you have any pointers."

"Oh, err…," Aden stammered, as his delight turned into embarrassment. He wasn't quite sure how Reynold Tam knew that he and Calvin were both gay or if he was implying that they were a couple.

Aden had no idea how to respond. His mind was already racing ahead to what it would be like to be on set with the senior actor—was he going to be awkward, or worse, actually homophobic?

"Of course we're happy to help, but there's so much we can learn from you too," Calvin replied diplomatically, though Aden noticed the corners of his mouth had turned down. He caught Calvin's gaze for a brief moment and gave him a nod of thanks before Kenny jumped in to steer the conversation back toward the script.

And then it was time for the table read to begin. Aden's character didn't appear immediately, so he got to observe the other actors transform into their on-screen personas for a while.

Eventually, it was time for his first scene, which happened to be with Calvin in the seafood restaurant. It wasn't exactly a romantic scene—though Aden knew exactly when those would come later—but it was a pretty decent meet-cute.

```
INT. SEAFOOD RESTAURANT—MORNING

Mok arrives for his first day at
work, tentatively opening the front
door of the restaurant. Inside, he
finds a typical Hong Kong-style banquet
setup, with large round tables, each
topped with a lazy Susan.

                MOK
Hello…? Is anyone here?


Unsure, he walks through the dining
room toward the kitchen, from which are
emanating a variety of loud shrieks and
bangs.

                MOK
Um, is everything okay?


Ting appears as a blur, running out
of the kitchen flailing a broom in front
```

of him, repeatedly trying and failing to hit a cockroach scurrying across the floor while shouting at it.

                    TING
        You little… I'm gonna get you!

As Ting runs between the tables, he spots Mok standing in his path. He tries to swerve left and then right. Mok moves as a mirror image, so he is still in Ting's way. Ting is running too fast and can't stop in time. He drops the broom but collides with Mok.

                    TING
              Aiiiiyaaaa!

They fall one on top of the other, onto a pile of tablecloths on the floor. After a beat, Ting springs up, embarrassed, with one of the tablecloths stuck to his back.

               MOK (smiling)
          Well, I guess you got me?

                    TING
        Ahhh, are you hurt? I'm so, so sorry.

He runs a hand through his hair nervously.

                    TING
        It's just… I've been after this cockroach all morning. Anyway, how can
                I help you?

<pre>
                    MOK
     Oh, I'm the new server. It's my first
     day, so I guess I'm here to help you.
     But maybe you can give me a hand first?
</pre>

Aden couldn't help but smile at the similarities between the scene and his and Calvin's own first meeting, though the writers had no way of knowing what had happened at the callback auditions all those weeks ago. Of course, Calvin had actually saved him from falling then, otherwise he might not be here today.

Later that day, with several more scenes to go, Kenny called a fifteen-minute break. Aden chugged the last of his sugar-free energy drink and went to fill up the empty bottle at the water dispenser. Next to it, he wasn't at all surprised to see Calvin staring at a vending machine full of snacks.

"Looks like I better be careful," Aden announced with a chuckle. He walked past Calvin with an exaggerated gingerliness, though this time there were no snacks on the floor, and it seemed he'd barely even registered Aden's presence. Aden filled his bottle with water, drank most of it, and then filled it again, while Calvin continued to stand next to the vending machine in silence.

Finally, Aden heard the telltale beep and thud of Calvin's purchase leaving the machine, just as his own stomach growled, reminding him it had been several hours since lunch. After retrieving a Kit Kat from the collection tray, Calvin turned to face Aden.

"Don't worry, I only bought one snack today," he said, his smile not quite reaching his eyes. "And before… it really was an accident, you know. I wasn't trying to sabotage your audition."

"Oh! Of course I know that. I'm sorry, I was only kidding." Taking a step closer, Aden reached out a hand to touch Calvin's arm reassuringly, then changed his mind and let it drop at his side. He realized that, though he and Calvin had both obviously recognized each other from the callback auditions when they were reunited as members of MK5, they'd never spoken about it until now. "And I'm sorry I was such a jerk to you that day."

"I get it. That audition was kind of a big deal." Calvin shrugged. He was quiet for a minute, then added, "I'm glad it worked out anyway."

"Me too." Aden had a feeling that he wasn't just talking about the audition anymore.

"Here." Calvin snapped the Kit Kat into pieces before opening the wrapper. Smiling fully now, he held it out toward Aden on an upturned palm. "A peace offering."

"Oh no, I couldn't," Aden refused automatically, though his stomach protested. Because of the table read, he hadn't had time to work out, so candy was even more out of the question than usual. When he got home, however late that might be, he would eat the healthy dinner his mum had prepared—rice, vegetables, a small amount of meat or fish.

"I know you're very anti-junk food, but I don't think a little chocolate will ruin your perfect dance body. Plus, who knows how much longer we'll be here tonight." Calvin paused, then puffed out his chest. "Don't want you to pass out, unless it's when my character is being a hero or something."

"Hmm." Aden frowned. Though his willpower was usually quite strong, he felt almost ready to give in to temptation. Then he registered that Calvin had called his body "perfect" and his brain froze.

"Go on," Calvin coaxed. He took a step toward Aden, moving his hand and the chocolate just a few inches from Aden's face. Aden glanced down at the sweet treat, then back up at Calvin.

Breathless, Aden opened his mouth, hoping to find the right words to refuse again. But before he could say anything, Calvin reached up and slipped one piece of the Kit Kat between Aden's lips, his fingertips brushing lightly against the soft skin as he held the candy in place.

Aden's eyes fluttered closed, and he momentarily stopped breathing. He knew he needed to take a bite of the Kit Kat so that Calvin could move his hand away, but it seemed he was paralyzed by Calvin's touch. Though he could barely taste the sugary chocolate wafer, his entire body lit up with pleasure. If anything was going to cause him to faint tonight, it would be this very instant, not hunger.

"Calvin, what are you doing out here? Where's my snack? Oh!"

At the sound of Christelle's excited trill, Aden broke the Kit Kat in half with his teeth and jumped backward, heart hammering against his ribs. He stared wide-eyed at Calvin as he popped the rest of the Kit Kat he'd been feeding to Aden into his own mouth.

"Practicing the kiss scene already, then, are we?" Christelle teased when neither of the band members spoke. Calvin stood by chewing thoughtfully, and Aden's mouth was full of chocolate that was proving impossible to swallow.

"No-o. Just trying to convince Aden to eat something before we get back to work," Calvin replied lazily. He reluctantly shifted his gaze to Christelle, then held out the three remaining pieces of Kit Kat. "Want some?"

Christelle surveyed Calvin skeptically, and Aden watched as the two old friends carried out a silent conversation with their eyes. Whatever had been said, Calvin seemed to come out ahead, and Christelle pushed past him with a shrug.

"I'll get my own, thank you." She sighed, considering the other options in the vending machine. "Aden, you want anything?"

"No thanks," Aden choked out. He gave Calvin a quick nod and slipped back into the conference room on shaky legs. After a few deep breaths, his pulse returned to a more normal pace, but his mind was still a mess. And though he'd technically eaten a snack during the break, Aden found himself even hungrier than before.

Morning Entertainment News Roundup
HK Star Watch
March 12

    Featured story: Action Hero Reynold Tam on his Latest Role: On-screen Lover and LGBTQ Icon
    >>Read more

    Music update: "YSim," MK5's First Single, Moves to No. 1 on Cantonese New Singles Chart
    >>See the full listings

    Photos: Behind the Scenes on Girl Group BB852's Debut MV
    >>Check it out

CHAPTER 7

THE FIRST day of filming for *Hooked on Love* fell on a Thursday, the day that Aden and Winnie had typically reserved for their morning workouts in the past. He snapped a photo of himself and his coffee in the taxi on the way to the studio and sent it to her with the message *Thinking of you.*

She didn't reply immediately, but around fifteen minutes later he got a photo of her dance sneakers in a pile on her bedroom floor.

No exercise for me today. My so-called friend / coach has ditched me for some guy he met in a band. Send coffee and pineapple buns to the rescue

Aden rolled his eyes. Though he'd been the one who'd first suggested their regular training sessions, Winnie had been equally as devoted to them. Like Aden, she'd relished the chance to practice more complicated, intricate dance moves, something she couldn't usually do when teaching classes for kids. She was more than capable of continuing without him, but he could see how it wouldn't be quite the same.

His heart ached. Though at times Aden was still pinching himself that this was his real life—he was in a band, he was on a TV show—he could admit that he missed spending time with his best friend.

Hang in there. I'm bound to have a day off eventually [prayer emoji]

Can't wait. Keep me posted in the meantime. I need details!!! [kiss emoji]

Aden nearly choked on his coffee, but somehow he managed to send Winnie a thumbs-up in reply. Since reading the script, he'd found himself picturing the upcoming kiss between Ting and Mok more than he wanted to admit.

Once he arrived at the studio, Aden's professional side took over, as he made his way to the building where the sets for *Hooked on Love* had been built on a soundstage. Just one floor below were the dressing rooms, as well as separate rooms for hair and makeup, wardrobe, props, etc.

In the long white corridor, Aden scanned each door he passed, searching for his name, and thus, the room he'd been assigned. A place where he could get ready each day or rest and recharge during breaks. A place that would be quiet and free of distractions when he reviewed his lines before filming began.

But when Aden found his dressing room, there was another name next to his on the door: Calvin Leung. Though MK5 was growing ever more popular, it seemed they hadn't yet reached the level of stardom that came with private dressing rooms.

Inside were two identical counters and mirrors with two matching swivel chairs, as well as a black leather sofa and a door that Aden assumed led to a bathroom. But he didn't spend much time looking around.

Instead, he tore off his hoodie and T-shirt, dropped onto the tile floor, and did so many push-ups that he lost count, until all he could think about was his screaming muscles. If he were tired enough, then perhaps his brain wouldn't fixate on what might happen between the two costars in such close quarters.

A glimmer of sweat had appeared on Aden's forehead, and his arms were beginning to tremble when the door opened. He froze in a plank position, glancing up as a man entered. Logically, he knew who it would be, but at first he didn't recognize Calvin—underneath his ball cap, his thick hair was no longer silver, having been dyed a more natural black for the show.

"Hey," Calvin said around a mouthful of food. It was more of a grunt than a greeting, perhaps due to the pastry he was eating, and Aden could sense that Calvin was making an effort not to look at him directly. Although that may not have been too difficult. His arms were full of several shopping bags, as well as his breakfast—a pineapple bun in a plastic bakery bag. Apparently they had the same taste in Hong Kong specialties.

"Hey," Aden replied, all too aware of his naked torso. Though he'd comfortably stripped down in countless dressing rooms in years of dancing and teaching, he was suddenly self-conscious. He wasn't sure how much skin he'd shown in front of Calvin before, or vice versa— surely he'd remember if he'd seen that tall, lean frame without clothes, even if he shouldn't think about such things. They'd shared a dressing room while filming MK5's music video, but of course Phantom, Mingo, and Shine had been there too.

Once Calvin turned away, Aden stood up quickly and pulled on his tight white T-shirt. He needed to change into his costume, but for now he was more focused on covering up his bare skin. After checking his hair in one of the mirrors, Aden turned around to find Calvin in the process of setting up his own personal snack bar on the other counter, filling up almost every inch of space that wasn't already covered by the vase of red roses, a welcome gift from the studio. Besides a variety of junk food including chocolate bars, chips, and instant noodles, Aden noted some less-processed options like dried fruit, nuts, and even coconut water.

"Wow," he breathed out, feeling a little bit impressed, not to mention guilty. He'd been quick to judge Calvin's dietary choices in the past, but obviously he knew how to eat well too. Just because Aden was overly strict with his own calorie count didn't mean he should expect everyone else to do the same.

"Okay now, don't freak out. As you can see, there's some healthy options too." Aden watched Calvin's brow furrow in the mirror, though his cheeks reddened slightly. "I just thought, err, you know, we might get hungry."

We. Oh. Were these shared snacks? And had Calvin bought healthier choices especially for Aden, even though he seemed to expect to be criticized for it? Aden winced, and at the same time his pulse beat the tiniest bit faster. This wasn't the first time that Calvin had gone out of his way to do something nice for Aden, and it always made his insides squirm. In a good way.

"You don't hear me complaining," Aden said warmly. "I was just surprised, but it's a good idea. Thank you."

He made a mental note to restock the snacks whenever they were running low. Not only was it the right thing to do, but he also didn't want Calvin to think he was a jerk. Quite the opposite in fact.

The room was quiet except for the sound of Calvin continuing to arrange the food, so Aden moved over to the clothing rack to find his costume for the day: fitted black trousers and a black button-up, a simple server's uniform. But his mind was stuck on how much Calvin seemed to like junk food, maybe more than anyone he'd ever met. He wondered if there was an explanation.

"Don't take this the wrong way," Aden began tentatively. "I swear, I'm just curious. Is there any reason you're kind of obsessed with snacks?"

"Oh." Calvin hesitated for a moment. "Aside from the fact that they're delicious? I guess they probably remind me of my dad."

That certainly wasn't an answer that Aden had expected. Calvin had never mentioned his father before, except when they'd talked about his parents' headline-making divorce.

"Really? How come?"

"Well, when I was a kid, I was always busy with after-school activities, so my dad used to pack snacks for me every day. My mum traveled a lot for work and still does, and whenever she was away, he'd always give me the best stuff." Calvin paused as a happy nostalgia crept over his face. Then he screwed up his lips wryly. "I know I'm gonna have to be more careful about what I eat someday, but I might as well enjoy it now while I still can."

Aden was intrigued to hear more about Calvin's dad, and he could certainly relate to the concept of being overscheduled, even as a kid. He'd had so many dance practices, music rehearsals, and plays, plus homework and supplementary English lessons, that it hadn't been uncommon for him to get home until well after dinnertime.

But it was what Calvin had said last that stood out to him most. In recent years, Aden had done a very good job of denying himself the little pleasures in life, like sugar and sex, all for the sake of advancing his career. That was what had gotten him where he was today, about to act in a TV show for the very first time.

And yet somehow Calvin had managed to make it to the exact same place without being quite so strict. As he pondered whether he'd pushed himself too hard, Aden turned his attention back to his costume. All black, it wasn't the most exciting of outfits, but he was pleased how the tailored trousers showed off his trim waist and hips.

Aden continued to face the mirror behind his dressing table, intentionally giving Calvin some privacy to change into his own costume. He averted his gaze when he heard the metallic clang of hangers on the clothing rack and the rustling of fabric, pulling out his phone to check the latest headlines about MK5.

There was a knock at the door, and Calvin opened it before Aden even had the chance to stand up from his makeup chair.

"Hey, boys, looks like we're neighbors for the next few weeks," Christelle chirped, and Aden glanced over to smile at her. The first thing he noticed was that her hair was no longer blonde—it was now black like Calvin's. But there was no way he could focus on her face peeking in through the crack in the door while Calvin stood behind it, sans pants, his long legs fully on display. He was just wearing the top half of his costume—a white button-up that covered only part of his dark purple boxer briefs.

Aden struggled to keep his facial expression neutral, though he knew he must've been blushing. If he'd been a cartoon character, his eyes would've popped out of his head and glued themselves onto Calvin's backside. It was just round enough that Aden could imagine what it would be like to bite it or how soft and smooth it might feel against his palm. He shuddered, chewing his bottom lip to distract himself as his thoughts threatened to move beyond what was considered appropriate for a colleague and friend.

As soon as Christelle said "See ya," Aden returned to staring at his phone. He heard Calvin close the door and finish getting dressed, but he wasn't taking any chances. He didn't move a muscle until Calvin was once again standing by the door, fully clothed and telling him it was time to head to hair and makeup.

LATER THAT day, Aden's scenes had been filmed, and he was free to leave after hanging up his costume. As he headed toward his and Calvin's shared dressing room, he toyed with the idea of finding an empty rehearsal space at the studio for a quick workout. He was tired, though it wasn't really that late—in fact, Calvin and Reynold Tam would be filming for a couple more hours. But Aden definitely hadn't been thinking about that, or how he and Calvin would both need to change clothes afterward, when he considered staying behind to exercise.

"Aden, wait!" Christelle called after him as she flitted down the hall. "What are you doing now? Wanna stay late with me for Calvin and Tam Sir's date scene? I bet it's gonna be super cheesy."

"Oh, err…." Aden stalled, wondering if Christelle had literally read his mind. Then again, she'd seen Aden with Calvin in several compromising positions now—glued to his body in the crowd at Tonic, eating chocolate directly out of his hand, trying not to ogle his ass. Maybe she was planning some sort of intervention, which would be awkward, but hopefully save Aden from any further embarrassment.

"Come on. What else do you need to do?" Christelle looked at him expectantly.

Work out. Eat dinner with his parents at a normal time. Sleep. Aden could think of plenty of things he should do, but instead he simply said, "Sure. Give me a few minutes."

After changing back into his fitted joggers and T-shirt, Aden grabbed two packets of unsalted nuts from Calvin's counter and stepped back into the hallway where Christelle was waiting. Before he could say anything, she silenced him by holding up one finger, then finished dictating a voice message to what sounded like her roommate in a mix of Chinese and English.

"Your Cantonese is really good for a...." Aden paused, remembering that some Westerners found the terms *gwai lo* and *gwai mui* offensive, even though to many locals they just meant "white man" and "white woman."

"For a *gwai mui*?" Christelle laughed, finishing his sentence. "Well, my mum's Chinese, but my dad's from the UK. Growing up, I spoke some Cantonese at home, and I even went to a local primary school for a while before I transferred to an international school. That's where I met Calvin."

"Right, of course." Aden nodded along as if nothing Christelle had said was out of the ordinary. And perhaps it wasn't, though expensive international schools geared toward expats weren't something Aden was at all familiar with. But suddenly some things about Calvin made a lot more sense—his willingness to pursue a career that his mother disapproved of, his outspokenness about LGBTQ issues. These things would come much more naturally to someone with a less traditional local upbringing.

On set, Aden and Christelle found a spot behind the camera, out of the way to one side. Calvin and Reynold were already in position, though filming hadn't begun. They sat opposite each other at one of the smaller tables in the fictional seafood restaurant. With two tapered candles and a bottle of wine atop a satiny cream-colored tablecloth, it looked a bit like a Chinese version of the date night in *Lady and the Tramp*.

Despite what he'd said at the table read, so far it seemed that Reynold wasn't having any trouble pretending to fall in love with another man. His acting and his attitude had been friendly and welcoming to Aden and Calvin both.

And yet Aden suddenly felt nervous, though he wasn't the one about to be on camera. He wondered if Calvin had seen him and Christelle, or if he even knew that she'd planned to watch this scene and had invited Aden along.

"Snack?" Aden asked, offering Christelle one of the packets of nuts as a distraction.

"Oooh thanks!" she squealed.

"You're welcome, though I can't really take any credit," Aden admitted wryly. "Calvin basically set up a tuck shop in our dressing room."

"That sounds about right." Christelle chuckled. "Naomi swears that Calvin should've auditioned for *Master Chef* instead of StudioHK, but I think *Supermarket Sweep* is probably more like it."

A vivid image of Calvin racing through aisles of food to a chromatic piano soundtrack—baggy trousers billowing out from his thin waist, brow furrowed in concentration—popped into Aden's head, and he couldn't help but smile. Christelle's suggestion was a good one, but who was Naomi? Oh yes. Calvin's other friend who'd been at Tonic.

"I would definitely love to see that," Aden agreed, though he was pretty sure he'd enjoy seeing Calvin do almost anything. He toyed with the remaining packet of nuts in his hand before continuing, "Is Naomi your…?"

"Girlfriend," Christelle almost shouted, though no one seemed to notice. The crew were still making final adjustments to the lighting and sound equipment before filming could start. "It feels so good to say that, even if it's taken forever."

"Really? How come?" Aden asked. Although he'd sworn off dating, he didn't mind hearing about other people's romances. And he was happier than he cared to admit to find out that Christelle was in no way interested in Calvin herself.

"Naomi and I have known each other for a long time, almost as long as I've known Calvin," Christelle explained, her eyes wide and shining. "I thought she was amazing from day one, and apparently she felt the same about me too. But neither of us said so for ages, until Calvin, the hopeless romantic, finally couldn't take it anymore and found a way to bring us together."

"Huh." Aden had known that Calvin wasn't anti-dating like he was. But Calvin wasn't in a relationship currently and had never talked about any recent dates or hookups. Aden hadn't expected him to be quite so sentimental, a matchmaker even. Apparently he was a man of many talents.

"Actually, it was the night we met you at Tonic. Naomi and I were dancing, and then, you know, one thing led to another…." Christelle trailed off dreamily, her gaze fixed at some faraway point. Aden, too, allowed his thoughts to drift back to that night and how right it had felt to be in Calvin's arms. But nothing good could come of indulging in such fantasies. He and Calvin were coworkers, and that's how it had to stay.

"Well, congratulations, then," Aden said, forcing himself back to the present, though Christelle was still lost in her reverie. She remained silent as he struggled to open his snack, finally opening the bag with a loud pop.

Aden winced, grateful filming still hadn't started, otherwise he'd have spoiled the take. As it was, he saw Calvin squint over at him in the semi-darkness beyond the brightness of the set lights. His surprise turned into a quiet smugness when he noted what Aden was holding. Aden smiled in return, sheepish, and tried to ignore the gymnastics taking place in his stomach.

Soon after, the director called "action" and Calvin was gazing at Reynold as he fed him dainty bites of all the restaurant's most expensive dishes using chopsticks. It appeared to be abalone, lobster, and scallops, but in reality Aden knew it probably wasn't anything nearly so elaborate.

Although Aden was perfectly capable of feeding himself, it did seem like a romantic Hollywood moment. Reynold as Mr. Yue was almost worshipping Calvin as Ting with his affections, and Aden found himself wondering what it would be like to really love someone that much. Or be loved in the same way.

The longer Aden watched, the stranger he felt as he got more wrapped up in the scene. At one point, Aden thought that Reynold was about to go off script and actually kiss Calvin, and he shuddered, glancing down at the floor. Careful not to make any noise this time, he popped a few mixed nuts into his mouth and chewed them roughly to distract himself from the emotions raging in his chest. He was uncharacteristically misty-eyed, full of longing, even envy. All for something that wasn't remotely real.

"Easy, tiger," Christelle said, lightly digging an elbow into Aden's ribs. "You know they're only acting, right?"

"Huh?" Aden blinked. Only when he spoke did he realize that, once he'd finished chewing, he'd continued to clench his jaw tightly. Forcing his facial muscles to relax, he shifted his attention from Calvin and Reynold, now chatting easily in between takes, to Christelle.

"You looked like you were trying to shoot death lasers at the famous Reynold Tam out of your pupils. Jealous much?" Her own eyes twinkled in amusement.

"What? As if." Aden shrugged. When Christelle crossed her arms in front of her chest, raising an eyebrow, he added, "I was just hyper-focused, trying to learn from one of the greats." He gestured at Reynold unconvincingly, and Christelle was having none of it.

"Uh-huh. Coulda fooled me."

"What's that supposed to mean?" Though Aden feigned innocence, he had a pretty good idea what Christelle meant. In an ideal world, he would've preferred not to have this conversation at all, but Aden was also relieved he wasn't officially acting right now. He was doing a fairly poor job of it.

"The way I see it, you and Calvin have been circling each other for the past few weeks and are about to take things to the next level on the show. Obviously, he's not my type—lesbian here—but objectively I know that he's pretty wonderful. If I were into him, I for sure wouldn't want to watch him be all lovey-dovey with anyone else."

"Hang on, weren't you just reminding me that this wasn't real life?" Aden asked, finally feeling as if he'd gotten the upper hand. For good measure, he continued, "Besides, Calvin and I are definitely just friends."

"If you say so." Christelle shook her head in disbelief, then grinned mischievously. "I guess we'll see what happens the day after tomorrow."

Aden gulped. Christelle may have been reading into his and Calvin's relationship a bit too much, but she was right about one thing. He and Calvin were filming the kiss scene in two days, and he was going to need every ounce of self-control he'd developed over the years to make sure he didn't get carried away.

Re: MK5 single week 1 recap
From: janus.so@studiohk.com.hk
To: peter.siu@studiohk.com.hk;
*   leon.ho@studiohk.com.hk;*
*   selina_mak@agentart.com.hk*
March 14 6:37pm

Dear all,

Attached please find the full week's report on the performance of "YSim," including the latest chart listings, video plays, and social media engagement. You'll see that all metrics have exceeded our expectations. To keep up the momentum, Marketing suggests launching the dance version of the single in the next week or two.

@Selina Please share the good news with the MK5 boys. Let's also remind them to continue posting about the band on their personal social media accounts even while working on their new separate projects.

The detailed promotion schedules for Phantom's first track, Mingo and Shine's show, and *Hooked on Love* are still being finalized, but I will update you all when ready. For now, a few key points and images will be included in a press kit to be distributed tomorrow.

Regards,
Janus

CHAPTER 8

ADEN HAD been staring at his mouth in the dressing room mirror for an unknown length of time. On the surface, his lips looked the same as always, maybe even better from all the lipstick he'd been wearing on set the past few days. So far they, and he, had managed to put on a good show for the cameras—smiling and frowning and reciting lines as directed in the script. In fact, though acting in a TV show was an entirely new experience, it was still a performance. And Aden was certainly familiar with those.

Today, however, he realized that it had been a while since his lips had done one thing in particular: kissing. He hoped they remembered how to do it properly, given there was no time to practice now. Not that he had anyone to practice with anyway. He wasn't about to suggest that to his handsome costar, even if the idea might've crossed his mind. More than once.

Aden's phone vibrated on the makeup counter and he jumped, startled out of his reflections. *Sell it, baby! Or should I say.... Kiss it, baby!* Somehow the encouraging words he'd loved hearing in the past didn't have the same effect this time. Then again, he wasn't usually nervous when people said them. But he'd never fake kissed anyone before, especially not an attractive colleague who needed to remain in the friend zone.

A noise somewhere between a laugh and a gasp escaped from his throat, and Aden quickly closed Winnie's message, darkening his phone screen before returning it to the table. He looked up to find Calvin eyeing him from his side of their dressing room.

"Everything okay over there?" he asked, amused.

"Yeah, just my friend—err Winnie, you met her at Tonic—being ridiculous." Aden shook his head, attempting to play it cool. He really didn't want to share the details of Winnie's message with Calvin unless he had to.

"Ready for today, then?" Calvin's face grew a touch more serious, though he was still smiling. "Do you think there's anything we need to, umm, talk about first?"

"Oh, I guess we'll be fine as long as we follow the script and Kenny's feedback." Aden stalled. Though he'd been thinking about the kiss scene all morning, and most of the day before if he was honest, the weight of it only hit him at that moment. This was so much bigger than him kissing Calvin and ideally not fucking it up. Even if Aden enjoyed it more than he was supposed to, he'd try his best not to let it have any weird effects on their working relationship. But it could have a huge impact on their careers. And their community.

"Of course! But that's not exactly what I meant…." Calvin trailed off, and his voice was pitched higher when he next spoke. Oh. Maybe Aden wasn't the only one feeling a little lost. "Do we need to, like, set any ground rules or anything?"

"Well, I mean, you did try to trip me once." Aden paused, waiting for a reaction. Once Calvin had pretended to scowl, Aden continued. "But we've done a lot of singing and dancing together these past couple of months, so I trust you."

Calvin nodded, and when he didn't say anything, Aden ventured on.

"My last test results were negative, and I'm not dating or kissing anyone but you." Aden laughed uneasily. "So there's nothing to worry about there."

"Same here." Calvin was smiling again, and this time it was almost radiant.

"Okay, then I guess we're good?" Aden asked, attempting to ignore the fluttering in his stomach.

"Yep," Calvin replied as he stood and opened the door.

```
     INT.   SEAFOOD  RESTAURANT  STORAGE
ROOM—EVENING
     Ting is tidying up near the end
of his shift, hoping to avoid the
attentions of one of the restaurant's
regular customers, Mr. Yue. Mok comes
in to check on him, laying a friendly
hand on Ting's shoulder.
```

<pre>
                    MOK
     Hey. Is everything okay? You've been
              in here a while.

                   TING
     It's fine. Has Mr. Yue left yet?

               MOK (nodding)
     Yep. It's just you and me, so the
               coast is clear.

                   TING
          Great, that's a relief.

                    MOK
     So... you don't like him, then?

                   TING
                    No!
</pre>

Mok cocks his head at Ting, then leans forward and kisses him. After a few seconds, Ting pushes Mok away in surprise.

Aden gulped. He and Calvin had finished running the pre-kiss dialogue, and it was almost time to move on to the kiss itself. Was it his imagination, or did the lighting suddenly seem unbearably hot? Across from him, Calvin leaned against one of the shelves on the storage room set, chewing fruit pastille after pastille like they were, well, candy. Though he wasn't hungry in the slightest, Aden found himself watching too attentively.

Soon enough, Kenny said "Places, please," and Aden and Calvin moved into position, while Calvin tucked the remaining roll of candy into his pocket. Their gazes met, and although Aden wasn't not nervous, at least he knew they were in this together. There was no going back now, for either of them.

At the word "action," Aden tilted his head to one side, still looking at Calvin and trying his best to make his face appear curious or intrigued. Then he leaned forward, closed his eyes, and placed his mouth on Calvin's. This close, he could almost taste the blackcurrant sweets himself, though their lips remained closed as directed—all the kisses in the script were chaste. Aden detected Calvin's familiar vanilla scent too, even if it was somewhat masked by the smell of hairspray and the various dry goods lining the shelves on set.

Before he could register any other sensations, Aden felt himself moving backward. Opening his eyes, he choked back a laugh at Calvin's over-the-top expression—mouth and eyes open wide in surprise. Okay, then. So far, so good. They'd broken the first kiss seal and the world hadn't stopped turning. Time hadn't stood still.

"Cut!" Kenny shouted, more out of habit than anger. "That was a good start, but let's hold the kiss just a bit longer, shall we? I think Ting should be too shocked by what's happened to react right away."

On the second take, Aden tried to repeat his movements exactly as before. But once he'd done his part, Calvin didn't move, even after several beats. Now Aden had time to notice that Calvin's lips felt soft and warm. But they were simply actors on a set, with probably more than a dozen other people in the room. Everything was surprisingly fine, except he was beginning to think that the kiss had gone on for too long.

"Cut!" came the director's voice again when Calvin still hadn't moved. "Okay, now that was a bit too much. This isn't a Category III film, and we don't want to scare away our more conservative viewers. Let's try it again."

Aden wondered whether he should check in with Calvin—maybe he wasn't okay—but the cameras had already started rolling. For the first time since he'd started obsessing about this scene, Aden realized that perhaps he had the easy part. He only needed to initiate the action, while Calvin had to react with a perfect mixture of emotions and movements at just the right time.

When Aden kissed Calvin for the third time, he was hyperaware in case something was about to go wrong. He thought that Calvin's mouth was opening against his, and his heart involuntarily sped up, even as alarm bells sounded in his brain. This wasn't supposed to happen. Was Calvin going off script?

But then Calvin was pushing him backward, looking hilariously confused, and Aden knew that everything had clicked into place.

"Cut!" This time Kenny's shout was one of satisfaction. "That was great. But let's get a few more takes so we've got lots of clips to work with."

So they proceeded to shoot the kiss scene several more times without interruption, until it felt just like any other scene and Aden had almost forgotten how keyed up he'd been earlier. After a while, his lips even started to feel tired from kissing—could that actually happen? He wondered if they were red and swollen, as Calvin's were, though that would only enhance their appearance on camera.

On what was surely the last take, Aden leaned forward to kiss Calvin once again. And though he'd performed the same motion just moments before, this time his body didn't quite cooperate. His alignment was the tiniest bit off, and his foot caught against a prop—a huge bag of rice on the floor—knocking him slightly off balance.

But Aden didn't fall over. He just fell into Calvin, pressing a lot more than their lips together. Yet the cameras kept rolling as Aden's entire body—his chest, his hips, his thighs—fitted neatly up against Calvin's frame. Aden could feel his heart pounding (or was it Calvin's?) as he remembered the only other time they'd been so close. The night at Tonic when everything had felt just as it should be.

A wonderful tingling feeling was building at the base of Aden's spine, and he was flooded with warmth. And then suddenly he wanted more, so much more. He was teetering on the edge of doing something dangerous and unscripted that he'd no doubt regret, like running his tongue across Calvin's inflamed lips and devouring his candy taste. Oh shit.

Aden heard a low grunt, barely even audible, and he wasn't entirely sure if it had come from himself or Calvin. Every single one of his muscles tensed, and he tried to think about anything except whatever was happening right now. If he concentrated hard enough, perhaps he could stop his blood from flowing to certain parts of his anatomy that would be all too revealing.

As the seconds ticked by, Aden didn't move, though he thought his hands were beginning to tremble. He didn't even breathe. At some point he sensed Calvin's hand on his shoulder, as he prepared to push Aden backward once more. Was there a strength, a pressure in his fingertips that hadn't been there before, as if he longed to pull Aden closer instead?

Or perhaps he just wanted to shove him away harder, which it felt like he did when he finally moved.

Though maybe Aden had only imagined it, stunned as he was by the heightened emotions of that last kiss. He shut his eyes as Calvin finished the scene, taking no pleasure in the fact that he'd been right to worry about it all along. For his sanity, Aden prayed that this would be the final take. He needed more than just a moment to remind himself that he and Calvin were actors, colleagues and nothing more.

"And cut," Kenny said in his most definitive tone. "Okay, that should do it for today. Great job everyone."

Around the set, people burst into applause punctuated with a few wolf whistles and cheers. Though he felt far from recovered, Aden knew he couldn't hide behind closed eyelids forever. He glanced up at Calvin and smiled weakly, in silent recognition of their hard work. But Calvin's mouth was set in a hard line, lips pressed together tightly, and his dark eyes bore no trace of their earlier amusement.

As the clapping continued, there was nothing left for the two young actors to do but take a bow. Aden flashed a brighter smile at the director and the crew, then bent low at the waist with a dramatic flourish of his hand. At least he hadn't lost the ability to give people a good show. Standing up, he turned toward Calvin again, only to see that he'd already left the set, and by the time Aden got to their shared dressing room, Calvin was gone.

For immediate release: MK5 Beyond the Music
March 15

As MK5's first single "YSim" continues to dominate the airwaves, StudioHK is pleased to announce that individual members of the band have embarked on the next steps in their journey to stardom.

The band's lead singer, Phantom Kwok, has started rehearsing his debut solo single, while Mingo Lee and Shine Cheung have been exploring Hong Kong and shooting segments for their new lifestyle magazine show. Aden Wong and Calvin Leung have been hard at work on one of StudioHK's sound stages as filming for the upcoming boys love TV drama *Hooked on Love* gets underway.

More details about these exciting new projects will be forthcoming.

Encl.:
Selection of approved photos
MK5 factsheet

Media contact:
Carmen Yau
pr@studiohk.com.hk
+852 2154 1888

CHAPTER 9

THE NEXT day, Aden arrived at the studio at his usual time, slightly early so there was no need to rush. He put on his same all-black costume and reviewed his lines, just as he'd done every day before this. But though he was following his standard routine, on the inside he didn't feel like the same person anymore.

He waited anxiously for Calvin to arrive, dreaded it even. After the final kiss the night before, something was off between them—it couldn't have been a coincidence that the only time Calvin had left without saying goodbye had been after filming such a significant scene. But why he'd rushed off, whether he was angry or upset or something else entirely, Aden had no idea.

Aden had spent the better part of the intervening hours trying, but failing, not to replay that last take over and over again in his mind. He told himself he was searching for a reason why Calvin might've freaked out, or at least numbing his senses so he'd be ready to film the next kiss scenes as they came along.

But the truth was that he wanted to lose himself in that moment, and all the accompanying delicious feelings, forever. He never wanted to forget just how exhilarating it had been to be pressed up against Calvin, igniting something deep within him he'd honestly never felt before. It seemed that his resolution to avoid men entirely until his career had taken off had temporarily slipped his mind.

The minutes ticked by, and still Calvin hadn't arrived. Aden picked up his phone to check the time, debating whether to send Calvin a text. He decided against it, not wanting to do any further damage, and returned his attention to the script. And that was when he realized he was doomed. There were no lines for Calvin's character in any of the scenes scheduled that day. He wouldn't be coming to the studio at all, and Aden was so worked up that he hadn't even noticed. He needed to get out of his head and into character and stop being so foolish.

After sighing heavily, Aden stood up and headed to hair and makeup. With any luck, he'd find out where things stood with Calvin tomorrow, but he had to make it through today first.

MUCH TO Aden's chagrin, the following day began much the same as the one before. He was a bundle of nerves as he waited for Calvin to walk into their shared dressing room. At times he wondered if he was overthinking what had happened—it was just a kiss, a scripted kiss, which had been cheered by the rest of the cast and crew. No actual lines had been crossed, except for possibly in Aden's fantasies, but Calvin had no way of knowing about that.

So there was a chance that Calvin would appear and everything would magically be fine between them. But as much as Aden hoped that was true, the fear gripping his stomach told him that wasn't going to be the case. He didn't let himself think too closely about the cause of his fears—whether he was concerned about what might happen to the show and the band if he and Calvin no longer got along or afraid of something much bigger developing between them.

The closer it got to call time, the more Aden's pulse fluttered. He decided that he couldn't stare at the script any longer, so he tried to use up his unwanted energy with a series of sit-ups and push-ups, even though he'd already worked out earlier that morning.

Finally, he gave in and left the dressing room. As he opened the door to hair and makeup, his eyes landed on Calvin in one of the chairs, already in full wardrobe and receiving the final touches on his face.

"Oh. Hey. You're early," Aden said, attempting to keep his voice neutral as he slipped into the empty seat beside his costar.

"Hey," Calvin grunted.

A makeup artist was applying his lip liner, and Aden wanted to think that was the only reason that Calvin didn't look at him and barely spoke. But given that Calvin had managed to miss seeing Aden in their dressing room entirely, it seemed unlikely. Since they weren't alone, Aden wasn't going to press him for any more details right now. He racked his brain for something else to talk about—the show, the band, even the weather—but he kept getting distracted by Calvin's painted mouth. Before he could say anything, the makeup artist was finished and Calvin left without another word to her or Aden.

Things between them certainly didn't improve on set, with Calvin seemingly becoming a master of microaggressions. As his character, Ting, trained Aden's character, Mok, in the basics of back-of-house restaurant prep, Calvin said all his lines as scripted, while taking many liberties with his actions. Instead of handing Aden a plate or bottle gently, he almost threw it. His elbows were everywhere, particularly in Aden's ribs, when they stood side by side folding napkins into complex designs.

Later, when Calvin barked orders into the "kitchen" and served the fictional restaurant's "customers," he did so with an edge that Aden had never seen before. And yet the director must've been happy with his performance, as filming continued according to plan. Aden was relieved, though he still felt like he was walking on eggshells.

At every break, not that there were many, Calvin managed to disappear before anyone else. Clearly, he was determined to be alone, so Aden made no attempt to follow him, though at times he was tempted. Calvin didn't even seem to talk to Christelle, and she could definitely tell that something was up.

"Lovers' tiff?" She grinned at Aden, and a nervous laugh burst out of his throat. For most of the day, he'd thought he was doing an excellent job of focusing on reasons why Calvin might be mad at him when he wasn't on camera. But now, thanks to Christelle, he was back to thinking about his costar in very unprofessional ways.

"Very funny," Aden grumbled once he'd recovered some of his composure.

"Have you tried talking to him?"

"Are you kidding me?" Aden made no attempt to hide his frustration. "How can I do that when he's actively avoiding me?"

Christelle's only answer was a slight shrug of her shoulders as she surveyed Aden with twinkling eyes.

"You're his best friend. Why don't you talk to him?" Aden sighed. His fingertips were inches away from his scalp, about to be shoved into his hair, when he realized what he was doing and jerked them away. He didn't need the hair and makeup team pissed at him too.

"I don't think I'll be much help in this case," Christelle said thoughtfully, as another grin spread slowly across her face. "But don't worry. I have a feeling everything will work out just fine."

This wasn't the first time that Christelle had not so subtly hinted that Aden and Calvin were more than friends, but Aden wished she'd just come out and say what she meant. Or what Calvin had told her. He didn't know her well enough to tell if she was being serious or if she, like Winnie, was merely prone to getting carried away by romantic ideas. But at the end of the day, it didn't matter. Once again, Calvin rushed off before Aden could even try to speak to him.

It was well after midnight, and Aden had just climbed into bed when his phone buzzed. He hesitated briefly before pulling it out from under his pillow. Reason told him that it wasn't Calvin texting him so late, but there was still a glimmer of hope in his heart that everything would be okay.

When Aden finally unlocked his phone, there were no messages from Calvin, as expected. But he had several from Winnie, and more notifications were rolling in.

Have you seen these?! People are seriously OBSESSED [shocked emoji]

Most of Winnie's messages turned out to be screencaps, and Aden found himself staring at a string of photos of him and Calvin from fan accounts on different social media platforms. There were several images of them from the set of *Hooked on Love*, which must've been released by the studio. Only these versions had been creatively edited—decorated with cartoon hearts and stars, plus speech bubbles or emojis. Someone had even taken a picture of Calvin's fictional romantic dinner with the customer and replaced Reynold Tam's face with Aden's own to adorable results. He inhaled sharply.

Scrolling through the rest of the photos, he saw that some had originally been pictures of himself or Calvin separately—including a few from their own social media feeds—which had then been placed side by side to show how they'd worn similar clothes or visited the same shop at different times. As if those everyday actions somehow meant they were actually a couple.

Out of all of them, he stared at an image from MK5's press conference the longest, though on the surface it was nothing special. Just a closely cropped photo of the two of them sitting at the table during the event.

But Aden had been uncharacteristically nervous that day, and Calvin had saved him from Helga Sze. Then they'd calmed each other on stage through the simple act of pressing their legs together. At least that's what Aden had thought they'd done, and even in the photo, Calvin appeared to be looking at him almost, well, tenderly. However, considering the events of the past couple of days, now Aden wondered if Calvin had just been annoyed with his fidgeting, or not even aware of what had happened.

Winnie was his friend, and Aden was momentarily tempted to share his worries about Calvin with her. But it was late, and there was nothing she could do to help. Not when even he didn't really understand what was wrong.

Wow, some people have too much time on their hands, he wrote back instead.

She sent him an eye-roll emoji. *You guys are cute, though (just like I said you would be btw). And so is your ship name. Caden!*

Aden sighed. He'd known that the MK5 fandom would take off as they became more famous—hell, K-pop idols were shipped by their fans all the time, though that didn't make it any less unsettling. Right now, the difference between these strangers' fantasies and his reality was too stark. At this point, he wondered if he and Calvin would ever get back to being friends, let alone anything else.

How was Caden's first kiss, then? Aden shuddered when he read Winnie's next message, thinking of the myriad ways to answer that question. Fine. Amazing. Confusing. Terrible. Stressful. Unlike anything he'd ever experienced before.

One down, several more to go, he said, followed by the peace fingers emoji. There was no way that Winnie would be satisfied with his reply, but it was all he was prepared to say for now.

Before putting away his phone for the night, he selected a few of the photos Winnie had shared and forwarded them to MK5's group chat. Just in case Selina hadn't seen them yet, it seemed like a good idea to let her know what the fans were saying about the band and the show.

Thanks, Aden, she replied almost instantly. Soon after, Mingo sent a GIF of his excited cat running in circles, and Shine attached the stickers he'd made out of some of the images (which Aden definitely didn't save on his phone).

So much for making headlines when my new single is released :/

Aden could almost hear Phantom moaning, and he chuckled for what might've been the first time all day.

By this time, it was closer to 1:00 a.m. than midnight, but Aden waited a few more minutes before fully committing himself to sleep. He wanted to see if Calvin would reply to any of the messages in the group, even if he was apparently not speaking to Aden directly.

Aden's eyes began to grow heavy, and more than once he nearly dropped his phone on his face as he started to drift off. The third time it happened, Aden gave in and decided to call it a night. He glanced at the group chat once more, noting with regret that Calvin still hadn't replied. However, he had liked a couple of the others' messages, and Aden really hoped that counted for something.

Re: MK5 sponsorship opportunities
From: janus.so@studiohk.com.hk
To: peter.siu@studiohk.com.hk;
*   leon.ho@studiohk.com.hk;*
*   selina_mak@agentart.com.hk*
March 16 5:25pm

Dear all,

Besides the upcoming partnership with YoYum, Marketing has come up with a number of other potential collaborations for MK5 to raise their profile and continue to build the fan base. These include a local instant noodle brand, several luxury and athletic apparel lines, and even a few options in the public service sector.

Please find the list of proposed partners in the attached. I will keep you updated if more details are confirmed.

Regards,
Janus

Chapter 10

When Aden had reviewed his schedule at the start of *Hooked on Love*, he'd been pleasantly surprised to see a few days off scattered here and there. Naively, he'd assumed he'd have some free time to see his family, or Winnie, or just be able to work out and practice at more normal hours of the day. He hadn't considered that the studio would find other ways to keep him occupied.

So the next day, though Aden and Calvin had yet to say anything to each other apart from a simple "hello" and their scripted lines since the fateful kiss scene, they'd be reunited with Phantom, Mingo, and Shine for the first time in a while. Instead of working on the music video for MK5's next single as Aden had hoped, they'd been booked on a promotional shoot for a new yogurt drink called YoYum.

"Long time no see, lover boy," Shine greeted Aden with a cheeky grin when he entered the band's shared dressing room, followed by a wolf whistle. Next to him, Mingo laughed and waved.

Aden felt his cheeks flush, though he was fairly sure Shine was just joking about the photos in the group chat the night before. Shine had no way of knowing the crazy ideas that had taken root in Aden's head, and Calvin hadn't arrived yet to reveal what had transpired on set. Neither had Phantom, but out of the corner of his eye, Aden thought Selina shot him a look over the top of her tablet.

"Yeah, yeah. It's called acting." Aden waved away Shine's remark, eager to change the subject. "How's life as a TV host? Are the fans shipping you two as well?"

"Not to my knowledge, but then again you never know." Shine chuckled.

"I mean, whatever makes them happy, I guess. The show's been really great so far!" Mingo exclaimed, his face lighting up. "We've done tons of cool stuff: singing, dancing, art jamming, beer tasting. I even got to drive a Ferrari!"

"For, like, five minutes only," Shine remarked dryly. When Mingo's smile fell ever so slightly, he was quick to add, "But obviously, it was amazing. We test drove several different cars." The contrast between their sweet little bromance and Calvin and Aden's tenuous situation made his heart ache. What would he do if Shine and Mingo's lifestyle magazine show was a hit but *Hooked on Love* bombed because two of its costars had a falling out?

"Niiice." Aden did his best to appear impressed at the photos Shine was swiping through on his phone. Although he'd never gotten around to, and wasn't interested in, learning to drive, he imagined that handling a luxury sports car would be like playing a top-of-the-line Steinway or flying first class—things he hoped would be part of his future as a successful entertainer. "So you've covered fast cars and bars, but what about women?"

For obvious reasons, this wasn't a topic that Aden had much interest in, but he figured the others would be happy to dish about their love lives, especially given some of Shine's previous remarks. Plus, it seemed like an easy way to keep the attention off himself and Calvin. So Aden was surprised when Shine, rather than puffing up his chest to brag about his latest conquests, appeared almost embarrassed. His lips quirked up, which he tried to hide by studying the floor.

"Well, I don't know what it's been like for you," Mingo began, and Aden couldn't tell if he was ignoring Shine's reaction or covering for him. "But there are pretty much girls everywhere we go. It was just a few at first, and now it seems like more and more each time we film in a new place."

Thus far, Aden and Calvin had been confined to the studio, but some of the upcoming scenes in *Hooked on Love* would be filmed on location. That included a few of their "dates," as well as the romantic finale when their characters got back together after temporarily breaking up. Although Aden rarely got stage fright, he wasn't keen on being hounded by eager fans and, most likely, the press while trying to do his job. Especially not when Calvin was being weird, and he was having trouble keeping his thoughts only on his career.

"Oh really? I—"

At that moment, the dressing room door opened and the two remaining band members walked in, very much in need of a shower. Aden barely registered Phantom's presence because the only thing he could see was Calvin, with his glistening biceps, skintight tank top, and low-slung athletic shorts. It was a very different look for him than at the callback audition or at Tonic, but he was just as gorgeous. His dark eyes seemed even bigger than usual, with the front part of his hair pulled up into a tiny topknot. Aden hadn't realized Calvin's hair was that long, but he was 100 percent here for it.

Aden's mouth hung open mid-reply, but he couldn't finish his sentence, even if he could remember what he'd been saying. Still, no one else was speaking, and he hoped they hadn't caught him staring. Aden forced himself to say something, anything, before things really got awkward.

"Hey, guys," he managed, barely above a whisper, then quickly looked away. As he turned his head, he noticed Calvin frowning at him. Great. Another day of not speaking to each other, even in front of the rest of the band and their manager.

"Think fast," Phantom called as he tossed the basketball he'd been holding to Shine, who caught it easily, then held out his free hand for a fist bump. Thank goodness Phantom hadn't thrown the ball to Aden. At the best of times, he wasn't sporty, but today he might've fallen over from sheer mortification.

"Nice of you to join us," Mingo said sullenly. "Guess our invitation to the game was lost in the mail."

Although he was still trying to recover his composure, Aden felt for Mingo, who obviously wasn't happy about being left out. For his part, Aden was neither upset nor surprised that he hadn't been asked to play. Even if things had been fine between him and Calvin, he wasn't interested and still hadn't spent that much time with the band outside of work. However, his ears pricked up as Phantom made his excuses.

"Sorry, dudes, my man Calvin and I needed to have a chat about—"

"About Phantom's new single, which is written by yours truly," Calvin interrupted in an overly loud voice. Did he sound nervous? "It's coming along really well so far, if I do say so myself."

Aden wasn't sure how anyone, even a talented songwriter like Calvin, could discuss music while playing basketball, which had a clear rhythm of its own. It was also unusual to hear Calvin praise one of his songs so directly. Even Phantom seemed taken aback, which made Aden think that they'd talked about something else. Perhaps *Hooked on Love* or, more specifically, him?

Phantom briefly raised an eyebrow at Calvin before shifting into his proud musician persona. He grinned. "Good? It's gonna be great, obviously."

"Which is more than we can say for this ad campaign." Shine sighed. Balancing the basketball on his hip, he toyed with the sleeve of a pale pink suit jacket hanging on a nearby rack, one of their costumes for the day in YoYum's signature brand color.

"Gentlemen, I know they're not creative or fun, but these promotions and sponsorships are just as important as making music or television," Selina announced, stepping into the center of the room from her half-hidden position in the corner. "Please don't forget that jobs like this help to build your brand and also fund the other riskier yet artistic projects that you like more."

"And you know, the yogurt isn't too bad!" Calvin said too brightly, his smile fading under Selina's disapproving glare.

"By the way, is there any particular reason you boys have arrived in such a fragrant state?" she sniffed.

"The showers at the court were out of order," Calvin explained in a more subdued tone.

"Lucky for you, and the rest of us, the ones here are not. May I suggest you get a move on, as we're meant to be starting soon?" Selina pointed toward the bathroom at the back of the dressing room, only lowering her arm once Calvin and Phantom began to move in that direction.

Not accustomed to being scolded, the diva in Phantom grumbled his disapproval as he went. Something like "too much to talk about" and "out of town," but Aden couldn't quite understand what he was saying or why Calvin was glaring at him.

After they'd cleaned up, all five band members donned their pink suits and headed to hair and makeup. Then they proceeded to a green-screen area, where they spent several hours posing with the yogurt, smiling, and pretending to drink it. The work wasn't as difficult as acting or dancing, but it was fairly continuous, which meant there wasn't much time for talking. Aden held out hope that the rest of MK5 wouldn't be able to tell that he and Calvin were on the outs.

Although the band weren't required to actually drink the yogurt during the shoot, they received plenty of free samples during breaks. Aden tried, but didn't even finish, his first bottle—it was far too sweet—and it seemed like Phantom, Mingo, and Shine weren't that impressed either.

Calvin, on the other hand, consumed enough YoYum for them all, but with no ill effects. He drank nearly every bottle that was given to him, though perhaps more out of distraction than enjoyment. Aden shuddered when he glimpsed Calvin's upturned chin and his long slender throat as he practically seduced the yogurt, even off camera. If the fans could see that, all the YoYum in the city would sell out immediately.

Most of the day, Aden had been trying to avoid being too close to or even looking at Calvin so he wouldn't be tempted to stare like in the dressing room. Today wasn't about them anyway—it was about MK5 and their newest sponsor.

But then the photographer asked Calvin and Mingo, the two tallest band members, to sit down, with the other three standing behind them. Unsurprisingly, Phantom claimed the center position, and since Shine was already near Mingo, that put Aden next to Calvin. It was the closest they'd been since the kiss scene. Aden tentatively rested his right hand on Calvin's shoulder as instructed, grimacing as he felt the muscles beneath his fingertips tense.

Aden let out a long exhale as he gathered the energy to pose once more. His cheeks ached, and he was tired, from the shoot as well as walking on eggshells around Calvin. He watched his breath ruffle Calvin's hair, and his heart skipped a beat when Calvin shuddered, the vibrations running through Aden's arm like an electric current.

"Okay, everyone, that's good. Now big smiles and eyes on me," the photographer called.

"That means you too, Mok." Aden jumped when Phantom hissed in his ear. He hadn't noticed he'd been looking at his hand on Calvin's shoulder instead of the camera. But apparently Phantom had, and for some reason, he'd said the name of Aden's character on *Hooked on Love* instead of his real name. How odd. Aden was surprised he knew it at all.

He decided to question Phantom about it later when the shoot was over, but then Selina cornered him in a secluded area of the now-empty set.

"Aden, is everything okay with you?" Her expression was friendly, but Aden could feel a weight to her piercing gaze. Inwardly, he squirmed.

"Sure, why wouldn't it be?"

"You seemed a little distracted today, and usually you're super focused, so I wanted to check in. I know yogurt commercials aren't exactly what anyone dreams of doing, but I hope you're enjoying *Hooked on Love* so far."

"Oh. Right." Aden hesitated. Until recently, his experience on set had been fantastic. Except, of course, for the past few days. But if he told Selina what had happened, would it make things even worse? He didn't want to give Calvin any more reasons to hate him when he had no idea what he'd done in the first place.

"How was the first kiss scene between you and Calvin?" Selina asked, as if she could read Aden's mind.

"It was…." Aden paused again. There were a lot of ways to answer that question, but he decided to go with a half truth. It seemed like a safe choice. "Good, I think? Everyone clapped for us when it was over."

"And how is Calvin?" Selina pressed. She wasn't smiling now.

"Err, shouldn't you ask him that?" he asked weakly.

"Of course." Selina laughed lightly. "I mean, how are you and Calvin? I know these particular roles may be challenging for you both as new actors."

Okay fine. Aden wasn't going to lie to his manager, and she wasn't giving up on her line of questioning. It was time to come clean.

"He's not really speaking to me right now, but I don't know why," Aden replied quietly, his eyes on the floor.

"I thought something seemed different between you two." Selina sounded satisfied, and her voice took on a gentler tone. "Let's give him some time, but please let me know if things don't work themselves out. You can come to me whenever."

"Thank you." Aden wasn't sure if he wanted to run away from Selina or hug her. He hoped he'd made the right decision in telling her, and at least she didn't appear too worried. Maybe he'd been making things out to be worse than they really were.

Tomorrow he and Calvin would be back on the restaurant set, and surely Aden could find a way to make things right. He certainly couldn't play basketball, but perhaps it would help if they sang or talked about music.

Oh. Of course. Aden couldn't believe he hadn't thought of it earlier. It was so obvious. What did Calvin love more than anything? Food. Aden could buy him some unhealthy, delicious treats as a peace offering.

"Aden?" Selina interrupted his train of thought.

"Sorry, what?"

"I was just saying that, in case this on-screen romance turns into something more, I expect to be informed A-S-A-P. Remember that the studio has very strict rules about dating fellow employees and things like that."

Jesus. First Christelle and Winnie, and now Selina—were her eyes actually twinkling? It was as if every woman Aden knew was playing matchmaker with him and Calvin. And even if the thought was more appealing than he'd expected, it was not a part of his plan for becoming one of Hong Kong's hottest new stars.

Aden nodded, relieved when Selina finished her interrogation. He made his way back to the dressing room to change, secretly hoping that the rest of the band had left. When he opened the door and saw Mingo and Shine still there, his heart sank.

"Hey, man, everything all right?" Shine asked, surveying Aden more closely than he would've liked.

"Yeah, sure. Why wouldn't it be?" Aden tried his best to sound casual as he removed his pink coat and tie. At least Calvin and Phantom had gone.

"We were just wondering where you went, that's all," Mingo replied. His tone was sweet and innocent as usual, though Aden may have detected a hint of uncertainty underneath.

"Oh right. I was talking with Selina about *Hooked on Love*."

Aden slipped out of his costume and into his own clothes as quickly as he could without looking too eager. He wasn't prepared to have any more awkward conversations today, though no doubt he'd be having one tomorrow.

But thankfully Shine and Mingo soon moved on to discussing the next episode of their TV show. They were going to do one of Hong Kong's most famous hikes, then perform the theme song to the classic TV drama *Below the Lion Rock*. Aden said his goodbyes and hurried home, trying not to think about how unlikely it was that *Hooked on Love* would be so popular. Especially not when two of its stars were barely speaking.

THE NEXT day, Aden and Calvin were back on the set of *Hooked on Love*, which had to be better than shooting promos for a yogurt drink. On the other hand, Aden had only just realized that they'd be filming another love scene, though the aftermath of the first one had yet to be resolved.

Before Aden even arrived at the studio, his day had gotten off to a bad start. As soon as he stepped outside his apartment building, he was soaked from head to toe by the heavy spring rain, despite using an umbrella. Although he was tempted to head back upstairs to change, he soldiered on to the taxi stand, after making a quick stop at his local bakery.

Now Aden was sitting in their shared dressing room, sipping his bottled milk tea and nibbling nervously at a pineapple bun. He'd decided he was allowed the occasional indulgence, having bought one for Calvin too. He just needed to work up the courage to give it to him.

Unsurprisingly, Calvin hadn't said anything to Aden when he arrived, with both his hair and flowy clothes looking more tousled than usual, no doubt thanks to the storm. He'd just collapsed into his chair and made a pillow for his head with his arms on the makeup counter, then sat there unmoving ever since.

When it was approaching call time, Aden walked over and tapped Calvin on the shoulder. Surprised, he jumped, then pushed up onto one elbow. Calvin squinted at Aden as he removed his earphones, from which came the cacophony of what sounded like a piano concerto—it was good Aden hadn't tried to talk to him earlier.

"I know you're not speaking to me or whatever, but I've got a present for you that should make you happy. Breakfast." Aden held up the remaining pineapple bun in its bag, dangling it temptingly in front of Calvin's face.

He hadn't expected Calvin to jump for joy, but ideally Aden was hoping for some sort of positive reaction. Instead, all he got was a pained expression before Calvin closed his eyes with a shake of his head. He seemed tired.

"I… err… thanks, but I've already eaten," Calvin finally said.

"*Chur.*" Aden groaned, narrowing his eyes. So much for a kind gesture to smooth things over. But he wasn't going to eat two pastries in one day.

"Well, I'm sure you'll be hungry later." Aden shrugged. He tossed the pineapple bun onto Calvin's makeup table and tried not to notice how his mouth seemed to tremble or his hair fell across his forehead so beautifully.

```
INT. SEAFOOD RESTAURANT
     Ting and Mok are in the empty
  restaurant changing a lightbulb above
```

one of the dining tables. Ting is
holding the ladder while Mok stands
on it. As he climbs down, Ting makes
his first move, showing Mok that he is
interested after all.

                    MOK
        Okay done! I'm coming down.

                    TING
        All right, please be careful.

                    MOK
    I'll be fine. Just don't let go of the
                  ladder.

                    TING
      (eyes twinkling as he purposefully
    shakes the ladder from side to side)
        Oh, it's shaking! Is there an
          earthquake? Or a ghost?

                    MOK
          Very funny…. Aiya!!!

    Mok's foot slips, but Ting steadies
him, then hugs him tightly from behind,
lifting him down off the ladder onto the
floor. They stay like that for a few
moments, Ting nuzzling Mok's neck.

                    MOK
    All right, you saved me. Now are you
            gonna let me go?

                    TING
          Nope. Never.

```
                MOK (smiling)
      Then how are you ever going to kiss
                     me?


      Ting loosens his grip, and Mok turns
      around in his arms. They kiss for a few
      seconds, only to be interrupted when
      Sher arrives at the restaurant.
```

When he'd first read this scene, Aden had thought it was almost too cute. Now, in the middle of it, he was more concerned that it wasn't cute enough. Calvin was all over the place from take to take, sometimes shaking the rickety wooden ladder violently, other times barely moving it at all. He never seemed to hug Aden tightly enough, as if he were afraid he might break or something, and they hadn't even made it to the actual kiss.

Aden wasn't worried about getting hurt, but his patience was wearing thin. More than that, it was growing obvious that the rest of the cast and crew could tell that something was off. Exactly what he didn't want.

"Okay, everyone, let's take fifteen and come back ready to do the whole scene." Kenny sighed wearily after Aden had slipped too much on the shaking ladder yet again.

Although beyond mortified that the director had called a break so soon, Aden was also relieved. He dogged Calvin's footsteps back to their dressing room, never letting him out of sight for a moment. As soon as the door closed behind them, Aden leaned against it, turning the lock before letting out all the frustrations of the past few days.

"Look, I don't know what's going on with you, but it's got to stop. Now." Although he wanted to shout, Aden tried to keep his voice down, knowing Christelle was probably next door. But he made no attempt to hide his anger. "I can handle you ignoring me or avoiding me if I have to, even when I try to be nice, but I'm not okay with whatever this is becoming a problem on set as well. And I think we both know that's what happened out there today."

Although Calvin had his back to Aden, his face was visible in the mirror. His lips were pressed together tightly, and he winced at the start of every sentence. He wasn't saying anything, so Aden continued, not quite realizing that his rant had taken on a more personal tone.

"Like, I know I don't taste of candy or naturally smell like vanilla, but I'm not exactly repulsive either. We're in a band together, we've danced together, and you literally saved me from falling before we'd even met. Is it really that terrible to hug or kiss me on camera?"

Calvin's eyes widened, and then he slowly turned around. He took one step toward Aden, then stopped.

"No." Calvin's voice was raspy, and the hair on the back of Aden's neck stood up. Even if Calvin was basically staring him down, at least they were speaking now. And it was nice to know that he didn't hate touching Aden either, even if it wasn't real.

"Good." Aden nodded, but he wasn't finished yet. He tried to sound more hopeful and less pissed off. "So please can we go back to how things were before? I thought we were friends."

"No," Calvin ground out, the muscle in his jaw twitching as he clenched his teeth. He stepped forward so they were less than a foot apart and Aden had to tilt his head up to see Calvin's face properly.

What he saw made his stomach drop and his heart speed up. Calvin's eyes were flashing, and his chest was heaving, but he no longer seemed angry, and maybe he never had been. He was looking at Aden like he was suddenly very interested in hugging or kissing him, almost as if he could eat him.

"Oh." Aden's lips parted, but even so, he could barely breathe. His mind raced back to the first kiss scene in the storeroom and how the last take had felt so different, so right. Apparently he wasn't the only one who'd thought so.

When Aden felt his fingertips brush against Calvin's, he realized that he'd unconsciously moved even closer. There was almost no space between them now. Calvin's breath was hot on his skin, and his heart pounded as they lingered on the edge of another point of no return. For real this time.

Aden met Calvin's gaze, and his lips quirked as he found the perfect thing to say—a twist on his last line in the scene they'd just been butchering. He had a feeling it would go a whole lot better in the next take.

"So when are you ever going to kiss me?" he quipped, just above a whisper.

Calvin's mouth descended onto his, and Aden's entire body lit up. He opened his lips, forcing his tongue greedily into Calvin's mouth and thrilling when he did the same. One or both of them moaned, and this time Aden only noticed that he wanted to hear and be the cause of all Calvin's sexy little noises.

Aden brought his arms around Calvin's neck, pulling him even closer as Calvin walked him backward, pushing Aden up against the door. He smiled into Calvin's mouth when he remembered that he'd already locked it, then gasped as Calvin ground their hips together and it was obvious how much they both wanted this.

Eventually Calvin broke the kiss, pulling away to nibble at Aden's neck, and Aden's hands wandered down Calvin's back to his waist. He'd untucked Calvin's white shirt and was about to venture lower when his fingers found something hard and plastic. The transmitter for Calvin's mic. Oh shit. Surely it wasn't turned on.

This time when Aden groaned it wasn't because of the incredible things Calvin was making him feel, though he was all too aware of his racing pulse and burning desire. What he'd momentarily forgotten was that they were still at work and expected to return to the set. How long had they been kissing? They needed to take a break before they tore each other apart, as tempting as it was.

With a moan, Aden shoved Calvin backward.

"Holy shit," he panted. "We have to stop."

"Right, of course." Calvin's eyes filled with hurt, and his shoulders sagged. He quickly looked down and moved away toward his side of the dressing room.

"Wait, no. Sorry. I'm not saying I want to stop, but like, I'm pretty sure it's past time for us to head back out there," Aden clarified, placing a hand on Calvin's arm. He cast an approving glance over Calvin's flushed cheeks and ruddy lips before gesturing toward his untucked shirt and the area where both their trousers were currently too tight. He cleared his throat. "And we're not exactly camera ready right now."

Seconds later, there was a knock on the door, and the knob turned back and forth a few times. Aden raised an eyebrow at Calvin as if to say, "I told you so."

"You guys ready in there? Open up!" Christelle called.

"Almost, but you go on ahead," Calvin replied, his voice on the shaky side. He gave Aden a small nod of understanding. "See you soon."

When the sound of Christelle's footsteps in the corridor had died down, Aden tugged on Calvin's arm, bringing him closer once more.

"Just to be clear, you're not mad at me and you don't hate me or anything?" Aden grinned, and Calvin rolled his eyes.

"No."

"So you were only acting weird because…." Although Aden was fairly sure he knew the answer, he couldn't resist the opportunity to tease Calvin a bit. After all, he'd made the past few days pretty miserable.

"Because I was trying not to think about doing this"—Calvin ghosted a kiss across Aden's lips—"or this"—he nuzzled Aden's jaw just below his ear—"and this"—he ran his thumb over Aden's left nipple, causing him to shudder.

"I need you to do all of those things," Aden purred, for the first time unbelievably happy that he and Calvin were sharing a dressing room, "but not right now. We've got to get back to work."

On set, Aden and Calvin nailed several great takes of the ladder kiss scene, though now Aden wasn't in any rush for it to end. He and Calvin were on the clock, getting paid to flirt and kiss, things it seemed they both wanted to do anyway. Kenny was pleased with their improved performance, but if he was curious as to the reason, he didn't ask. Christelle, on the other hand, definitely smirked at them every time she broke up Ting and Mok's tender moment as directed.

They filmed a couple more scenes that day as scheduled, though as usual everything took longer than expected and it was late when Aden and Calvin were alone in their dressing room again. Aden locked the door behind them as he'd done earlier that day and leaned up against it.

"So…," Aden said, surveying Calvin at a safe distance. He itched to be infinitely closer yet didn't want to presume. There'd been enough misunderstandings for one day.

"So…." Calvin bit his lip, and Aden's heart melted a little.

"About earlier," Aden began, and he didn't miss the way Calvin's face fell. He hurried to add, "I didn't imagine it, right? That really happened?"

Calvin smiled weakly, looking relieved. He nodded and took a step toward Aden, then stopped. For a minute, or maybe longer, they simply gazed at each other, registering the myriad emotions of the day: anger, frustration, and confusion that had given way to longing and so much want.

When Aden couldn't bear it anymore, he loosened the top two buttons of his black shirt, thrilling at the heat in Calvin's stare. He grabbed Calvin's tie, tugging him closer, and once again they were nose to nose.

Then they were kissing, tongues tangling and hands exploring, and somehow it was everything, and not nearly enough at the same time. Aden was trying to decide whether to take off his own clothes or Calvin's first when a screech in the hallway startled them both.

As Calvin pulled away, eyes wide, Aden froze, tightening his grip on Calvin's waist and clinging on as if for dear life. In reality, he knew they were safely behind a closed and locked door, but the interruption was as unnerving as it was inconvenient.

A moment later, they heard the telltale sound of a wet mop hitting the linoleum floor, and Calvin let his forehead drop against Aden's in defeat.

"*Diu.* The janitor," Aden whispered before letting out a slight giggle. The horrible sound must've been the wheels of the cleaning cart as it was pushed down the hall.

"That means the studio is closing," Calvin moaned. What he didn't say, but they both knew, was that it also meant their time together that evening was running out. They needed to leave, and soon.

"But it will be open tomorrow," Aden murmured before touching his lips to Calvin's for one last kiss.

Letters: What's happening at StudioHK?
HK Entertainment 101
March 19

I refer to the previous articles about the latest offerings coming out of StudioHK, including the new wave of Cantopop groups such as MK5 and BB852, as well as the upcoming TV drama, *Hooked on Love*.

It appears the company is dead set on corrupting the youth of this city. Not only have they introduced a new generation of highly sexualized pop stars as supposed role models for our children, some of the same musicians will star in a free-to-air television show featuring a homosexual romance. Just what example are they trying to set?

Marcus Lam
Hong Kong Christian Family Society

***

There's been a lot of negativity surrounding the recent reports of changes that StudioHK is bringing to the local music and television industry. But all the naysayers need a refresher on their Cantopop history.

Leslie Cheung was wearing red high heels at his concerts all the way back in 1997, and two years earlier, Anita Mui's "Bad Girl" was banned in China because it was considered too titillating. Yet these are some of the city's most famous and beloved icons, and StudioHK's new stars seem relatively tame in comparison.

Besides, isn't it time for Hong Kong to join the 21st century? Our children need positive role models of all genders, ethnicities, and sexual orientations in order for us to build a truly inclusive society.

Kelvin To
Sheung Wan

CHAPTER 11

THE NEXT morning, Aden woke up to a message from Winnie that sent chills down his spine. It was a link to a photo with the caption "Caden's first kiss," and for a few terrifying seconds, he began to panic that someone had found out about his and Calvin's off-screen kiss(es) the day before. On closer inspection, he realized the picture had been taken on set during the first kiss scene, most likely one of many promotional images for the show.

Still, Aden considered his reply to Winnie carefully. Although she'd lose her mind if she knew the truth about him and Calvin, this was probably the kind of career-ending secret he could only share in person, if at all. Besides, it was possible that yesterday's turn of events had been a fluke, so he'd hold off on telling Winnie until he knew for sure.

Later he'd see Calvin in their dressing room and they could… talk? Although if Aden was honest, he had better ideas about what they could do, and he really hoped Calvin would be on board. He hadn't had his fill of his costar yet.

But when Aden checked his schedule, he found that neither he nor Calvin would be at the studio that day. It was their first on-location shoot, and as it turned out, they wouldn't have a dressing room at all. They would simply get changed, separately, in the tiny bathroom at a rabbit café: the site of Ting and Mok's first date.

Aden had taken a taxi to the address in Mong Kok, one of the city's busiest districts, known for touristy stalls in Ladies Market, pet shops in the Goldfish Market, and plentiful restaurants as well as street food. Even earlier in the day, it could be crowded, so he wore a black bucket hat, sunglasses, and a face mask to disguise his appearance.

Still, he managed to attract the attention of a few passersby nosing around the vans, from which the crew were unloading costumes, makeup, and sound and lighting equipment into the street lined with cafés and noodle shops. Knowing his photo would likely be all over the internet by the end of the day, Aden straightened his shoulders and tried to walk at a normal pace, doing his best to ignore the strangers calling his name.

He was relieved once he made it inside, though with floor-to-ceiling windows at the front, the small café didn't really provide much sanctuary. In fact, for rising stars like Aden and Calvin, it was a bit like their own version of the kennels used for the café's furry occupants.

Still, it was obvious why the producers had chosen this location. It was absolutely adorable, its white walls decorated with childlike garden-inspired displays that kids, teenagers, and most adults would love. In the cages near the back were more than fifteen cuddly bunnies in all shapes and sizes, from the tiny spotted dwarf, so delicate that Aden was almost afraid to touch it, to a huge brown lop-eared angora that would nearly fill one of the café's round tables.

Not that the rabbits were allowed on the tables—even on camera Aden and Calvin could only handle them one at a time on the bright green fake grass in the play area, with a staff member hovering nearby just out of the shot. After a series of test bits with different animals, the director settled on a white rabbit with pink eyes named Cony after one of the Line Friends mascots.

```
        INT. RABBIT CAFE—AFTERNOON
        Ting and Mok are sitting on the
   floor, happily besotted, with one rabbit
   between them. As they take turns petting
   it, their fingers brush together and
   they exchange longing glances.


        TING (in baby talk)
     Aren't you just the cutest, wutest
         bun-bun there ever was?


             MOK
   Are you talking to me or the rabbit?
     You know, my buns come highly
            recommended.


             TING
      Is that so? I'm gonna need you to
             prove it.
```

In some ways, Aden couldn't have written the scene any better himself. It was almost perfect—with two handsome stars and an adorable animal, the fans would eat it up. He certainly didn't hate (pretending to?) romance Calvin, even if all the cameras and crew made it seem like they were under a microscope.

What Aden was less keen on, however, was the torture of flirting while being unable to do anything else that usually went with it. There was no scripted kissing in store for Ting and Mok today, and given they weren't sharing a dressing room, Calvin and Aden hadn't even talked about what had happened the day before, much less acted on it.

But the chemistry between them was palpable. It seemed as if Calvin was back to his old self, and every time he delivered his flirty lines, Aden got real shivers up his spine. He was having a hard time remembering that this was only for show.

For someone who'd actively avoided romantic entanglements for much of his life, he was suddenly very eager to spend more time with Calvin. Preferably alone. And naked. Doing any variety of things that Aden shouldn't be thinking about right now.

At the end of the take, he sighed wearily, then resumed petting Cony's soft fur so that he didn't do anything he shouldn't with his hands. She placidly nibbled a bit of hay, blissfully unaware of her human costar's increasing frustration.

"Relax, it's just a few lines of dialogue," Calvin said in a low voice, but from his tone, Aden wasn't quite sure who he was trying to reassure.

"Right, I know." Aden pressed his lips together tightly but let out a gasp when Calvin's fingers brushed against his own. "But that doesn't mean it's not driving me a little bit crazy."

"Well, then…." Calvin took on a teasing, suggestive tone. "Maybe we need to find something to distract you for a while."

"Such as?" Aden raised an eyebrow, then nodded at Cony. "If this cutie doesn't help, nothing will."

"What if I tell you that I hate your costume today?" Calvin grinned, a mischievous gleam in his eyes at Aden's confusion. While he wouldn't have chosen the pale green polo shirt for himself, the sleeves hugged his biceps just right. Meanwhile, Calvin was looking scrumptious in a periwinkle short-sleeved button-up with, what else, tiny gray bunnies all over it. "I think you should probably just take it off."

"*Diu*," Aden moaned. "You are the absolute worst."

Though, of course, he didn't mean it. He was, in fact, delighted to learn that Calvin was equally as interested in picking up where they'd left off the night before. Still, the next time Kenny called "Cut," Aden left Cony with Calvin and rushed over to the café's drinks counter to try to clear his head.

"Can I get a hot lemon water, please?" he asked Sung, the young barista standing behind the silver espresso machine. He was on hand to make beautifully crafted coffees for Ting and Mok, as well as provide more standard refreshments to the cast and crew in lieu of their regular catering. With shaggy hair peeking out from a beanie and denim shirtsleeves rolled up to reveal strong tanned forearms, he was ruggedly handsome, though he didn't quite match the cute decor of the café.

"Sure, I can do that. But don't you want something a bit more exciting?" Sung offered Aden a sexy smile as he reached for a teacup and saucer.

"No thanks. I've had more than enough fancy drinks today. I don't eat much sugar, really," Aden replied. All day, he'd been taking the tiniest sips of the lattes Sung had served and barely nibbling at the matcha shortbread cookies that Ting and Mok were meant to share on their date. Calvin, on the other hand, had probably eaten more cookies than Aden had all year.

"Is that because you're so sweet already? Or is it just an act?" Sung raked his gaze over Aden shamelessly, then turned to fill the blue cup with hot water.

Aden gulped. Sung openly flirting with him wasn't the breath of fresh air he'd been hoping for. Sure, the guy was good-looking, if slightly rough around the edges, and a few weeks ago Aden might've been flattered, though uninterested. Now, in his keyed-up state, he was even more flustered at the unexpected attention.

And if Sung had managed to figure out that Aden wasn't merely playing a gay role in *Hooked on Love*, what else had he noticed exactly? Aden hoped that the crew, or anyone watching or taking photos outside, wasn't nearly as observant. He didn't want to give the Caden fandom anything else to speculate about, even if there might be some truth to it.

So far the outcry against Hong Kong's first gay TV drama had been fairly minor, and it would be best to keep it that way. Presumably that's why the studio had limited the on-screen physical affection between the love interests, and there was no need to add any real-life rumors into the mix.

When Sung placed Aden's drink on the counter, he blurted out a quick "thank you" and hurried away. With trembling hands, he sank onto the wooden stool opposite Calvin, who had moved from the rabbit play area to one of the café's low tables. Aden's relief at escaping Sung quickly evaporated when Calvin narrowed his eyes at him.

"So after all the obscene looks that barista was giving you, you only got plain lemon water? Surely you could've managed a little latte art or something with whipped cream on top. If not for you, then for your costar," Calvin grumbled, and Aden wasn't entirely sure if Calvin was more annoyed about the flirting or the lack of sweet treats. Either way, it was a good look on him.

"Now who needs to relax?" Aden teased, bumping his foot against Calvin's under the table.

"Hmm." Calvin sulked, his bottom lip protruding in an oh-so-tempting pout as he toyed with his empty potato chip bag.

"There's only one person here I want to flirt with, and it's not Sung. But if it happens again, I promise to bring you the sickliest, sweetest drink there is, even if it's bad for you." Aden picked up his teacup and blew cool air across the water's surface. His blood ran hot as Calvin tracked every movement of his mouth. "Or perhaps I can find a way to make it up to you later."

Though Calvin was still frowning, Aden could tell that he liked the sound of that from the slight flare of his nostrils. But before either of them could say anything else, the director clapped his hands to signal the end of the break.

"Okay, everybody, let's get started again. Places, please," Kenny called out.

Reluctantly, Aden headed back to the rabbit play area and resumed his position on the floor. Calvin followed close on his heels and sat down cross-legged to his right. All they needed was Cony, and Aden made sure to avert his gaze when Sung placed the little guest star in position.

Once he'd left, Aden began to stroke Cony with his right hand, holding his left arm out as a barrier in case she tried to hop away. Although the cameras hadn't started rolling, Calvin too began to pet the rabbit, taking the opportunity to brush a finger lightly against Aden's hand.

"How about tonight?" Calvin whispered to Cony's back.

"What?"

"You can make it up to me tonight," Calvin explained, and though he shrugged, Aden thought he almost seemed hesitant, unsure. "My mum's away, so I've got the apartment to myself. It's not too far from here."

Aden's eyebrows shot up in surprise, which quickly turned into excitement when he considered all the things they could do in Calvin's bed. It would certainly be more intimate than a dressing room and a definite improvement on the hourly love hotels where people their age often met their boyfriends or girlfriends in private. Aden wasn't sure he'd been to any of his previous partners' homes before or if he'd even wanted to, but he couldn't wait to visit Calvin's.

Besides being thrilled at this unexpected opportunity, he also wondered how the apartment might be a reflection of Calvin or his distant mother. Was it messy or tidy? He guessed messy. Was it packed with musical instruments or snack foods or both? How many childhood photos could he shamelessly admire?

The click of the assistant director's clapboard brought Aden back to the rabbit café, and he realized he hadn't replied to Calvin's invitation. With the cameras set to roll any second, Aden gave him a quick, smiling nod. The sooner they got back to filming, the sooner they'd be finished and Aden and Calvin could finally be alone.

By the time filming wrapped later that night, the busy district of Mong Kok had quieted considerably, though it was rarely totally deserted. After changing back into his own clothes, including the same black hat and face mask for camouflage, Aden slipped outside to wait for Calvin in the alley next to the café.

It wasn't completely dark, but it was somewhat sheltered from the colorful neon signs and lights of the main street. It seemed unlikely anyone would spot him, as there didn't seem to be any eager fans or reporters lingering nearby. Even Sung had been too busy tidying up to attempt any further flirtations. So besides a few late-night commuters, the only activity was the crew packing up their equipment.

Still, Aden didn't feel entirely at ease. He wasn't anxious exactly, but something like nervous excitement was rushing through his veins. And he didn't like the anticipation of waiting, not even for something he knew would very much be worth it.

"Ready?" Calvin had somehow snuck up on Aden without him hearing. He was so close his breath tickled Aden's neck, sending a shiver down his spine, though there was only a slight chill in the air. Without waiting for a reply, he tugged on Aden's arm, pulling him toward the street, presumably in the direction of his apartment.

Once they were on the well-lit sidewalk, Calvin let his hand drop and they walked side by side at a friendly distance. It was the sensible thing to do, yet Aden hated how much he noticed the absence of Calvin's touch. He was frustrated that they still weren't alone, and a small part of him didn't even care what the studio might think if they got caught.

A few minutes later Aden's nostrils were assaulted by the faint, then overpowering smell of stinky tofu and grilled innards—traditional local foods he hadn't eaten in years. Calvin's steps slowed to a stop as they reached a stall selling a variety of savory snacks, next to an old-school juice stand. At this hour, the stall was deserted except for its elderly owner.

"Hang on, let's make a pit stop. I'm starving," he said, looking as excited as a kid in a candy store.

"When are you not?" Aden chuckled. As eager as he was to get to Calvin's apartment, he knew there was no way he could win over Calvin's empty stomach. Plus he may have felt a bit hungry too.

"Auntie Tse, long time no see." Calvin surprised Aden by addressing the tiny white-haired proprietress by name. She smiled so wide her eyes were barely visible.

"Out late again, Little Leung? Don't work too hard," Auntie Tse replied, fussing over Calvin like he was her long-lost grandchild. Since Calvin was probably two heads taller than her, Aden could only assume it was the childhood nickname of a faithful customer. "What would you like? Curry fish balls, pig intestines, tripe? I'm out of *siu mai*, I'm afraid."

After Calvin ordered at least half a dozen different skewers from the sizzling grill at the front of the stall, he turned to Aden, motioning him to come closer.

"Want anything? I know you probably don't eat this stuff, but it's been ages since we had dinner on set." Lowering his voice, he added, "And we've gotta keep our energy levels up."

Heart racing at Calvin's words, Aden took a step forward and gestured to the white rice noodle rolls in a steamer next to the cash register. "Just some *cheung fun*, please."

"Oh!" Auntie Tse exclaimed on seeing Aden close up. Behind her, near the back of the stall, Aden spotted an old TV, no bigger than a rice cooker, which somehow still worked and was currently showing StudioHK's late news program. Had she seen him in some of the studio's publicity efforts? "Is this one of—?"

With a nod, Calvin placed his index finger over the area where his lips should be, though they were hidden by his own protective face mask.

"That's right, Auntie. This is my band mate Aden." He spoke clearly yet quietly, and Aden was almost disappointed to be introduced as merely a colleague. "But remember, it's better not to tell anyone about us. If people find out how much I love your stall, I'll never be able to come here again!"

"Okay *la*! Here you go," Auntie Tse handed several paper bags of skewers to Calvin, then placed Aden's plastic container of rice rolls on the counter. Despite their protests, she wouldn't accept any payment and simply waved them away. As there was no seating area, Aden followed Calvin round the corner to another darkened alley, where they leaned against the wall and devoured their snacks.

At first, Aden was wary of removing his mask in case anyone walking by might see. He'd felt a little uneasy at being recognized by Auntie Tse, though Calvin seemed to trust her completely. But after his first chewy rice roll smothered in peanut and chili sauces, he was only concerned with finding the shortest path from the plastic container to his mouth.

"Mmm," he moaned in between bites. Apparently he was hungrier than he'd thought.

"Good, right?" Calvin laughed, sounding pleased with himself. "I knew I'd wear you down eventually."

"Huh?" Aden only managed a monosyllabic reply around a mouthful of the delicious snack.

"So far, I've convinced you to eat chocolate on more than one occasion and now street food, even though you're a health nut. I got you to go out drinking at a bar and even seduced you in our dressing room. Right under the studio's nose," Calvin explained as he nibbled at his chewy cuttlefish. "Maybe Aden Wong isn't as much of a workaholic as everyone thinks."

Aden rolled his eyes, but he couldn't deny there was some truth to what Calvin had said. He had been thinking a little bit less about his career these days, though perhaps it was because he was finally doing the things he'd always dreamed about—singing in a band, acting on a TV show. Surely it wasn't only due to a certain handsome musician with a junk food obsession. Hmm.

Lost in his thoughts, Aden wasn't quite sure when they started walking toward Calvin's apartment again. And then they were running through the relatively quiet residential streets beyond Flower Market Road. They passed an occasional pedestrian on the sidewalk, and there were just a few cars, mainly taxis, on the road lined with gated courtyards, each containing a medium-sized tower block. Aden could hear his ragged breath, but he was so keen to reach their destination that he didn't feel his burning lungs or aching legs.

When Calvin stopped suddenly outside one of the gates, Aden was moving too fast to avoid bumping into him. Once they were so close, he didn't want to pull away. As Calvin fumbled for his keycard, Aden crowded against him from behind, nuzzling his neck. It was only when Calvin whirled around, pushing Aden up against the brick wall, that he realized neither of them had been masked since they left Auntie Tse's stall. But any panic that Aden felt was only fleeting as his mouth met Calvin's in a heated kiss.

They broke apart when Calvin beeped his keycard, opened the gate, and pushed Aden through ahead of him. Although there was no security guard on duty this late, Aden knew there could be cameras in the courtyard, as well as inside the lobby and lifts. So he kept his hands to himself for a few painful minutes more as they passed the parked cars and entered the building, making their way up to Calvin's empty apartment on the 16th floor.

"Here we are."

Facing Aden, Calvin stood in the middle of the living room and shrugged his arms wide. No lights were on, but both he and the room were bathed in a warm yellow glow filtering in the big picture window from the streetlamps below. A cursory glance revealed the apartment was larger than Hong Kong's standard 400 square feet, but Aden was more focused on the man in front of him.

"Lovely," he murmured. Calvin was like an angel glimmering in the night, even without his previously silver-gray hair. On the day they'd met, Aden would've never believed that he and the beautiful stranger from his audition would end up here, or even considered it a possibility. But deep down, he sensed that a part of him had wanted this all along.

"Really? It's a bit hard to see anything in here," Calvin teased.

Although Aden was happy admiring the view, he suddenly wanted a much better look. He pulled off his hat, tossed it onto the floor with his shoulder bag, and moved to stand directly in front of Calvin. He brought his hands up into Calvin's glorious hair, knocking his baseball cap askew in the best possible way.

"It's perfect," Aden whispered, his lips hovering just below Calvin's mouth. In that instant, he could've said the same thing about Calvin.

Calvin wrapped his arms around Aden's waist, pulling him even closer.

"Yeah," he hummed, gazing into Aden's eyes before leaning down to kiss him tenderly. And Aden was swept off his feet all over again. Although their lips had met both on and off screen already, somehow this was different. Here, alone in the dark, they could be sweet and sensual and leisurely, with the promise of more to come.

But after a day of waiting, Aden wasn't satisfied with taking things slow for very long. He tilted his head to deepen the kiss, tugging more roughly on Calvin's hair so his hat fell to the floor. Calvin let out a playful growl, smiling as he dipped his tongue into Aden's mouth. And then they were locked together in a dance of flurried movements—hands exploring, hips grinding, hearts racing.

Calvin began to walk them backward, presumably to his bedroom, though objects in their path—a potted ficus, a rug—kept getting in the way. They didn't go far before Aden's foot collided with something hard and the kiss was broken as he swayed off balance. He didn't fall, and this time Calvin didn't catch him. He just ended up leaning onto a smooth wooden surface, and soon Calvin was back on him with an even greater intensity than before.

With Calvin pressed up against him, Aden was almost sitting on a large piece of furniture that he couldn't quite identify. Maybe a desk or a sideboard. As he leaned back slightly, a sharp corner dug into his ribs along with the sound of papers rustling. Oh. There was only one thing it could possibly be: a piano.

Gasping with delight, Aden flung his arms around Calvin's neck and wrapped his legs tightly around his waist. Doing sexy things with a sexy pianist on an actual piano had never played a part in his fantasies before, but right then he couldn't imagine anything more wonderful except perhaps whatever came next.

Eventually Calvin's hands found their way down to grip Aden's ass, and he lifted him off the piano, finally carrying him the short distance to another room. After setting Aden down gently on his feet, Calvin loosened one hand and flicked on the bedside lamp to reveal his childhood bedroom.

It was larger than Aden's room, and the walls were lined with shelves full of memories and clues about Calvin's life that Aden would certainly inspect at some point—photographs, sheet music, trophies, old CDs and records, even a ukulele. But right now, the most important thing was the bed.

"You have a piano and a double bed," he breathed, craning his neck to take everything in without moving from Calvin's embrace. In his apartment, the only bedroom that could fit more than a twin bed was, of course, his parents' room. "Good luck getting rid of me now."

For a brief moment, Calvin's face bore an expression Aden couldn't quite read. Then he dropped a kiss onto Aden's forehead, murmuring, "Actually, you could stay over some time, if you want. My mum's been on tour for a while now and probably won't be back for a couple more weeks. As usual, she's picked up more gigs along the way."

The tone of Calvin's last few words shifted toward resentment, and though Aden was beyond pleased at the idea of sleepovers in Calvin's empty apartment, his heart ached. Calvin was so strong, actively pursuing a career that his mother didn't approve of, one that was already starting to attract the attention of the tabloid press that had made his parents' divorce even more traumatic. Yet he was still willing to take a huge risk just by being here with Aden. He hoped they wouldn't live to regret it.

Aden wanted to say something encouraging or comforting, but talking about family issues didn't exactly fit the mood. He squeezed Calvin's waist tighter and nuzzled his ear, as Phantom's comment from the YoYum shoot about being out of town flickered through his brain. Again Aden wondered if Calvin had been asking Phantom for advice about him that day.

"Well, then, I better make sure you don't get lonely," he whispered, nibbling his way down Calvin's jawline.

"Yes, please," Calvin replied, sliding his hands under Aden's shirt and tracing the lines of his muscles. He slowly guided the shirt up and off, trailing kisses onto Aden's abs, pecs, and collarbone along the way. Aden groaned at the exquisite torture of it.

Once his arms were free, he ripped Calvin's black long-sleeved shirt off, then stripped out of his skinny jeans as fast as he could. Calvin chuckled at his frantic movements but grew silent and serious as his eyes locked onto Aden's one remaining article of clothing: his purple boxer briefs, now extra tight. Although this wasn't the first time they'd seen each other mostly naked, it was the only time so far that day.

"Like what you see?" Aden reached out to stroke Calvin's hip bone, dipping his fingers below the waistband of the gray wide-leg trousers that were keeping too much hidden away.

Yet instead of undressing, Calvin dropped to his knees, and Aden soon discovered that his long, delicate fingers and luscious mouth had talents far beyond playing the piano and singing. In what had to be a first, Aden almost felt like he might pass out, though in a very good way. His chest was heaving, and his breath was coming in unsteady gulps in between the moans escaping from his mouth. Clearly it had been a while since he'd done this, and right now he couldn't remember why he'd been dead set against it for so long.

"*Diu*," he swore under his breath as his toes began to tingle and his legs shook. He wasn't going to last much longer, but Calvin was still partially clothed, and that was a problem. Shifting his hips backward, Aden reached down and stroked Calvin's cheek, then tugged him up to standing.

With swollen lips and mussed hair, Calvin was even more beautiful than usual. Although many of MK5's fans idolized them both from photos alone, Aden had a front-row seat to the real thing. He suddenly felt protective and, at the same time, jealous. Girls, and perhaps boys, across Hong Kong could openly worship Calvin or Aden, but according to Selina and the studio, they shouldn't be here together at all.

Aden's heart was in his throat as he leaned up to kiss Calvin, slowly and deeply, like it might last forever. Then he guided them toward the bed, pushed Calvin down gently, and finally removed the rest of his cumbersome clothes. Aden's mouth watered at the sight laid out in front of him, but surprisingly, his previous urgency had faded now that he had Calvin at his mercy.

He took his time to worship Calvin's body, giving him a taste of his own agonizing pleasure while savoring every moment himself. At first

Calvin was almost reverently still, which Aden hoped was due to wonder rather than disappointment. But soon Calvin's hands were in his hair, his transported expression not too dissimilar from how he sometimes looked when playing the piano.

Afterward, Calvin sighed blissfully as Aden made his way back up the bed to snuggle in beside him. Aden rested his head on Calvin's chest, content with simply listening to the sound of his beating heart. Calvin brushed soft fingers along Aden's back, and he was in danger of drifting off to sleep.

His eyes flew open as he found himself flipped onto his back with Calvin on top, grinding their hips together and kissing Aden like his life depended on it.

"My turn," Calvin said breathlessly before proceeding to blow Aden's, ahem, mind. Any thoughts he'd had of the fans, the studio, or Calvin's horrible mother ceased to exist as his brain practically short-circuited.

After Calvin pressed a final kiss to Aden's hip, he flopped down next to Aden and pulled him close, as if this were something they'd always done. Aden was in no state to consider if it might become a regular part of their future, though his body would be more than willing. After a few minutes anyway.

"Unghhh," Aden grunted. He hadn't recovered the ability to speak, and he couldn't have moved if he'd tried.

"What was that?" Calvin grinned.

"Hhmg." Aden's mouth could only form another nonsense syllable. So much for his career as a singer and an actor. He mouthed a kiss to Calvin's pec as he struggled to drag an arm across it.

"Well, it's good to know there's no way we can do that in between takes. Even if we didn't get caught in the dressing room, you'd totally give us away by not being able to say any of your lines," Calvin teased.

Aden shoved him half-heartedly in response, surprised when Calvin heaved a big sigh.

"What?"

"Oh, nothing really. I was just thinking that today was… nice," Calvin mused. He almost seemed sad, but Aden couldn't figure out why.

"Which part?" Aden smirked. Now that he'd somewhat rallied after one of the best blow jobs of his life, he was prepared to do a little teasing of his own. "Shooting on location where people could see us the whole time, or not being able to kiss for hours? Though I suppose there were snacks, which would make you happy."

"Ugh, no. Obviously I meant the flirting and the sex." Calvin pouted, and Aden felt like a jerk.

"Okay, fair enough. No arguments there," Aden murmured, kissing his way across Calvin's chest as an apology.

"In fact, it was probably the best date I've had in quite a while, even if it wasn't real." Calvin scrunched up his face, and a part of Aden winced at what he'd said, though it was the truth.

"Well, most of it was scripted and staged by professionals, so I don't think it's really comparable," Aden replied. Then he shrugged. "But I suppose it's the same for me as well."

"Why am I not surprised?" Calvin laughed. "When was the last time you went on a real date anyway?"

"*Chur*," Aden groaned. He rolled onto his back and brought a hand to his heart dramatically, buying time to consider his answer. Although he could mention Simon or other guys he'd casually seen before, he'd mainly met them to work out or go to bars. He didn't think he'd arranged a proper date for someone for years, if at all. "I want to be offended at that, but also I don't exactly remember."

Calvin shook his head and rolled his eyes. Aden expected to be pushed to share more details, but then Calvin was blanketing his whole body instead.

"Luckily we were on camera so you won't forget this time," he said. "Still, maybe I need to make it extra special just to be sure."

And then he was kissing Aden deeply, as if it wasn't well past midnight and they hadn't been working all day long. Aden's pulse was racing, and his spine was tingling, and he could've easily stayed in Calvin's bed, in his arms, for the rest of the night.

But even though Aden's parents had long been asleep, they expected him to come home eventually, and he didn't want to worry them. So he managed to tear himself away at some point, somewhat consoled that he'd see Calvin again on set in a matter of hours.

No matter what, Aden wouldn't need the cameraman's video footage to remind him of anything about this day. It would be imprinted in his brain, and on his heart, forever.

Re:"YSim" dance version marketing plan
From: janus.so@studiohk.com.hk
To: peter.siu@studiohk.com.hk;
*   leon.ho@studiohk.com.hk;*
*   selina_mak@agentart.com.hk*
March 22 11:23am

Dear all,

Attached please find the marketing plan for the release of the "YSim" dance remix later this week. The original single and video continue to perform well, though the initial hype has tapered off a bit.

As mentioned in today's call, the promotion schedule for Phantom's debut will be shared tomorrow.

@Leon Please make sure to update all teams once the next band member's solo release is confirmed. Results of the focus groups show that fans are keen to see more of everyone in MK5 and also anything that highlights their unique skills (e.g. Calvin's songwriting, Aden's dancing, Mingo's vlogging, Shine's rapping).

Regards,
Janus

Chapter 12

THE NEXT two days saw Aden and Calvin continue to film on location. First, they browsed for souvenirs in a crowded street market, delighting locals and bewildering foreign tourists with their over-the-top haggling and ridiculous purchases (a foam dart gun for Ting and a *Drunken Master*-style kung fu outfit for Mok). Then they rode through the streets of Hong Kong Island in a slow but iconic *ding ding*—one of the city's old open-air two-level trams that was still the cheapest form of public transport.

They were even more exposed than at the rabbit café, and their presence was far from unnoticed, with crowds of onlookers gathering even as shooting stretched well into the night. Aden barely felt comfortable chatting with Calvin during breaks with so many people around, much less showing any signs of affection or leaving with him afterward.

But soon they were back at StudioHK, reunited with the rest of the cast for more scenes at the seafood restaurant and in the apartment that Ting and Mok would come to share. Even better, Aden and Calvin were once again sharing a dressing room. They did their best to maximize any spare minutes behind closed doors, where Aden quickly learned to relish the feel of Calvin's ribs under his fingertips, Calvin's hands on his back, Calvin's tongue in his mouth.

When they were alone, he could almost forget about MK5 and their careers outside of *Hooked on Love*, not to mention the studio's strict no-dating policy. There was no label yet for what Aden and Calvin were doing, but it was a definite violation of their contracts. Surprised at how easy it was to ignore this major red flag, Aden told himself it was fine because, for now at least, it affected his and Calvin's work in a positive way.

And yet, like many TV shows in Hong Kong, *Hooked on Love* was only scheduled to run for one short season. Filming would last two months at most, and after that, Aden and Calvin would return to being two members of what was rapidly becoming the city's most popular five-person boy band. Who also happened to be hooking up. What could possibly go wrong?

"So you guys wanna go to Tonic tonight?" Christelle asked Aden and Calvin around a mouthful of stir-fried cabbage. The three of them sat at a small folding table just off set, draped in protective napkins while eating takeaway lunches during a break. "We could make a double date of it before you're off to shoot on location again next week."

Aden choked on the rice he'd been in the process of swallowing, and his eyes watered. Though he'd seen Christelle shooting them suggestive looks over the past few days, the bluntness of her question caught him off guard. It was one thing for him and Calvin to break the studio's rules in their dressing room, but telling another person was a whole new level of risk.

Across the table, Calvin pressed his knee against Aden's out of sight, but he kept his expression neutral.

"That could be fun, but...." Calvin traced his foot slowly up Aden's shin, then licked his lips. One glance at Calvin's burning gaze and Aden knew that what he'd taken for a calming gesture was, in fact, a suggestion of things to come later that evening. Now that they had returned to the studio, he'd be able to make his way back to Calvin's apartment discreetly. He couldn't wait.

"I'm not sure that's a good idea," Aden interrupted. In truth, he would've loved to go to Tonic with Calvin again, not to drink but to dance. But it was also a PR disaster waiting to happen. There was no way Aden would be able to keep his hands, or his mouth, to himself, and then it would only be a matter of time before the Caden fandom really blew up. This time with photos of Aden and Calvin doing things in real life that, as far as the studio was concerned, were supposed to remain on set.

"Hmm." Christelle pouted. "Guess someone really is all work and no play, just like Calvin said. Still, I'm pretty sure that you two have been having plenty of fun these past few days."

Calvin rolled his eyes as Aden opened his mouth to protest. Before he could say anything, Christelle held up her wooden chopsticks, demanding silence.

Lowering her voice, she said, "Relax, don't freak out. I'm the only one here who can tell the difference between Calvin's pining crush face and Calvin's post-kiss face. At least I was until recently."

Christelle looked at Aden pointedly, and he flushed as he pictured the expressions she'd referred to—one was sweet and dreamy, the other rumpled and blissed out. For selfish reasons, he preferred the latter, but he'd take either, if they were directed at him.

Under the table, Calvin bumped his leg against Aden's again, playfully this time. Their eyes met, each asking the same unspoken question. Aden nodded, and Calvin bit his lip shyly, sending a thrill up Aden's spine.

With a sigh, Aden turned his attention back to Christelle. "Please don't tell anyone. This is… I mean, we've only just…."

Aden broke off, unsure what to say. It had been about a week since he and Calvin had first kissed for real—far too soon to define a relationship under normal circumstances, even if they'd had the time to talk things through. But in this case, maybe they needed to be totally up front to avoid any misunderstandings or scandals that might jeopardize their careers.

"Seriously, not even Naomi," Calvin added, surveying Christelle closely. "You know all about the studio policy, as well as the crazy fans. It would be very bad for us both if this gets out right now."

"Okay, okay. I promise. I know I'm a chatterbox, but I'm not an idiot." Christelle held out her palms in defeat. Then her face softened into what could only be described as the heart-eyed emoji. "I'm just so happy for you guys."

Aden could feel himself blush even more, though it likely wasn't visible because of his stage makeup. But for the rest of the day, he felt slightly on edge, even if his and Calvin's on-screen chemistry resulted in several near-perfect takes.

That night in their dressing room, Aden quickly changed out of his server's uniform into his own fitted joggers and T-shirt. Calvin, on the other hand, was taking his time, leisurely removing his makeup and snacking on chocolate cookies while wearing only a pair of wide-legged black trousers, the waistband of his hot pink boxer briefs just barely visible.

Normally, Aden would've relished the view of Calvin's smooth, firm chest and toned arms, especially now that he didn't have to pretend not to notice. But he kept thinking about their conversation with Christelle earlier. What would happen if the studio knew too? Would they be fired? It seemed unlikely that production of *Hooked on Love* would be halted— they were more than halfway through—but it wasn't unheard of to find replacements for members of a boy band.

"Stop staring and come over here," Calvin said, startling Aden out of his reverie.

"Okay, but—" Aden hesitated.

"I don't bite." Calvin crunched into another cookie with a smirk. "At least, not hard."

Aden took a step closer, and though still unsettled, he was suddenly more interested in the chocolate crumbs at the corner of Calvin's mouth. And not because he was hungry.

"I won't even force you to eat junk food." Calvin placed the packet of cookies on his makeup counter and slid it away, looking far too pleased with himself.

"I'm not worried about that." Aden laughed nervously.

"But something is wrong?" Calvin slipped his arms around Aden's waist and pulled him close, dropping a series of kisses down Aden's neck that made him shiver.

"It's just… talking to Christelle earlier has got me thinking," Aden began, his fears already starting to fade in Calvin's arms.

"Ahh." Calvin took a step backward, and his face darkened. "I should've known you'd get all weird at some point, though maybe not so soon. We can go back to being friends and bandmates if that's what you want."

Calvin put his hands up and raised his shoulders casually. Still, Aden could see that he was upset. "But, hey, it was fun while it lasted."

"What? That's not what I…." Aden shook his head, then reached out to grab Calvin's hand. He laced their fingers together and was rewarded with a small smile.

"I mean, I actually don't mind if Christelle knows, but what if more people find out? Are we crazy for even thinking about doing… whatever this is?" Aden asked quietly, attempting to keep the panic out of his voice. He was intentionally vague, avoiding words like "dating" or "boyfriend," though weirdly he didn't hate the idea of either.

"Honestly?" Calvin snorted, then rolled his eyes. "I never expected to… I mean, I can't quite believe that you're okay with any of it to begin with."

"Well, it definitely wasn't part of my long-term plan, but neither was doing a boys love show. And that's turned out fine, so…." Aden shrugged.

"Just fine? Really?" Calvin scoffed, feigning offense, but Aden was relieved to see his eyes beginning to twinkle.

"Better than fine," Aden corrected himself, tugging Calvin toward him for a quick kiss.

"I'll say," Calvin murmured against Aden's neck, nibbling his jaw until he shuddered.

"We need to be so, so careful," Aden rasped, though his brain was quickly becoming more interested in Calvin's mouth than this conversation.

"Believe me, I know. I absolutely don't want to be part of another celebrity scandal." Calvin's voice hardened, and Aden felt a twinge of guilt. He'd been so concerned about their careers that he'd forgotten Calvin's horrible experience with the tabloids during his parents' divorce. He pulled away slightly to meet Calvin's gaze.

"So we'll keep things quiet, then. Besides Christelle, who knows?"

"I haven't told anyone. You?"

"Well, my parents have noticed that I've stayed out late, but I didn't tell them why exactly. I'm pretty sure Winnie will figure it out, though."

"Right, that should be okay." Calvin leaned forward to resume kissing Aden's neck.

"Oh." Aden suddenly remembered his conversation with their manager when Calvin hadn't been speaking to him. "I think Selina may suspect something already. She was asking me questions about us and the show after the YoYum shoot."

"Really?" Calvin gulped. "How perceptive of her."

"Yeah."

For a moment, they were both silent, and though Aden didn't know what Calvin was thinking, he could make an educated guess. On more than one occasion, Selina had told the members of MK5 to be discreet about their love lives and to inform her if they were ever in a serious relationship. Obviously Aden and Calvin hadn't quite gotten there yet, but they were still in direct violation of one of StudioHK's rules for their employees.

"Speaking of which, I might've said something to Phantom that day too," Calvin admitted sheepishly, and Aden's heart fluttered. He'd had his suspicions, given everything that Phantom had said at the shoot, even calling him by his character's name.

"Is that so?" Aden clasped his hands around Calvin's neck and batted his eyelashes. He was being dramatic, though in truth he was delighted. "What did you say to our colleague about me, then?"

"That's enough questions for one night," Calvin growled, pulling Aden fully against his bare chest, and Aden instantly regretted getting changed so quickly. "I can think of plenty of better ways to use our time before we're back here tomorrow. Come home with me?"

Before Aden could answer, Calvin had claimed his mouth in a searing kiss, and as much as Aden wanted to go back to Calvin's apartment, he wasn't sure he could wait that long either. As he considered whether to strip off his shirt then and there, he realized with dismay that he wouldn't be doing either.

"*Diu*," Aden swore as he regretfully broke the kiss. "I would love to, but I really can't. I just remembered I'm off tomorrow, and I'm meeting Winnie in the morning. So I should probably go home tonight."

"*Diuuuuu*," Calvin moaned, and even in his distress, he was adorable. "Tomorrow night, then?"

"Can't wait," Aden replied, indulging in one last lingering kiss before tearing himself away.

ADEN WOKE up the next morning feeling more rested than he had in ages, even after he'd gone to bed extremely late. His mind and body were lighter, and though Calvin was most likely the reason, it didn't make any sense. How could being with someone who was very much off-limits make him feel anything but uneasy? Taking a risk with his career was not something he would normally have felt so happy about.

On the other hand, he should've been thrilled to have a full day off, a rare event in his busy schedule. But in fact Aden almost wished he was working. Then he could spend the whole day with Calvin, instead of waiting until evening to see him.

With hardly a thought about the calorie count, Aden selected two pineapple buns from the bakery near his apartment before taking a taxi to the ballet studio where Winnie worked. He paid the driver, then picked up two coffees—an iced latte for her and a soy version for himself. Thankfully, no one paid him any special attention, but he wondered if there would come a time when he'd be recognized almost everywhere, even with his now customary face mask and hat.

Aden was surprised to see that the gate to Sally Wu's studio was already open, and all the lights were on, though it was too early for classes to begin. The unlocked door gave way at his push, and he walked inside hesitantly.

"Winnie?" The reception area was deserted, but Aden could hear sounds of movement in the distance. Just when he was beginning to think he'd imagined it, Winnie appeared in the hallway that led toward the classrooms.

"Aden? Oh!" Though she tried to hide it with a smile, Aden had a feeling that Winnie hadn't been expecting him. It wasn't like her to forget their friend dates, especially now that they were so infrequent, but even her clothes gave her away. Unlike him, she wasn't wearing workout gear, but had on a delightful powder-blue dress with a full skirt. Her long hair, too, wasn't in the usual braid or bun, but hung loose and curled down her back.

"Good morning, Alice. I'm here to see my friend, Winnie, but I think she's forgotten about me," Aden teased. "Did you hide her behind a looking glass?"

"*Chur*." Winnie clicked her tongue as she waved away Aden's question, but she couldn't hide her rosy cheeks.

"Seriously, I mean, that is a killer dress. Although it's probably not great for dance aerobics. What's the occasion?"

"I…." Winnie's blush deepened, and she stared at the floor. "I have a, err, meeting soon. It's possible I overlooked the fact that you were coming this morning."

"Is that so?" Aden smirked, watching her closely. He was slightly annoyed that he'd turned down a night at Calvin's when Winnie hadn't even remembered their plans, but mostly he was curious. Winnie looked awfully pretty, excited even, about the prospect of a client meeting, yet as far as he knew she didn't exactly like her job or her employer. Perhaps the "meeting" was really a date, but then why would she hide it? Unlike Aden, Winnie had never sworn off love and romance, despite having very good reasons to.

"I suppose you've already had breakfast as well, then." Aden held up the coffee tray in one hand and the bag of pineapple buns in the other. Winnie's eyes widened, and she blinked rapidly several times.

"Yes," she admitted guiltily. "But this looks great. Why don't you come on back for a chat anyway? I've got a few minutes."

Once they were in an otherwise empty studio, Winnie set out a couple of folding chairs, and Aden placed his purchases on top of the stereo cabinet before digging in. It didn't matter if Winnie was eating or not; he wasn't going to wait. He hadn't had anything except water since the night before.

Aden took a huge bite of his pineapple bun and washed it down with a gulp of latte. In contrast, Winnie sipped at her coffee, merely nibbling at the pastry before tucking it back into the bag and staring out the window dreamily. It was almost like she'd forgotten about Aden, though he was sitting right next to her.

After a few more bites in silence, he asked, "Are you okay? What's going on with you?"

Startled out of her reverie, Winnie took another drink, then played with the straw almost tenderly. She replied softly, "I'm fine… really good actually. At least I think so. I hope so. You?"

Aden raised an eyebrow skeptically, and they both laughed. Whatever Winnie wasn't telling him, at least it seemed to be something good. So he decided not to pry, given his own recent foray into keeping certain things quiet.

"I'm great," he said around another mouthful of breakfast. Winnie glanced back and forth from Aden's contented face to the remains of the pineapple bun in its plastic bag. Then she let out an ear-piercing squeal.

"Oh my god! You have news, and it must be good for you to stuff your face like that. Is it about your single? Or you're doing a movie? I haven't been online yet today." Aden smiled, amused, but made no attempt to reply as Winnie rushed on breathlessly.

Although *Hooked on Love* was going well, Aden didn't have any other career updates to share—the leaked photos from the most recent on-location shoots weren't terribly interesting. In terms of music, Selina had informed MK5 that morning that Calvin would release a solo single next. That meant Aden still had to wait his turn, but he was proud that he hadn't felt even a bit jealous.

"Wait, I know." Winnie placed her coffee down and spread her palms out dramatically. "It's Calvin! Please tell me you finally got over your stupid hangups and got with him instead."

"I think it's perfectly reasonable to focus on my career and follow the studio's policies," Aden replied primly, but he couldn't stop himself from breaking into a wide grin. "And also rather impossible, as it turns out. But this is top secret—I shouldn't've said anything, and you definitely can't tell anyone."

"Ha! I just knew you guys would end up together. How perfect! You must really like him to…." Aden felt himself beginning to redden at the truth of Winnie's statement, but she didn't even notice, distracted by a series of notifications appearing on her phone. Her eyes were sparkling when she returned her gaze to Aden. "I'm so glad things seem to be working out for both of us, and I want to hear all about it. But not today, I'm afraid."

She stood up, and Aden followed suit.

"Okay, I can take a hint," he said, collecting his rubbish and wondering how to fill the hours till he saw Calvin again that evening. "Since I always put work first, I know I can't be too upset if you do. But maybe the next time I see my best friend it'll be for more than five minutes."

"I'll try my best," Winnie promised, then practically pushed Aden out the door.

Once he was outside at street level, he paused, considering where to go next. The former industrial district, where shiny new office buildings had sprung up alongside repurposed warehouses home to dance studios and creative spaces, was fairly quiet between morning rush hour and lunchtime. Still, Aden hoped a taxi would drive by before he had any surprise fan encounters.

As he searched for a ride, his eyes snagged on a bright orange sports car parked nearby that was either really cool or terribly ugly. Definitely expensive. And also familiar somehow, though Aden didn't know anyone who'd bought a new car recently. Shine and Mingo had done some test driving for their show, but surely they hadn't gotten a free car as part of the deal. That wasn't quite the same as some gratis yogurt or sportswear.

With a shrug, Aden flagged down an approaching taxi and headed home. Since Winnie had ditched him, he'd work out at the gym at his apartment complex instead. Afterward, he might even take a nap. He certainly didn't want to be tired when he saw Calvin in the evening.

Morning Entertainment News Roundup
HK Star Watch
March 26

Featured story: Hongkongers Anita Leung, Harry Mo Headline Piano Gala in Salzburg
>>Read more

Music news: Just 1 Week Until Phantom Kwok of MK5 Drops his Debut Single
>>Watch the teaser

Photos: MK5's Aden Wong and Calvin Leung Looking Cute on the Set of *Hooked on Love*
>>Check it out

Chapter 13

IT WAS after midnight when Aden punched the code into the downstairs keypad and made his way up to Calvin's apartment. Before he could knock, the door flew open to reveal Calvin, freshly showered after a day of filming, looking delicious in nothing but a pair of low-slung gray sweatpants.

For a moment, Aden was speechless. Even though he'd seen Calvin without a shirt countless times, plus fully naked days before, he was still in awe of the beautiful lines of his body.

"Wow," he breathed, eyes glued to Calvin's toned chest. His heartbeat quickened, yet the excitement he'd felt all day gave way to a sudden nervousness about everything, even his clothes. He was wearing tight jeans and a white tank, with a black floral short-sleeved shirt on top, unbuttoned, something a bit nicer than his usual sporty gear to go with his special plans for the evening.

"Wow yourself." Calvin raked his gaze across Aden's body approvingly. When he saw the multiple bags Aden was carrying, he raised an eyebrow. "What's all this?"

It was a fair question. Standing in the middle of Calvin's living room like an overdressed delivery boy, Aden felt rather sheepish, though earlier he'd been convinced it was a great idea.

When Selina had informed the MK5 group chat that Calvin would be next to launch a solo single, after Phantom, Aden had remembered two things: how upset Calvin had been when his lyrics had been changed and how little his mother thought of his career. So he'd decided to make sure that Calvin celebrated this important win. A small part of him hoped that it might count as their actual first date too. Not that it could compare with Ting and Mok's visit to a rabbit café, but at least it would be real.

Aden was still surprised he wasn't upset at having to wait even longer for his own musical debut. And here he was, the master of keeping things casual, trying to do something nice for someone he liked. A lot. Yet for some reason, Aden was currently more worried about how Calvin would react than what he might be doing to his career.

"Well, someone is going to record his first song soon. And I believe that same someone also talked about how he hadn't been on many good dates recently," Aden began hesitantly. "It's too late for dinner, but I brought snacks and movies, and even champagne."

He held out two bulging plastic bags to Calvin, who looked at them with watery eyes.

"Thanks," Calvin whispered, placing the bags on the dining table without even peeking inside.

Hmm. Aden wasn't sure he'd seen Calvin sad in the presence of junk food, and it certainly wasn't the reaction he'd expected. But before he could give any more thought to the matter, Calvin had pinned him against the door and was kissing him hungrily.

Aden gasped, partly in relief, and angled his head to deepen the kiss, though he was finding it difficult to breathe. Calvin's weight was crushing Aden's spine against the backpack he still wore that contained some other items he hoped to use during their "date": condoms and lube. Still, Aden made no attempt to push Calvin away, instead hooking a leg behind his thigh to pull their hips flush.

With a growl, Calvin ground down into Aden, who was definitely regretting his decision to wear tight jeans now. His wandering hands dipped into Calvin's loose sweats, and he moaned loudly when he discovered there was nothing underneath. Aden toyed with Calvin's waistband suggestively, any thoughts about the evening's other possible activities forgotten.

Calvin broke their heated kiss only to nibble at Aden's neck and the sensitive skin near his collarbone. He brought his hands to Aden's shoulders, attempting to slide off his outer shirt, which got tangled in the straps of his backpack. After a fair amount of wriggling that put far too much distance between them, Aden managed to free himself and send his shirt and bag onto the floor with a thud.

"What was that?" Calvin rasped, his breath hot on Aden's neck as he moved in closer again.

"Oh nothing. Just my bag," Aden muttered, more interested in chasing Calvin's mouth than talking. Suddenly he realized that, though he'd packed to stay overnight, Calvin hadn't explicitly invited him to. He'd only mentioned the idea in passing. Maybe he'd even forgotten. Yet somehow Aden had gone from barely making time to hang out with his friends or colleagues to wanting to spend a whole night with one of them. In bed.

"More snacks?" Calvin asked breathlessly, though he didn't seem at all interested in food. Slowly, he dragged his hands down Aden's chest, tracing the contours of his muscles through the tight tank.

"No-o," Aden gulped. "I, err, brought a few things from home. A change of clothes, a toothbrush." He leaned his head back against the door and lowered his voice. "And, ahem, other supplies...."

Calvin's eyes went wide, and Aden wondered if it was time to start panicking. Perhaps he'd made too many plans and assumptions for one evening.

"You know, because I promised to keep you company and everything," he hurried to add. "But of course, not if you don't want—"

Aden broke off as Calvin laid a finger on his lips. He really hoped Calvin wasn't upset because that simple gesture set his whole body on fire.

"Oh, I want." Calvin smirked. "But who are you, and what have you done with Aden Wong?"

Aden blushed all the way to the tips of his ears. There was no denying that his former self would be shocked at everything he was doing right now. He parted his lips as if to reply, but instead sucked Calvin's finger into his mouth, delighting in the sounds he could conjure with just a swirl of his tongue.

And then Calvin was dragging him toward the bedroom, though this time they managed to avoid colliding with the piano or any other home decor. When Calvin gently pushed Aden down onto the bed, he bit his lip in anticipation. But instead of following his slow, almost torturous pace from a few nights before, Calvin moved with an urgency that Aden had never seen.

In seconds, the rest of their clothes were off and scattered on the floor. Their mouths met in a heated kiss as Calvin covered Aden's body with his own, and Aden actually whimpered with need. In response, Calvin got to work with his talented hands and tongue in all the right places. When Aden almost couldn't take it anymore, he remembered that his backpack, and its very important contents, was still in the living room by the door.

"Gahh. Wait, wait," Aden panted in frustration as he eased Calvin back up to eye level. "You need to, ahh, stop that for a minute. Plus, I've barely gotten to touch you yet." He sighed ruefully, nodding toward the door. "Also, my bag's out there."

Calvin chuckled against Aden's lips. "Don't worry. I did some shopping too." He reached over to the nightstand and grabbed a small plastic bag from the top drawer. After taking out a condom and a bottle of lube, he kissed his way down Aden's chest and returned to what he'd been doing moments before.

Aden's blood fizzed, and his muscles slackened as Calvin's touch opened him up in all the best ways. Everything felt incredible, and for the life of him, he couldn't remember why he'd been so against dating for so long. And once Calvin was fully inside him, Aden ceased to think about anything at all except to register the tenderness in Calvin's eyes, the salty sweet taste of his skin, the sound of their breathing growing ever more erratic.

Although it had been quite a while since he'd had sex, Aden wasn't sure it had ever been anywhere near this good. He was filled with an overwhelming sense of completeness, as if Calvin had shined a light into all the places he'd kept closed off for ages. Despite the very real possibility that this amazing thing between them could threaten everything they'd worked so hard for.

Later, once Calvin had returned from the bathroom, Aden snuggled up against him, so close that he could feel as well as hear his stomach when it inevitably rumbled.

"Hungry? Maybe now you'll want the snacks I brought that you didn't even look at," Aden teased, though he was still curious about Calvin's earlier mood.

"I… well," Calvin hesitated, sounding uncomfortable.

"Hey, I'm only kidding." Aden pushed up onto an elbow to see Calvin's face more clearly. He looked much sadder than anyone should be after what they'd just done. "And I'm, err, sorry if I did something to upset you. You know I don't do this much, so…."

"Oh no!" Calvin exclaimed, shaking his head from side to side.

"So what's going on, then?"

"It's nothing," Calvin sighed.

"Hmm." Aden was rightfully skeptical.

"It was just hard," Calvin explained. "You being so nice, when you have every right to be jealous that I get to release a single before you."

Aden scoffed, mostly pretending to be offended, but Calvin wasn't finished.

"My mum, on the other hand, is supposed to be supportive, but she basically ignored my message about the song to update me on her latest travel plans. And now she's pissed because she thinks I didn't tell her about *Hooked on Love*."

"But you did?"

"Maybe not in great detail, but yes." Calvin nodded solemnly. "It's not exactly the easiest thing to talk about via text, you know? Though since she's not home much anyway, I can't see why it even matters."

Aden's heart ached. Although Calvin's mum wasn't the worst he'd encountered—some of his queer friends had been kicked out or disowned by their parents—she obviously wasn't the greatest either. He wished she could recognize her son for the incredible abilities he had, not what she wanted him to be. There were plenty of trophies for songwriting and talent shows on the shelves in Calvin's room, as well as piano competitions.

"Oh, babe, I'm so sorry. That's awful." As soon as he spoke, Aden's cheeks began to burn. He'd never called anyone "babe" before. It had just slipped out. He wasn't sure if Calvin would mind, but he didn't want to keep staring at him until he found out. At least now he knew why Calvin hadn't wanted to celebrate.

Aden was starting to lie back down when Calvin pulled him on top of his long frame instead.

"Hang on, what did you just say?" he demanded eagerly.

"Umm, that I'm sorry?" Aden gulped, squeezing his eyes shut tight.

"No-o." Calvin stroked Aden's cheek gently with his thumb until his eyes fluttered open again.

"Babe?" Aden asked tentatively. He searched Calvin's face for signs of displeasure, and though he found none, he still chewed his bottom lip nervously.

"Hmm, I'm not sure I heard correctly." Although he tried to seem doubtful, Calvin couldn't keep a smile from tugging at his mouth. "Say it again."

Aden was about to comply, but then a better idea occurred to him.

"What are you gonna do if I don't?" he asked playfully, slowly tracing a finger across Calvin's bare chest. As he grazed each nipple, Calvin shuddered, and his nostrils flared with want.

Aden smirked, though he too would've been unable to resist Calvin's touch. But he didn't remain smug for long. The next instant, he found himself flipped on his back with Calvin on top, wearing an expression that was equal parts delight and desire.

"Then I'll just have to find a way to make you," he countered, moving his pelvis against Aden's in tantalizing circles.

"Oh really? I thought you wanted something to eat," Aden teased.

"Maybe I've got a better idea," Calvin murmured before attacking Aden's mouth.

Their all-consuming kiss quickly progressed into round two, and it wasn't long before Aden was whispering "babe" and "Calvin" along with strings of indistinguishable swear words as once again the snacks he'd brought were forgotten.

TRUE TO his word, Aden spent most of his free time over the next week at Calvin's, though it was an easy promise to keep. At first he'd felt guilty telling his parents he might not make it home for several days, without explaining exactly where he was going. But Evelyn must've sensed that he had a good reason because, for possibly the first time ever, she didn't ask a single question about it.

Each day Aden went to and from Calvin's apartment and the studio alone. Although it was unlikely someone would notice if they arrived in the same taxi—the StudioHK complex had multiple buildings with hundreds of employees—Aden wasn't taking any chances. And when shooting on location, they needed to be even more careful.

Winnie had already sent him several photos circulating in the Caden fandom from other scenes between Ting and Mok in *Hooked on Love*—Calvin and Aden walking hand in hand along the harbor front, Calvin shoving Aden playfully during a lovers' tiff, Aden looking at Calvin full of longing. What Aden and Calvin knew, but thankfully the fans did not, was that the last one wasn't in the script. It had been taken after the cameras had stopped rolling.

Aden had expected Winnie to tease him endlessly when he told her, but she'd simply replied with two emojis: a fishhook and heart eyes. It wasn't like her to pass up an opportunity to remind him that he'd been wrong about something, especially when it came to romance, but perhaps she was waiting to gloat in person. Or she had other things on her mind, like whatever had distracted her the last time they'd met up.

But Aden didn't spend too much time thinking about Winnie, as he was making memories with Calvin.

One day stood out most in his mind. They'd spent a few hours filming another date scene on the banks of the Shing Mun River, cycling up and down the tree-lined bike paths on a beautiful spring evening. The air was fresh and clean, and though it was impossible to escape Hong Kong's humidity, a gentle breeze tousled their hair.

Calvin, with rosy cheeks and shining eyes, was radiant in the pinks and golds of the setting sun. And the more Aden repeated his lines—Ting and Mok were talking about their dreams and loves—the less he knew whether he was speaking as his character or as himself.

Out in the New Territories on a weeknight, it was quiet and peaceful, a welcome change from the city. Unlike a Sunday afternoon, which would've been packed, there was no one around besides the two actors and the pared-down crew, plus an occasional jogger or lone fisherman. Because they had to stop filming when it got dark, they actually finished work at a reasonable hour.

"Dinner?" Calvin asked. After changing out of their costumes in one of the studio's vans, he and Aden had left the crew to pack up their gear. They were walking toward the nearest taxi stand, a perfectly acceptable distance between them as they neared a rundown *cha chaan teng*.

In the past, Aden would've headed straight to the gym on a free evening, despite getting plenty of exercise on the bike. Instead, after a quick glance from side to side, he nodded and said, "It's a date," his heart full and his smile wide behind his face mask.

It seemed plausible, safe even, to eat dinner together after work in a place that looked like it could've only been new when Aden's grandparents had been young. There was an old-fashioned pastry case of metal and glass near the entrance, mostly empty at this time of day. Behind the cashier's counter a red incandescent lightbulb glowed over the small shrine to Kwan Kung, the Taoist kitchen god. Slow-spinning fans hung down from the high ceilings, a relic of days before air-conditioning, and the small multicolored tiles covering the walls had long since faded from their original bright blues, reds, and greens.

Aden had wanted to take Calvin on a real date, and unexpectedly they'd stumbled into one. Even if the old café could hardly be considered a suitable location by the average person, much less a celebrity. Then again, perhaps that made it perfect for two rising stars who very much didn't want to be seen. But once their server, a grumpy middle-aged woman who appeared to be the owner's wife, had unceremoniously deposited their food on the booth's linoleum table, Aden wasn't sure whether to laugh or cry.

Over the sound of orders shouted in the open kitchen at the back came the strains of "YSim" playing on the restaurant's old crackly radio. It seemed they couldn't escape reality even here, and Aden froze with his rice spoon halfway to his mouth.

He looked around nervously, waiting for the other diners to recognize the young musicians in their midst. Then there would be whispering followed by the clicks of phone cameras. Across from him, Calvin pulled his baseball cap down lower and sat up straighter, in the process leaning away from Aden and sending a pang straight to his heart.

But the other customers were mostly older manual laborers tired after a hard day's work. They sat by themselves, watching racing news on the muted TV and eating heaping plates of stir-fried noodles with beef or pork chops with rice and brown gravy. Meanwhile, the staff were fully occupied serving food and bussing tables during the evening rush. Apparently no one was aware that two of the voices coming over the airwaves had also been audible in the restaurant.

To be safe, neither Aden nor Calvin spoke as MK5's song continued to play. When it had finished, Aden bumped his knee against Calvin's under the table, and they grinned at each other stupidly for a few moments.

"You smile, I melt," Calvin said in a low voice, and Aden thought his heart might stop beating.

He was in danger of melting himself, or doing something stupid like jumping across the table to kiss Calvin senseless. He dropped his gaze to his chicken in black bean sauce and shoved a spoonful of rice in his mouth.

They ate in silence during the commercial break. Then the station played one of Calvin's songs, though Aden could only identify it due to some internet sleuthing. Besides the several chart-topping hits Calvin had told him about, he'd written dozens more. They'd been recorded by several different Cantopop artists, first for Phantom's dad's company, MusiCity, and later at StudioHK. Before that, he'd won a teen radio songwriting competition three years in a row. Aden stared at Calvin, waiting for him to react, but it took a while for him to look up from his cheesy baked seafood spaghetti.

"What? Don't you like the food?" Calvin finally asked, his mind as ever on his stomach.

Aden rolled his eyes. "A song that you wrote is currently playing on the radio, and you're not even going to say anything?"

Calvin seemed surprised, as if he hadn't expected Aden to make the connection, then frowned at his plate.

"Well, I thought we were trying to stay incognito," he said around a mouthful of pasta. "Besides, it seems you already knew, so I didn't need to bring it up."

"Okay, but you still can. It's impressive, and more people should know how amazing you are," Aden replied warmly. He was pleased to see Calvin's cheeks pinken in response. But as the song continued in the background, Aden began to feel sad. It was a ballad, like much of Calvin's catalog, slow and melancholy. "Do your songs… are they all as emotional as this?"

Calvin shrugged. "Possibly. You know how much people love to wail their hearts out to sappy melodies at karaoke."

"Hmm," Aden wondered aloud. "Is that the only reason?"

Calvin cocked his head, listening to the lyrics, though Aden found it hard to believe he didn't remember them. The song was about a high school student in love with his best friend, who was always going on dates with other people while he sat by silently and pined. It wasn't totally unlike how Calvin had hidden his feelings for Aden until he couldn't control them anymore.

"If you're asking if this song was based on my life, then no." Calvin's face twisted wryly as he considered. "But sure, I'm not above using my own experiences in a song, if it works."

"Then if you ever write a song about me, it had better be happy," Aden joked, then instantly regretted it. He and Calvin may have been on an impromptu date, but they hadn't reached the stage in a relationship that included love songs, especially not ones with happily ever afters.

Calvin raised an eyebrow, but underneath his cap his eyes were smiling. Aden blushed, then hurried to change the subject.

"How did you get into songwriting anyhow?"

"In the most embarrassing teenage way possible," Calvin groaned, ticking off the reasons on his fingers. "My parents getting divorced, all the related tabloid coverage, pressure from my mum, having my heart broken more than a few times."

"Oh," Aden replied, slightly stunned. He didn't want to think about a miserable young Calvin even more than he hated to imagine him getting his heart broken. "How many times?"

"Too many!" Calvin let out a fluttery laugh. "My mom did a great job of scaring off all the boys I liked, as well as some of my friends, when I was younger. Then with all the practicing she made me do, I barely had time to meet people." Calvin lowered his voice and looked at Aden pointedly. "Not to mention the fact that I have a tendency to want people I can't have."

Now it was Aden's turn to flush and inwardly squirm, but in the best of ways. Knowing that Calvin wanted him was never going to get old.

Although he and Calvin had talked about their romantic pasts when they'd first bonded as the two gay members of MK5, now Aden had a more personal interest in Calvin's previous boyfriends. He listened attentively as Calvin described some of the worst offenders—a high school crush who left to study in the UK without saying goodbye after receiving an earful from Calvin's mum, a university fling who mostly wanted free tickets to piano concerts, a finance bro who'd been great in bed but a jerk everywhere else.

He went from feeling sad to being angry, then racked with guilt. Given his own dating history, or lack thereof, Aden couldn't claim that he'd be any better than Calvin's dickhead boyfriends, even if he wanted to be. Still, he'd always been able to perfect new dance moves and tricky vocal techniques—practicing was something he was good at. Maybe if he tried hard enough, being with Calvin would be the same? Although that wouldn't change the fact that, in the studio's view, they weren't supposed to be together at all.

A new song came on the radio, and Aden recognized Phantom's debut single—this station really had a thing for MK5, or they were really just that big now. Then he realized that Calvin had stopped talking and was now waiting expectantly.

Aden took a deep breath and cleared his throat.

"Okay, I know it's my turn to share, but my stories aren't that interesting. They all pretty much have the same ending," he said in a rush. He hung his head and continued just above a whisper. "The one where I'm the cause of the breakup, though I'm not sure you can even call it that when you've never dated anyone seriously."

"Really? You, a workaholic, weren't a great person to be in a relationship with?" Calvin pretended to be shocked, and when Aden managed a small smile, he added, "I figured."

"I'm sorry," Aden murmured. He almost felt like he might cry. "Please don't think that I—" He broke off, trying to find the right words. "I would never, I mean, I really hope this time will be different."

"It's fine," Calvin replied gently, and then Aden was surprised to find he was smirking. "Anyway, you'll have a chance to see how it feels pretty soon."

"What?" Aden choked, though he'd long since pushed the remnants of his food away.

"Don't you remember? We'll be filming Ting and Mok's breakup in a couple of days." Calvin's tone was light, but Aden thought he could detect a hint of worry in his eyes. For both of them, acting in a fake relationship while also navigating a real secret romance was uncharted territory.

"*Diu,*" Aden moaned in relief. He kicked Calvin underneath the table, though he really just wanted to leap across and hug him.

"Let's get out of here," he said, hurrying to pay the bill so they could head back to Calvin's apartment once more.

Weekly Cantopop chart listings
April 3

	Artist	Title	Release Date
1	MK5	YSim (dance version)	March 8
2	Phantom Kwok	The Dream	April 1
3	BB852	(Be My) Hong Kong BB	March 15
4	Cherie Lam	Lucky Charm	April 1
5	Jacky Lee	Rapsody	March 1

CHAPTER 14

ADEN'S EYES burned thanks to the menthol stick he'd been given by the makeup crew, but the truth was he didn't need any help crying. Today they were filming the breakup between Ting and Mok, and for maybe the first time in his life, Aden was on the receiving end.

He'd always tried to let people down gently before, with his many career-related reasons, but now he realized it didn't make much difference. Being dumped by someone you cared about felt awful, regardless of the explanation. Even if it wasn't real.

"And cut," Kenny said for what felt like the hundredth time. "Take a minute to grab a drink or wipe your eyes before we reset."

Aden was sure the director was calling more breaks than usual, and though he was grateful, he couldn't figure out why. He hoped it was due to the generally depressing mood in the studio, not because Kenny had figured out that the two young actors were suffering more than if they'd been just friends.

At least it wasn't because Aden and Calvin were failing. In fact, Kenny had praised both their performances. Still, Aden was worried. Not only had Calvin done an excellent job of breaking his heart on set, he'd also kept his distance all day, even when the cameras had stopped rolling. In the same storeroom where Calvin had acted so strange after their first "kiss," it felt all too familiar.

Aden knew one of the reasons why he'd been performing so well— it was easy to appear brokenhearted when he had actual feelings for his costar. Feelings that were amazing and wonderful and frightening and terrible, feelings that he wasn't supposed to have at all. But surely Calvin wasn't channeling a real desire to end things with Aden when he said Ting's lines. Right?

```
INT. SEAFOOD RESTAURANT—EVENING
Ting finds Mok in the restaurant
storeroom after hours. He tells him he
has decided to end their relationship
```

but withholds the true reason (he wants
to start his own business, a coffee shop,
but doesn't want Mok to help because of
the many risks involved).

                MOK (sadly, quietly)
        Wait, what are you saying, then?

              TING (holding back tears)
        I just think it might be best if we're
        not together for a while. I… I don't
              want to be with you anymore.

                   MOK (pleading)
        But why? Have I done something wrong?

        Ting   shakes   his   head   sadly   but
        doesn't reply. He turns to leave.

              MOK (grabbing Ting's arm)
        No, please don't go! I love you.

Every time Aden said that line, he thought his heart might actually stop beating. He wasn't used to saying those three words to anyone except his parents. But when they came out of his mouth, even in character as Mok, it did crazy things to his insides. Part of him wanted to say them to Calvin for real, and the rest of him was beyond shocked at the idea.

Aden shook his head. It was far too soon to be thinking about that. Although behind closed doors he and Calvin had done plenty of hooking up and sleeping over, to the rest of the world, minus Christelle and Winnie, they were just colleagues and friends. Aden didn't have a clue what they were going to do when they finished filming *Hooked on Love* the following week.

Lost in thought in his designated director's chair, Aden jumped when an arm settled on his shoulders. His frown deepened. Although he would've loved nothing more than a hug from Calvin at that moment, they were far from alone. He turned his head to find it was only Christelle, who'd just arrived. At the end of the scene, her character would step in to comfort Mok after Ting had left him devastated and alone.

"Someone's looking rather blue today. I guess that means I've got some cheering up to do off set as well," she teased, squeezing Aden tight while waving to Calvin at the snack cart with her free hand.

"Shh," Aden warned, in case Christelle was about to get carried away and say something too revealing, though his heart warmed at her kindness.

Calvin walked toward them slowly, lips pulling on the straw of his carton of lemon tea, and came to a stop next to Christelle. She slipped her other arm around his waist, then asked brightly, "Drinks tonight? I'm sure you boys will want to do something fun after this."

Calvin gave Christelle a pained look but otherwise made no reply. Aden wasn't sure if he was upset by the grueling scene or something else entirely.

"Oh, that's sweet of you," Aden said sincerely, though he wanted to spend the evening alone with Calvin like they'd discussed that morning in his apartment. At least he hoped that was still their plan. However, he was more open to socializing after work than in the past, before Calvin had shattered his resolve to focus on his career. All the time.

"Great! Can't wait!" Christelle seemed to think Aden had accepted her invitation and hugged them both even tighter. Aden winced. But before he could correct her, Christelle bounded away to greet the rest of the cast and crew, leaving him alone with Calvin, who was now glaring down at him.

"Why on earth did you agree to that?" he hissed. Perfect. Now, in addition to avoiding Aden all day, Calvin was mad at him too.

"We-ll, I didn't mean to. I was trying to be nice yet vague, but apparently it didn't work." Aden sighed. For once he was relieved when the break ended so there was no time to get into a fight.

Later that night, Aden found himself sitting across from Christelle in a dingy dive bar as she kept up a running commentary on everyone else in the darkened room. None of whom seemed to have noticed the stars in their midst.

There was a group of middle-aged men playing darts, blatantly smoking indoors despite the long-standing ban. At the front, some drunk young women were singing karaoke, near a couple who'd inexplicably brought their toddler along. The tables surrounding the three actors were filled with people playing liar's dice, shaking their dice cups and shouting their bluffs.

But the noise level wasn't why Aden only halfway listened to what Christelle was saying. He was mostly focused on Calvin's anxious movements on the stool next to him.

Soon after they'd arrived, Calvin had downed most of his bottle of beer in a hurry and was now spinning it round and round on the table in silence. Below, his leg was bouncing up and down like his life depended on it. More than once, Aden had tried to calm him by pressing his own thigh close, to no avail.

There were a few remaining beers in their shared bucket of six when Aden drained the last of his vodka soda. Almost instantly, Calvin started putting on his face mask to leave.

"Wait!" Christelle grabbed Calvin's arm before he could stand up. "There's something I want to ask you both."

Aden gulped. Surely Christelle wasn't going to put them on the spot about their secret romance, or the weirdness between them today, in public.

"So there's a Pride concert that's happening in a couple of months," she explained shyly. "Naomi's volunteered to be one of the organizers, and I'm part of the lineup."

"That's cool, congrats. Can we go now, please?" Calvin asked, and Aden shot him a look from under the brim of his hat. He was being rude, but at least he'd said "we." It seemed they would be leaving together as planned.

"I thought," Christelle began, toying with her empty beer glass, "that maybe you guys would like to join? It could be like a *Hooked on Love* reunion. Or maybe even a chance to promote the show."

Aden stared at Christelle, eyes wide. He'd been shocked to find out he would star in a BL drama, but the idea of performing at a queer event, as himself, was almost impossible to imagine. Next to him, Calvin scoffed.

"Well, even if the Caden fandom would love that, I'm not sure the studio would go for it," he said dryly. "It wasn't that long ago that they sanitized the lyrics to my songs, you know."

"Oh," Christelle replied, deflating. "I forgot about that."

"But if the show goes well, maybe things will be different," Calvin added wistfully.

"Yeah, let's see," Aden managed, though his gut response was more along the lines of "no way." He'd already strayed from his intended career path more than he'd expected. He wasn't sure he was ready to add even more risk into the mix, especially not when he didn't know where things stood with Calvin.

A quiet melancholy fell over the three actors, in spite of the din and the booze. Not long after, Christelle was waving Aden and Calvin out the door. Then they were in a taxi together, and Aden said a quick prayer to the universe that they still hadn't been recognized.

There was an uncomfortable silence between them the whole ride back to Calvin's apartment, only the sounds of late-night talk radio and the whir of the taxi meter in the background. Aden spent most of the time debating whether he should've gone home instead—it'd been a few days since he'd slept in his own bed anyway.

When they reached Calvin's floor, he made Aden wait outside the apartment while he went in alone. Aden shifted on his feet in the hallway, unsure what to expect. Subconsciously, he held his breath, more from anticipation than the strong smells of a neighbor's incense burner.

Surely Calvin wouldn't have brought Aden back to his apartment if he didn't want him there. But then why was he being forced to stand out here?

Although it was late, Aden looked around nervously. He kept expecting the elevator to open with a ding or for a resident to choose this moment to put their trash in the stairwell. What would they think when they saw him hovering on Calvin's doorstep? He didn't want to imagine the field day the tabloids would have with such a picture.

After a few very long minutes, Calvin finally opened the door, and Aden felt like he might cry yet again that day. On the table, next to the champagne he'd bought that they still hadn't drunk, was a huge bouquet of red roses, a handful of flickering tea lights, and a stuffed bunny that looked surprisingly like their guest costar Cony from the rabbit café.

"Oh." Aden blinked, swiping the corners of his eyes with his thumbs. "I guess you're not trying to get rid of me."

"What?" Calvin frowned.

"Well, you were acting kind of strange today." Aden tried to smile, but he couldn't keep his voice from cracking. Again, just when he'd expected the worst, Calvin had surprised him by being perfectly wonderful. "And technically you did break up with me. More than once."

"On camera!" Calvin protested. He opened his arms, and Aden practically fell into them, burying his face in Calvin's neck. Although they'd both acquired an odor of stale secondhand smoke at the bar, he drank in any trace that remained of Calvin's familiar vanilla scent.

"Today was rough." Calvin sighed, his hands tracing circles on Aden's back.

"Yeah. It felt a bit too real." Aden squeezed Calvin even tighter, like he could crawl inside his skin and live there forever.

"As an actor, I'll take that as a compliment. But as myself...." Calvin hesitated, loosening Aden's grip and taking a step backward. He found Aden's gaze and continued, "I think it, err, doesn't have to be. Umm, real, that is. I know we haven't talked about us much, but maybe we should?"

Aden smashed his mouth into Calvin's, pulling their chests together so fast that the other man let out a startled "mmpf." In fact, Aden surprised himself with the force of his response, but the emotional roller coaster of the past several hours had him pent up and eager for release. Now that he knew Calvin was still his, talking could wait. At least for a bit.

Once he'd recovered from his initial shock, Calvin proved more than willing to forget about everything but the man standing before him. He dug his hands into Aden's hair and gasped into his mouth as they both worked to erase the stress of the day by losing themselves in each other. As their movements became more frantic, Aden anchored himself with the taste of Calvin's lips and the feel of his tall, lean frame pressed up against his own.

Although Aden could never truly get his fill, eventually he forced himself to end the kiss. The thoughtful, talented man in his arms had gone to great lengths to make sure that Aden wasn't upset about their on-screen breakup. He certainly deserved a real answer to his suggestion.

"Yes," Aden murmured as he leaned their foreheads together.

"Yes to what?" Calvin asked breathlessly.

"To dating, boyfriends, anything. Whatever you want." Aden's words tumbled out in a rush, and then Calvin laughed outright. "What?"

"I mean, technically I only said that I wanted to talk." Calvin smirked, and Aden's heart clenched.

"Uhh...." Aden began to move away.

"Hey, I'm just kidding." Calvin's face fell, and he reached for Aden quickly. "That was a lot easier than I expected."

Aden thought back to the (many) times he'd proudly proclaimed he was focused on his career, how he'd scoffed when the other members of MK5 had delighted in the prospects of dating as they became well-known. Maybe Calvin had a point.

"Fair enough." Aden pouted. "But that may be the only thing that's easy about this."

Calvin sighed. "Don't remind me. And speaking of which, my mum's plans have changed again. She'll be back in a couple of days, instead of a couple of weeks from now."

"*Diu*," Aden moaned. Although he'd always known they couldn't keep pretending like Calvin's family apartment was their own, he hadn't wanted to think too much about when this honeymoon period might end. Then another thought occurred to him. "Oh! Then she'll be around for the award show in a couple of weeks."

"In theory, yes, though I wouldn't count on it," Calvin replied grimly.

The StudioHK music awards were one of the biggest nights of the year in the local entertainment industry. This year, MK5 would attend for the first time, though their debut single had just missed the cut-off date to be considered in the judging process. Still, it was a good opportunity to mix and mingle and highlight the stars they were becoming.

Selina had decided that the young men weren't allowed to bring dates, which might distract from their growing fame. Instead, their families were invited to join. Aden's mum had been looking forward to it for ages, but he wasn't surprised that Calvin's didn't feel the same way. He tried not to think too much about how surreal it would be to meet each other's parents as a couple, at a black-tie event.

"We have a meeting with Selina about that in a couple of days," Aden mused. She planned to brief the band at her office before their red-carpet debut, which also presented Aden and Calvin with an opportunity. If they were really serious about this. "She might have time for a chat."

Calvin's lips parted in a surprised O for a moment. Then he asked shakily, "You mean you want to tell her? About us?"

"Might as well?" A part of Aden was aware that his brain had obviously left his body—in no world would Aden Wong consider a romantic relationship that might distract from or interfere with his career—but somehow he didn't care. He only knew that he didn't want a repeat of the horrible feelings from his and Calvin's fake breakup, which left them no choice but to find a way forward together. Preferably one where they were no longer in violation of their contracts.

This time it was Calvin's turn to answer with a kiss. But where earlier Aden had been almost aggressive, now Calvin moved with a tenderness, a reverence that took Aden's breath away even more than the evening's surprise romantic gesture. His heart was full of emotions that he wasn't quite ready to put into words, and that he was not at all prepared to lose.

Hongkongers Head Over Heels for MK5
HK Entertainment 101
April 5

It's been less than a month since new Cantopop sensation MK5 burst onto the scene with their hit single "YSim," but it seems like they're everywhere you turn—from the top of the charts to the cover of your favorite magazine, not to mention on every bottle of YoYum you drink.

With the band now appearing in campaigns for their music and various side projects, as well as yogurt and other products, local teenagers have started congregating at prominent outdoor advertisements around the city. After posing for photos with their favorite idols, they share the images on social media in hopes that the new stars may one day take notice. Gifts of flowers, candles, and other trinkets have also appeared like shrines below the ads as fans express their adoration.

But are the handsome hunks of MK5 already romantically linked? On a few occasions, both Phantom Kwok and Shine Cheung have been spotted out on the town with unknown yet beautiful female companions.

There have been no sightings of the other three members: Mingo Lee, Calvin Leung, and Aden Wong. However, certain fans have begun to speculate that Calvin and Aden, commonly known by their ship name "Caden," are an item in real life, not only on the set of *Hooked on Love*, where they play Hong Kong's first gay male TV couple.

Is there any truth to such rumors? There has been no comment from StudioHK.

CHAPTER 15

THE NEXT morning, Aden opened a series of messages in MK5's group chat with bated breath. It had been a few days since Winnie had shared any paparazzi photos of him and Calvin, and he felt on edge. What if someone had spotted them at the shitty dive bar the night before? At least Christelle had been there, except when they'd stupidly taken a taxi back to Calvin's apartment together as a couple.

But what Aden saw was unexpected: a blurry image of Shine leaving an apartment building with a mystery girl, an orange sports car parked nearby. Shadows cast by the streetlights obscured her face. Still, something about the night scene was strangely familiar, though Aden had never been to Shine's home.

Aden spent so much time considering Shine's unidentified love interest that he was late leaving for StudioHK. So late that he and Calvin ended up in the same taxi again and barely made it out of hair and makeup by call time. He hoped this inauspicious start to the last day of filming *Hooked on Love* wasn't some sort of bad omen.

```
        INT. SEAFOOD RESTAURANT—EVENING
        Ting and Mok have given their notice
    to their employer. They say goodbye to
    their colleagues and regular customers,
    including Mr. Yue, after working their
    last shifts at the seafood restaurant.


            MR YUE
    You're sure you don't want to stick
    around a while longer? Until your new
        business has really taken off?


            MOK
    I don't think so, Mr. Yue. We've got a
        lot of work to do.
```

                         SHER
          I'm gonna miss you both soooo much.
                 You better come visit.

          She wails, and Mr. Yue sniffs, as
       if about to cry, then pulls Ting into
       a hug that appears more personal than
       professional.

                        MR YUE
           I can't believe my two favorite
        servers are leaving me. In case things
           don't work out, you know I'll always
                   be here for you.

        TING (pulling away to grab Mok's hand
               and beam at him adoringly)
        Thanks, Mr. Yue. We really appreciate
        it, but as long as we're together, Mok
                and I can do anything.

"And that's a wrap," Kenny declared at the end of the final take, after which everyone on set cheered. Calvin gave Aden's hand a final squeeze before letting go to join in the collective round of applause.

A minute later, the bright lights were switched off and the cameras were moved back as the whole crew made their way into the fictional seafood restaurant. On one of the larger round tables, bottles of champagne and paper cups materialized for an impromptu celebration, though an official cast party was already scheduled for another day. Then Kenny began popping corks as his assistant hurried to pour the fizzy liquid into enough cups for the twenty-plus people assembled.

Between spending the majority of his time at the studio or at Calvin's, Aden hadn't had many opportunities to work out recently, though some of what they did in private could probably be considered exercise. Yet as much as he wanted to avoid the extra calories, he couldn't refuse a drink from Reynold Tam himself.

"Cheers, lads," Reynold said to Aden and Calvin, passing them each a paper cup. "It's been a pleasure."

"Tam Sir," Aden replied, using a more respectful form of address. Even now he couldn't bring himself to call the senior actor by his given name. "You're too kind. Thank you so much for everything, and for all your faith in us."

"Here's to season two of *Hooked on Love*." Calvin grinned, giving Aden his own special wink. Then he raised his cup to touch those of his costars.

But either Calvin's cup was too full or his movements were too forceful because champagne sloshed everywhere—on his costume, on the floor, even on his fellow actors somewhat. Without a second thought, Aden grabbed a handful of tissues from a nearby supply cart. After passing a few to Reynold, he began drying off Calvin, the wettest of the three. First his hand, then his sleeve and finally his shirt and tie near his abdomen, where the thin white material was clinging to his skin.

"There, that's better," Aden fussed, low and tender and very much in Calvin's personal space. Although he may have sounded like a mother hen, there was nothing maternal in his look or his touch, and he couldn't even blame it on the champagne. He hadn't taken a drink.

"*Aiya,* sorry," Calvin apologized to Reynold sheepishly. He took a slight step away from Aden, somehow managing to remain as cool and collected as usual.

Only then did Aden realize exactly how obvious he was being about something that was supposed to remain a secret, at least for now. Quickly he turned his attention to drying his own hands and wiping up the mess on the floor.

Once he'd stood up again, Aden was pleased to see that Reynold wasn't angry at being unexpectedly damp. Yet he was surveying the two young actors with a great deal of interest.

"If I didn't know any better…," he mused, his gaze flicking back and forth between Calvin and Aden.

Shit. Aden really hoped that Reynold wasn't going to finish that sentence. He couldn't believe that he and Calvin had managed to hide their relationship from everyone involved in the show, except Christelle, only for him to screw up on the very last day of filming.

"More champagne?" Christelle trilled, holding up a bottle. For once, she was interrupting at the perfect time, and Aden felt so relieved that he could almost kiss her. He wasn't sure if she was trying to be a distraction or if it was just a lucky coincidence, but he shot her a grateful look as she refilled Calvin's cup. Shortly after, he left his three costars behind to make the rounds of the party, hoping to avoid any more situations that might give too much away.

ADEN LAY in Calvin's bed later that night, listening to the sound of his boyfriend's soft breathing in the dark. His boyfriend. It had been a very long time since he'd had one of those, but that wasn't what was bothering him now.

Calvin had fallen asleep soon after they'd wrecked the bed, and Aden knew he should be sleeping too. However, he couldn't shake the sense that tonight had felt too much like saying goodbye.

After a couple of farewell drinks on the set of *Hooked on Love*, and thankfully no more close calls, Aden and Calvin had snuck back to his apartment separately. And though at first they'd kissed eagerly and hurriedly, still flushed from the champagne, in the end it had been Aden who slowed things down to a more leisurely pace. Not because he wasn't dying to taste Calvin or feel him everywhere, but because he wanted to make the precious moments last as long as possible. He needed to memorize each detail—from the curve of Calvin's lips to the reverent way he whispered Aden's name—before it slipped away.

In the morning, Calvin's mum would be back in Hong Kong, so it was their last night in his bed for the foreseeable future. Soon after, Calvin would start working on his debut single and Aden would begin whatever project the studio had lined up for him before MK5's next group rehearsals. Then they'd have even less alone time.

Logically, Aden knew that these weren't real endings, just changes in the circumstances of their relationship. Still, in the short term, everything was only going to get more complicated, and he felt sad and nervous and terrified all at once.

Tomorrow they planned to tell their manager that they were more than just colleagues and friends. She wasn't the first person to know, but she would be the most important one so far. After Selina, they'd tell the studio and the band, and then…? Aden and Calvin hadn't really talked about if or how to go public about their relationship. They needed Selina on their side first.

Not that Aden expected her to have a problem with it. She'd even hinted at the possibility of them being together during the YoYum shoot, as had Phantom. Technically, the studio supported diversity and inclusion, so that shouldn't be a concern either. Except that Aden and Calvin had been violating the no-dating policy for the past month or so, but surely they wouldn't be too harsh on two of their hottest new stars. Right?

When Ms. Yeung from HR had first told the band about that rule back in February, Aden had downright scoffed. He'd been so convinced that dating anyone, let alone a fellow StudioHK employee, would never be an issue that it had seemed like a waste of breath to even discuss it. Turns out he couldn't've been more wrong.

He'd gotten his big break and found his first real romance at the same time. Now he finally understood why Winnie had been so enamored with the idea of being in love all these years. Although he and Calvin hadn't said as much to each other out loud yet, there was no other word to describe how Aden felt. He had no clue how he'd gone from always putting his career before his love life to merging the two together, but there was no going back now. He just hoped there wouldn't be too many hiccups along the way.

THE NEXT day, Aden was wedged between Calvin and Phantom on the maroon leather sofa in Selina's office. Across from them, Selina sat at her mahogany desk containing a laptop, a tablet, multiple monitors, and far more client folders and assorted music publications. On either side, Mingo and Shine, the last to arrive, were perched on folding chairs that didn't appear entirely stable on the ornate Persian carpet.

Although this wasn't the most important meeting of Aden's life—most of the information would also be emailed to the band with their detailed schedules and rundowns—he should've been paying closer attention. Now that his main responsibilities for *Hooked on Love* had ended, it was time to learn what would happen next.

But so far, Aden had been doing a terrible job of listening to anything that Selina was saying. He caught bits and pieces of her instructions but didn't quite grasp the details. His mind was elsewhere.

"Phantom… new female star…. Calvin… theme song…. Mingo and Shine… interview with…. Aden…."

When Selina said his name, Aden sat up straighter, and somehow he was able to smile and nod as she told him his duties for the next few weeks: choreographing dance breaks for some of StudioHK's newer acts, a guest appearance on Shine and Mingo's lifestyle show with Calvin. Nothing about when it would be his turn to release his own single, which was slightly disappointing.

So Aden's thoughts drifted away from Selina's voice and returned to focusing on all the places where his body was currently touching Calvin's: shoulders, elbows, knees. Their hands were less than an inch apart, and it would be so easy for Aden to reach over and lace their fingers together, but he couldn't. Not yet.

As soon as Selina finished her briefing, Aden and Calvin would tell her that they were dating. For real, not just on TV. Until then, they had to sit side by side and pretend that they hadn't been doing a whole lot more than acting during their time on *Hooked on Love*.

"Aden."

Aden jumped at the sound of his name on Selina's lips again. From the way she was looking at him, it wasn't the first time she'd said it either. Shit. He quickly reached out to grab whatever it was that Selina was holding out toward him. Oh. The three event passes that would grant him and his parents entry to the StudioHK music awards as well as the receptions before and afterward.

As he leaned back against the squeaky sofa cushions, Aden swore he saw Phantom smirking at him. It might've just been his usual smugness, or perhaps Phantom had managed to catch one of the longing looks that Aden had stolen at his boyfriend.

Finally the meeting was over and the others were standing to leave. Mingo and Shine headed out first, no doubt relieved to be rid of their uncomfortable seats. But Phantom hung back, watching as Aden made too much of a fuss over his duffel bag while Calvin hadn't even moved.

"You guys coming?" Phantom asked.

"No actually, we're not quite finished," Calvin replied, waving Phantom away a bit too eagerly. "See you later."

Phantom's gaze flicked between his old friend and Aden a couple of times. Then without another word, he grinned and turned to leave.

"All right, you two. What's up? I'm pleased to see that you're on speaking terms again," Selina said once it was just the three of them.

Biting back a laugh, Aden glanced over at Calvin, whose eyes were twinkling, and then they both turned to Selina, who was waiting expectantly. It was now or never. Although Aden was surprisingly calm—he was more worried about Selina being angry than the studio's dating policy—he didn't quite know how to begin. In their excitement, he and Calvin hadn't planned out the details of how to have this conversation.

"I—" Aden started at the same time Calvin said, "We."

"Go ahead," Aden offered, blushing.

"No, you." Calvin knocked his knee against Aden's, and Aden used his hand to push it away playfully.

"Oh for goodness sake, stop. I don't have time for this," Selina groaned, reaching for her mouse. "Either tell me that you guys are dating or whatever the problem is now so that I can get back to work."

"Right. In that case…."

"We are?"

Aden held his breath.

"I see," Selina sounded stern, but her lips twitched. "And just how long has this been going on?"

"About a month?" Aden cringed. He wondered if Selina remembered exactly when she'd interrogated him about Calvin before.

"It seems everyone's falling in love this spring," she mused almost dreamily before fixing Aden with a steely gaze. "Wait. Isn't that when you all filmed the YoYum commercial? I hope you weren't lying to me then."

"*Aiya*. Nothing had happened at that point, I swear!" Aden protested. Although he was telling the truth, it wasn't by much—he and Calvin had kissed and made up the day after he'd told Selina there was nothing going on between them.

"Honest," Calvin concurred when Selina raised a skeptical eyebrow at him. "We weren't together until after that."

On her desk, Selina's phone vibrated once, and she picked it up to read the notification.

"Well, given what I've seen and heard about you both over the past couple of months, I can't say I'm surprised," she said without looking up. "In fact, I spoke with StudioHK's HR about this possibility already."

"Huh?" Aden croaked, unsure whether to feel relieved or worried.

"What did they say?" Calvin asked quietly.

"I need you both to listen carefully," Selina said, surveying them with a furrowed brow. "The studio and I value you for who you are without question, though I know the same can't be said for everyone else. Now there's paperwork that you'll need to fill out and some things we should probably discuss, such as how to handle the press—"

"Wait, you mean we can be out to the world as a couple?" Calvin interrupted, sounding hesitant yet hopeful. But Aden couldn't quite believe that could be true. It was an outcome far beyond what he'd considered, one he wasn't sure he was ready for.

"I think we're going to need to come up with a plan and share it with the studio, not just to HR but also the PR folks, so that everyone is on the same page," Selina explained. It wasn't a yes, but it wasn't a no either.

Before Aden could think of anything to say, Calvin continued, "We've also been asked to perform in a Pride concert."

Apparently he'd decided to turn the meeting into a full-court press like the basketball player that he was. It was ballsy and probably not necessary. Aden should've been annoyed, but he was mostly turned on.

Selina's phone vibrated again, and she frowned. Aden hoped it was because of the message she'd received, but he wasn't so sure. Nor would he get to find out, as just then Selina's phone started ringing in earnest.

"Good talk, boys, but I've got to take this," she said, her thumb hovering over the Call Accept button. "Let's circle back and get everything sorted once things settle down. I'll be in touch later, and until then, let's keep this quiet."

She shooed them away. The next thing Aden knew, he and Calvin were standing shoulder to shoulder in the hallway, waiting for the elevator. Although his feet were touching the ground and the duffel bag he was carrying wasn't light, Aden felt like he was floating.

"So that went well, right?" Calvin asked.

"Yes."

"Then why are you trembling?" Calvin sounded concerned.

"Oh, umm." Thanks to a mixture of adrenaline, shock, and something very much like joy, Aden's entire body was buzzing. He hadn't realized it wasn't just a feeling, but a visible physical reaction to their meeting with Selina.

As he waited for a reply, Calvin brushed his knuckles across the back of Aden's hand. Presumably it was meant as a comforting gesture, but it sent a jolt of electricity straight to Aden's heart and further south too.

"Oh my god, don't," he gasped.

"Right, sorry." Calvin bit his lip, then shook his head. Aden wanted nothing more than to wrap him up in a hug, press him against the wall, and shove his tongue down his throat.

"If you do that again, there's no way I can stop myself from kissing you," he said through gritted teeth.

"Oh. Shit." Aden glanced up to see Calvin's cheeks darken under his black baseball cap and quickly looked away again. After a brief pause, Calvin asked, "What are you doing now?"

"Err, heading home I suppose. I need to drop this off"—Aden gestured to the bag he'd packed earlier full of various clothes he'd left at Calvin's apartment over the past couple of weeks—"and I told my mum I'd be back for dinner."

"Well, it's only four thirty now. I'm going to the studio to work on another song for BB852 and maybe rehearse my single." Calvin lowered his voice. "You know, some of the practice rooms are soundproof, and of course they all lock."

Aden inhaled sharply. When the elevator doors opened a few seconds later, he'd never moved such a short distance so quickly in his life.

Re: MK5 schedule
From: janus.so@studiohk.com.hk
To: selina_mak@agentart.com.hk
Cc: peter.siu@studiohk.com.hk;
leon.ho@studiohk.com.hk
April 6 4:45pm

Dear Selina,

As previously discussed, attached please find the list of MK5's upcoming commitments and appearances for the coming few weeks. Appreciate your help to share with the band. Just let me know if you have any concerns.

Regards,
Janus

MK5 schedule

April 6-15:	Mingo and Shine filming at various locations [With Aden and Calvin as guests on April 8]
April 6-20:	Calvin songwriting (see full list of songs required in attachment)
April 8-11:	Rehearsals + recording Phantom's duet with Cherie Lam @StudioHK
April 8-25:	Aden @StudioHK as guest choreographer
April 20:	MK5 and families @StudioHK awards [Detailed rundown to be provided]
April 23-29:	Calvin @StudioHK recording debut single
May 1-7:	Calvin MV shoot in Taiwan

Chapter 16

IT TOOK all Aden's self-restraint not to throw himself on Calvin's lap in the taxi they shared to StudioHK. Thankfully, he'd had a lot of practice in denying himself over the years. Plus, there was no traffic, so it was a relatively short journey to keep his emotions in check. Still, his heart pounded in his ears due to a combination of relief, anticipation, and most of all, excitement.

But even if they had just told Selina about their relationship, that was only the first step. She'd been very clear that they needed to fill out the proper paperwork and make a plan, a fact Aden was reminded of almost the instant they set foot inside the studio's main music building.

"Fancy meeting you two here." In the otherwise empty hallway, Phantom greeted Aden and Calvin with a waggling of his eyebrows. "We could've waited if we'd known you guys were headed this way."

"We?" Aden asked dumbly.

"Yeah. Shine, Mingo, and I came from Selina's office together. I've got to talk to Leon about my duet with Cherie Lam, and they're getting ready to film another episode of their show soon." Aden nodded blankly, suddenly aware how much he'd missed during the meeting. Maybe Phantom wouldn't notice how clueless he was if he pretended to agree. "But I don't think Selina mentioned either of you coming to the studio today?"

Aden's stomach dropped, and out of the corner of his eye, he saw Calvin wince ever so slightly. Obviously they couldn't tell Phantom the truth—planning to hook up in a practice room was something that no one else needed to know about.

Besides, Selina had asked them to keep their relationship quiet, even if it felt wrong to hide something so important from a fellow band member. Although, given Phantom's actions so far that day, it seemed like he already had some idea. It didn't help that Aden was holding a large duffel bag, which he wouldn't normally bring to Selina's office or the studio.

"Oh, I'm going to get a head start on writing some new songs…," Calvin said, his voice pitched higher than usual.

"The boys love theme song?" Phantom grinned suggestively.

Aden couldn't tell if Phantom was just making a stupid joke or if Calvin had indeed been given the opportunity to write the TV show's theme. He really should've listened to Selina more carefully during the meeting.

"Yeah, maybe. Let's see." Calvin shrugged.

"Wait, what? Really?" Aden asked before he could stop himself.

"Selina literally just told us all about it. You were there." Phantom sighed dramatically.

"I—I must've missed that." Aden wasn't sure whether he was more surprised or embarrassed, or even proud.

"I guess so." Phantom smirked. "Maybe you were too busy thinking about some of Calvin's *other* talents. Speaking of which, are you here to inspire him to write the song?"

"Huh? No, I…." Aden paused, though he could do nothing to stop the blush spreading across his cheeks. He needed to think up an excuse to be at the studio and fast, before Phantom could make any more innuendo. Avoiding Phantom's eyes, he spotted a poster on the opposite wall, stuck onto a noticeboard alongside a copy of the company newsletter and several outdated job ads. It announced the latest free gift for new members of the MK5 fan club: a mini plush doll of the band member of their choice.

"I just stopped by to get some band merch for my friend. Winnie."

Adding Winnie's name was an afterthought, one that Aden hoped would make his white lie more credible. Yet Phantom gave him a rather skeptical look.

"Riiiight." Phantom's gaze darted between Aden and Calvin in amusement. "You wanna grab dinner with us later?"

"Maybe." Calvin was noncommittal, whereas Aden replied with a definite "No." At least Phantom wouldn't think that was anything out of the ordinary. Apart from the night at Tonic, he still hadn't spent much time with the band outside of work.

A few awkward minutes later, Phantom headed to Leon's office, and Aden and Calvin continued down the hall in the opposite direction toward the practice rooms. Aden was equal parts excited and nervous at what they were about to do, so much so that he'd barely even thought about what might happen if they got caught.

He was more concerned with the possibility of running into someone else along the way, resulting in further delays. He debated whether to put his hat and face mask back on, in case Shine, Mingo, or another familiar face were to appear.

And though he was tempted to break into a sprint, Aden forced himself to walk at a normal pace. As studio employees, he and Calvin had every right to be on the premises, and as bandmates and costars, it wasn't unusual for them to be together. Still, he held his breath until the practice room door closed and Calvin locked it with a flick of his delicate wrist.

Finally they were alone, really alone, though the space in no way compared to Calvin's bedroom, crowded as it was with assorted mics, music stands, and a piano. But given that Aden wasn't sure when he'd see Calvin again in the near future, it was definitely better than nothing.

"You really didn't know that I was going to write the theme song for *Hooked on Love*?" Calvin asked. Aden almost thought he was angry until he found himself being pushed down onto the padded piano bench, and then Calvin was in his lap, straddling his legs.

"Sorry, babe. I was super distracted in today's meeting. All I could think about was talking to Selina after." Aden slipped his arms round Calvin's waist like he'd been aching to for hours. "That's really awesome, though, and I know whatever you write will be amazing."

"It's fine," Calvin hummed, brushing their noses together. "But I think Phantom might have the right idea. You can be my inspiration for the song. Starting now."

Calvin ghosted a kiss across Aden's lips, leaving him more full of want than before.

"Is that what we're calling it these days?" Aden chuckled, in spite of his frustration. He grabbed Calvin's ass and melded their hips together as Calvin began kissing his neck. Aden tilted his head to one side, relishing the light scratch of his boyfriend's day-old stubble, still barely there.

Even the tickle of Calvin's lips couldn't shake the guilt Aden felt about their encounter with Phantom earlier. With a sigh, he pulled away slightly. "I hate that I lied to another member of the band about us, though."

"He'll find out soon enough, and until then, I'm sure he'll live." Something almost like a growl escaped from Calvin's throat. "Which is more than I can say for myself if you insist on talking much longer."

Then Calvin placed his hands on either side of Aden's face and kissed him. Deeply and intensely, as if they hadn't woken up together that morning and made good use of Calvin's bed one last time before his mother returned.

Aden parted his lips eagerly, and his whole body thrilled with pleasure as their tongues intertwined. He was briefly reminded of the first time he'd been to Calvin's apartment—when they'd first done anything more than kiss on a set or in a dressing room—and how they'd ended up in a similar position with him gloriously sandwiched between the Leung family piano and Calvin's lanky frame. He'd been just as desperate for Calvin's touch then, but far less assured.

Now Aden knew just what to whisper in Calvin's ear and when to give that extra something that would make him shudder. More than that, he knew how wonderful it felt to be in Calvin's arms, in his life, and to let himself finally admit that he'd wanted this all along.

With a moan, Aden shoved his fingers into Calvin's hair, attacking his mouth even more hungrily than before. Angling his head to one side, he gasped at the feeling of Calvin's hands sliding under his shirt as he ground down in Aden's lap.

"Wha—?" Aden asked in a daze as Calvin stood up, breaking off when his boyfriend's long fingers gently grazed his lips.

"Shh," Calvin whispered before dropping to his knees and showing just how skilled he was at making Aden come undone.

But as Aden returned the favor, his thoughts drifted from the muffled sounds that Calvin was making—thank goodness for soundproofing—to the reason for their sexy celebration. Today they'd started down the path toward their future as a couple, two of StudioHK's hottest young stars who also happened to be extremely hot for each other. In the not-too-distant future, Aden might really have everything he'd ever wanted, along with something he'd never dared hope for: a career and love both.

A few days later, a taxi dropped Aden off at a famous egg waffle shop on Hong Kong Island. His stomach rumbled at the sweet smells filling the night air, and he remembered he hadn't eaten a full meal since breakfast.

He'd spent the day at StudioHK working on choreography for BB852, and now it was time to film his guest appearance on Shine and Mingo's TV show.

Despite the lateness of the hour, the short side street was crowded, though that wasn't necessarily unusual. The small shop, no more than a stall really, was extremely popular. Hungry diners frequently filled the sidewalks as they waited in line for delicious (and photo-worthy) snacks.

Tonight, however, the only customers were the hosts and their film crew, who'd attracted more than a few MK5 fans eager to glimpse their idols in person. A series of shrieks spread through the crowd as they recognized Aden underneath his hat and mask, making his way toward his fellow bandmates.

"Hey, guys." Aden came up between Shine and Mingo from behind, draping an arm across both their shoulders as they bent over their scripts. Calvin was standing opposite him, and despite his casual nod in greeting, Aden didn't miss the brief look of longing that passed across his face.

Thanks to their busy schedules—with Calvin focused on his own and other people's songs and Aden getting back to his dance roots—they hadn't seen each other since they'd made creative use of the studio's practice room. But in the presence of their colleagues and countless fans, Aden was determined to keep a sensible distance between himself and his still mostly secret boyfriend, even if he wanted to do exactly the opposite.

That proved even more difficult than he expected once they started filming. As special guests, Aden and Calvin were placed in the center of the shot, with Mingo and Shine on either side. The four of them squeezed in tightly together as they chatted with the shop owner and sampled the different egg waffle flavors available—plain, dark chocolate, stinky durian, and black sesame-filled, among others.

Aden found himself pressed up against Calvin's side, like he'd been many times before, usually naked. His mouth watered, though he was no longer hungry.

"You know, you guys should've asked Calvin for street food recs," Aden suggested. During a pause between takes, Shine and Mingo were listing off the rest of the foods they'd be trying that night. "There's a place near his apartment that's…."

"Here, don't you want the rest of this? Since you didn't have any dinner," Calvin said too loudly. He shoved the rest of his purple taro waffle into Aden's mouth, cutting him off. Aden gasped in what he hoped would appear to be surprise, not simply the thrill of Calvin's fingertips on his lips.

As he struggled to chew the oversized mouthful, Aden realized his mistake: implying that he'd been to Calvin's apartment. Especially when he'd never accepted previous invitations to the other band members' homes to play video games or chill.

Shine snorted and surveyed the two bandmates with twinkling eyes. His tone was more than a little suggestive. "Really? And how would you know?"

Mingo, on the other hand, didn't seem to think anything strange or awkward had just happened. He turned to Calvin innocently.

"Oh yeah? You know a great street food stall?"

"You're kidding, right?" Aden couldn't help but laugh, while still trying not to choke on the waffle in his mouth. "Surely you haven't forgotten that Calvin is obsessed with all kinds of junk food."

"*Hai yaa*, that's true. But I don't think we have time to go anywhere else tonight." Mingo looked incredibly disappointed to miss out on something he'd only heard about a moment before. "Maybe we can try to film there another day if you want."

"No thanks, man." Calvin shook his head, glancing around at the crowd. "Then I'd never be able to go there again without getting mobbed or something."

"Fair enough," Mingo sighed. "After our last episode, it's almost impossible to buy my favorite ice cream because it's always sold out."

"I know we should be flattered at how much the fans love us, but…." Aden stopped, not quite sure how to proceed. He hated to criticize anyone who had contributed to the success he'd always craved, but at the same time, they were also partly why he and Calvin had to be so careful.

"Yeah, it's not quite as awesome as I thought it would be. Not now that I'm…." Shine paused to pull out his phone, positively lighting up when he saw whatever was displayed on the screen.

"Crushing hard on a special someone?" Mingo helpfully supplied.

Shine tried to scowl at him, but it was obvious that he was still grinning.

"Oh really? Who is she?" Calvin asked. "Have you told Selina or the studio?"

Aden, too, wondered who had managed to convince MK5's stud rapper to settle down, though he'd had an inkling that Shine was a bit of a softie all along. He certainly wasn't in a position to judge anyone for changing their views or habits where romance was concerned.

"Err, actually…." Shine hesitated. He shifted his gaze to Aden, who detected a hint of uncertainty in his bandmate's eyes. Shine looked down at his sneakers and then back up. "Aden, I—"

But Shine couldn't say anything else about his new love interest because the cameras started rolling again. Then once they'd gotten enough footage, the band members were escorted through the crowd into a waiting van and the topic was forgotten.

They visited three more locations that night—a stall with sizzling skewers of juicy meat, seafood, and vegetables; another selling sugar cane juice; and lastly one of the city's few remaining all-night *dai pai dongs*, a type of outdoor restaurant. At each one, they ate and chatted and mostly had fun while technically working, albeit with too many onlookers in the background.

After the final take, Aden was absolutely stuffed yet far from satisfied. At least he was scheduled to run through choreography with another of StudioHK's musical acts again the next day. He could dance along with them in hopes of burning off the evening's excessive calories, as well as his current frustrations. He'd been near Calvin all night but unable to do or say any of the things he yearned to. It was excruciating.

And it seemed that Calvin had similar feelings. Although they hadn't discussed it beforehand, they both urged their fellow bandmates to take the first taxis that arrived, content to remain behind a little longer.

Mingo was the earliest to leave, followed by Shine, loudly griping about how he should've driven his own car instead despite the crowds. And then it was just Calvin and Aden, along with the crew packing up their equipment and a few lingering diehard fans.

"You can take the next taxi," Aden offered, keeping his attention on the mostly deserted street to avoid ogling his boyfriend. As late as it was, he was more interested in these few minutes they had together than heading home.

"I wish you could come with me," Calvin whispered. "But my mum…."

"I know." Underneath his mask, Aden smiled weakly. Even if Calvin's apartment had been empty and available, it wasn't a good idea for them to be seen leaving together. "Is she coming to the StudioHK awards with you next week?"

"I think so. Selina made me put her on the phone the other day, and from what I could hear, she agreed to it. Who knows what Selina said to convince her, but I wouldn't put it past her to threaten bodily harm, or worse."

They both chuckled, though Aden wondered if there was any truth to Calvin's statement. Selina was intense and demanding, and he certainly didn't want to cross her in any way. Ever.

"I'm sorry in advance for all the awful things my mum might say." Calvin shook his head as his face fell, and Aden wanted to hug him so badly.

"Don't worry. I'll be fine. Provided that I can make it through this week first," Aden replied wryly. He'd gotten so used to seeing Calvin nearly every day while filming *Hooked on Love* that the thought of spending another stretch of time apart was almost as bad as meeting his boyfriend's scary mother.

"*Aiya*, don't remind me. But Selina said she's almost got the paperwork ready, so we shouldn't need to wait much longer."

Calvin bumped his shoulder into Aden's in a friendly gesture, and Aden leaned into his touch. It wasn't much, but it was all he'd get for a while.

"Here's hoping."

Moments later another taxi slowed to a stop near where they stood, and Aden regretfully nudged Calvin toward it. He clapped one hand on Calvin's shoulder in farewell as he got into the car and tried not to think about how easy it would be to slide in next to him.

The next morning, Aden had a message from Winnie, the first she'd sent in a while. It was a photo of Calvin feeding him a piece of waffle from the night before. The caption from one of the Caden fan accounts read "Egg waffle? More like wedding cake." Winnie had written her own commentary below.

Gee thanks for the invite. And you didn't even ask me to be MOH! Or did you say something you shouldn't have?

Aden rolled his eyes, though he was alone in his bedroom. He could sort of see a similarity between Calvin feeding him a waffle and newlyweds smashing cake in each other's faces, but it was a bit of a stretch. Not to mention the fact that Winnie seemed to think that Aden was the bride in this scenario, if she was the maid of honor. Yet gay marriage wasn't even legal in Hong Kong.

As he tried to come up with a snarky reply, another thought struck him. There could be any number of reasons why Calvin had shoved food into Aden's mouth. How had Winnie guessed something so close to the truth? Sure, she was his best friend, though it almost felt like she knew more than she was letting on. But what?

Aden and Calvin,

Looking forward to seeing you and your families tonight at the awards event. Here's another reason to celebrate!

I've been in touch with Ms. Yeung from StudioHK HR and she's finalized the paperwork for you to officially declare your relationship to the company. Please take a look at the attached document and read it carefully to make sure you're fine with all the terms. Then we can arrange a date for you both to sign and figure out the next steps.

Cheers,
SM

Chapter 17

A week later, as Aden dressed for the StudioHK awards, he paused to survey himself in the mirror hanging on his wardrobe. He wasn't sure he'd ever feel comfortable in evening wear—he preferred dance chic—but he had to admit he looked good. His black trousers were perfectly tailored, and the ruffles down the front of his white shirt felt more fun than formal. A matching black jacket and deep red bow tie hung over the back of his desk chair, and a box on his bedroom floor held his shoes for the night: a pair of black patent leather oxfords.

One of the many perks of being a pop star was that designers were keen for Aden and the rest of MK5 to be seen in their clothes. So Selina had arranged coordinated tuxedos for the awards at no cost. It was a sweet deal for the brands too, as once photos from the event were posted online, the products would very likely sell out.

On his desk, Aden's phone buzzed, and his heart raced just thinking it might be Calvin. Perhaps a photo of him looking dashing in a similar tux or, even better, before he'd put it on. Aden's mouth watered.

Although he and his boyfriend had done plenty of texting and calling since filming Shine and Mingo's TV show, they hadn't found any time to be alone together. Not only were they busy with separate projects—for Calvin, music and for Aden, choreography and promo shoots for a few dancewear brands—they both still lived with their parents in none-too-spacious Hong Kong apartments. At this rate, they might not get to have sex before Calvin headed to Taiwan to film the music video for his new single.

Aden shuddered at the thought, but Calvin's body wasn't the only thing on his mind. What he was really waiting for was an update about Calvin's mother—if she was definitely coming to the awards and, more importantly, how she'd reacted when Calvin had told her about their relationship.

Now that the paperwork was finalized so they could officially date—they just needed to sign it—Aden and Calvin had decided to tell their parents that they were an item. They'd agreed that they didn't want to lie to them or otherwise do anything that might result in a bad first impression at the awards.

Although from what Calvin had said before, Aden wasn't sure that anything he did would be considered right by Anita Leung. He wasn't exactly looking forward to meeting her for the first time. He gulped.

Excited for your date tonight?

Aden frowned when he saw a message on his phone from Winnie, not Calvin. But he wasn't going on a date. Maybe she'd sent it to him by mistake.

He sent back a string of question marks.

Aren't you and Calvin going to the music awards tonight?

Huh. Aden hadn't told Winnie about the event, but it was going to be televised. She'd probably read about it online or something.

Yes, he replied. *But we have to bring our parents as our dates. Studio's orders.*

I know but your bf will still be there.

Aden rolled his eyes. Of course Winnie was right, even if she was one of the few people who knew. At least Selina and Ms. Yeung were in the loop now. Aden's parents would be too, by the time they arrived at the awards that evening. He needed to hurry up and talk to them before it was time to leave. But the next instant he was distracted by another message from Winnie.

And so will mine! [sweating emoji]

Below the text was a photo, similar to one that had been shared in the MK5 group chat a couple of weeks earlier, but more zoomed in. Looking closely, Aden could just make out that the girl next to the orange sports car was Winnie. Oh. Now he knew why the apartment building had seemed so familiar, plus what Shine had been trying to tell him about his crush at the egg waffle shop.

Apparently Aden and Winnie had more catching up to do than he'd thought, but that was a topic for another day. He put down his phone and picked up his tie to focus on getting ready for tonight.

Aden and his parents were waiting for their ride, a private car and driver arranged by the studio, in the covered drop-off area outside their building. The weather forecast included a chance of rain, which luckily had held off so far. Yet the air was close and the humidity high, unusually warm for April.

With three people rushing around at the last minute to use the apartment's single bathroom, Aden's skin was already flushed. He was relieved he hadn't tried to straighten his naturally wavy hair. Still, sweat was starting to form on the back of his neck and under his arms, and it didn't help that he hadn't had time to talk to his parents.

He needed to brief them about what to expect at the awards. Not to mention tell them about Calvin, who, Aden realized with a tightness in his stomach, he had yet to hear from.

As per her usual habit, Aden's mum was now peppering him with questions, and he couldn't get a word in edgewise. He was trying, and failing, to be patient. But their car would be arriving soon, and Aden certainly couldn't say everything he needed to in front of the studio's driver.

"So all the members of MK5 will be there, right?" Evelyn asked. "Besides you there's Phantom, Calvin, Shine, and Mingo?"

"Yes." Though he was verging on annoyed, Aden couldn't help but be impressed. He didn't think he'd ever done more than mention the names of his bandmates in passing, and probably only at first, months ago. His mum must've done some pre-event research of her own.

"And they're all bringing their parents?"

"That's the plan, as far as I know." Aden shot a weary look at Desmond Wong over the top of Evelyn's head, but his dad merely shrugged as if to say, "You know what she's like."

"What are their names?"

"I have no idea, Mum." Aden sighed. That wasn't exactly true—he knew Calvin's mum was called Anita and had heard Phantom's dad's name before—but it wasn't like he'd ever met them.

"And what about—"

"Mum!" Agitated, Aden cut her off too forcefully. Desmond's eyes narrowed, and Aden tried to use a more apologetic tone when he continued. "Can you just hold on a minute? There's something important I need to say."

"Of course, dear," Evelyn replied, while Desmond nodded his approval.

"You know that Calvin is also my costar in *Hooked on Love*, right?" Aden asked.

"Yes."

"Well actually, he's a lot more than that." Aden glanced around nervously, making sure there was no one else nearby. Still, he took the extra precaution of lowering his voice further. "He's my… boyfriend."

"Oh!" Evelyn's eyes went wide for a few moments, but she soon recovered and was smiling at Aden. "I wasn't expecting that, but... it explains a lot."

Aden blushed, knowing she had to be thinking about all the times he'd stayed out late while filming *Hooked on Love* or slept over at Calvin's and not come home at all.

"Wow, really?" Desmond asked softly. He'd always been a man of few words, except perhaps with Mimi, but that didn't mean he wasn't observant. As usual, what he did say was to the point. "The last time I remember you having a boyfriend, you were in secondary school."

Aden gulped. He knew he hadn't talked about his love life with his parents in a while, but until recently, he'd never felt the need. It had been more years than he'd thought since he'd been serious about anyone.

"Well, he's been busy with his studies and his career," Evelyn offered sympathetically, though they seemed like poor excuses to Aden now. She frowned, placing a hand on Aden's arm. "Does anyone else know about this? It seems like it could be rather complicated."

"It wasn't part of my plan to make it big, that's for sure." Aden laughed, shaking his head in disbelief. "Right now we've only told our manager and a few friends. So please don't say anything to anyone else. But Calvin's so great, and I really lo—" There was that word again, but Aden managed to stop himself before he said it. Scary as it was, he should really tell Calvin how he felt first. "I mean, we wanted you to know before you all meet tonight."

"Oh, Aden." Evelyn pressed her lips together, on the verge of tears. Desmond, too, looked more than a bit emotional. As much as Aden wished Calvin was his date for the awards, he was incredibly glad his parents could join him. They'd always been so supportive, and now they had the chance to mingle with the city's hottest stars. And also meet the man he... loved. There was no other word for it.

Aden wrapped an arm around Evelyn's shoulders and gave her a light squeeze, careful not to wrinkle his jacket or her silky white cheongsam with royal blue flowers. Misty-eyed, he was relieved to see a black van approaching to take them to the award ceremony.

OUTSIDE THE Hong Kong Coliseum, a small crowd of fans had gathered in the piazza, undeterred by the cloudy sky that made it seem rain was imminent. Some people held up signs for MK5, while others were waiting for a glimpse at any number of Cantopop icons in attendance. Thankfully, the Wongs' arrival was fairly painless. The van provided by the studio had inscrutable tinted windows, and temporary metal barriers prevented bystanders from entering the drop-off area.

Aden had been to the unique building—a huge white inverted trapezoid rising above the harbor in Hung Hom—as a paying customer at music events in the past, but this was his first time as an invited guest. The fairly basic entryway had been transformed into a space worthy of the stars, with red carpeting on the concrete floors, elaborate floral displays and photo backdrops, even an open bar.

As he entered the pre-award reception with his parents, Aden toyed with the gold and silver stacking rings on his fingers—another element of MK5's coordinated outfits from a different designer. He wasn't exactly nervous, though there were plenty of celebrities and journalists in the lobby of the city's iconic concert venue.

He couldn't help but dream of some day in the future when he'd return to the Coliseum and take the stage with MK5 for their own concert, surrounded by legions of adoring fans. But mostly he was excited, and maybe a little bit anxious, to see Calvin for the first time in almost two weeks, and for his handsome boyfriend to meet his parents. He was trying not to think too much about meeting Anita.

The Wongs made their way to the photo area, where a professional photographer took several formal shots, followed by a series of funny ones using cheesy props. The images were printed instantly for them to take home as souvenirs. In Aden's favorite, his mum was pretending to hold a plastic rose in her teeth as he struck a matador's pose. His dad, on the other hand, was simply looking at Evelyn with so much adoration that Aden almost teared up.

Instead, he started scanning the area for anyone he knew. Although he saw famous rockers and pop stars of all ages, he had more difficulty finding any members of MK5.

Eventually Aden spotted Phantom and his industry exec father at the far end of the room. He was standing on his tiptoes, straining to see any of the others, but mainly Calvin, when he noticed someone standing right in front of him.

He blinked and took a few steps backward to get a better look. This had to be his manager, but in a skintight black sequined dress and sky-high platform heels, Selina was hardly the same person Aden was used to seeing in her office. There, she was professional and intimidating; here, she was stunning.

"Wow. Selina?" he asked uncertainly.

"Good evening, Aden." She chuckled. "Aren't you going to introduce me to your parents?"

"Right, of course. Mum, Dad, this is my manager, Selina Mak." Aden watched as they all shook hands and exchanged pleasantries, but only a part of him was paying attention. His eyes kept drifting around in search of Calvin.

Aden half listened as Evelyn talked Selina's ear off about how she'd always known her son had the makings of a star and how excited she was to be in the presence of so many greats, while Desmond stood by, mostly silent. He was surprised but grateful how patient the usually brusque Selina was with his excited mother, and supposed he should be the same.

"Aden, I can't believe you haven't pushed Selina harder about the schedule for your first single," Evelyn said, sounding bemused but almost annoyed, and Aden forced himself to focus on their conversation. "She said you've barely asked about it at all, and that just seems so unlike you."

"Oh well, you know, I've been quite busy with *Hooked on Love* and other things recently," Aden stammered as his cheeks heated. He wasn't sure what was worse—his mum calling him out for being less career-driven than usual or the accidental double meaning in his reply. Selina seemed to be enjoying this a little too much. "But we're done filming now, so I can work more on music—"

Aden broke off as he saw Calvin (finally!) walk in the door, looking every bit like the Cantopop star he was. His tux was black, just like Aden's, and perfectly tailored to the long lines of his body. Underneath the jacket, he wore a silver waistcoat to match his silver bow tie, and he'd even styled his dark hair with some kind of metallic spray. It was swept back, glittering and shiny, reminding Aden of the day they'd met.

When he eventually brought his awareness back to Selina and his parents, Aden was relieved that they already knew about his secret romance. There was no hiding it now, not when he'd been caught ogling Calvin from afar and they were all surveying him with twinkling eyes.

"Be right back," Aden murmured, already walking in Calvin's direction. As he got closer, he registered the woman holding on to Calvin's arm stiffly. She wore a beautiful floor-length gown in purplish gray silk, with a matching lace bodice that covered her delicate arms down to the wrists. With her tall frame and similar bone structure, she could only be Calvin's mother, Anita.

And now Aden could admit that maybe he was a little freaked out after all. It had been a long time since he'd met anyone's parents, and this might be more like a confrontation than an introduction. Nor was he sure exactly what Anita knew about him.

Still, Aden wore a stupid grin when he stood next to Calvin and said, "Hi."

"Hey." Calvin smiled back guardedly, but the corners of his mouth dropped as he pivoted toward his mother. "Mum, this is—"

"The young man who turned my son's head, I suppose," Anita interrupted with an air of disdain, or perhaps it was only boredom. Aden wondered if this was how she'd reacted when Calvin had told her their news. He shot his boyfriend a questioning look, but Calvin was now staring at the floor like he wished it would open up and swallow him whole.

"And where are your parents, then?" Anita asked crisply. "I must meet the producer who convinced Calvin to throw away all his classical training for a career in pop music. Even though writing sappy love songs about your crush does not make you a composer."

Oh. Anita seemed to think that she was speaking to Phantom. From the look of Calvin's ears, which had gone bright red, she was right in believing that her son had once crushed on his friend. Aden filed that interesting tidbit away for later. He still wasn't sure what Anita thought about him, but regardless, he wasn't going to let her demean their work.

"I mean, technically speaking, anyone who writes music is a composer." Aden made no attempt to hide the sarcasm in his voice. When he saw a worried Calvin shaking his head, he stopped himself before saying anything offensive. He chose his next words carefully. "But you must be thinking of someone else. My dad's not a producer, he's a civil engineer. I'm Aden, from MK5 and *Hooked on Love*."

Aden held out his hand, and Anita took it, arching an eyebrow at him.

"The boys love show? You must be brave, then," she said. Nothing in her tone, which was more doubtful than impressed, implied she knew that Aden had practically been living in her apartment a few weeks ago. Aden was more disappointed than he expected when his suspicions were confirmed. At the same time, he could see why Calvin would be wary of sharing anything personal or special with his mother.

"I've already told Calvin I can help him fall back on the piano if it turns out to be a disaster, or in case of a scandal. What will you do as a backup plan?"

"Nothing. The show's not going to fail," Aden said quietly, though right now he wasn't so sure. He had an ache in his heart that hadn't been there before.

"Aden is an amazing dancer, Mum," Calvin offered, his pleading gaze on Aden.

"Ballet?" Anita asked, peering at Aden intently.

"Not anymore," Aden said. It was true, though he'd given up ballet for more modern types of dance in early secondary school. Anita's face clouded, and Aden had a sudden desire to be a little bit evil. He didn't want Calvin's mother to hate him, even if she only knew him as Calvin's colleague, not his boyfriend. But he also didn't like being made to feel that the things, and the person, he loved were somehow less worthy.

Ernesto had once invited Aden to pick up extra shifts at a private ballroom dance club, where sometimes the members paid for a lot more than just dancing. Although he'd never considered it, Aden was tempted to tell Anita that he could easily find a job there, or as an exotic dancer for private parties.

But then he saw Helga Sze approaching out of the corner of his eye and shuddered. Starring in a boys love TV show and dating his male costar were risky enough—Aden didn't need the tabloids spreading rumors about him becoming a sex worker too.

"Anita Leung! It's been such a long time," Helga crooned. Once again her long manicured nails matched her outfit, a silk pantsuit, both in an eye-watering shade of lime green.

"Ms. Sze," Anita replied curtly. She drew herself up to her full height, taller than Aden in heels. Yet the tiny reporter didn't appear the least bit intimidated by one of her former subjects.

"It must be wonderful to see your son doing so well in his career. He and MK5 are everywhere in the papers these days," Helga said sweetly. On the face of it, her remark was just what any parent wanted to hear. But Aden wondered if somehow Helga knew about Anita's dislike of all things trendy and modern, including her son's life choices. He couldn't wait to see how she'd react.

"Why yes, that's right," Anita said coolly, her eyes narrowed and her lips tight. After a long, tense beat, she looked away, jaw clenched below her even paler skin.

Apparently Anita did have feelings, if seeing Helga Sze was so painful after all these years. Aden almost felt sympathy for her, though he wasn't exactly sorry that someone who'd caused so much discomfort to Calvin was now the uncomfortable one.

"Calvin, Aden. Lovely to see you both again." Helga nodded at them.

"Hello, Helga." Aden hoped he wasn't smiling too wide. It was important to remember that Helga wasn't necessarily a friend, even if she had put an end to Anita's interrogation.

But it seemed that Helga wasn't too interested in Aden, Calvin, or Anita. She drifted away, possibly toward Shine and Mingo, and soon after Aden rejoined his parents to lead them to their assigned seats for the evening.

Since neither he nor MK5 had any vested interest in the awards that night, Aden contented himself with listening to the sounds coming from his mum beside him, little squeals and sad sighs, as she alternately delighted in other musicians' wins or mourned their losses. It was cute, and Aden hoped that next year she'd be right here to celebrate whatever awards he or any of his bandmates might win.

Although he wasn't particularly competitive by nature, Aden had always been determined to be the best. He didn't need trophies to prove that he or MK5 were a success, but they wouldn't hurt either. Especially not if he wanted to do more controversial things like *Hooked on Love*, or possibly Christelle's Pride concert. Or for that matter, generally be a bit more open about who he was outside of work.

He glanced down the row to where Calvin sat between his mother and, as it turned out, Phantom. As much as Aden wished he was sitting next to Calvin instead, it was better to keep a safe distance for now. Maybe next year they could be each other's actual dates to the awards, or any other formal event. They could sit side by side, holding hands or sharing a celebratory kiss, just like an ordinary couple. Aden exhaled loudly. Maybe.

When the ceremony was over, everyone moved back into the lobby for the post-event reception. The five band members and their families remained clustered together at first, though it was really too awkward to talk in such a big group.

Phantom's dad was the first to break away, no doubt in search of his own clients, and Phantom went with him. Anita strode off soon after, long silky hair flowing behind her. At least she hadn't had the chance to argue with the Kwoks about the superiority of classical music.

But Aden's heart sank as Calvin followed his mother sadly, lips pursed as he nodded at Aden in farewell. As expected, they wouldn't have an opportunity for any stolen sexy minutes alone.

Next Shine announced that he had somewhere to be—from his cheeky grin, Aden assumed it could only be a date. With his best friend. Weird. He needed a bit more time to get used to this new way his worlds had collided. Nor did he trust Shine's fancy sports car on a dark, possibly rainy night.

"Be careful in this weather!" Aden called after him knowingly, and Shine winked.

Aden sighed wistfully. Not that he begrudged Shine or Winnie the chance at romance. He just wished it wasn't so hard to find the right time and place for his own.

Then Mingo and his parents left, presumably to look after their viral cat, and Aden was about to suggest that he, Evelyn, and Desmond head home too.

But then there was a hand pressing against the small of his back and a sweet vanilla scent in the air, and Aden's body knew Calvin had returned before he even caught a glimpse of him.

"Mr. and Mrs. Wong, I didn't want to leave without being properly introduced," Calvin said as he stepped forward, shooting a quick smile at Aden. "I'm very pleased to meet you."

Calvin bowed slightly to show respect for his elders, which sent Aden's heart fluttering. He couldn't help but beam at this gorgeous man who was secretly his. Once again he was so glad he'd told his parents the truth about their relationship.

"Oh, Calvin, you're even more handsome in person than in MK5's music video," Aden's mum fussed in her excitement. "And there's no need to be so formal. You can call us auntie and uncle."

Then she proceeded to do what she did best, ask Calvin too many questions, while Aden and his father stood by in silence and the crowd around them slowly began to thin. Calvin, however, continued to reply to Evelyn patiently. If Aden hadn't been so delighted that his boyfriend had come back, he might've been annoyed that Calvin was mainly speaking to his mum, not him.

At the same time, he felt a twinge of sadness at the contrast between this moment and his meeting with Anita earlier. Sure, he wanted her to know the truth and to like him. More than anything, his heart ached for Calvin. Although Anita had deigned to attend the awards, thanks in part to Selina, she'd shown little interest in her son's colleagues and friends.

"*Sai lo.*" Evelyn seemed to remember that Aden existed, calling him "younger brother" like she would at home, though his sister wasn't around. "We'd better be off soon. Would you like to invite Calvin over for a drink?"

Aden blinked rapidly a few times, trying to process what his mum had said. He hadn't been expecting it, but Evelyn's offer was too good to pass up. If Calvin came over for a nightcap, then he could also venture into Aden's bedroom. Preferably naked, though he did look great in his tux. Slightly stunned, he turned to face Calvin and was met with a pair of eyebrows raised in a silent question.

Then Aden's gaze was drawn to a patch of bright green over Calvin's shoulder and his stomach tightened. Not far away, Helga Sze was talking to a StudioHK executive but also appeared to be watching them closely. What if she saw Aden and Calvin leave together?

Aden flinched. Although it seemed unlikely that Helga knew anything about him and Calvin, the thought of it was terrifying enough. If she leaked a story about them before Selina had submitted their signed paperwork to the studio, it could be an absolute nightmare. And here was Evelyn, out of pure goodness and love, inviting Calvin over like it was no big deal, in plain view of someone who made a living ruining careers by breaking juicy scandals.

"Oh, that's very kind of you to offer." Calvin broke the silence hesitantly when Aden didn't reply. His beautiful dark eyes were still fixed on Aden, waiting for an answer. A glimmer of hope flickered there, along with something like understanding and maybe even worry.

Despite the unease in his stomach and the tension in his shoulders, Aden couldn't resist the pull of finally being able to kiss his boyfriend again. It felt like it had been forever. So he found himself saying, "Great idea, Mum. Let's go."

Helga might have been lurking nearby, but Aden's focus had narrowed to include Calvin and no one else, in particular, his glowing face. Aden hoped he'd have no reason to regret this crazy decision in the future. For now at least, Calvin's expression alone was completely worth it.

Low Pressure System to Bring Plenty of April Showers
852weather.com
April 20 6:30pm, Updated 10:46pm

THE HONG Kong Weather Service has issued a thunderstorm warning for the territory, which will remain in effect for most of the evening. Residents are advised to prepare for heavy rainfall, thunder and lightning conditions.

Although temperatures will remain moderate, around 20-25 °C, there is a chance of hail. People should remain indoors wherever possible and stay tuned to local news outlets for further updates.

As of 10:00 p.m. this evening, the landslip warning was also in effect. Not only has flooding been observed in low-lying areas in the New Territories, but there have also been reports of streets overwhelmed with water due to poor drainage. For safety, motorists should slow down and avoid driving on roads where water appears more than 10 cm deep.

<u>Click here</u> for photos of the latest storm damage around the city.

Chapter 18

WHEN ADEN, his parents, and Calvin made their way outside the Hong Kong Coliseum, the weather was even worse than expected. The heavy rain fell in sheets, slanting sideways in the strong wind, so the building's unique overhang provided little protection from the elements.

As they waited for their driver, Aden debated whether Calvin should take a separate taxi to the Wong family apartment. Anita had already departed in Calvin's studio-provided car, leaving her son semi-stranded. Yet because of the storm, public transportation would be difficult to come by.

So Aden decided on the easiest, and most dangerous, option. When the van arrived, he pulled Calvin inside and prayed that Helga Sze or her contemporaries weren't close enough to see it. They sat in the back seat, with Aden's parents a row in front for what felt like an interminable ride home. The car was quiet for most of the journey except for the clattering of the rain, and Aden trained his eyes on the road ahead. He didn't trust himself to even look at Calvin when they were so close, but not exactly alone.

When Aden's front door finally closed behind the four of them, Desmond was surprisingly the first to speak.

"Whiskeys all round?" he offered. Neither of Aden's parents were really big drinkers. Still, there was always a bottle of Chivas in one of the glass-fronted cabinets in the living/dining area. Desmond set the bottle on the table, placed four cut-glass tumblers next to it, then poured a shot in each.

With hot blood already rushing through his veins, Aden had no desire to throw any liquor into the mix. But in theory his parents had invited Calvin over for a nightcap, so he dutifully took the glass his father slid toward him and sat down after removing his jacket and loosening his tie.

As before, Aden's mum kept up a steady conversation with Calvin, asking a series of questions and sometimes barely pausing to hear his replies. But as far as Aden could tell, Calvin didn't seem to mind. He mainly sounded bemused, except when the whiskey's burn made his throat rasp.

Across the table, Desmond mostly listened, throwing in an occasional murmur or other sound of acknowledgment. Aden, meanwhile, alternately sipped and swirled his drink, staring through the glass tabletop to the floor, where his socked feet were mere inches away from Calvin's.

All he wanted was for his parents to leave him and Calvin alone, but he also couldn't quite believe his boyfriend was actually here. Since he'd gotten serious about dance in high school, Aden had rarely asked anyone over, even friends. He'd certainly never brought any of the guys he'd casually dated home to meet his parents. This was suddenly a lot.

When Aden finished his whiskey, he set his glass down with a clang that made everyone jump. Although it hadn't been intentional, given his parents' reactions, Aden wished he'd done it sooner.

Evelyn broke off midsentence, then asked, "Oh my, it is getting late, isn't it?"

"Yes, dear," Desmond replied mildly. As he stood up, he pushed the bottle of Chivas toward Calvin. "Good night, and please help yourself."

Then Aden's parents went into their room, and his pulse spiked.

"Do you want another drink?" Aden asked, willing Calvin not to say yes. He toyed with the whiskey bottle anxiously, spinning it round and listening to the clink of his rings on the glass.

"No," Calvin said. He reached out to still Aden's hands, taking them both in his and squeezing gently. There was a hint of concern in his voice as he asked, "Do you want me to go?"

"What? No!" Aden exclaimed. "Why?"

"I don't know. Because you're pissed at me for not telling my mum about us?" Calvin almost whispered.

"I mean, I won't say that it didn't hurt a little bit. But after meeting her tonight, I totally get it," Aden replied dryly.

"I'm sorry." Calvin hung his head, though Aden almost felt like he should be the one to apologize. "So what's wrong, then?"

"Well…." Aden thought back over the evening so far: meeting Anita and trying to avoid Helga Sze's scrutiny. But the reason he was stressing out was sitting right next to him. Yet instead of telling Calvin that he never brought guys home or introduced them to his family, Aden smiled slowly. "You mean, aside from the fact that we're still out here, and not in my bed?"

Calvin's head snapped up in surprise, eyes wide and mouth open. And then Aden was on his feet, racing the short distance to his bedroom with Calvin following right behind.

Somehow Aden managed to close the door quietly despite his hurry, but he didn't stop to turn on a light. He just smashed his mouth onto Calvin's, kissing him deeply, almost roughly, to drown out all the other thoughts circling through his head.

Although the whiskey lingered on Aden's tongue, he relished in the taste of Calvin that he'd been craving for the past two weeks. He lost himself in Calvin so much that he almost had to remind himself to breathe. At the same time, being here with Calvin was just the breath of fresh air he needed.

Chest heaving, it was Calvin who pulled away first. In the minimal light coming through the half-opened curtains, his hair was now deliciously tousled despite the generous coating of silver styling spray. Needing a better view, Aden stepped away to turn on his desk lamp.

When Aden faced his boyfriend again, Calvin's eyes were glassy and even darker than usual. He was in the process of trying to simultaneously loosen his tie and undo the buttons of his waistcoat, rings glinting on his long, slender fingers.

"Wait," Aden growled, batting Calvin's hands away. Most of the evening, he'd tried his best not to look at Calvin, in an attempt to avoid any temptation or embarrassment. Now that they were finally alone, he needed a second to take everything in. It wasn't every day he got to see such a handsome man in a tux. Or invite his boyfriend into his childhood bedroom.

"What? What's wrong?" Calvin's eyebrows drew closer together the longer that Aden stared at him.

"Nothing." Aden blushed, his throat unexpectedly tight. "Just admiring the view, babe."

Calvin chuckled. This time his hands moved to Aden's neck, where he slowly began to remove his tie. "You know we'll be going to many more events for the band, the show, and who knows what else. That means many more chances to see me in beautiful but uncomfortable clothes."

"Is that a promise?" Aden murmured, his head swimming at the prospect and the feel of Calvin's delicate fingers on his throat.

Calvin's only reply was to kiss him with such tenderness that Aden almost thought he might cry. Once Calvin had dropped Aden's tie on the floor, he moved on to his shirt, though the frills of fabric meant that the buttons were rather too well-hidden. Eventually, enough of them were undone that Calvin was able to slide the shirt over Aden's head, and only then did Aden begin to undress him, while keeping their lips locked.

Naked from the waist up, Aden guided Calvin toward his single bed, never more grateful that the simple wooden frame included only a headboard, no footboard. Since Aden was only average height and usually slept alone, the size of his bed had never mattered much before. But with the addition of Calvin's tall frame, it was going to be a tight squeeze. Aden took the place closest to the wall, and Calvin slipped in beside him, his feet almost reaching the end of the mattress.

Although he didn't seem to mind the small space and, in fact, scrambled even closer to Aden for another kiss. Aden ran his hands over Calvin's smooth chest, still not quite convinced the moment was real.

He kicked off his trousers and tugged at Calvin's waistband, encouraging him to do the same. Instead, Calvin searched his pockets, tossing a packet of tissues and his keys on the floor, until finally he held out a condom and travel-sized lube.

"Here," Calvin said breathlessly, handing them to Aden before wriggling out of the last remaining piece of his tuxedo.

"Someone was well-prepared." Aden smirked. He rolled onto his back, pulling Calvin on top of him into another heady kiss. He wrapped his legs around Calvin's slim waist, dragging his hips down until their bodies were joined in all the right places. He was deliriously happy, and though it was a weird time to be thinking about this, beyond grateful for his mum's kind yet risky invitation.

Calvin gasped into Aden's mouth, and suddenly he had another reason to worry. Not about tabloid journalists or career-ending scandals, but his parents, who were trying to sleep in the next room.

"Shh," Aden said, a reminder to both himself and Calvin. Their lips had only just met again when another unwelcome noise came over the sounds of their labored breathing. Now it was Aden's turn to groan.

At the same time, he and Calvin turned to look at their clothes on the floor. Somewhere in the pile of expensive fabrics, one of their phones was vibrating. Aden couldn't imagine who would be calling either of them in the middle of the night. Surely it was a mistake or a drunk dial. Unless it was something really important.

"Ignore it," Calvin urged, nibbling at Aden's jaw, and Aden found himself unable to protest. He dragged Calvin's mouth back to his, kissing him desperately so that they could forget about anything and anyone outside this room.

At some point, Aden reached up to tug on Calvin's hair and realized he was still clutching the supplies in his fist. He tried to press them into Calvin's hand, encouraging him to move things along and fill the aching need within him. But Calvin had other ideas, flipping them both so that Aden was on top.

"Your bed, your turn," Calvin whispered in Aden's ear, his breath hot on his neck.

Positively giddy, Aden let out a small laugh as he ground his pelvis deeper into Calvin's. He wondered if this man would ever stop surprising him in the very best of ways, but so far it seemed the answer was no.

Although he was a big fan of being in control in his daily life, it wasn't usually Aden's preference in the bedroom. But it wasn't like he'd never topped before, and if that was what Calvin wanted, he was more than happy to oblige. After two weeks of waiting, he was so glad to be reunited that he'd do almost anything.

As much as he wanted everything right now, Aden took a deep breath and forced himself to move slowly, carefully and lovingly, not to mention quietly. There was no reason to rush. And when he could finally see Calvin coming undone beneath him, he was awestruck all over again. At the flush that bloomed from Calvin's round cheeks to his slender neck, at the way he bit his trembling bottom lip, at the sound of Aden's name on his lips just before he carried them both over the edge. It was better than he'd ever imagined.

Afterward, they lay together mostly in silence for what could've been minutes or hours—a boneless, sticky heap in a too small bed. It was nothing short of perfection, and Aden never wanted it to end. Of course, they couldn't lie there forever, as appealing as it might be. Even if Calvin stayed the night, he'd have to go home or to work eventually. It was probably best for them both, and their careers, if he didn't do a walk of shame from Aden's apartment in a tuxedo.

Beside him, his boyfriend stirred, and Aden wondered if he was thinking the same thing. A glance at Calvin—eyebrows slightly furrowed, lips tight—meant the answer was probably yes.

"Babe." Aden threw one leg over both of Calvin's, then pressed his forehead into Calvin's chest in an attempt to pin him to the bed for a little while longer. Calvin brought his free arm—the one not trapped under Aden's body—up to stroke Aden's hair gently.

"I should go. It's late," he said sadly, then reached for the packet of wet tissues on Aden's nightstand. "My mum will expect me home at some point."

At the mention of Anita, Aden was reminded of a part of their meeting earlier that actually hadn't been too unpleasant. When she'd confused Aden for another member of MK5.

"Speaking of which, your mum said something interesting before." Aden lifted up onto his elbows. He needed an unobstructed view of Calvin's face when he teased him. "About Phantom."

Calvin rolled his eyes, but his cheeks pinked.

"I knew it," Aden gloated. "You totally had a thing for him, didn't you?"

"Phantom is my friend," Calvin said, not quite meeting Aden's gaze. "And in case you hadn't noticed, he is very straight."

"Mm-hmm." Aden wasn't fooled. Besides, Calvin was far from the first gay guy to fall for his straight best friend.

"Okay, I'll admit it's possible. But not since…." Calvin paused, his blush deepening.

"Since when?" Aden held his breath.

Calvin closed his eyes before he replied, "Since the day I almost ruined both of our auditions."

"Oh, babe," Aden whispered. He could feel Calvin's heart beating against his chest as if it were his own, and in a way, it almost was. He'd handed over his own heart to Calvin long ago. Although they'd only been official boyfriends for a short while, maybe he needed to say so out loud. He took a deep breath, summoning the courage to tell Calvin how he really felt.

"I—" Aden paused as the pile of clothes started vibrating once more. Maybe it hadn't been a junk call or a misdial earlier. Maybe someone really was trying to reach them.

With a moan, he pushed himself off Calvin's warm body and searched for the offending phone. He found his first, in the pocket of his trousers, though it didn't seem to be the source. By the time he located Calvin's in a waistcoat pocket, the caller had hung up, but there were a slew of notifications on the lock screen.

Aden handed over Calvin's phone carefully, fighting the growing sense of foreboding beneath his ribs. Calvin sat up and listened to his voicemails, first halfheartedly, then intently, his face undergoing a series of transformations from confused to stunned to something Aden hadn't seen before: scared.

Once finished, Calvin let his hand drop to his side, almost lifeless yet still maintaining a tight grip on his phone. He didn't move, just sat on the bed, naked and seemingly helpless.

"Calvin?" Aden asked tentatively after a few long beats. He moved to kneel between his boyfriend's legs, with little thought for his bare skin on the cold tile floor. Setting Calvin's phone aside, he clasped his hands tightly. "Babe, what's the matter?"

"That was the accident and emergency department at Victoria International Hospital," Calvin said slowly, his voice strained. This close, Aden could see his cheeks were streaked with silent tears. "My mum was in a car wreck on the way home from the awards. She's in surgery now."

Aden hauled Calvin to his feet and into a bear hug, the press of their bodies physically similar, yet not at all the same as before. In his arms, Calvin seemed to sway, tremble even, and the skin gradually grew wet where Calvin had buried his face in Aden's shoulder.

Although he had no such terrible reasons to be upset, Aden was uneasy, or at least bewildered. He had no idea what to say when your boyfriend's difficult mother, who'd seemed less than kind earlier in the evening, was in critical condition. He'd never even seen Calvin cry before, except perhaps on set. But he resolved to do his best to support him until the worst was over.

When Aden was sure that Calvin was able to stand on his own, he flew around the room grabbing any of his own clothes that might fit his taller boyfriend. There was no way he was letting him go to a hospital, even an exclusive private one, in a flashy designer tuxedo. He found the longest pair of athletic shorts he owned, a T-shirt that was baggy on him, his spare bucket hat and roomiest hoodie. No doubt it would be cold in the air-conditioned hospital.

After tossing the clothes to Calvin, Aden dressed himself in record time in similar but better-fitting attire. He was heading toward his bedroom door when he realized that, still in shock, Calvin hadn't moved a muscle. Like a young child, he needed Aden's help to put on every article of clothing.

Finally they were ready, and Aden led the way out of his apartment building in silence. They waited alone at the taxi stand in the semi-darkness of Hong Kong's light-polluted night. At least the rain had stopped, though the air was still warm and humid, oppressive even.

Briefly, Aden wondered if he should send Calvin on his way by himself. One celebrity at a hospital, no matter the time of night, was likely to cause something of a stir. When that celebrity was accompanied by another, in this case his on-screen love interest, it would definitely be more newsworthy.

But after a glance at Calvin's pale face and tired eyes, Aden knew this wasn't the time to be thinking about himself or his career. His boyfriend was hurting, and he needed him. It was as simple as that.

In the taxi, Aden messaged his sleeping mum to let her know he'd most likely be out all night. He contacted Selina and the band's group chat too, as Calvin's family emergency would impact them all. If he took time off to be with Anita during her recovery, the others would have to cover for him at public appearances and press events. Someone might need to take his recording sessions at the studio as well.

With a sinking feeling, Aden remembered their plan to meet with Selina the next day. Or, given the time, later that day, but obviously it wasn't going to happen. He sighed, disappointed that he and Calvin would have to wait to make their relationship official with StudioHK. Hopefully not for too much longer, and before their secret got out.

When they arrived at the hospital—after a longer journey than expected due to flash flooding from the recent storm—a few more second thoughts flitted through Aden's brain. He forced them away as he opened the door and helped Calvin out of the car.

The hospital was on a relatively secluded hillside, with mostly trees and no other buildings nearby. The two young stars wouldn't be easily recognizable in the dark, while also wearing hats and masks. Plus, it seemed unlikely that any journalists or fans knew they were coming. Yet.

Still, Aden hurried them inside, away from the possibility of prying eyes. There were hardly any people near the entrance at this hour, but you could never be too careful.

Anita's divorce had once been fodder for the tabloids, and now her son was frequently in the news. It was only a matter of time until a story about the accident appeared. Whether Aden would end up in the copy, described as a supportive colleague or something closer to the truth, remained to be seen.

Morning Entertainment News Roundup
HK Star Watch
April 21

Breaking news: Local Pianist Anita Leung Hospitalized after Traffic Accident During Thunderstorm
>>Read more

Music update: All the Winners at StudioHK's Annual Music Awards
>>See the full list

Photos: Hong Kong's Hottest Celebs Walk the Red Carpet at StudioHK's Annual Music Awards
>>Check it out

CHAPTER 19

IF THE floor of Anita's hospital room had been anything other than tile, Aden was sure Calvin would've worn a hole in the pale green surface by now. Since they'd arrived, he'd been pacing almost nonstop, from the bed where his mother lay unconscious and unmoving to the sofa where Aden sat, almost dizzy from Calvin's repetitive movements.

Besides the regular sounds of his boyfriend's footfalls, the sharp chirp of Anita's heart monitor echoed in the quiet. There were some occasional noises from the hall, but for the most part they hadn't been disturbed since a nurse had led them to the room a couple of hours ago.

In that time, Calvin had only stood still to speak to Anita's surgeon, a Dr. Chow, when she'd checked on her high-profile patient postoperatively. But if Dr. Chow had been surprised to find two young pop stars in the room of a well-known classical pianist, she hadn't shown it.

Instead, she'd gently explained to Calvin that his mother had needed surgery to stabilize a compound fracture in her leg. It was likely she had a concussion too, but Dr. Chow would perform a more detailed examination once the anesthetic had worn off. There had not, however, been any damage to Anita's piano-playing hands, something Calvin had double and triple checked.

According to Dr. Chow, the studio-provided car—the car Calvin would've been riding in if he hadn't stayed behind to meet Aden's parents—had been hit by a hydroplaning vehicle on a partially flooded road. The studio's driver had then called Selina as well as 999, and they'd managed to send Calvin's mum to the most exclusive private hospital in the city, a highly unusual arrangement. Emergency cases were typically handled in the public healthcare system.

"Come try to sleep before the person in the room below makes a noise complaint." Aden patted the sofa next to him and hoped that Calvin would take the hint. For now, it was still dark outside the window above his head. But it was approaching an hour that would be considered early rather than late, and neither of them had slept.

Not that it would necessarily be easy to get any rest in Calvin's current state. He was anxious and upset, as Aden would be in a similar situation. Although Evelyn seemed to have a whole lot more going for her as a mum than Anita.

But Aden sensed there was something more that his boyfriend wasn't saying. In fact, they'd barely spoken since they'd arrived.

At the sound of Aden's voice, Calvin paused, narrowing his eyes for a moment before resuming his path around the room.

"Worrying yourself sick isn't going to make her wake up any faster."

This time when Calvin stopped walking, he looked devastated, like he was ready to crumble. Aden dragged him onto the sofa, lifting his legs onto the footstool and removing his shoes—an old pair of Desmond's loafers, which, though ratty, had been a better alternative than the dress shoes Calvin had worn with his tux.

After taking off his own shoes, Aden slotted his body in next to Calvin's and covered them both with an extra blanket he'd found in one of the cabinets. He eased an arm around Calvin's shoulders and tucked him into his side.

"I'm not worried," Calvin finally said, far from convincingly. Aden raised an eyebrow. "I mean, that's not the only problem."

"Then what is?"

"I can't stop thinking about how things might've been different if I'd convinced her to stay at the awards a bit longer." Calvin squeezed his eyes shut and swallowed. "And about the fact that I was supposed to be in the car too. She already thinks I'm not a very dutiful son, but now…."

With his free hand, Aden reached for Calvin's and laced their fingers together, his heart in his throat. He'd had similar thoughts more than once since their arrival but had tried not to dwell on them. Later, he would be sure to thank Evelyn for inviting Calvin to their apartment and unknowingly keeping him out of harm's way.

"You being there wouldn't have stopped the rain from falling or other cars from crashing into things they shouldn't," he said gently. "If you'd been in the car, then you'd both be injured, and it would be all over the news by now."

Aden's voice broke on the last sentence, but in his head he had more to say. *And I might never be able to tell you that I love you.*

"I'm sure it will be soon anyway." Calvin bit his lip and glared up at the white ceiling tiles. "Helga Sze is going to love this, just another reason for my mum to be upset with me."

Aden decided now wasn't the time to point out that Calvin's parents had attracted plenty of media attention with their divorce before he'd been the least bit famous. Instead, he said, "Or perhaps she'll find a reason to be grateful. That you're okay."

Calvin's eyes welled up, and blinking furiously, he buried his face in Aden's neck. Aden hugged him tighter, rubbing his back and stroking his hair until Calvin's sobs eased and they both drifted off into an uneasy sleep.

ADEN WASN'T quite sure where he was, but he knew that he was cold and uncomfortable and something was missing. He drew the blanket closer around him and tried to snuggle into Calvin yet found only empty space on the sofa next to him. Calvin couldn't've gone far, though, because Aden was sure he could hear his voice.

Opening an eye halfway, Aden took in the sterile environment—white walls, white linens, white fluorescent lights—and remembered he was in Anita's hospital room. Now that he was more awake, he could see that Calvin was sitting at his mother's bedside. She appeared to have woken up too.

Calvin was holding her hand, and they were speaking in hushed tones. Aden was relieved that her face, though tired and strained, showed nothing but fondness for her son. She didn't seem angry, as Calvin had feared, or even distant and disdainful, as she'd been at the awards.

Aden closed his eyes again, feigning sleep to give Calvin and Anita some semblance of privacy. But that didn't stop him from hearing at least some of what they were saying.

"I'm so sorry…."

"Accidents happen…."

"I have no idea what I would do if…." Calvin sounded distraught, and Aden's heart ached. He didn't want to think about how he'd react if one of his own family members, or Calvin, had been injured.

"I'm just relieved that you're safe." Anita seemed equally upset. Just as Aden was beginning to reconsider his opinion of her, she said something that set him on edge. "But it wasn't the best idea to bring your *friend* to the hospital with you."

The disapproval in her voice was unmistakable.

"Aden's not only my friend. He's my boyfriend," Calvin replied warmly. Aden could picture just how his eyes sparkled when provoked. He fought the urge to rush to Calvin's side and squeeze him tight. "There's no way I would've made it here tonight without him, Mum. I… I lo—"

Aden held his breath in anticipation, but Calvin never got the chance to finish his sentence.

"How you feel is beside the point," Anita interrupted curtly. "It was a big risk, and I can't imagine it's going to end well for any one of us."

Aden shuddered, willing himself to fall back asleep soon. He didn't want to listen to any more of this conversation. It was unpleasant, and as much as Aden hoped Anita was wrong, what if she wasn't? She may not have been the most enthusiastic or supportive mum for her son. Still, Anita obviously knew a thing or two about the music industry and the media. He really hoped her prediction didn't turn out to be correct.

THE NEXT thing Aden was aware of was the sound of the door opening and closing, possibly more than once. At first he wondered if Calvin had gone in search of snacks or even breakfast. What time was it anyway? Then he felt Calvin's head on his shoulder and relief flooded through him. His boyfriend was finally getting the rest he'd need to deal with the days, and likely weeks, ahead.

But if Aden had heard the door, that meant someone else was in Anita's hospital room. And that person, or people, had seen him and Calvin cuddled together on the sofa, looking far too cozy to be just friends. Shit. Aden took a deep breath and forced himself not to panic. As much as he felt the urge to move away, he didn't want to wake Calvin even more.

Nervously he glanced up to find Selina leaning against the built-in cabinet across from Anita's bed, typing furiously on her phone. Next to her, Phantom, Shine, and Mingo were standing around awkwardly, an assortment of shopping bags at their feet. They'd brought all of Calvin's favorites—chocolate, gummies, instant noodles, chips—as well as other healthier foods, toiletries, and even spare clothes.

Now Aden was even more relieved. He and Calvin hadn't been caught by anyone but their colleagues. Not only had MK5 shown up at the hospital the morning after Aden's late-night updates, despite their busy schedules, they'd come bearing gifts too.

Aden's heart was full. He was debating what to say to everyone or how he could ever thank them when Phantom caught his eye, looking particularly smug. Like he'd known all along that Aden had lied that day at the studio. Aden tried not to squirm, but he certainly felt sheepish.

When he'd messaged Selina and the group chat the night before, Aden had been so focused on helping his boyfriend that he hadn't stopped to think about what else he might be revealing. Like why he was spending time with Calvin, but not any other band members, after hours.

Little had he known that Selina was already well-informed about Anita's accident by the studio's driver. Then again, Selina knew the true nature of his and Calvin's relationship and even had the paperwork to prove it. Once it was signed, they would've told the rest of the band eventually. Or as it turned out, today.

After adjusting Calvin's head so it rested on the sofa instead of his shoulder, Aden crept out from under the covers and stood up. He readjusted the blanket, tucking Calvin in snugly and brushing a lock of still-silvery hair away from his face.

"Hey, guys, thanks for coming," Aden whispered as he walked toward the visitors.

"How is she? Have you seen the doctor this morning?" Selina asked, as if Aden hadn't just obviously been asleep.

"Calvin spoke to Dr. Chow soon after we arrived, and I heard him talking to his mum sometime in the night." Aden felt his cheeks redden at the admission, though everyone knew he'd been at the hospital for hours. "Anita may need more tests later today, and I think she'll be here for the next few nights."

Selina nodded but made no reply, and for a few seconds no one said anything. Phantom's smug expression had transformed into a full-blown smirk, and even Shine seemed rather amused.

Mingo, on the other hand, was as sweet and innocent as always. He fixed Aden with an earnest look as he asked, "And what about you? How are you holding up?"

"Oh… err." Aden shrugged as if he weren't blushing even harder than before. Since he couldn't meet Mingo's wide eyes, he ended up glancing over to Calvin, still sleeping peacefully on the less-than-comfortable sofa. Aden hoped that the relative calm of the morning would last after the chaos of the previous night. But even if it didn't and Aden and Calvin became the subject of unwanted headlines, at least they had each other. And everyone else in the room too.

Aden's thoughts were interrupted when Phantom stepped in close, blocking his view of his boyfriend. He realized he'd been staring for too long, and Phantom chuckled at the guilt written all over his face.

"Told you they were together!" Phantom declared proudly, holding his palm out toward Mingo and Shine. "Now pay up!"

Aden gaped at the three of them in surprise. Selina merely shook her head without looking up from her phone.

"As if." Shine shoved Phantom playfully. "I'm sure I didn't agree to such a thing. I'd never take a losing bet."

"Well, the other week at Happy Valley…," Mingo began, but Aden held up his hand and shushed him.

He didn't need to hear about Shine and Mingo's adventures at the Wednesday night horse races, no doubt another filming location for their TV show. Nor did he care if the others had been speculating that he and Calvin were dating. They hadn't necessarily done the greatest job of hiding it anyway. He just wanted everyone to keep their voices down so that Calvin wouldn't be disturbed.

Soon after, Aden saw the handle of Anita's door turn, but he hoped Dr. Chow hadn't chosen this moment for her late-morning rounds. Calvin and his mother were both still asleep. Selina hadn't moved from her position by the cabinet, but the four members of MK5 were now clustered around the small table between it and the sofa, speaking in subdued tones.

"Breakfast is served," a familiar female voice called, Aden's curiosity quickly giving way to concern at the disruption. Especially when Shine jumped up, his chair squeaking on the tile floor, to hold the door open for… Winnie?

Aden's jaw dropped at the sight of his childhood best friend standing in the doorway, a tray of coffees in each hand and bakery bags dangling from her elbows. He was happy to see her but mostly confused.

"Hey, Win. Wow, thank you," Aden stammered. He knew he'd messaged Christelle the night before but couldn't remember contacting Winnie as well. Maybe he'd been too frazzled to notice, or perhaps Winnie had found out from someone else. Like the Caden fan accounts she was always sending him links to. Oh no. Perhaps Anita had been right after all and Aden shouldn't be here.

"How did you…?" Aden struggled to form words as he tried not to panic. He watched as Shine gently unburdened Winnie of her packages, placing them carefully on the table before offering her the chair he'd been sitting in. He stood behind her, his hand resting just above her shoulder. No, on her shoulder.

Winnie beamed up at Shine before turning to grin at Aden. Suddenly he remembered their text conversation from the previous day, though it felt like years ago now. Winnie and Shine were dating, which explained a lot—the orange sports car outside Sally Wu's ballet studio, Winnie's uncanny knowledge of Aden's schedule, even Selina's cryptic comment about love being in the air that spring.

"I have my sources." Winnie laughed, looping an arm around Shine's waist.

"Right, of course." Aden shook his head, still somewhat bewildered. He was happy for Winnie and Shine, but his brain was overloaded from the whirlwind of the past twelve hours. It must've shown on his face too. The next thing he knew, Winnie was fussing over him, handing him the food she'd brought.

"Here, take this. Eat something," she said softly. And Aden did, too exhausted to care about the calories in the delicious pineapple bun or the exercise he'd need to do to burn them off. He was simply grateful for the support of yet another friend.

It was afternoon, and the members of MK5 (plus Winnie) were entertaining themselves with a never-ending game—listing celebrities based on the first letter of the previous celebrity's surname—as Selina hovered nearby on her phone. She'd been hard at work all day, rescheduling their most urgent commitments while keeping a close eye on the news.

The only coverage of the accident so far had been a basic report about the crash included in a wrap-up of the record-breaking storm.

Although it had referred to Anita by name, there had been no mention of her famous son or StudioHK. Yet.

Aden was pressed against Calvin on the sofa. There was no real reason for him to be at the hospital at all, but he hadn't even thought about leaving. His boyfriend, his best friend, and his closest colleagues were all together. Except for probably the gym, there was nowhere else he needed to be. He wished they were all hanging out under different circumstances but was more than glad to support Calvin, despite the risk.

Earlier, Aden's sister Mimi had popped in with trays of assorted sushi before the beginning of her shift, another unexpected surprise. Aden had been so busy with his own career that he'd forgotten Mimi had a new job and remembered none of the details. Evelyn, however, had asked Mimi to check in on her little brother if she got the chance.

As a nurse at a private hospital, Mimi could enjoy a higher degree of prestige and earn more compared to her previous position in an urgent care clinic. But to Aden, it felt a little bit like fate that his sister was working at the same hospital where Calvin's mum was now a patient.

Throughout the day, Dr. Chow and multiple nurses had checked on Anita, while she drifted in and out of sleep due to all the pain medication. When she was awake, she'd been surprisingly civil to the band members, given her dislike of popular music. She and Calvin had seemed almost affectionate.

Of course, Anita had noticed that Aden was still in her room. He'd caught her surveying him closely a few times, like when he touched Calvin's leg or passed him some food. But she hadn't made any more negative comments or given him any dirty looks. Perhaps it was because of the medication, or maybe she was feeling better. Although it would've been nice, Aden couldn't quite believe she'd warmed to him so soon.

Calvin himself had been fairly quiet since he'd awakened earlier in the day, but obviously he had a lot on his mind. The presence of MK5 and Anita's promising recovery had done much to lighten the mood. Still, they were in a hospital only hours after a dangerous accident had occurred.

"Okay, Calvin, I don't want you to worry about a thing," Selina said. She spoke more gently than usual as she slipped her phone into her handbag in preparation to leave. "You just focus on taking care of yourself and your mum and let us handle everything else."

Beside him, Calvin bit his lip and nodded, and Aden squeezed his knee reassuringly. Although Calvin wasn't as career-obsessed as he was, he'd still worked hard to get to where he was. It wouldn't be easy for him to give everything up, even temporarily.

Selina turned to the other members of MK5, resuming her usual clipped tone. "As for the rest of you, I've cleared your schedules for tomorrow as well. Meet me in my office at eleven and we'll sort out how to cover Calvin's upcoming commitments."

Aden gulped. He didn't want to think about all the *Hooked on Love* promotions he might have to do without Calvin by his side. Not that he wasn't perfectly capable of doing interviews on his own or with other cast members, but he'd been hoping to see his boyfriend more in the coming weeks. He was getting used to having a partner, and not only thinking of himself.

Once Selina left, the rest of the band members went their separate ways, first Phantom, then Mingo, and lastly Shine and Winnie together. Then Aden and Calvin were alone, except for Anita, who was sleeping again. Which Aden wasn't sad about. He snuggled closer into his boyfriend, resting his head on Calvin's chest, and closed his eyes.

"You must be exhausted. You should go too." Calvin stroked Aden's hair tenderly. It would've been so easy to fall asleep in his arms, except his tone seemed off. Aden tried not to overthink it. As tired as he was, Calvin was equally as sleep-deprived and under a lot more stress.

"Are you sure? I can stay as long as you need me," Aden murmured into Calvin's neck, lips brushing the soft skin. Yet he felt his boyfriend tense beneath him, not at all the response he'd expected.

"No, it's fine. Christelle will be here soon anyway," Calvin replied too quickly. That evening, he and Christelle were going back to his apartment to collect things that he and Anita might need for the next few days in the hospital. Aden had considered doing it himself, but Christelle was eager to help and probably wouldn't attract as much attention. Or, Aden realized bitterly, she might even be a kind of diversion. "Besides, Dr. Chow seems to think my mum is doing well, so hopefully everything will be okay from here on out."

"Good. I hope so." Aden shifted so he could see Calvin's face more clearly, though he was reluctant to leave his embrace just yet.

"Maybe you can drop by tomorrow or something. Let's see. I'll call you, okay?" Calvin's weary eyes found Aden's for a moment, but he looked away again almost immediately.

"Yeah, sure. Of course I will, babe," Aden agreed, though he felt strangely unsettled. He also didn't want to overstay his welcome.

Rising to leave, he dropped a peck on Calvin's cheek. When he turned to walk away, he found himself being dragged into Calvin's lap. Then Calvin was kissing him hard and digging his fingers into Aden's hips like he was determined to leave bruises.

Aden couldn't hold back a gasp, and though it was mostly due to surprise, it didn't take long until he was fully on board with this impromptu make-out session. He sank his hands into Calvin's hair and relished the scratch of their stubble, not even noticing that neither of them had brushed their teeth for who knew how long.

But as amazing as it felt, something about the way Calvin was kissing him seemed different. Although Calvin's hands and tongue were moving so fast that Aden could barely keep up, this wasn't only a wild, passionate kiss or a kiss seeking comfort. It bordered on desperate.

Still, Aden had done his best to take care of his boyfriend so far. If this was what Calvin needed right now, Aden would certainly give it to him. Provided that Anita didn't wake up as they got each other off in her hospital room. But as it turned out, that wasn't going to happen.

Just as suddenly as he'd begun the kiss, Calvin broke away. He eased himself out from underneath a breathless Aden, moving carefully now that they were both very obviously turned on. Then he stood abruptly and handed Aden his hat before practically forcing him out the door.

In the taxi heading home, Aden pressed his lips together behind his mask, still feeling the burn of Calvin's searing kiss. As he tried to process what had just happened, his thoughts kept returning to the last time he'd been kissed like that—when he'd ended things with Simon.

But this was different. Aden and Calvin were about to sign paperwork for the studio that would allow them to continue their relationship, not break up. Given Anita's accident, they'd have to wait a little longer to make things official, but probably only a few days or, at most, weeks. It was more likely that Calvin was simply overwrought after the upset of the previous day. Right?

The Official MK5 Fan Club

Home > Fan Forum > Thread: Anita Leung was in an accident?!

calvin4evr
April 22 11:36am
OMG u guys! I m so worried rn. Poor Calvin T_T

CLfan1
April 22 11:39am
I knowwwww. What can we do to help? [prayer emoji]

MK5life
April 22 11:40am
Just so grateful that he is OK! But what's gonna happen to the band now?

Not_that_Jackie_Chan
April 22 11:58am
Can u believe what ppl are saying? About him/about his mum. DLLM >_<

CantoStan
April 22 12:01pm
I hd no idea abt Calvin's parents and their very public divorce. No kid shd have to go thru that!

Caden888
April 22 12:05pm
Pls pls say this wont change anything re *Hooked on Love*. Im dying.......

CHAPTER 20

"Before we get started, there are some things I need to show you all."

Selina turned her desktop monitor to face the four members of MK5 in her office. Shine and Mingo were in their usual places on folding chairs, but the normally crowded leather sofa felt too spacious with only Phantom and Aden sitting there.

Aden gripped his knees with his hands, bracing himself for the worst. He purposely hadn't read any news since leaving Anita's hospital room the day before, knowing that Selina would be refreshing all the feeds on a near-constant basis. It didn't seem like a good sign that she wanted to discuss whatever she'd found at the beginning of the meeting.

On the screen, Aden saw an article by who else but Helga Sze: "Boy Band Member Eludes Car Crash that Injures Mother, Pianist Anita Leung." Shit. This was exactly the type of story that Anita had been worried about. From the multiple tabs open in Selina's browser, it looked like every tabloid in town had their own version.

Even worse, Helga's article implied that Calvin was a less than dutiful son for not riding in the car with his mother, something Anita might also be inclined to believe. Although the truth was that she'd pretty much abandoned Calvin after the awards ceremony. At the bottom of the page, there were even links to archived coverage of Calvin's parents' divorce. Yikes.

The good news was that Aden's name wasn't mentioned anywhere. Yet. But once an enterprising reporter figured out that he was the reason Calvin hadn't been in the car with Anita that night, he was bound to be drawn into the story as well.

"*Diu,*" Phantom muttered, but Selina wasn't finished.

A photo of Aden leaving Victoria International Hospital the day before appeared on the screen, though the headline only said that he'd been visiting Calvin and his mum. Next there was a similar photo of Christelle. The headline asked "Childhood Friend or Girlfriend?" and Aden felt like he'd been punched in the gut.

He'd wondered if something like this might happen, and he knew he should be grateful that his and Calvin's secret hadn't been revealed. But he didn't like how people automatically assumed that Christelle and Calvin were an item just because she was a woman. And he was beyond annoyed that, though the rest of MK5 had been at the hospital too, there were no photos or mentions of Phantom, Mingo, or Shine. Or for that matter, Shine and Winnie.

"So far most of this is just speculation, but I hope I don't need to remind you boys to be careful," Selina said as she moved her monitor back to its original position. "A scandal is certainly not what Calvin and his mother need right now, especially not given their previous experience with the media. I suggest we all give them some space."

Selina turned pointedly toward Aden, and he nodded. He'd promised to visit Calvin at the hospital later if he asked, but that might change based on the news he'd just seen.

"Okay, now let's move on." Selina folded her hands on her desk and surveyed MK5 as if she were a principal about to tell her students something important. "Obviously, we'll need to delay the band's next single a bit until Calvin is ready to come back. But we've got plenty of individual projects for you all. Plus, each of you will need to help cover some of Calvin's commitments."

Selina pulled out a list and started going through each item one by one. Aden listened as best he could, trying not to think about how Calvin was holding up or how he might feel when all his responsibilities had been reassigned to the other band members.

Because Shine and Mingo were still filming their TV show, they were given the smallest roles—a cartoon movie voice-over, a new product endorsement, a lifestyle magazine interview. It also made sense that Phantom, the sporty one, would take Calvin's place in a charity basketball tournament and a sports drink advertisement, though Aden's biased view was that he didn't look nearly as good all sweaty and flushed.

As for himself, Aden wasn't surprised to hear that he'd be joined by Christelle or other cast members for any *Hooked on Love* promotions in the near future. But with at least a month to go until the show's premiere, Calvin would probably be back to work for the most important launch events.

"Okay, so the last change is that Calvin won't be the next one of you to record a solo single," Selina said once she'd reached the bottom of her list. Aden held his breath.

"Phantom has already released his first song, and Shine and Mingo's schedules are quite packed. So that means all the recording sessions and the Taiwan shoots we'd originally booked for Calvin are yours, Aden. You start tomorrow. The studio has okayed the music, and I'll email it to you right after this."

"Wow," Aden whispered as both his mind and heart started to race.

He couldn't believe it. Except for maybe starring in a film, releasing his own song was the only mark of being a Hong Kong entertainer that he hadn't tried yet. It was what he'd been waiting for since MK5 had first formed, since before he'd even auditioned for StudioHK. Even more than being in a band or on a TV show, a solo song would help to make him a real star.

Although it wasn't ideal that Aden had only gotten his break because Calvin was unavailable. Or that he would take his boyfriend's place in the recording studio while Calvin stayed at his mother's bedside. But Calvin was reasonable, and he cared about Aden. Maybe he wouldn't be too upset, especially since he'd get another opportunity down the line. And Aden would be helping to protect Calvin's image as a good son, even if Anita might've chosen her work over him in the past.

A better boyfriend would probably have said something like "Are you sure?" or "Is this a good idea?" but Selina had sounded firm. Anyway, it was the studio's decision. Who was Aden to question it? Besides, the arrangements had been made, and no doubt deposits paid, months in advance. The studio would lose money if he didn't step up when he was asked.

"That's gonna be a fun conversation later," Phantom commented dryly. "Good luck."

Aden glared sideways at him, though internally he fully agreed.

"No, Phantom. I'll handle this," Selina said sternly. "Aden, you don't need to say anything to Calvin that will cause him any more stress. Everything we're doing is meant to make his life easier right now."

In his pocket, Aden's phone vibrated. Glancing away from Selina, he saw a message from Winnie. He let out a loud groan, and everyone stared at him.

"What?" Phantom asked, but his eyes widened as he took in the image on the screen. A photo of Aden and Calvin arriving at the hospital together, alongside another of them leaving the StudioHK awards in the same car. This time the headline was a lot closer to the truth: "Caden Spotted Together Off Set: Are the *Hooked on Love* Costars More Than Friends?"

Winnie's accompanying message read, *Don't panic. You know you've made it when the juicy rumors start.* Aden shuddered, thinking back to what Anita had told Calvin that night when Aden had pretended to be asleep. Maybe she was right and it had been a mistake for him to go to the hospital. But what kind of boyfriend would he be if he hadn't?

Aden grimaced, wondering if he'd somehow tempted fate by thinking that the other headline about Christelle had gone too far. He placed his phone in Selina's outstretched palm, and she sucked in a breath.

"In case I wasn't clear earlier—" Selina's voice was deadly serious. "—none of you are to visit Calvin and his mother in the hospital from now on, unless we all go as a group. And no meeting him anywhere else either."

Aden watched as his fellow band members nodded, then asked, "So… what are you going to do?"

"Nothing," Selina said.

"Nothing?" Aden blinked. That wasn't the answer he'd expected, even if it was probably unreasonable to think that Selina, or StudioHK, could come up with a crisis communication plan on the spot.

"The way I see it, we have three choices. One, we can deny it, which may not be believable and will only make things more difficult for you later on."

Aden gulped, but he knew Selina was right. Since he and Calvin had technically been out before they joined MK5, it wouldn't be that difficult for someone to find photos of them with past boyfriends that would make any denial seem implausible. In a way, Aden was almost surprised that some old images hadn't been reposted online already.

"Two, we can admit the truth, but the studio isn't going to love the timing, since it's before *Hooked on Love* has premiered. Nor do I want to give the press a chance to say that Calvin chose romance over family."

Again, Aden didn't disagree. Filial piety was one of the most important traditional Chinese values, even in the 21st century. He wasn't sure how bad it would be for Calvin's reputation if he were branded a bad son, but it couldn't be good. Still, it didn't seem fair how much their personal lives could have an outsized impact on their careers. That was why he'd been so resolved not to date in the first place.

"Or three, we do nothing and let the rumors run their course. Once things have settled down, you and Calvin can sign the official paperwork for the studio. Then you can decide when and how you want to say anything to the general public about your relationship, if at all."

As much as Aden didn't want to stand by helplessly while people said who knows what about him and Calvin, it was the best worst option. It might be painful in the short term, but if Aden kept his distance for now, then maybe everything would work out fine eventually. Preferably without him being blamed for causing problems in the Leung family.

WHEN THE meeting was over, Aden holed up in a practice room at StudioHK, steering clear of the one he and Calvin had used a few weeks ago. In fact, he avoided that hallway entirely. He needed to concentrate.

He had mere hours to learn an entire song before rehearsals and recording sessions kicked off the next day. It would've been a tall order no matter what, but it didn't help that he'd been mostly acting, not singing, for the past month and a half.

Yet that wasn't really the problem. Even with his phone on airplane mode to avoid distractions, it was no use. Aden's mind wasn't on the music. He sat at the piano, listening to the demo of the poppy dance tune without really hearing it.

If Aden wasn't thinking about the most recent photos of him and Calvin online, then he was replaying their unusual kiss the day before or imagining how his boyfriend would react when Selina briefed him. That was before he considered what Anita might say about the news coverage, or even Aden himself. Not to mention the potential fallout among their fans.

Aden's gaze strayed from the lyrics in front of him to his phone every few minutes. Now it was only playing the killer beat of his new track, but once off airplane mode, he wondered yet dreaded what missed calls or messages might be waiting. He hated not knowing how Calvin was doing. More than that, he hated to think about what came next.

Sure, Selina had said that the latest headlines would likely blow over. And she'd assured Aden and Calvin that they could be together on their own terms. Once they finally signed the official paperwork, they'd make a plan and share it with StudioHK. But Aden was beginning to think it wouldn't be as easy as that.

Even if they no longer had to hide their relationship, they'd always be in the public eye, fair game for the tabloids. Calvin had already endured enough scandals for one lifetime. Now, partly thanks to Aden, he was back under the media's spotlight. At the same time his boyfriend had inadvertently stolen a major career opportunity out from under him. Maybe Calvin was going to hate him, but Aden didn't even know because he had to wait for Selina to talk to him first.

When Aden had decided to put his career over love, he'd only been concerned about losing his drive or precious time he needed to perfect his craft. Now he realized there were so many complications he'd never considered. Competing for roles or awards with the person he loved would be awkward at best, but keeping things from Calvin and stirring up bad press were far worse.

Aden's brain and his heart were both a mess, and he had no idea what to do. He felt like he was being pulled in multiple directions at once. In some ways, he was almost grateful for his hectic schedule the next two weeks—if his body was fully occupied, he wouldn't have to think about anything else.

When Aden finally gave in and checked his phone, it was approaching evening and there was a stream of messages from Selina in MK5's group chat. She'd shared each band member's revised schedule, along with the latest updates about Anita's recovery. That meant she'd talked to Calvin, and he knew exactly how Aden and the others would be covering for him.

Replies from Phantom, Mingo, and Shine had followed, full of support and encouragement, so Aden quickly sent some generic well wishes of his own. Switching over to his private chat with Calvin, he typed and deleted at least half a dozen different messages. But there were so many things he wanted to say, to explain and apologize for, that he couldn't get it right. Even a voice message didn't seem sufficient.

With a sigh, Aden set his phone down and went back to practicing his new song. This time he managed to focus, rehearsing without a break right up until the studio closed for the night.

When he checked his phone again, Calvin still hadn't been in touch. So Aden decided to call him, telling himself that he was just being sensible. If there was a chance that Calvin wanted Aden to come to the hospital, it was better to know before he ordered a taxi home. But as he waited for Calvin to answer, a part of Aden wondered if he should prepare for the worst.

"Hey, babe." Aden tried to sound cheerful when the line connected. Although he was alone in the practice room, he still felt nervous saying the term of endearment out loud.

"Hi," Calvin said flatly, and Aden's stomach tightened.

"I—I just wanted to check in on you, after everything that's happened today."

"I'm fine," Calvin sighed.

"Okay, that's good." Aden pretended to believe him. "But I need to tell you that I'm so, so sorry about the photos of us and the recording sessions, all of it really. I totally understand if you're mad at me, but I hope that you won't be forever."

"I don't know what to think, to be honest." Calvin sounded exhausted or overwhelmed, but not necessarily angry. "This is a lot to take in."

"Well, do you wanna talk through it together? I know Selina said not to, but I could stop by the hospital now. Or whatever you need, really. I'll do anything you want because I lo—"

"No!" Calvin almost shouted before Aden had finished.

"Oh. All right, then." Aden wasn't sure what was worse: being rejected by his boyfriend or not even being able to say "I love you" properly. He'd been so sure that Calvin felt the same way—he'd heard him almost say the L-word to Anita two nights before—but maybe this wasn't the best time to talk about things like that.

"My mum, err, I think it might be best if we don't see each other for a while." It seemed like Calvin was sniffling, as if he were crying. As Aden considered the possible reasons why, he had the strangest sense of déjà vu.

"Right, no secret hospital visits. Got it," Aden replied shakily, hoping that his growing anxiety was unwarranted. It was probably wise to follow Selina's advice anyway.

"No, not just that." Calvin's voice trembled from a distance. "I mean, maybe we should—" Sniff. "—take a break or something." Sniff.

"Oh," Aden managed to croak. He was grateful he hadn't left the practice room, and for the piano bench that was the only thing holding him up. He was beginning to realize what was happening and why it seemed familiar. Calvin was ending things between them, but this time it wasn't a scene in a TV drama. "Is that really what you want?"

There was a pause. For a while all Aden could hear on the line was Calvin's uneven breathing, occasionally punctuated by various beeping sounds from Anita's hospital room. He bit his lip, waiting for Calvin to say something, anything to give him even the slightest of hopes.

Instead, it was Calvin's mother who broke the silence with a series of muffled words that Aden couldn't understand. The next thing he knew, Calvin was saying "Yes, Mum" and "I've got to go," and then he was gone.

Aden was so stunned that he wasn't sure how he made it out of the studio and onto the street. When he climbed into the taxi he had no memory of ordering, he noticed his legs were shaking uncontrollably, and his face mask was soaked with tears. Although it didn't make any sense given the throbbing ache in his chest, somehow his heart was still beating.

Today he'd gotten something he'd always dreamed of: the opportunity to record a song as a solo artist, another step on the path toward becoming one of Hong Kong's new generation of entertainers. At the same time, he'd lost something he'd grown to want more than he'd ever thought possible: the man he loved.

When Aden arrived at his apartment complex, he said a silent prayer that Evelyn had gone out for dinner or was playing mahjong with her friends. He didn't want to speak to anyone. At least Desmond would already be in bed. But when he opened the door, Aden saw not only his mum but also his sister sitting at the dining table.

"What are you doing here?" he asked glumly, too wrecked to care how rude he might sound.

"Nice to see you too." Mimi rolled her eyes. She gestured to an empty bowl next to packets of tissues and throat lozenges on the table. "Mum made me congee since I'm getting sick. One of the hazards of being a nurse, you know."

Aden winced. In his misery, he'd temporarily forgotten that Mimi worked in the same hospital where Calvin was spending most of his time these days. Maybe she'd dropped in to see him or Anita again. Had it been before or after Calvin had broken Aden's heart?

Not that it mattered. Aden wasn't ready to accept what had happened, let alone share the details with anyone else. He was trying to find an excuse to say good night when Evelyn asked him the worst possible question.

"Did you visit Calvin and Anita today, then? How are they?"

"I don't know," Aden muttered, clenching his teeth to hold back any sad, embarrassing noises he might make. Still, he didn't miss the concern on Mimi and Evelyn's faces.

"I wondered if I'd see you at work today," Mimi said. "Why didn't you stop by?"

"It's complicated." Aden glared at the floor, determined not to cry. At least not until he made it to his own room. And yet he didn't move toward his door.

"You wanna talk about it?" Mimi asked gently. She pushed out an empty chair, and Aden found himself sinking into it. He rested his head in his hands and looked down at his feet, trying but failing not to think about when he'd sat in the same place with Calvin by his side.

Slowly he began to describe what he'd been dealing with that day: the news articles about Calvin and Anita, Calvin and Christelle, Calvin and Aden, plus all the extra work he was taking on in the next few weeks, including a trip to Taiwan. As he spoke, his words tumbled out faster and more heated. But he resolved not to tell his mum and sister everything, stopping himself just before he mentioned his final phone call with Calvin earlier that evening.

"Try not to worry, dear," Evelyn said in her most soothing voice when Aden had finished. "I'm sure the studio has everything under control."

"Mum's right. All you guys in MK5 are so popular right now. You'd have to do something way worse to really mess up. It'll all be fine in the end."

"No, I don't think so," Aden choked out.

"Why not?" Mimi laid a hand lightly on his shoulder, and Aden crumpled forward so his head rested on his forearms.

"Because Calvin may never forgive me," he wailed, each word clawing at his throat. Although saying it out loud would make it all too real, he couldn't seem to hold back any longer. "He—he wants to take a break, whatever that means."

The room was silent except for the soft sounds of Aden's sobs, but eventually his eyes ran out of tears. When he managed to sit up, Mimi handed him one of her tissues.

"You know that going on a break isn't necessarily the same thing as breaking up," she pointed out.

Aden scoffed and shook his head. Admittedly, he didn't have a lot of experience in the dating department, but it certainly felt like he'd been dumped.

"Your sister is right." Evelyn nodded encouragingly. "I know I've only seen you and Calvin together briefly, but I think it's pretty obvious how he feels about you, and you him."

"Yeah, you guys looked ridiculously cute on the hospital sofa," Mimi added. "I almost couldn't believe it."

Aden groaned. A few months ago, he also wouldn't've believed that he'd spend an uncomfortable night in a hospital room to support a handsome, wonderful man who was his boyfriend. Now, for more than one reason, he wouldn't be doing that again.

Although his family was only trying to make Aden feel better, somehow it was having the opposite effect. As soon as he could, he escaped to take a shower and crawl into bed. Surely he couldn't be utterly miserable if he was asleep.

For immediate release: StudioHK and MK5 Support One of their Own
April 23

MK5's Calvin Leung will be taking a step back from his duties with the band after his mother sustained injuries from an automobile accident earlier this week. StudioHK offers Calvin our full support at this difficult time, along with best wishes for his mother's speedy recovery.

To allow Calvin to focus on his family, StudioHK has reassigned his upcoming responsibilities to other members of the band. Importantly, no projects have been canceled, though some rescheduling may be required.

For now, the studio is pleased to announce that Aden Wong will be the next MK5 member to release a solo single. The groundbreaking boys love TV drama *Hooked on Love*, starring Calvin and Aden, along with action hero Reynold Tam, will air next month as planned.

Other MK5 members—Phantom Kwok, Shine Cheung, and Mingo Lee—will continue with their current projects as scheduled.

Encl.:
Updated list of MK5 activities

Media contact:
Carmen Yau
pr@studiohk.com.hk
+852 2154 1888

CHAPTER 21

THE NEXT day, Aden endured a punishing rehearsal schedule, including practice time with backup singers and musicians, as well as drop-ins from Leon and several other StudioHK producers. Somehow he managed to get into the right headspace to learn the music and lyrics for his new single, though his heart was shattered.

At first glance, it appeared that Aden's years of hard work and preparation had finally paid off. But deep down, he knew the song was pretty simple. It was a dance track, so the vocal lines were straightforward. In the end product, they'd be supported by backing tracks, pulsing beats, and no doubt a high-energy music video.

During every break (not that there were many), Aden checked and rechecked his phone to see if Calvin had been in touch. Although he'd been pretty clear when they'd talked the day before, Aden held on to the tiniest ray of hope that it had all been a mistake, a misunderstanding. He couldn't figure out how his boyfriend—the same wonderful human who'd helped Aden right before his own audition and repeatedly stood up for himself and his beliefs—had seemingly changed overnight.

More than a few times, Aden was tempted to message Calvin, only to talk himself out of it. Sure, he wanted to ask a million questions and wasn't opposed to begging, but he also wanted to know if Calvin was okay.

However, he wasn't totally clear what it meant to be "on a break." As much as Aden longed to speak to the man he loved, he didn't want to push or somehow make things worse. He was even more on edge than when he'd waited to hear from StudioHK about his callback audition all those months ago.

At the end of a long day, Aden's phone finally sprang to life. But sadly the messages weren't from Calvin. They were from Winnie.

OMG. I just heard the news. Are u OK??????

Aden's heart rate increased slightly. What now? He hadn't been online all day. He gulped, not wanting to consider how close the media coverage or fan theories about his and Calvin's relationship might've come to the truth by now. But at the same time, he hadn't had any updates from Selina.

Umm, can you be more specific? he asked.

Shine said that you and Calvin are on a break [sobbing emoji]

Oh. Aden had only told his mum and his sister what had happened. He hadn't said anything to the other band members, or even Selina, but apparently Calvin had.

Out of anyone, Aden would've expected Calvin to tell Phantom first. But if he'd told Shine, had he told Mingo as well? And why? Had he been sad and in need of comfort or just keeping the rest of MK5 updated?

The only way to find out was to ask, but Aden wasn't prepared to do that. At least Winnie had used the words "on a break" rather than "broken up" in her message.

Still, Aden hesitated before sending a reply. He didn't really want to discuss the details of his sorry love life via text. He told Winnie that he'd explain everything later, in a few weeks once he'd returned from Taiwan. Maybe his head and his heart wouldn't hurt so much by then, though it seemed unlikely.

But he should've known his best friend wouldn't rest until she knew everything, especially not when she'd waited so long for him to fall in love. After a great deal of pestering and in spite of his packed schedule, Aden agreed to meet Winnie the following morning at Miss Sally Wu's World of Dance, for old time's sake.

In an alternate reality, the first time the two friends returned to their routine of exercising and catching up would've been a celebration. Of Aden's career successes, of their blossoming romances. Aden would definitely have taken pineapple buns as a special treat, along with coffee or maybe even something stronger.

Instead, tomorrow he'd be spilling his aching guts to Winnie and asking her for any and all advice she had to offer. Aden wasn't sure he'd ever feel like celebrating again.

Although he wished they were meeting up under different circumstances, as it turned out, Aden was glad to dive into a hard-core dance workout with Winnie. Not that he'd let himself go while filming *Hooked on Love*, but a few extra cardio sessions would help make sure he was ready to sing and dance at the same time in his first solo music video. Of course, his vocals would be recorded separately in the studio; still, he needed to look comfortable singing on camera.

"*Diu*," Aden swore as he flubbed the footwork of the jazz swing combination they were working on and nearly ran into Winnie. The moves were familiar; he'd probably done them hundreds of times in his life. But his mind wasn't on his feet or even rehearsals later that day. Aden was distracted by what he'd been thinking about nonstop for the past forty-eight hours: Calvin.

"Okay, break time," Winnie announced. She walked toward the stereo cabinet in the corner of the studio and sat down on one of the folding chairs. "I'd ask how you're holding up, but I think I already know the answer."

Aden sighed as he sank into the chair next to his best friend.

"Have you seen the latest rumors?" Winnie looked at Aden nervously.

"Unfortunately yes." He nodded, pinching the bridge of his nose. That morning he'd awoken to several updates from Selina in MK5's group chat. Since Aden and the others had been staying away from the hospital as directed, there hadn't been any more leaked photos of Calvin or the rest of them.

Normally that would've been good news, except that some of the stories circulating in the online fandom had taken a surprising turn. Now a few people were calling Aden a terrible boyfriend, someone who'd abandoned his partner in need. They were upset, but not for the reason everyone had worried about. There had been very little discussion of Aden's sexuality, only his behavior.

"What people are saying really sucks, obviously, but it's also kind of good, right?" Winnie asked hopefully as she unscrewed the cap of her water bottle.

"You mean because most people don't seem to care that I'm gay?" Aden shook his head, relishing the slight breeze on his sweaty scalp. Those were words he'd never imagined saying out loud.

"Yeah, exactly. It's not what I would've expected, but maybe Hong Kong is more progressive than we thought."

Aden grimaced. He didn't disagree, and somewhere in the back of his mind, he realized that *Hooked on Love* might be a bigger success than anticipated. That would only be good for his career and the LGBTQ community—perhaps Christelle's suggestion of performing at a Pride event was worth considering after all. Except she'd invited Aden and Calvin to participate together, and right now that wasn't going to happen.

He knew he should feel grateful at the lack of any bigoted outcry, but it was rather difficult when his heart was in tatters.

"Maybe so. But it's pretty ironic, though," he said.

"What do you mean?" Winnie cocked her head, and her long braid swung behind her.

"Well, all this time I didn't date because I wanted to focus on my career. No distractions, no scandals, no prejudiced idiots, nothing," Aden explained. "Then once I actually had a real relationship with someone, not only did I maybe get dumped, but now I'm being criticized for something that wasn't my choice. There's no way to fix it even if I wanted to."

"*Pok gai,*" Winnie swore under her breath.

"Exactly."

They were quiet for a while, each lost in their own thoughts. Aden spent a long time riffling through his bag in search of his own water bottle. He wasn't particularly thirsty, nor did he mind sharing a companionable silence with his best friend. He was just going through the motions like he'd done every second since his last phone call with Calvin.

Finally, Winnie mused, "I find it hard to believe that Calvin really wants to take a break. From what I can tell and everything Shine has said, he's head over heels for you. It was pretty obvious even that night at Tonic months ago."

"That's what my mum thinks too." Aden shrugged, though he was painfully aware it didn't matter what anyone else thought. Only Calvin knew the true reasons for his actions.

"So are you going to win him back, then?"

"Umm…." Aden hesitated. He had no idea what Winnie was suggesting exactly, but the way she'd worded the question was interesting. She hadn't asked whether it was a good idea for Aden to try to reconcile with Calvin, only if he planned on doing it. Was it really that simple? "Hang on, what if that's not what Calvin wants?"

"Well, you'll never know unless you try," Winnie said encouragingly.

"But…." Aden tried to object yet found himself at a loss for words. His heart was too eager to believe that Winnie's idea just might work.

"Aden Wong, for once in your life, you have to be a total romantic!" Winnie exclaimed. She was excited now.

"And how do you propose I do that?" He hoped he sounded skeptical, and not how he truly felt—like he was grasping at the last straws of hope.

"I guess you can't go running through the streets to beg for a second chance." Winnie paused, considering, and Aden shuddered at the idea. If he, or any member of MK5, walked around openly in public, they could easily be surrounded by fans within minutes. Dropping down onto one knee and making a romantic speech would cause absolute mayhem. "But maybe you can show you care in other ways?"

Aden's thoughts flashed back to how he and Calvin had first started to reveal their feelings for each other—extra help with dance moves, thoughtful snacks, nothing too showstopping. Then he remembered the early episodes of *Hooked on Love* where Reynold Tam as Mr. Yue tried and failed to woo Calvin as Ting. The huge bouquet of flowers on the waterfront promenade, special deliveries of gourmet food during his lunch break, matching bracelets, each with one half of a heart charm.

Perhaps Winnie was onto something, even if there was no way to give Calvin any gifts in person. Selina had banned all one-on-one meetings until the news cycle had shifted. Not that Calvin would've agreed to see Aden anyway. But if Aden ordered everything online, he could simply have it delivered to Anita's hospital room or the Leungs' apartment. Or there might be an even better way.

Aden pulled out his phone and furiously typed a message to his sister. *What's your work schedule this week? May need your help with Calvin*

"Hey. What's going on?" Winnie asked suspiciously, but not unkindly.

"Huh?" Aden faced her, puzzled.

"You're smiling." Winnie poked him in the ribs, and Aden nearly laughed, a foreign sensation. "Just before you looked like death, and now you almost seem happy. How did that happen?"

"Well, like you said, maybe there is a way to get Calvin back," Aden said as his phone buzzed again. He held his breath when he saw Mimi's message. She'd sent him a screencap of her upcoming shifts as well as a short reply: *Just tell me what you need and when. Let's do it!*

"Oooh yes!" Winnie squealed after she'd leaned over to read Aden's phone. "Fix it, baby!"

Aden rolled his eyes at the ridiculous twist on the dance mantra of their childhood. It was cheesy, but at the same time, he felt more in need of encouragement than he ever had back then before a recital. Secretly, he hoped that Winnie's revised cheer would bring him all the luck he needed to make things right.

THE REST of the week passed by in a blur of early-morning workouts and late-night rehearsals at StudioHK, punctuated with soaring melodies and high-speed footwork. Aden went through many of the same routines as for MK5's first single and *Hooked on Love*—costume fittings, hair and makeup stylings, sound checks.

Although the studio's producers had the final word on every detail, Aden was allowed a surprising amount of input on his debut. He wanted (and got) warm brown highlights in his hair, helped select a few different outfits for the MV, and even enhanced some of the choreography. He poured everything he had into his new song and all the accompaniments, but not necessarily because he was aiming for greatness.

Not that Aden didn't want to do his best under the circumstances. He'd dreamed of and worked toward this since he was a teenager, or even younger. But he was hurt and confused, still trying to figure out what had gone wrong with Calvin. He was also coming to terms with the fact that he cared about their relationship as much as, if not more than his career, something he'd never thought possible.

He wanted to believe that if he was busy enough and tired enough, he'd stop holding his breath every time he checked his phone, on the off chance that he'd received a message from Calvin. That if he threw himself into work as he'd always done, he'd manage to fill the gaping hole in his heart.

Of course, Aden was wrong, but only because he'd never been in love before. No amount of overtime or hoarse throats or blistered feet could distract him from the current situation. Things between him and Calvin were screwed up, with no signs of improvement. He wondered how long he'd have to endure feeling so miserable.

And yet Aden hadn't quite given up. With Mimi's help, he'd arranged a series of deliveries to Anita's hospital room for his (ex?)-boyfriend. Everything was sent anonymously, but the sender would be obvious from the items he'd chosen: a tabletop vending machine full of mints and fruit pastilles, a bouquet of eighty-eight red roses with a stuffed white rabbit in the center, local pastries and sweet coffee drinks for breakfast, even baked seafood spaghetti from the *cha chaan teng* they'd visited in Sha Tin. But if Calvin had figured out the origin of the gifts, he hadn't said anything to Aden about it.

He had, however, posted some pictures of them online, along with images of the many cards, balloons, and trinkets he'd received from members of MK5's fan club. Which had also been Aden's doing. It was him, not Selina or anyone from the studio, who'd asked the fan club to support Calvin during his mother's recovery as well. But the captions for all of Calvin's posts were maddeningly generic, positive and grateful, without any hint of his true reactions or feelings.

Even the following week when Aden was in Taipei, accompanied by Selina, Calvin was never far from his thoughts. As he moved to the beat with a great crew of backup dancers, Aden remembered the sparks between them at a dance rehearsal for "YSim." While recording a Mandarin version of his new single, he imagined the sound of Calvin's soft voice singing in another language. At the city's famous night markets, he longed to share unhealthy treats like spring onion pancakes and fried chicken with the man he loved. Aden may have been in another country, but his heart had never left Hong Kong.

More than a few times, he'd sworn that Selina was about to scold him for looking anything less than delighted on camera or out in public. Or even raise the subject of the latest online rumors, which Aden had tried to avoid as much as possible. Instead, she didn't say Calvin's name for the entire trip.

For the most part, Aden was grateful, though he could've used some comfort or encouragement. At the same time, he was curious, wary even. He'd never told Selina that he and Calvin weren't speaking, but it seemed that she already knew. Could she tell from Aden's subdued demeanor, like when she'd noticed their rift at the YoYum shoot? Or perhaps Calvin had said something to her as well.

After another whirlwind of rehearsals and recordings, when all footage had been shot and all tracks finalized, Aden and Selina boarded a plane back to Hong Kong. They sat in first class, if more for the added privacy than the luxury. On a flight that was barely two hours long, there wasn't much time to enjoy the amenities.

Especially not when Selina was determined to multitask by briefing Aden about his upcoming commitments. So far, there were still no concrete plans for MK5's next single. But everything was set for the launch of his own—all he needed to do was share the content from StudioHK on his social media accounts once the release date was confirmed. That was a good thing because, with the premiere of *Hooked on Love* approaching, Aden would be busy with the final round of promotions.

Aden could feel Selina's eyes on him as she described the press conference, interviews, and other activities arranged by the studio to increase the hype around the new BL drama. Most of the events would feature all the main cast members and StudioHK's own media channels. But just a few actors were scheduled for online live streams, fan competitions, and even a sit-down with Helga Sze herself.

As he listened, Aden experienced conflicting emotions. He was excited to promote his first-ever TV role but understandably nervous about the public's response to the controversial subject matter. Most of all, he was anxious to know how much Calvin might be involved, worrying his bottom lip until it was raw. He waited and waited for Selina to mention Calvin's name yet was still caught off guard when she did.

"Calvin's going to be there for all of this," Selina said carefully as she was wrapping up. Aden's heart flew to his throat, and his stomach tightened as he waited to hear what came next. "He's had a rough few weeks but is more than ready to get back to work now. I believe he's looking forward to seeing you too."

Selina was smiling at Aden now, in that uncanny, knowing way of hers. If she hadn't been looking at him so kindly, he might've thought that she'd intentionally saved this particular piece of information until the end just to torment him.

Either way, all he could do was blink and attempt to nod his understanding. He was grateful for the mask covering the bottom half of his face, which hid at least some of his surprise. Something like hope was blossoming in his chest, though his brain was having trouble catching up. Had his plan to win back Calvin actually worked? Or had the past couple of weeks really been some kind of misunderstanding?

But ignoring Aden for an extended period of time didn't seem like the behavior of someone who wanted to work together again, let alone renew any sort of romantic relationship. A part of Aden wondered if he should still be apprehensive or terrified to see Calvin, or even angry given all the heartache he'd endured.

Yet as long as Aden didn't have a meltdown or cause a scene on the plane, it didn't matter what thoughts were raging inside his head. The important thing was that Calvin wouldn't be able to avoid him for much longer, and maybe, just maybe, they could find a way to move on. Preferably as a couple, but at least as amiable colleagues, if not.

Re: Hooked on Love promotions
From: selina_mak@agentart.com.hk
To: leon.ho@studiohk.com.hk;
    peter.siu@studiohk.com.hk;
    janus.so@studiohk.com.hk
May 7 9:32pm

Dear all,

I've briefed Aden and Calvin separately about the various promos and events leading up to the *Hooked on Love* premiere. Though Calvin is still taking it relatively easy as his mother's condition continues to improve, he is looking forward to getting back to work. Aden is as hardworking as ever.

Just one point of concern. I realize that Helga Sze is considered the best in the biz, but I assume no one has forgotten her less-than-friendly history with Calvin's family. I trust she'll be well-prepped by PR about what questions are appropriate and what we're expecting in the final piece. This needs to be a positive preview, not an exposé.

Cheers,
SM

CHAPTER 22

A FEW days later, Aden sat across from Calvin at one of StudioHK's conference tables, with Selina and Carmen Yau from PR off to one side. Except for the briefest "hello" to the room when he arrived, Calvin still hadn't spoken to Aden at all since suggesting they take a break.

Yet now they were waiting to start a joint interview with Helga Sze in the same room where they'd first officially met months earlier. Afterward, they'd attend a screening event for the cast of *Hooked on Love*, their families, and select members of the press. Aden was no media relations expert, but it didn't seem like a great idea for the two costars to dive into all that on uncertain terms. However, neither Selina nor Carmen had even tried to break the ice between them.

Aden could tell that Calvin didn't exactly seem happy, but he wasn't sure if he was upset or something more like embarrassed. Perhaps he was anxious, understandable given his family's previous experiences with Helga. Aden knew he probably should be more wary of the tabloid journalist who, it seemed, was running late, or annoyed at Calvin for ignoring him, but mostly he was just delighted they were in the same room again.

Even if so far Calvin was doing a good job of pretending that Aden didn't exist, avoiding his gaze as well as the whole area of the room where he was sitting, whereas Aden could barely keep himself from ogling the man in front of him.

He observed with some dismay that Calvin looked tired—his big eyes seemed to have lost a bit of their sparkle, and his cheeks weren't as full. But he was as handsome as ever in his oversized black tunic and round silver glasses, perhaps even more so now that his tousled hair was dyed silver once again.

"Let's kick things off with something fun," Helga said brightly after she finally arrived and set up her digital recorder. She rubbed her hands together, long red nails flashing dangerously.

Aden was immediately on edge, suspicious of what a reporter considered "fun." Although he'd just seen Selina and Carmen give her a list of topics that were off-limits, including the band members' personal lives.

"I know that Aden is a wonderful dancer and Calvin is a talented pianist. But who's the better—" Helga raised her eyebrows in amusement as she paused. Oh no. Surely not. Aden gripped the arms of his chair until his knuckles turned white, his own terror reflected back at him in Calvin's face. Whereas a few weeks ago this question would've been awkward, now it was not only humiliating but heartbreaking too. No small part of him wished that Selina or Carmen would end the interview right now before it even began.

"—cook? Did you learn any culinary skills while pretending to work at a restaurant?" Helga finished, her eyes flicking between Aden and Calvin as her pen hovered over a lined notebook on the mahogany table.

Aden let out a long, shaky exhale. He'd been so certain she was going to say "kisser" (impossible to answer) or even "actor" (still tricky), but apparently Helga was playing nice today.

"Definitely not me." Calvin laughed nervously. "I love food, but I can't cook to save my life. Not even on a set."

Aden managed to smile as images of Calvin flashed through his mind—balancing cup noodles on his music, feeding Aden chocolate at a vending machine, eating street food in the dark of night. The sound of Selina's phone vibrating on the table brought Aden back to the present, and he realized Helga was waiting for his answer.

"Actually, my mum taught me and my sister to cook, though I rarely have time to practice," Aden said. "But Calvin pretty much set up his own tuck shop in our dressing room, and we ordered a lot of takeaway with our colleagues, so we never went hungry."

He couldn't be sure, but Aden thought he saw traces of a blush appear on Calvin's cheeks. He seemed lighter than before, less closed off even. In that moment, Aden decided to do something that he probably should've cleared with Selina and Carmen first—use his replies to Helga not only to test the waters with Calvin, but to show just how much he still cared too.

The next several questions that Helga asked were pretty standard—about their favorite scenes, their daily routines while filming, their other costars—and Aden did his best to answer truthfully. Although for obvious reasons it was better not to mention *everything* he and Calvin had done while making the TV show. He spoke fondly about his experiences, and he felt heartened when Calvin did the same.

"As you well know, this program is pushing boundaries in Hong Kong. Were there any other shows or films that you turned to for inspiration when preparing for these roles?" Helga asked.

"Well, of course there are other BL dramas around Asia," Aden began, though in fact he'd never been that interested in them. He'd always been too busy focusing on his own career to watch much TV.

"Right, like *2gether* from Thailand and all the yaoi manga from Japan," Calvin elaborated when Aden didn't say anything else. "And, maybe it's stating the obvious, but Leslie Cheung was a pioneer in gender-bending roles going back more than thirty years ago with *Farewell My Concubine*."

Aden frowned. He wasn't very familiar with Calvin's first two examples. But the film he'd mentioned, though visually striking and internationally acclaimed, was at heart a tragedy.

"I mean, all of *gor gor's* work is iconic, but I think I like him better as Sam in *He's a Woman, She's a Man*," Aden said, looking straight at Calvin. He hoped he didn't sound argumentative, though he couldn't quite control his voice. His chest felt tight, but he pressed on, forcing out each word. He needed to explain, to Calvin more than Helga, why he'd name-checked this particular romantic comedy. "What does he say at the end that's so powerful? Something like it doesn't matter if you're a boy or a girl. I only know that I love you."

Calvin's mouth fell open, and then Aden really was unable to speak. They just stared at each other in silence as Aden willed himself not to lunge across the table at the man who was finally looking at him, all wide-eyed and flushed and perfect. As if nothing had changed.

Thankfully, Helga didn't seem to notice the unspoken conversation between them. Her attention was trained on Aden, waiting for him to continue. He cleared his throat, though it did nothing to calm his pounding heart. "Anyway, I hope that's the message we're sending and that the fans are on board with it too."

"Does that mean *Hooked on Love* has a happy ending?" Helga smiled slyly, knowing she'd laid a trap. The studio had been adamant that no one involved in the production reveal any spoilers.

"I guess you'll just have to wait and see," Calvin said dreamily, gazing at Aden with what seemed a lot like adoration. God, he wished they were alone.

"Speaking of things working out well, I hear your mum is doing much better now," Helga said, too sweetly.

Aden watched as every muscle in Calvin's body tensed, and inwardly he cursed Helga for ruining the moment.

"Yes, thank you," Calvin said through clenched teeth.

"I also heard that you were a big help to your costar during this difficult time." Helga turned to Aden, and he braced himself for what was to come. He didn't think the studio had released any specifics about his upcoming single, but Helga probably had her sources. Or was she going to mention the photos of them at the hospital, though they were old news now and surely on the forbidden list? Either way, it would do nothing to ease the tension in the room, or between Calvin and Aden.

"Food deliveries, beautiful flowers, encouraging the fan club to send all those cards to Calvin as well as the medical staff." Helga listed off the many surprises that Aden had arranged when he couldn't visit the hospital. "It seems far beyond what most people would do for a colleague."

Oh. Aden hadn't even told Winnie the extent of what he'd done, much less Calvin. He wondered how Helga had found out, but he definitely needed to thank her for digging up this particular information.

Calvin's jaw softened, and his lips parted slightly. He blinked watery eyes at Aden a few times before peering down at his lap with great interest. All Aden could think about was taking Calvin in his arms and kissing him and eventually forcing him to explain whatever had been going on the past two weeks.

Before Aden managed to form a reply, Helga had more to say. She sounded as if she were thinking aloud, except there was a devious glint in her eye.

"And yet, I also saw a few people being rather critical of your behavior online, Aden. Something about you being a bad boy—"

"Nope, let's move on, please. Nothing too personal, Helga, unless you want this interview to end earlier than expected." Selina cut her off before she could finish, though Helga's meaning was clear to everyone in the room.

Yet Helga wasn't a bit flustered and had clearly only raised the subject to get a reaction. She didn't seem in a rush to ask her next question and took some time to review her notes.

Across from Aden, Calvin sniffed and raised his head. Then he began to speak quietly but firmly.

"There's no doubt that these past few weeks have been hard, but absolutely none of it is Aden's fault, and I won't let anyone criticize him while I'm around. As you said yourself, Helga, he did a lot for me and my mum, much more than I ever expected." Calvin's gaze found Aden's as he proved that he too could use this interview to say things that needed to be said. Now they were both on the verge of tears. "He's the best, and I consider myself lucky to have met him."

Aden thought Selina let out a heavy sigh, and he knew that Helga had to be watching them closely. But all he cared about was the fact that Calvin had praised him, defended him, practically declared his love, and in front of a journalist no less. Surely he wouldn't have taken such a risk if it didn't mean something, if he'd decided he didn't want to be with Aden anymore. Aden felt like he should hold on to his chair tightly, in case he floated up into the clouds.

"Anything to add, Aden?" Helga interrupted his thoughts.

Aden swallowed, keeping his focus on Calvin's face, partly to avoid whatever angry glares Selina or Carmen were throwing his way. They wouldn't like what he was about to say, no matter how much he tried to make it sound like he was talking about *Hooked on Love* rather than Calvin himself.

"Well, like I said before, the show is all about love." Aden attempted to keep his voice steady, though it felt like his whole body was trembling. "And for me, it's important to bring more of those positive words and deeds into our daily life as well. You know, love not hate, being there for one another, and so on."

Helga was surveying Aden intently, but not unkindly. Then she scribbled some notes on the paper in front of her, murmuring something that sounded a lot like "Hooked on love indeed."

Soon afterward, Selina nearly pushed Helga out the door, muttering harsh warnings about the content of the article the whole way. She asked Carmen to escort Helga to the studio's main entrance. Then once the three of them were alone, she stood at the head of the table and scowled.

"That was some smooth-talking, both of you, though I don't think it was the smartest thing you've ever done. A heads-up beforehand certainly would've been nice," she said, but to Aden it seemed that she was only trying to sound stern. "I assume you have some things you want to say to each other, but you're just going to have to wait."

Calvin heaved a frustrated sigh, glaring at Selina before staring at Aden. His eyes were dry now, but Aden could see something in them like hope and gratitude and maybe even desire that made it hard for him to breathe. Aden did his best to silently return all the same feelings, but he didn't get the chance to say anything.

"The reception before the screening starts in less than half an hour, and you've got to get changed." Selina told them how to find the dressing room with their clothes for the event, coordinated suits from yet another designer eager for a celebrity endorsement. Then she shooed Aden out of the room, making an excuse about needing to discuss something with Calvin. Although it was possible she just didn't trust them to be alone together, and Aden couldn't exactly blame her.

ADEN FELT hot in his suit, and not in a sexy way, but the midnight-blue silk jacket and trousers fit him perfectly. More like his tie was too tight, though he'd tied it himself, and the room was too crowded, yet it wasn't even full.

After hurriedly changing into his formal clothes, Aden had met his parents in the reception area outside StudioHK's screening room, an atrium-type space that normally only held a few plants and leather sofas. Tonight, several rectangular tables filled with food and drinks lined the walls, and a portable sound system had been set up at one end for celebratory speeches.

Although Aden hadn't had even a drop of champagne, his cheeks were flushed, and his heart was racing. His entire body was buzzing, but he wasn't nervous about the screening. He wasn't thinking about *Hooked on Love* at all. His mind was still in the conference room from earlier.

People kept coming over to say hello or congratulations—the director, the rest of MK5, even Ms. Yeung from HR—but it was all a bit of a blur. For once, Aden was grateful that his mum was so chatty. Next to him, Evelyn looked radiant in a knee-length cheongsam-inspired dress of multicolored floral silk and never seemed to tire of talking to anyone who stopped by. At her side, Desmond remained mostly silent, sporting a very dad look in tan trousers and a navy blazer over a blue-and-white striped button-down.

It seemed like Aden had spoken to everyone in the room, except the person who mattered most. He'd been casting impatient glances at Calvin out of the corner of his eye every chance he got, though he too was surrounded by well-wishers. Even without looking, Aden could sense Calvin's presence nearby, yet not nearly close enough. Aden wanted a better view of him in a similar midnight-blue suit and rainbow striped tie almost as much as they needed to talk.

Aden was rather surprised to see that Anita had made it to the screening, her bulky cast peeking out from under a long gown of pale pink chiffon. He was pleased that Calvin's mother appeared to show more support for her son now than at the music awards. Even better, Anita sat in a wheelchair accompanied by a nurse's aide. Calvin wouldn't need to stay with her all night, if Aden could find a way to get him alone.

"How was the interview?" Aden jumped at his dad's question, realizing it had been a while since he'd shaken any hands. He wasn't sure how long he'd been staring into space thinking about the man he loved.

"It was… better than I expected," Aden murmured as a small smile crept over his lips.

"Go on, son. Your mother and I are fine here, and this is a big night for you both."

Aden shot his dad a surprised look, but Desmond only chuckled and nudged Aden in Calvin's direction. He was about to set off when the sound of someone tapping a microphone echoed around the room.

"*Dai gaa ho.*" The MC for the night welcomed the audience to StudioHK. After a few words, she passed the mic to Kenny, who gave a brief introduction before directing people to take their seats in the next room. Aden had never seen the studio's private movie theater, but he followed the crowd inside and found the three leather seats assigned to him and his parents.

They were in the second row, along with other key members of the cast. The first row was reserved for studio executives and other VIPs. Yet for some reason Calvin was sitting in the very front, all the way at one end. Aden was about to feel slighted—after all, they had equal billing—when he saw Anita being wheeled into the accessible area next to her son.

Once the room had filled up, the lights went down and a video began to play on the big screen. What Aden and the audience saw first wasn't the opening scene of the show but the titles, accompanied by one of the cutest, sweetest theme songs he'd ever heard. It was just a demo—with a simple piano accompaniment rather than a produced backing track—and the male voice singing was intimately familiar. The lyrics were all about hope and young love, and Aden adored it, even if it also made his stomach twist in all the wrong ways.

When the theme song ended, Aden was able to lose himself in the story of *Hooked on Love*, despite his nervous energy and aching heart. Although he already knew the plot and still remembered many of his lines, it was different with all the scenes put together for the first time. He loved seeing the narrative and the characters come to life—the meet-cute between Calvin and Aden as Ting and Mok, Christelle showing off her talent for singing in the restaurant, Reynold Tam's very public declaration of love to Ting on the waterfront promenade as the episode ended.

At the time, when Aden had watched Calvin and Reynold film that scene, he'd found it sweet, if a bit ridiculous. He'd also felt something like jealousy, though he never would've admitted it then. But Reynold's fictional displays of affection had come in handy over the past couple of weeks as Aden tried to prove his love to Calvin from afar. He only hoped that he'd be more successful.

As the end credits rolled on the first episode of *Hooked on Love*, the audience clapped and cheered, though Aden was more interested in the return of the wonderful theme song. Beside him, Evelyn dabbed at her eyes, and only then did he notice his face was also wet with tears. Tears of joy and pride, but mostly longing, that blurred all the words on the screen in front of him. He'd have to ask Kenny who'd written the music later.

He stood up, preparing to move back to the reception area with everyone else. Then he saw Calvin wiping his eyes too, and he couldn't stand to wait anymore. Tonight was supposed to be all about their groundbreaking TV show, but Aden didn't want to celebrate alone if he didn't have to.

Aden fought his way through the flow of people to where Calvin still stood in the front next to Anita and her aide. With the briefest of nods at Anita, he grabbed Calvin by the elbow and pulled him out of the theater through a side door in the opposite direction as the reception.

Neither of them spoke, even when they ended up in an empty hallway next to the toilets and… oh. A vending machine. The exact place where they'd first run into each other.

With a slightly hysterical gasp, Aden positioned Calvin on the far side of the vending machine against the wall, though it seemed unlikely anyone from the event would venture nearby. Once they were facing each other, he let go of Calvin's arm, immediately regretting the loss of contact.

And perhaps Calvin felt the same way. His gaze lingered on Aden's hand for a second before shifting to his face. He looked at Aden expectantly, maybe even hopefully, and suddenly Aden's mind went blank. He'd dragged Calvin away from the screening without a clear plan of what to do afterward.

"You look amazing." Aden blurted out his first coherent thought. Maybe not the best thing to say under the circumstances, but it was true. Even in the most basic of corridors and lackluster lighting, with traces of dark circles visible under his eyes, Calvin was perfect. Perhaps not quite as angelic as on the day of the callback auditions, given his suit was dark blue, not white, but equally as stunning. And more irresistible than ever after too much time apart.

"I suppose that's an improvement over what you once said to me here," Calvin remarked dryly. Aden cringed, remembering how he'd been so quick to think that Calvin was trying to sabotage him, the competition, that day.

He searched Calvin's face for any sign that he was displeased or upset but found none. Calvin certainly made no attempt to leave. Still, neither of them said anything for several moments, the air around them growing thick with anticipation. Then Calvin placed a hand on Aden's bicep, sending his pulse racing. Not unlike when Calvin had steadied him in the same location in the past.

"So umm…," Aden began tentatively at the same time Calvin, in a wobbly voice, said, "I can't believe…."

Aden let out a nervous laugh and stared at the tile floor.

"We need to…." He tried again without looking up just as Calvin moaned, "I never wanted—"

There was another pause, and then Calvin's fingers dug into Aden's arm, tugging him gently so that their noses brushed and their chests were almost touching.

Aden gulped, his mouth suddenly dry. He'd been trying to bring up what they'd both said, and left unsaid, in their interview with Helga. But now he couldn't speak. Nor did he want to, with his lips hovering just below Calvin's, even if he still had no idea where things stood between them.

Before Aden could overthink it, he leaned the slightest bit forward, and the next instant their mouths were crashing together. Calvin smelled like vanilla and tasted, rather appropriately, like mint, and Aden felt like he was coming home far more than when he'd flown back from Taipei. With a strangled cry, he shoved his trembling hands into Calvin's hair, kissing him with every emotion he'd stored up over the past few weeks. He registered that someone might see, but somehow it didn't matter.

To Aden's delight, Calvin seemed equally eager and gave as good as he got. His hands were everywhere—on Aden's shoulders and his chest, then under his jacket and even on his ass. His hot breath was in Aden's mouth and on his neck, and his gasps were none too quiet, especially not when Aden pushed him against the wall and ground their hips together.

For a minute, Aden considered dragging Calvin into the toilet and tearing off all his clothes. He wanted to feel and taste and see him everywhere. At the same time, something about this amazing kiss was too similar to the last time they'd made out—the wildness, the uncertainty. He wasn't entirely convinced it was a makeup kiss.

The only way to know for sure would be to talk things out, to ask Calvin if they were still "on a break" or what. Yet every time Aden tried to break away, he couldn't bear the thought that this might be his last chance to feel Calvin's lips against his own. So he didn't.

It was Calvin who eventually pulled back, chest heaving and cheeks flushed.

"I'm sorry," he rasped, sounding rather desperate. "So, so sorry."

As Calvin's eyes sparkled with moisture, Aden's blood ran cold. Was he about to be officially dumped? He attempted to take a step backward out of self-preservation, but Calvin's arms held him firmly in place.

"I honestly don't know what I was thinking when you called me that day, and I've missed you so much." Calvin's voice cracked, and he hung his head sadly. Aden held his breath. "My mum was really freaking me out about the rumors and the media and everything, but I know that's a terrible excuse. I wanted to call you back almost as soon as I hung up, but I… I was afraid."

"Afraid?" Aden echoed, confused yet encouraged.

"Ye-ah. In case you wouldn't forgive me, or if you'd changed your mind about the whole dating thing and decided you didn't want to be with me after all." Calvin made a low wailing sound. "I was such an idiot."

"Because you made us go on a stupid break and didn't talk to me for two whole weeks?" Aden pouted. He paused, waiting for Calvin's sheepish nod of acknowledgment, though he was far from upset. "Or because you pretty much outed us in front of the queen of all gossip reporters?"

Calvin bit his lip anxiously before nodding again.

"Well, you're right about the first thing, and I'm going to at least pretend to be mad about it for a while," Aden teased, thrilling at the little grumbling noises Calvin made in protest. He wanted to kiss them away, but not yet. "But both of us may have gotten a bit carried away in the interview today."

He paused again, still mainly for effect as he tried to seem serious. It was difficult because he hadn't felt so happy in, well, about two weeks. Lowering his voice, Aden continued roughly, "I would do it again if I had to, though."

"Me too." Calvin squeezed Aden closer, murmuring in his ear, "It was so worth it, and I am absolutely never letting you go. Ever."

"Yeah?" Aden shivered. "Just to be clear, that means we're no longer on a break or broken up or whatever?"

"Definitely not. Worst idea ever." Calvin sighed.

Inwardly, Aden agreed. But now that he was in Calvin's arms again, he didn't want to think about the past anymore. He tucked his head onto Calvin's chest, nuzzling his neck and listening to the sound of his steady heartbeat, wishing they could stay like this forever. Tightening his grip around Calvin's waist, he took a deep breath.

"I love you," Aden said. It didn't feel nearly as scary as he thought it might, given how rarely he'd said those words to anyone besides his parents before. Then again, it was the truth.

"I love you too." Calvin sniffed. "More than anything."

Hearing Calvin saying it back to him should've made Aden positively giddy, and his heart was so full. But when Calvin's snuffling noises didn't ease up and he felt a slight dampness on his skin, Aden lifted his head in concern.

"Babe," he said at the sight of Calvin's trembling bottom lip and the wetness on his cheeks. "Those better be happy tears."

"They are, mostly," Calvin mumbled.

Aden stood on his tiptoes and gently began to kiss away the salty droplets on Calvin's reddening face. He was in no rush to return to the screening after-party, but they certainly couldn't go back if Calvin looked like he'd been crying. As Aden's lips continued to brush against Calvin's soft skin, his breath quickened, and he found himself wondering if they could ditch the celebrations entirely.

As he considered whether to turn up the heat of his kisses, Aden heard footsteps behind him and froze, his lips still on Calvin's cheek. For a split second, he had a fight-or-flight urge to wrench himself away. But it quickly changed into something more like pride—that Calvin was his boyfriend, that Aden had finally let himself fall for someone in the first place.

He decided that if they were indeed about to cause a scandal, they were going to do it in style. He grabbed Calvin's face with both hands and planted a loud, wet kiss on his lips, resulting in a shocked moan that would've been oh so tempting, if they hadn't had an audience.

"So this is where you two snuck off to. People have been wondering why you aren't at the reception," a familiar female voice said. "I'm glad to see that you're back to being hooked on love in real life too."

Aden turned around to see Christelle grinning at them, arms folded across the front of her silver satin gown. Relief washed over him, and he chuckled. Christelle's sense of humor may've been cheesy, but she wasn't wrong.

"Mmm," Calvin hummed his agreement as he drew Aden's back toward his chest.

"You know, for a while, Naomi and I thought we might need to do something really drastic to get you two to sort things out."

"Such as?" Aden asked, though he was more focused on the weight of Calvin's chin on his shoulder.

"We hadn't decided, but I wasn't opposed to faking another car accident or celebrity scandal if it would help." Christelle's eyes twinkled mischievously. "Or maybe locking you in a room and forcing you to write love songs about each other."

Aden rolled his eyes as Calvin swallowed loudly in his ear.

"Right… well… as you can see, there's no need." Calvin's reply was stilted, as if he were embarrassed, but Aden wasn't quite sure why.

"Oh my god! Of course!" Christelle squealed. She covered her mouth with her hands, which did nothing to obscure the fact that her cheeks had gone pink and her eyes glistened. Was she crying? "I can't believe I didn't realize it earlier."

Aden felt Calvin nod, the smoothness of their cheeks brushing together pleasantly, as he confirmed whatever it was that Christelle was suggesting.

"That's adorable," Christelle murmured.

"What is?" Although Aden knew they probably looked delightfully loved up, he could tell he was missing something.

"Apparently Calvin has already written and recorded a song for you." Christelle sounded too pleased. "So now you basically have to sing it together at the Pride concert next month."

For the second time in this hallway, Aden felt like he was floating. He hadn't thought it was possible for this evening to get any better, at least not until he and Calvin were naked together somewhere, but he was happy to be proven wrong. He twisted his head around to find Calvin blushing, a little bit chuffed but mostly mortified.

"Babe," Aden whispered around the lump that was forming in his throat. Calvin had once told him that he'd started writing songs because of teenage breakups, after which Aden had refused to be the subject of a sad song. But a song that Calvin had composed in the past two weeks was more likely to be full of heartache than anything else. "Is it a heart-wrenching ballad?"

Calvin looked at him curiously for a moment, brows furrowed, then shook his head. Now it was Aden's turn to cry.

"A happily ever after?" He sniffed into Calvin's neck.

"Err yes," Calvin almost sounded sheepish. "Weren't you paying attention at the beginning of the screening?"

Oh. The theme song's beautiful words about true love. They were all from Calvin. For Aden. He'd completely forgotten that Calvin had been assigned to write the music before the award show and all the chaos that came after. And even with Anita in the hospital, Calvin had still managed to find time to complete it.

Aden thought he might faint or his heart might explode. In all his years of performing for cheering audiences, he'd never felt anything like this. It was brighter than any stage lights and more beautiful than any song. Except perhaps the one that Calvin had written for him. He was almost ready to agree to Christelle's suggestion of singing it together on stage for the whole of Hong Kong's LGBTQ community.

"Okay, I can't handle any more of this disgusting cuteness," Aden heard Christelle say, as if from a distance, while his entire body turned to mush in Calvin's arms. "But if you guys don't get back in there soon, I think people will really start to talk."

Christelle was probably right, but Aden couldn't bring himself to care about the reception, or even her, right now. Vaguely aware that Christelle had left, he lifted his head off Calvin's chest so they faced each other once more.

"You wrote me a song," Aden murmured dreamily.

"I mean, I had to write it for the show anyway," Calvin said airily. "As it turned out, I had a lot of free time on my hands and no one to share it with."

He brushed a kiss onto Aden's forehead, working his way down to his cheek and his jawline.

Aden shuddered, feeling frustrated and turned on at the same time. He slipped his hands down to squeeze Calvin's ass, pulling their hips flush.

"Wish we had some of that right now." He moaned just before Calvin's mouth landed on his. Aden's lips parted instantly, and then Calvin's tongue was sweeping against his own. Where their previous kiss had been wild with heat and pent-up longing, this was slow and sensual. When they finally came up for air, Aden's knees were weak.

"Come on," Calvin said, pushing Aden backward gently. "We better go before we do something scandalous right here in the hallway."

As tempting as that sounded, Aden knew that Calvin was right. He followed him back through the theater into the reception, where they were greeted by enthusiastic clapping as soon as they arrived.

Aden froze. As much as he wanted to jump for joy that Calvin was still his boyfriend, he'd hoped to sneak in discreetly. He squeezed Calvin's fingers, which only caused him to panic even more. They were holding hands. In public. His face flushed, and his eyes darted around the room, but he didn't pull away.

At the front, Kenny stood with a mic in his hand, flanked by Peter Siu and Leon Ho. Behind them, one of the rectangular tables was now covered in a red silk tablecloth, topped with three whole roast pigs, bowls of fresh fruit, and jars of incense sticks.

Oh. Aden realized that the director must've just given a speech before the traditional pig-cutting ceremony for good luck. The applause was for him, or the screening itself, not the two costars who'd reappeared hand in hand like a young couple on their wedding day. Although Aden and Calvin were probably supposed to join the senior production team at some point for a photo op.

Seconds later, Phantom materialized in front of them, smirking even more than usual. Still, he looked dashing in a suit of slate gray, that evening's color of choice for the three members of MK5 not in *Hooked on Love*.

"Looks like you two are having a good time," he said, reaching up to smooth a few of Calvin's stray silver waves back into place.

Aden cringed at how rumpled they both must be in a room full of studio employees and reporters. Reluctantly, he let go of Calvin's hand and set about straightening his tie, then buttoned his jacket and smoothed the lapels.

"Well, tonight is all about celebrating, right?" Calvin grinned, and Phantom rolled his eyes.

"Hey! Where have you guys been?" Mingo asked as he and Shine approached. He was even more cheerful than usual, perhaps a result of the now-empty champagne glass in his hand. "This is some party. Everyone is raving about the show and how popular it's going to be."

"Shame that two of the guests of honor missed most of it," Shine remarked dryly. "Nice of you to finally join us."

"Err, sorry. We were, uh, busy," Aden stammered. Then Winnie stepped out from behind her boyfriend, and suddenly he was a lot less embarrassed.

"Oh. Hey. What are you doing here?" Aden asked. Although he should've been pleased at his best friend's presence, he felt strangely annoyed.

"Nice to see you too." Winnie arched an eyebrow.

"She's my date, duh," Shine said, as if it was obvious, though this was the first time a member of MK5 had brought someone besides their parents to an official public appearance.

"What?" Calvin sucked in a breath. "We're allowed to have dates?"

Aden turned toward him, eyes flashing. Although they hadn't spoken in two weeks, during that time Calvin had written a song about him. Surely he hadn't been dreaming of anyone else. Right? "And just who exactly were you thinking of inviting?"

Calvin's lips parted as a pained expression crept across his face. He didn't say anything, and Aden didn't get the chance to apologize.

"Woah, dudes, relax." Shine held out his hands. "It's only because we got the all-clear from Selina yesterday. Technically, I don't think we had to tell her about us, since Winnie's not a studio employee or some other conflict of interest. But my girl is legit, so I figured why not?"

Oh. Aden winced. He'd forgotten that he and Calvin couldn't just get back together on their own—they still had some hoops to jump through. Not only did they need to update Selina, they had to finally sign the studio's paperwork. Hopefully she hadn't thrown it out.

Shine slid an arm around Winnie's waist, and she beamed. "Otherwise I would've been on my own like these two." He jerked a thumb at Phantom and Mingo, both eagerly watching as the roast pigs were carved into crispy bite-sized pieces.

"*Diu,*" Calvin swore. Then he grabbed Aden by the hand and dragged him through the crowd almost at a run. Aden had no idea what was happening—if they'd missed their cue for part of the ceremony or if Calvin just couldn't wait to try the roast pork—but he tried his best to keep up.

In his blurry peripheral vision, Aden thought he saw his parents standing near Anita, talking and laughing like old friends. Huh. Next they zoomed past a cluster of entertainment journalists, including Helga Sze. But if any of them noticed the two young costars of *Hooked on Love* acting strangely, they didn't say a word. Christelle seemed to give them a thumbs-up as they passed.

Then the sounds of clapping echoed around the room again. Aden knew it was just another part of the evening's celebrations, but he couldn't help imagining what it would be like if it were for him and Calvin instead. The thought of doing something crazy like kissing at the front of the room was both terrifying and thrilling, though it was clear now that they weren't headed in that direction.

"Where are we going?" Aden finally asked, breathless and bewildered.

Calvin whirled around abruptly, and Aden almost ran into him.

"To find Selina, of course," he said. "I think we've waited long enough to get the studio's approval. If Shine can date Winnie, then I sure as hell get to date you too."

Aden blinked. Of course. He shouldn't have doubted Calvin even for a minute. He squeezed his boyfriend's hand tightly, and then it was his turn to lead them the rest of the way toward their manager at the far end of the room.

Selina, again, was almost unrecognizable in a hot pink cocktail dress with tiers of ruffles. But she had no more warnings about what they'd said in the interview, and she didn't bat an eyelid at the sight of their joined hands. Unsurprisingly, she was already holding her phone, so it took just a few clicks to reschedule the meeting where they'd make things official.

Aden and Calvin were now free to enjoy the rest of the party, and in a few days' time, they could start planning for their future. Not just as musicians or actors, but as a couple.

The Official MK5 Fan Club
Home > Fan Forum

Most Discussed Threads

Still waiting for MK5's next single
Started by MK5life on May 12

Anyone down for a Hooked on Love watch party?
Started by BL Boi on May 19

Who is Shine's new gf? They're inseparable….
Started by Shine_army on May 25

Caden are performing at a pride event. IS IT LOVE?
Started by Caden888 on June 1

MK5 concerts announced for this autumn!
Started by Ho Chok on June 7

CHAPTER 23

IT WAS barely after 8:00 a.m., but Aden was already starting to sweat as he waited near the Star Ferry entrance in Tsim Sha Tsui. Victoria Harbor was picture-perfect on this hot summer morning under a clear blue sky, though Aden wasn't admiring the view. Below the brim of his black bucket hat his eyes were on his phone, skimming the headlines for any mentions of the *Hooked on Love* episode that had aired the previous evening.

It had been a week since the premiere, and so far the response to the city's first BL drama had been better than anyone had expected. The number of viewers and fans seemed to increase with each passing day, turning Aden and Calvin into household names even more than before. Even Anita, now cast-free, had begrudgingly praised both the show and her son's performance when the Wongs and Leungs had watched the first episode at Calvin's apartment.

But that didn't mean everyone in Hong Kong's conservative circles had suddenly embraced the LGBTQ community. More than one church leader had condemned the studio and the show, and a politician had even tried to make the case that it would lower the city's birth rate—as if by supporting same-sex relationships, *Hooked on Love* could impact a sociodemographic statistic that had pretty much been declining since the 1960s.

This morning, however, the online conversation seemed to be focused on harmless topics like where certain scenes had been filmed and what brand of clothes the actors had worn. So Aden scrolled on to the other entertainment news. He'd just spotted a ridiculously cute photo of Shine and Winnie at a new rooftop bar when he felt a strange yet pleasant tickle at the back of his neck.

With a gasp, Aden jumped forward, clutching his phone as he nearly collided with the stream of commuters en route to the ferry. He stepped backward just as quickly, and at the same time a strong hand grabbed one of his shoulders, turning him around. He looked up to find

Calvin, dressed all in white except for his black ball cap, laughing behind his round sunglasses and face mask.

"Good morning, birthday boy," Calvin giggled. "Breakfast?"

With his free hand, he held up a plastic bag containing two pineapple buns that, given the condensation inside, were freshly baked and still warm. Aden wasn't sure whether he wanted to punch his boyfriend for scaring him to death, kiss him for trying to help, or simply fall into his arms like he had when they first met all those months ago.

"Hey." Aden exhaled slowly, still slightly shaken. He put his phone in his pocket and readjusted his hat, now askew. Only when his heartbeat had returned to a more normal pace did he try to speak again. "I suppose I should thank you for bringing me food, but then again, you very nearly killed me so...."

"It's not my fault you freaked out when I kissed your neck." Calvin rolled his eyes.

"That's certainly not what it felt like," Aden retorted.

"Well, the mask kind of gets in the way." Calvin shrugged, but he wasn't wrong. Still, all five members of MK5 always wore them in public now. Even then, there was no guarantee they wouldn't be recognized in a crowded place, like the Star Ferry at morning rush hour.

"Right. Well, those look great, but let's get this over with first."

"Fine." Calvin sighed dramatically, but he followed Aden down the busy sidewalk without further protest. They passed bustling convenience stores and bakeries, as well as newsstands selling papers and glossy magazines, some featuring their own faces on the cover.

Near one store in particular, Calvin stopped. Planting his feet firmly on the ground, he leaned forward to whisper in Aden's ear.

"Listen. Can you hear that? What is it?"

For a few seconds, Aden strained to hear the sounds of anything unusual—a siren, a cry of distress—but there was nothing except the typical noises of the people and traffic around them. Then something else caught his attention: the store's radio. With a groan, he shot Calvin a pretend glare. "Ohmigod, stop."

"Wait, I know. It's me and the man I love singing the song I wrote. About him."

Calvin's eyes danced behind pink-tinted lenses as they listened to the *Hooked on Love* theme song, his soft, smooth voice on melody with Aden in perfect harmony. After the screening, they'd hurried to record the official version together, and it had debuted at number one when the show had premiered.

That meant Aden's first single, which had come out several days before, had been pushed to the number two spot. No doubt it would fall at least one position further when Calvin released his own solo song in a few days' time.

Months ago, Aden would've been beyond annoyed at the thought of anyone, let alone a boyfriend he never expected to have, even joking about trying to outshine him professionally. But now that he'd finally allowed himself to care about someone, he realized there was room in his heart for so much more than a desire to succeed.

"Babe, come on." Aden tugged at Calvin's sleeve, anxious to avoid attracting a crowd of fans, from which it wouldn't be easy to escape.

"What?" Calvin folded his arms across his chest, and though his mouth was hidden under a mask, Aden knew his lips had formed a dramatic, kissable pout. "You always told me I needed to be more vocal about my skills as a songwriter. Now you've changed your mind?"

More than once, Calvin had teased Aden about how he'd reveal the true story behind the theme song someday. So far he'd never followed through, but a part of Aden almost wished he would. They'd signed their relationship paperwork for StudioHK, so they could tell the whole world if they wanted. But they hadn't, so most people assumed the song was about Ting and Mok, and that Aden and Calvin were just good friends.

"I didn't say that, but right now we're supposed to be taking pictures." Aden turned on his heel and resumed walking.

He stopped when he came to a huge billboard bearing an image of himself with the message "June 8 Aden Day | Happy birthday, Aden Wong!" in a bright pink font. For his twenty-fourth birthday, MK5's fan club had sponsored celebratory ads in several places around the city, so Aden's face was more visible than ever.

Now Aden was here to acknowledge their efforts, strategically choosing a time of day when no fans would be lingering nearby to spot him in person. He took off his hat and face mask and handed his phone to Calvin, who snapped a series of photos for Aden to share on social media.

"Okay done. Can we eat now?" Calvin whined. He waved Aden's phone toward him while peering longingly into the bag of pineapple buns.

"Not yet." Aden's fingers wrapped around Calvin's outstretched wrist and pulled him forward. "Let's take some photos together."

Calvin raised an eyebrow but didn't object. Since the premiere of *Hooked on Love*, there had been renewed speculation in the Caden fandom that the costars were a couple in real life. Although they'd done nothing to confirm those suspicions, Aden and Calvin hadn't necessarily tried to hide their relationship either. They took taxis together now without a second thought, and they were both performing with Christelle at the Pride concert later that week. They'd even talked about singing a duet of Calvin's song "No Other Love" with the original lyrics, since MK5 had ultimately never recorded it.

Once Calvin had removed his hat, sunglasses, and mask, he reached out one long arm to take some selfies. Squinting at the two smiling faces on his phone screen, Aden's heart caught in his throat. Since he and Calvin had made up, and in the glow of their combined successes, life had been almost perfect. At the same time, something was missing.

When Calvin dropped his arm and tried to return Aden's phone the second time, Aden refused it again. There was another way he wanted to remember this morning with his boyfriend.

"I know it's your birthday, but that doesn't make me your personal paparazzi. Let's go. We've got rehearsal for the Pride concert soon." Calvin brought his lips closer to Aden's ear and lowered his voice. "And if we find an empty dressing room beforehand, I'll give you a special birthday treat."

"I like the sound of that." Aden smirked, though there would be plenty of celebrating in the five-star hotel suite that Calvin had booked for them that evening. He might even allow himself to eat cake, especially if it happened to be smeared all over his boyfriend's smooth chest. "But let's take a few more first. Just to make sure."

"Ugh. Whatever." Calvin was beginning to get hangry, but he brought Aden's phone into position again.

This time, Aden snuck an arm round his waist and pulled him sideways until they were touching from shoulder to knee. Then before he could overthink it, he reached up to kiss Calvin on the cheek, praying that he wouldn't be so surprised that he forgot to take what should be an unforgettable picture. An echo of Ting and Mok's happy ending in *Hooked on Love*, what had brought them together in the first place.

But it seemed that Calvin had a similar idea. Aden's lips landed on Calvin's mouth, not his cheek. Either one or both of them gasped, but then Calvin was drawing Aden closer, and Aden's hands were cupping Calvin's face. And though it was a fairly brief, chaste kiss, given the very public setting, it was the best birthday present Aden could've wished for.

"Umm… wow." Calvin laughed breathlessly when they broke apart, somewhat stunned. He switched Aden's phone from camera mode to the photo reel, holding it where they both could see. The picture was even better than Aden had hoped for, so full of love and joy that for a short while he was speechless. He wanted to live in this moment forever.

The repeated blare of an impatient taxi horn brought Aden mostly back to earth.

"Okay, now we can go." Aden grinned as he put his hat and mask on again.

"I think we better, otherwise we might have an audience pretty soon." Calvin glanced around nervously, and all too soon he covered his flushed cheeks with his mask. Still, Aden could tell that he was just as pleased.

"You know what, let them look, as long as we don't, like, get mobbed or something." Aden didn't see anyone obviously watching them—most people were rushing toward buses or the ferry—but it was certainly a possibility. He took his phone from Calvin's outstretched palm, then reached out his other hand to interlace their fingers together. Calvin inhaled sharply. "Maybe I'll even kiss you on stage in a few days. If you're lucky."

"Are you feeling okay? Has the sun gone to your head already?" Calvin asked, flipping up the brim of Aden's hat and touching the back of his hand to his forehead.

"Not the sun," Aden shook his head. "Just you, babe."

"Aden Wong, it's your birthday, which means that I'm supposed to sweep you off your feet. Not the other way around." Calvin pretended to sound stern.

"Calvin Leung," Aden mimicked his boyfriend's tone, "you've been doing just that for the past several months. Besides, there's nothing I want more than to be here with you, the man I love."

Past Aden would've been incredulous at the words that had just come out of his mouth. But they were true. It was as simple as that.

"Me too, sweetheart. Well, except to also eat breakfast at some point, but y'know…."

Apparently some things, like Calvin's obsession with food, would never change. Aden chuckled and squeezed his hand, thrilling when Calvin returned the simple gesture and made no move to pull away.

At the start of the year, Aden could never have imagined he'd be standing here in public holding hands with another man. In front of a billboard of himself. His path to stardom in Hong Kong's entertainment industry had not gone as he'd expected and would likely continue on a different course now that he was with Calvin. But he'd realized that different didn't always have to be bad. In fact, it could be even better than what you'd always dreamed of.

Keep reading for an excerpt from
The Temple of Heaven
by Z. Allora!

CHAPTER 1

Dear future Husband,

Maybe it's silly that I've been writing and drawing pictures for you since I was twelve years old. I know currently you don't exist in my world, but you're never far from my thoughts. I'm convinced you're somewhere out there waiting for me. At night I catch myself looking at the stars, wondering if you're seeing the same sky... making the same wishes I make.

I wonder if you'll love me as much as I know I'll love you.

God, this is dumb. I should stop, but I'm lonely, and I can share things with you I can't tell anyone else.

Sometimes I fantasize about what you'll look like. I don't really have a type, but I do appreciate—

Jordon's cell vibrated with a notification.

Following the alert, he checked the in-box on his laptop. *A new Made in China clip. Yes!*

He sprawled out on the red leather couch outside the Dark Angels' practice room. His brother would be in there for at least another hour, so he might as well enjoy his beloved band. He cast a gaze toward the closed door. Make that his *second*-favorite band.

He followed the link to Youku, the Asian version of YouTube. Humming a few bars of a Made in China song, he waited for the video to buffer, then hit Play.

His laptop screen filled with the bass player chasing the keyboard player while the drummer and lead guitarist made music accenting the silliness. The twenty-second clip ended with a brief flash of the singer chuckling and holding a mic. He asked in English, "Now are you ready?"

Fuck, yeah! Jordon was more than ready as that deep voice reached inside him and soothed empty spaces. He pulled at the front of his suddenly too-tight jeans because he couldn't pretend Tian Di's androgynous sex appeal didn't flip all his switches.

God, what was wrong with him? Crushing on the singer in a band. Was there anything more clichéd?

He grabbed his sketch pad and pencils from his bag, then started to draw. He was on his fifth sketch before he realized he'd done one study after another of the singer.

Damn, he needed to stop or check into a groupie recovery program. He went back to his laptop, but instead of returning to the letter he'd been writing, he allowed the sirens to call him to the other videos of Made in China.

Jordon had seen each video and snippet about a hundred times, but he rewatched the trailer clips of the South Korean game show *Knock Your Socks Off*. Made in China would compete against the reigning champs from Korea. Of course, Made in China had no shot at winning the rigged game show, but the exposure for the band would be great, and watching them play Rip Tear or Suck and Blow would be… stimulating. He couldn't wait for someone to post the episode.

Clicking through the videos, he came to his favorite trailer of the band. Goddamn, Youku limped along, taking forever to load. When the clip finally finished buffering, Made in China's driving sound blared out of his computer and slo-mo images of the band posing for pictures morphed into individual head shots of each member.

Then the picture twirled into a still of the drummer and the lead guitar player. They hugged and blushed in a way that almost made Jordon gag with its sweetness—or was that just him choking on jealousy? Their foreheads touched while they stared at the space between them as if they were going to share their first kiss. The tabloid blog rumors painting them as lovers must be true.

The screen image morphed into the bass player holding the keyboard player by the hair. Far from struggling to get away, the keyboardist wore a demonic smile of lustful joy.

Jordon's breath caught. Those two were totally hooking up.

The band's singer, Tian Di Zhao, reappeared on the screen in a long red jacket with an embroidered white rose pattern running along each side, tight black pants, and knee-high boots. His raven hair cascaded in gentle waves over his shoulders and down to the middle of his back. His eyes were closed, and he held a white rose like a microphone. Some might label his high cheekbones, delicate mannerisms, and lean body more feminine than masculine, but Jordon's fingers itched to draw the perfection of him.

Biting back a moan, Jordon wet his lips and tried not to be envious of the petals that caressed the singer's full red-lipsticked lips. Tian Di's long lashes fluttered, and he opened his mesmerizing brown eyes. He stared into the camera with such longing that Jordon's heart ached.

The screen flashed to a group shot of the band and then panned in for close-ups on their mouths. Jin, the guitar player, gripped and tore a piece of paper that Styx, the drummer, held between his lips.

Jordon's stupid heart triple-timed its beat when Tian Di's glossed lips came into focus. He clamped his straight white teeth down on the paper before tearing a piece away from the drummer. He turned to Li Zhehao, the bass player, whose mouth grazed his chin before severing the paper close to Tian Di's mouth.

Indigo Young spun Li, playfully subdued his struggles by wrapping him in an embrace, and then kissed him full on the mouth. After a long lip-lock, Indigo pulled back and blew the slip of paper out of his mouth.

Ah, Asian bands understood fan service.

The clip ended with the two couples hugging on either side of the singer. Tian Di glanced to his right and then to his left. Finally he stared directly into the camera and gave an empty look that gutted Jordon. Tian Di grabbed for a microphone as if it was the only thing consistently there for him.

A silly need to be there for Tian Di slashed through Jordon's soul. Yeah, like an international star like Tian Di Zhao wanted Jordon Davis to rescue him from the loneliness of falling into bed with his worshippers. Jordon dismissed his feelings as a crush.

Who wouldn't have a wicked case of heat over the guy? Tian Di had the voice of an angel and looks to match. He wasn't just a pretty face. Jordon had listened to Tian Di's interviews—okay, quite possibly Jordon heard or read every interview the guy had ever given—and Tian Di presented himself as quiet, intelligent, and driven, with a tease of irresistible hidden depths.

His deep speaking voice held more confidence than Tian Di showed onstage. Knowing the music industry, the Tian Di Zhao Jordon thought he knew could all be branding. Made in China didn't have the benefit of a record label or management behind them dictating an image.

Indigo was no stranger to the music scene; his father was well connected in LA. According to Dusty, Jordon's oldest brother, who knew just about everyone and everything, the guy's father was a guru who worked tirelessly behind the scenes, setting the direction of many pop icons. Maybe Tian Di's persona was a creation—so Jordon might be crushing on someone who didn't exist.

Why did Jordon always overthink things?

Tian Di was hot and provided Jordon with jerkoff fodder. Wasn't that enough? Why did he have to take his fantasies further? Why couldn't he revel in some mindless sex? Everything in him rebelled against that idea. Maybe that would explain his lack of experience and his silly need to write to a nonexistent husband.

He clicked on the link to Tian Di's website. No new pictures since the last time Jordon checked… yesterday.

There were cute pictures of Tian Di as a kid of five or six. One or two of them showed him as an awkward teen—maybe he hadn't grown into his height—but everything else was still in the range of delicious. Jordon scrolled through the numerous head shots. And the rest were posed pictures of Tian Di around Hong Kong and Shanghai.

God, what would it be like to be curled up in his arms? Maybe reading or watching a movie. He'd love to kiss those lips and maybe even stroke his cock.

Right. The way Jordon's brothers kept him sequestered ensured that type of encounter would never happen even though Made in China was going to be the opening act on the Dark Angels tour. His brothers were the biggest cockblocks in the world. Not only were they overprotective, but seeing their successful relationships set the standards pretty high for what Jordon expected in a partner.

He couldn't dwell on the fact that Made in China had been signed for the entire Asia leg of the *Life's a Drag* tour, because it was like letting the artist Pollock loose inside Jordon. His mind melted into all spatters of happiness and vivid colors. He'd get to meet the man who had haunted his dreams for well over a year.

Maybe he and Tian Di would hit it off. *Ha! What a freaking imagination.* He should stick to art. Tian Di Zhao probably wasn't even gay, or if he was, he wouldn't be into Jordon. *Whatever.* It was a great daydream.

The practice room door banged open, but no one appeared.

Jordon put his computer aside and grabbed his sketch pad. Maybe sitting outside while his brother and the Dark Angels practiced wasn't the best time to contemplate all the things Tian Di's glistening lips invited Jordon to do.

No, definitely not the best time.

He looked around, and his gaze landed on one of his abstract pieces that hung outside the practice space. Over the last several years, Jordon's canvases had replaced and now dominated the area. Some were earlier abstracts he'd given the band and original sketches from the first Dark Angels manga he'd penned backstage at one of their shows.

He opened his work sketch pad and paged past the character sketches of the various designs he'd yet to draw into his Manga Studio program. His characters were born on paper with pen, an essential step for Jordon to connect with his subjects. Only fully realized images found their way into his computer.

Angel strutted out, followed by Darius and Dusty. Angel pointed to Jordon's computer. "You perving on our opening act again?"

Jordon was compelled to cut Angel down. He had known his brother's best friend forever, and Angel had always been good to him. Maybe the overcompensation was to ensure Angel never discovered that at twelve Jordon had crushed on him for an entire year, or that he had wished to be more confident like Angel. Eh, or maybe God put Jordon on earth to keep Angel Luv's ego from overwhelming the band.

"Nah, listening to your replacements." Direct hit, if Jordon could go by Angel's injured expression. "You do know Made in China's singer has a larger range than yours?"

Dare rushed over and hip-bumped Angel. "Hey, in terms of size, I've got no complaints. Besides, their singer's good, but he's not Angel Luv."

Angel shrugged and gave his boyfriend a sparkly smile for a moment. "The guy's amazing, which is why Made in China will be opening our show. And I wish them every success."

"Don't forget about the drummer." Jordon winced at Dusty's frown. Why did he still play the role of the bratty kid brother? Damn, but every interaction forced him to slip into the familiar role and into saying words scripted years before.

Dusty admitted, "The kid's impressive. No doubt."

"Yeah, but he doesn't have your experience." Jordon tried to find something Made in China's drummer didn't have over his brother.

"Ha-ha. Yeah, I'm close to another birthday. Thanks for reminding me." Dusty waved him off.

Damn it, Jordon needed a tongue transplant. "No, that's not what I meant. You know how to drive the crowd with the drums. It's because you can read them, and you got that from years of experience in front of an audience."

Dusty twirled his drumsticks. "He'll learn. Made in China is still relatively new."

God, Dusty's easy agreement, which helped Jordon's careless words cut him, made Jordon sick.

Robin came into the room, fixing his hair, with a smirking Josh. Robin's gaze zeroed in on Jordon. "Who needs a cuddle?"

Ever since the night Jordon's mother had thrown him out at age sixteen, Robin, the keyboard player for the Dark Angels, seemed determined to give him some much-needed mothering. He loved that Robin didn't just accept him, he celebrated who Jordon was and, best of all, who Jordon was trying to become. Robin even knew two of Jordon's deepest secrets, and he didn't tell anyone, not even Josh.

Josh growled, which forced Jordon into an automatic response. He raised his hand like he desperately needed a pass to the bathroom. True, there used to be pleasure in making Josh jealous, but baiting him stopped being fun a while ago.

Just another thing Jordon did out of habit. Maybe he needed to figure out a way to break these patterns.

Robin settled onto the sofa next to him and murmured low enough so no one else could hear, "I loved your—I mean, Sakura Rose's latest volume of *Tricks and Treats*."

"Thanks. I mean, yeah. It's good work. But Sakura's having trouble with the next story." That was a damn understatement. Jordon sighed, shut his sketchbook, and set the pad aside.

Robin eased Jordon's head down into his lap and played with Jordon's hair. "I'm sure Sakura Rose will figure it out. Sakura is extremely talented."

Jordon drank in Robin's kind words. "Sakura Rose has hit a major creative blockage… I've heard."

Why couldn't Jordon admit to his brothers he'd been drawing for a Japanese yaoi publishing house since he was sixteen? It wasn't like Dusty or Zack could ground him. For fuck's sake, he was twenty years old. But the confession would be delivered with an admission he'd lied by omission, or at least wasn't honest with them. They'd be disappointed in him and hurt. Avoidance was easier.

"I'm sure SR will find a way." Robin patted Jordon's cheek with a little frown and a glint of determination in his eyes, like he'd fight the dragons of artistic constipation for Jordon.

Josh crushed in next to Robin and threw a territorial arm over Robin's shoulder. "Who are you talking about?"

"A yaoi artist I really enjoy." Robin didn't exactly lie, but his inventive use of the truth made Jordon feel shitty nonetheless.

He inhaled Robin's vanilla-lavender calming scent—which was always mixed with Josh's—and found comfort. Even though Jordon's brothers kept him like a sequestered nun, he'd always enjoyed Robin's platonic touch.

What did Tian Di smell like? He probably smelled edible. Now was not the time to think about the deliciousness that was Tian Di.

Jordon jumped off the sofa and knocked over his sketch pad in the process. It landed on his latest storyboard for *Tricks and Treats*.

Josh grabbed the sketch pad from the floor and stared at the scenes of Tricks on his knees providing a *treat* for one of the main characters. "This isn't for a Dark Angels manga, is it?"

"No. It's for something else I'm working on." He snatched the pad back and clutched his secrets to his chest.

Josh was way too perceptive to have missed the "SR" scrawled at the bottom of the sketch; his look of understanding was clear in his gaze.

Shit.

Some silent communication went back and forth between Robin and Josh until Robin caressed Josh's hand, then turned his attention back to Jordon. "Any new Made in China videos?"

"Yeah, actually, there's a couple. One is a trailer for a game show they'll be on, and a few others are just silly." Jordon loved when someone shared his… interest.

Josh shifted and patted the place between him and Robin. "Well, let's see it."

Jordon eased back down and clicked on the Rip Tear trailer with the speed of a skilled stalker.

By the time the clip ended, Dare, Dusty, and Angel had all squeezed in around him and his laptop, watching the trailer.

"Hey, wait. Let's see this one again. It's my favorite." Angel reached over Dare and Robin and tapped the curser on a music video.

The video opened. Made in China took to the darkened stage in traditional Chinese opera costumes, each band member standing in a spotlight, holding traditional instruments. The bottom left identified the song as "Evolution."

"Evolution" was the first video Jordon had showed the Dark Angels. Angel credited the band's viewing of "Evolution" as the moment that convinced them to consider Made in China for an opening act for their upcoming tour. Jordon should be content knowing he helped draw attention to Made in China's talent, and if his involvement impacted his crush in a positive way, all the better.

The video started with flutes and plucking strings on a *ruan*, or Chinese guitar, accompanying Tian Di as he glided toward center stage, trailing the hem of a light pink embroidered robe across the floor. Colorfully stitched birds perched on cherry blossom branches covered the expanse of silk. As he reached the spotlight, he thrust his arms up, and white waterfall sleeves shot out of the jacket and into the air before the silk gracefully fell in ripples at his sides.

Flowers dangled from the ornamental sticks holding his ebony hair in a knot at the back of his head. His makeup blurred the line between Goth and Chinese opera, heavy black eyeliner making his eyes appear huge.

How many times had Jordon caught himself sketching Tian Di Zhao?

He couldn't deny he was drawn to gender ambiguity, Goth, and tradition. Maybe he tried to capture Tian Di's essence so he might be able to understand why a man half a world away enchanted him.

"Geez, if I didn't know he was a guy…," Dare said to no one in particular. "The singer's movements are graceful, and the way he wears that kimono—"

"In China it's robes," Captain Know-It-All Dusty corrected.

Angel pulled Dare against him. "He's got a voice, no doubt about it."

Dusty shook his head during an unexpected drum solo that cut into and around the traditional flute and ruan. "I can't imagine doing that in those heavy robes."

As if the statement was a decree, the traditional Chinese clothing vanished with a bit of choppy editing. The band appeared, wearing black T-shirts and jeans, playing their usual instruments. The beat increased in intensity and speed.

"I love how they keep the same melody while rockafying it." Robin's label of the style was accurate.

The guitar, bass, and keyboard gave the song a driving, almost heavy metal sound.

"The evolution is really good. Get it? 'Evolution' is the name of the song." Josh apparently got Dare's meaning, because they fist-bumped.

Beep.

At the simultaneous announcement of a text message, Angel and Dusty pulled their cell phones out of their pockets.

"Fuck!" Angel glared at his phone.

"She'll fix it," Dusty said.

Jordon's stomach dropped. "What?"

"One of Made in China's band members is having trouble getting a visa for travel outside of China because his mother wasn't married to his father when he was born. Apparently certain paperwork and identification cards are necessary to get a passport."

Josh scoffed. "What kind of backward shit is that?"

Robin petted his hand. "It's how they do things in their country."

Originally from small-town Missouri, ADA PIPER moved to Hong Kong in 2010. She only planned to stay for a year, but then she fell in love with a boy (now her husband) and the city itself. She's a fan of Hong Kong arts and culture, especially food, movies, and all things related to Mirror, a Cantopop boy band.

A lifelong reader and writer, Ada discovered her love of romance, particularly MM romance, during the pandemic. In her free time, you can find her cooking, doing yoga or Pilates, traveling around Asia, or hanging out with her family.

To learn more, visit her website at adapiper.com or follow her on Instagram (@adapiperauthor).